The Last Train From Mombasa

by Louis Segesvary

ISBN: 0-615-28889-8
EAN13: 9780615288895

Visit www.booksurge to order additional copies.

Gutiri mundu wonaga wega wake, no kuonwo wonagwo.

"Nobody can see his own goodness. It can be seen only by others."

(KIKUYU PROVERB)

GREAT FALLS PRESS

Louis Segesvary served as a career American Foreign Service officer for 22 years, with assignments in Latin America, Europe, Africa, and the United Nations during the 1980s and 1990s. He holds a Ph.D. in Romance languages and literature and writes from Northern Virginia, where he resides with his wife, Beata, a teacher and performer of the violin.

PREFACE

Africa has often been presented in travel books as a magical destination, where sweeping savannahs and imposing mountain ranges serve as a backdrop to an exotic assortment of vegetation and wildlife and lithe men and women with rhythm in their veins and dancing in their feet.

In these agreeable books, little or no effort is made to acknowledge the less pleasant scenes of endemic poverty and sporadic violence that can easily crowd out these idyllic impressions, disfiguring the physical landscape with endless rows of flimsy shanties and piles of garbage in its cities and weighing down its people with wounds so brutal and burdens so great they are hardly imaginable in today's industrialized world.

It is here in this continent, after all, where alongside its raw beauty and native cultural charms that the African "big man" emerged in a number of the former British, French, Portuguese, and Belgian territories to replace the repressive colonial governors. The "big man" wasted no time in leaving his legacy, whether it was in the Congo, Uganda, Angola, or elsewhere, which was a level of corruption and cronyism that in some cases has set back social and economic development by decades.

It is also here in this African continent that rape takes place on a disturbing scale and where per capita income rates are the lowest in the world.

But the worst, the very worst scenes remain those of genocide, where tribal, internecine warfare becomes a zero-sum game, in which the annihilation of an enemy ethnic community played out to the last man, woman, and child becomes the goal.

And yet the pretty scenes offered in the travel magazines are not as disingenuous as they would seem on first glance. The beauty and majestic power of the continent's natural landscape are entirely real, as real as the energy, courage, and devotion of its people dispersed through hundreds of distinct ethnic communities that often cross the national borders laid down by the colonial powers. And it is there, among the many tribal communities which exist in Africa, that the region's defining struggle to become full partners with the modern industrial world is taking place.

It is my hope that this book will contribute to an appreciation of what this struggle actually entails in the deeper reaches of the human spirit, and that it will complement in its own modest way the considerable writing that already exists about the continent's political, economic, and sociological problems. A standard litany of solutions to these problems has been proposed by one donor country after another, usually focused on building civic society and strengthening the rule of law, promoting democratic governance and institutions, curbing corruption, building a market economy, and bolstering education and health. Over and over this has been set forth as Africa's way out of poverty and violence to a prosperous future.

As the chief speech writer on African issues at the American Embassy in Nairobi, Kenya from 1994-1997 and for two more years after that at the Africa Bureau in the State Department in Washington, D.C., I laid out this formula in different variations on numerous occasions.

But eventually I wanted to go below the surface of the traditional norms of political, economic, and social analysis. This was not because this time-tested approach doesn't merit our full respect; not because it doesn't explain a great deal about the challenges confronting the continent; and certainly not because the solutions proposed have no merit. They do indeed have merit, enormous merit, and do to this day.

Nonetheless, I wanted to draw on the insights into the interior dimension of life as it is lived in sub-Saharan Africa that I had gained after five years of extensive engagement with its people and land, including traveling from its southern tip in South Africa to its northern regions in the Sudan. My experience has been that they are the kind of insights that do not always wind up as part of the conventional discourse about Africa.

This book, then, is an attempt to make that interior realm come alive, with each character and each relationship that is depicted representing either a detour or a signpost to Africa's true destiny, as some of the finest African and Western minds I have encountered themselves see it.

As a result, I have tried to represent symbolically, which is one of the great prerogatives of literary fiction, not only the social qualities that play such an important role in the affairs of a community and its relations to the rest of the world but the qualities of the individual will and spirit as well.

Some of these representations will be clear at once, while others will be cloaked in various attitudes and actions. They apply to the full cast of characters, whether they are from Africa or other parts of the world.

I invite the reader to explore with me this fascinating, sometimes hidden interior landscape, where Africa's future is being slowly but surely forged. In some cases for the worst, but I believe in most cases for the better.

How well I remember a brilliant sun-drenched day in Tanzania as I was on my way to see Kilimanjaro with my lovely musician wife and our fine young boy. Our creaky four-wheel drive pitched and rolled, over one crater and washed-out gully after another, its whining motor keeping time with every shake and rattle, when this massive mountain suddenly loomed in the horizon, a sight so majestic it can turn groans into sighs of wonder.

There Kilimanjaro was -- towering, snow-capped power emerging from a hot and dusty land, the destination point of our pockmarked highway. And now in retrospect, after recalling that scene many times, I know what it means. Africa is that road, and that grand mountain represents its hope.

Does this seem too impractical a notion in view of the harsh social conditions prevailing in so much of the continent? I don't think so. It can help to turn to our unfettered imagination if we are going to cope with the troubles that confront us, wherever and whatever they are. But while there are times we need to let our imagination dance freely, we also need to remember when it needs to be done respectfully and with great care. *Mcheza hawi kiwete, ngoma yatak matao,* goes the Swahili saying, or "A dancer should not be crippled, for dancing calls for grace." I have endeavored to keep the wisdom of those words in mind in writing this book.

Louis Segesvary
July 2011

CHAPTER 1
ON RULAWANDA STREET

∽

It was the month of November in 1997 in Kenya. The second rainy season of the year had begun weeks earlier, but the equatorial sun, a shimmering ball of fire suspended in the sky, had lost none of its power. As noonday arrived, it had already burned off the morning haze hanging over Nairobi, Kenya's capital city, while the tin roofs of buildings scattered around the civic center turned warm in its rays.

Alain Sardou, on assignment in Nairobi to cover East Africa for Agence France-Presse International, had just left his office in Chichester House in the downtown area of the city to take a break and get some fresh air. As he strolled toward Moi Avenue he heard piercing, high-pitched screaming in Swahili.

"*Hapana, hapana*...No! No! I wasn't doing anything. Please stop it! Please stop! Someone help me! Please help me!"

Before he knew it, Alain was on the sidewalk of Moi Avenue, swept up into a crowd of angry faces forcing its way in the direction of the wailing voice.

"No! Please. Don't punish me. I didn't mean it. Please! I'm just a poor street boy, just a poor boy!"

As he drew closer to the cries, he could tell they were coming from Rulawanda Street, off to the right. Soon, he could see the outer wall of the layers of jostling people surrounding the trapped boy. Pushing his way through the packed crowd, Alain was able to catch a glimpse of a skinny body in a smudged tee shirt, torn jeans, and sandals probably made from a rubber tire.

A visibly irate, heavyset woman in an awkwardly-fitting, one-piece print dress, with its unraveled hem dragging in the dirt, caught his eye. Her brightly-colored headdress dripping with sweat, she was tugging fiercely at the boy's ear while others jeered and spat on him.

"*Mwizi, mwizi*...Thief, thief!" she was screaming at the top of her lungs. "You stole my earring!"

"We will punish you!" rang one voice, while another shouted, "You will pay for what you've taken. We will teach you! We know who you are and where you are from."

By now the boy was shaking and sobbing uncontrollably, begging the crowd to let him go as they pulled and tore at his grimy clothing.

"Please! Please stop! Yes, yes, I took the earring."

He reached carefully into his left pocket and pulled it out to show them. "Here, take it back," he wailed as he held up the round silver earring. "I needed to get some *kitu kidogo* for my mother and father. They sent me to the streets...We have nothing...I have to help them."

"Liar, liar!" a voice roared back. "You were stealing so you could buy more glue to sniff, not to help your parents!"

A long brown hand emerged from the crowd. Alain recognized it as a man's hand, extending from the arm of a summer sports jacket, torn right up to the elbow and spattered with remnants of grease and food. But the hand didn't reach for the earring in the terrified boy's hand. Instead, it reached into the right pocket of the boy's tattered jeans and pulled out a small cardboard roll.

"You see! Here, in his pocket, I have found the proof! This is what he used to sniff the glue," yelled the voice attached to the long hand. "Someone, anyone, bring the paraffin!"

Alain shuddered as he heard the word. Paraffin in Kenya meant kerosene.

"I'm getting the paraffin!" another voice rang out.

2

"Hurry, hurry!" several voices demanded almost in unison.

"Yes, be quick about it!" another voice urged as the crowd continued slapping, kicking, and spitting at the boy, whose hands flew up and down without stopping as he tried to protect his face and his shins at the same time.

Jolted by a sudden surge from behind, Alain felt himself being pushed forward by the crowd, almost losing his footing. He knew if that happened he was done for. He also knew that he needed more room if he wasn't going to be crushed and began shoving both his elbows around him as hard as he possibly could. The pressure relented for a moment, and as he began to catch his breath, a large, rectangular can reeking of paraffin appeared, passed along over a series of shoulders by one pair of hands to another until a scowling man right next to the boy caught it and held on to it.

"Quick, now!" a voice demanded.

"I know what to do!" the man holding the can retorted. "Somebody, give me a match!"

Alain numbly watched as a box of matches was thrust into the paraffin man's right hand. Suddenly, Alain felt himself lose his balance from the jostling of the crowd. Forced to his knees in the middle of a tangle of bodies pressed against one another, he blindly thrust his left hand out for support and managed to grab the rear pocket of a pair of pants. His right hand then grabbed a belt of someone else's pants, and he was able to slowly pull his way back up to his feet.

Once standing, he felt the crowd pressing around him even harder, trapping him so tightly that he could hardly breathe or see ahead. As he gasped for air, a body ahead of him shoved another body to the side, allowing him to see splashes of paraffin landing on the boy, with the fuming, stinking liquid drenching what was left of the boy's tattered tee shirt.

An elbow caught Alain hard on the right side of his face, sending a streak of pain through his cheekbone and a wave of nausea to his stomach while the agitated voices of the crowd joined together in a crescendo of shouts and screams that dazed his mind.

He put his hand to his throbbing face and rubbed it. Suddenly another elbow crashed into the left side of his face, sending him reeling and his knees buckling. After steadying himself, he crouched down to avoid getting hit again and managed to push himself forward closer to the boy.

His cries had now become a combination of pathetic sobbing, wailing, and pleading.

"Please, please stop! No, no, don't kill me; don't kill me like this! Please take the earring back. Somebody take it from my hand. Please give it back to the owner."

"I don't want it now!" the woman who had owned the earring screamed. "He spoiled it for me with his dirty hands."

"Please take it back," the boy pleaded. "I have no parents. They both died from slim disease...I lied because I was afraid...I take glue so I don't feel so sad."

"You liar, you thief!" rang another voice. "We know who you are and where you are from. You are a thief. You like to steal. And now you will be punished!"

"What are we waiting for?" still another voice shouted. "Burn him, burn him! Turn him into ashes! He will see what we do to thieves."

As the crowd continued to grow in number and fury, with waves of shouting rolling into one another so that Alain could no longer tell when one ended and the other began, he was startled by a still louder but much stranger sound. It was an earsplitting hum, which sounded like the same kind of electrically amplified sound he had heard earlier in the day while sauntering through the small grassy area that passed for a noon-time park on the rear side of Moi Avenue.

A row of stores and eateries lined the little park, which was cordoned off by barbed wire on short pegs. A preacher had stood on a wooden crate there, holding a microphone hooked up to a worn black box with dials connected to a long patched-up cord leading to a nearby grocery store. Wearing a faded charcoal suit that was too small for his tall body, he had managed to draw the attention of five or six people who had stopped to hear him.

This was a real Bible-thumper, Alain remembered thinking at the time, struck by his face, lean as rawhide, hands huge, and eyes gleaming.

By now, the hum from the amplifier had turned into a commanding, resonating voice, overwhelming every other noise on the street.

"Stop, please stop in the name of God!" a deep bass voice boomed.

Alain could see out of the corner of his eye that it was the same preacher from the grassy patch now standing on his crate off to the side of the crowd, with the amplifier right before him. He wondered who had given him the power outlet for it.

"In the name of God, I beg of you to stop this evil now. It's not too late for you to stop. But you must stop now!"

"Somebody make him shut up," a voice from the crowd shouted. Two men rushed toward the preacher, but before they could reach him he jerked the cord that connected the amplifier to the outlet, coiled it up as it curled toward him, and then unfurled it, whipping and lashing the men and the rest of the mob without mercy. The cord cracked sharply and danced wildly in the air, raining lash after lash on the mob as the preacher's jacket flayed in unison to the furious movement of his outstretched arms.

Many in the crowd were now screaming and wrapping their hands around their heads in self-defense as they tried to escape, some tripping and falling on their faces then getting up and running even harder, until they scattered into the adjoining streets and alleys.

In all the turmoil, the paraffin can, now nearly empty, dropped to the sidewalk with a clang, spilling what was left on the ground, while the boy took flight, scampering away as fast as his bruised legs could carry him. As Alain watched the boy disappear into the distance, he heard the welcome sound of sirens and screeching tires. Four Kenyan policemen in blue uniforms, revolvers in hand, poured out of two late-model Japanese cars.

The few remaining members of the mob stumbled over each other trying to reach the same corner the boy had slipped behind. Some were too slow. Alain watched the policemen catch up with several fleeing men, whom they tackled, hand-cuffed, and threw into the back seats of the police cars.

Once the police left and the street slowly returned to normal, Alain brushed off his clothes and looked around for the preacher. He saw no sight or trace of him. Nor did he see the amplifier and cord.

He looked up at the sky. It had become overcast, and big drops of rain were beginning to fall from above. First, it was one drop, then another and another, until they were splattering all around him, forming tiny craters in the dust along the edges of the sidewalk, which then blended into rivulets of sticky brown mud.

The sun was long gone with dark clouds crowding out the last remaining patches of blue in the sky. He stopped walking and began running back to his office, the soles of his soft leather loafers picking up bits of the mud seeping onto the sidewalk. He didn't have an umbrella and didn't want to get drenched any more than he was, not with all the unfinished business waiting for him.

CHAPTER 2
SOUNDS OF THUNDER

☙

The hands of the plain clock on the wall were juxtaposed in a thin, inverted Roman numeral V pointed downward at exactly 5:35 p.m., while shadows were creeping their way to the baseboards of the white walls in Alain Sardou's office. One and a half hours had passed since he had resumed the session with the two Kenyan women who ran his office for him. He was beginning to squint and should have put on his glasses, but he remained too preoccupied to take them out of his shirt pocket.

The movement of feet along the corridor outside had ceased some time ago, as many of the correspondents and staff in the building had already gone home. But while the corridor traffic had abated, the angry verbal exchanges between these two employees sitting before his desk hadn't. Besides the words, the tension was so palpable it seemed to fill the room to the exploding point.

He didn't like finding himself being swayed by the passion of their outbursts. He didn't like being distracted from the rational merits of the arguments they were pressing on him. And, most of all, he didn't like feeling more helpless by the minute in simply trying to determine who was telling the truth.

"But didn't you admit earlier that you had been telling other employees in the building that Roselyne was trying to get you fired? That's spreading gossip and undermining morale. I won't tolerate that."

Alain was now speaking firmly, unequivocally, to Ann, leaning forward to emphasize his words as he struggled to resist the temptation to get up from behind his desk and pace the room in circles around her.

"Please explain," he continued. "Help me get to the bottom of this."

"It's true that I did talk to Njeri and Sally about my problems with Roselyne," Ann answered haltingly, "and I'm sorry for that. But she'd been making my life miserable while you were traveling."

Alain sighed under his breath as he abruptly turned toward the wall where he thought he had just seen a mosquito quietly alight. Mosquitoes were rare in Nairobi due to its cool altitude, and the ones around were not as a rule malarious. But he knew of a case where an expatriate had contracted the disease after going to the train station to pick someone up arriving from Mombasa on the Indian Ocean coast, where malaria-carrying *Anopheles* mosquitoes abounded. The man had been bitten by a female mosquito of the genus, which had found its way onto the train and emerged in Nairobi at just the right time to land on him and pass the parasite into his blood.

It was his bad luck that he was the one bitten and not the passenger he was meeting. And it was more bad luck that he had gotten the virulent cerebral variety of this plague and was close to joining the over-one-million Africans who died from malaria every year. But he survived, and that was the only kind of luck that counted in the end.

He looked more closely at the wall. Not seeing any mosquitoes, he turned back to look again at the two women before him. What must they think of my bruised cheeks, he wondered, but then dismissed the thought.

He leaned forward, focusing on Ann. "Yet you two had been getting along so well for the previous months. Roselyne took you under her wing and showed you everything you needed to know to serve as her back-up. I know that you're not of the same tribe, but at times I thought you were. You two acted just like sisters."

"That's what makes me so angry with Ann," replied Roselyne. "She has no gratitude and everyone could see that she was no longer satisfied with her position and wanted mine."

"Ann says that you yelled at her and threatened to get her fired."

"That's not true. I did no such thing!" Roselyne exclaimed indignantly.

"Yes, you did!" Ann retorted, her voice rising to match Roselyne's. "I was afraid to tell Alain because you've been his assistant ever since he came here, and I knew that he relied on you. But that's not all people were saying."

"Stop it," Alain interjected, his annoyance growing. "That's a ridiculous suggestion. I'm not the issue: you two are."

He paused and continued. "I want the truth and I want it now. Ann, what about the personal telephone calls Roselyne says you were making while I was gone?"

"I did make some, but not nearly as many as Roselyne says. My children were sick and I had to look after them. That meant calling home sometimes during the day, just for a few minutes each time, though. You understand, don't you, Alain?"

"Ann," Alain whispered, calmly enunciating each word. "I don't know if Roselyne has been abusive with you. I do know that you started complaining to the others without coming to me. That's not helpful. It's also your responsibility as the new member on the team to respect the older players. Roselyne has been here in this office for more years than you have and has done an outstanding job. You have to give her credit. So this is what I want you to do. Apologize and begin acting in a civil way with her again. Surely that's not so hard to do. You can do it, can't you?"

"Yes, Alain, I can do that. Oh, yes I can. Roselyne, I apologize. I really do. I won't talk about you again."

"I don't know if I can believe you," Roselyne replied, her eyes narrowing, lips curling upward. "You've lied too many times before."

"No, I haven't lied," responded Ann. "And I'm apologizing, even though you were abusive with me."

"No, I was never abusive with you!" Roselyne retorted angrily. "Where's your proof?"

"Stop it, stop it!" Alain interjected again. "Roselyne, please listen. Ann has apologized. Will you accept her apology?"

"Oh, all right, Alain," Roselyne answered with a sigh. "I will give her one more chance."

"Roselyne, it's your responsibility as well never to abuse Ann. I know you say you didn't. But I'm repeating this as a matter of policy, not as a matter of judgment. Is that clear?"

"The policy is clear, Alain, though I never abused her."

"Roselyne, you did. But I'm still sorry," Ann muttered.

"No, I didn't, but we'll see if you really mean it," Roselyne answered.

"All right, I think that's enough. I can see that we've gone as far as we can." Alain was now visibly tired and his voice was beginning to trail off. "It's late and you can both leave now. Tomorrow you can come in later since I will be in the field for the day. Goodnight Roselyne, Ann."

"Good night, Alain."

"Have a good trip, Alain."

Without waiting for them to close the door as they left his office, Alain started to clear his desk. He threw several papers into his briefcase, ran out to the parking lot, climbed into his old Subaru sedan, and headed for the exit, waving to the parking attendant who was already lifting the barrier to let him out onto the street.

It was nearly dusk as he left the city's business center and headed toward his bungalow on the outskirts of the city. First, he made his way through Kenyatta Avenue to Ngong Road, and then onto Kabarnet Road, passing piles of rotting garbage, smoldering outdoor cooking fires, and flimsy huts made from scrap wood, cardboard, polyethylene and tin, silhouetted against the smoky sky. Every few seconds he had to brace himself as he swerved to avoid a pothole. When he did hit one, the chassis of the Subaru shuddered from front to end, the vibrations running up his hands and through his forearms.

He brought the Subaru to a stop at the Karanja Road intersection, where several street children in dirty, ragged clothes rushed to his car, their grimy faces peering at him as they pounded on the windows with their fists, demanding money. One, whose age he guessed to be about 13 or14, was waving a banged-up aluminum cup and hopping from car to car on a deformed leg as thin as a twig and half as long as his other leg. Another seemed to look just like the child he had seen nearly burned to death earlier in the day.

He took a quick look at his car doors to make sure they were locked. He had been persuaded several weeks ago by a colleague to stop giving money to child beggars because it only encouraged them to stay on the streets. "Don't give, no matter how much they beg," he had said. "Giving just makes them want to continue begging from passersby, and the nuisance to us grows."

As he caught the look of annoyance in his colleague's eye, Alain understood the argument. It was logical. It made perfect sense if avoiding being bothered was the issue. But he had also caught the look of desperation in the eyes of some of these children as they flitted from car to car. Did avoiding them make sense if survival itself were the issue? Where could they go? Who would take them in? Were there enough shelters?

He knew of one shelter for AIDS orphans founded by an American priest/doctor who left a successful medical practice in America to come here. But he knew that the needs of these

11

many children went far beyond what this one gallant man or the few other shelters could meet.

When the light changed to green, he gunned the accelerator and sped across the intersection. He was thinking too much about his session with Ann and Roselyne to pay any attention to Nairobi's street life this evening. The angry exchanges between Roselyne and Ann had been pressing on his mind more than the violent images and sounds of the near-lynching of the young glue-sniffer earlier in the afternoon on Rulawanda Street. He still had no idea which of the two was being truthful; or more to the point, what might have been the true parts in their stories.

It was nearly dark by the time he reached his one-story bungalow in what Kenyans considered one of the better residential districts of the city, though still inferior to the exclusive area where most of the expatriate community lived. The uniformed security guard sitting on a bamboo chair at the entrance to the driveway stood up as he saw Alain's car approaching and fished the keys out of his gray trousers to open the heavy, one-piece metal gate to let him enter.

Alain waved to the saluting guard and parked his Subaru in front of the garage. He grabbed his briefcase and walked to the wall in front of the main entrance to the bungalow and passed through its two-piece iron-barred gate. At his request, Rebecca, his housekeeper, always left it unlocked, which allowed the partitions to separate and open when he came home.

After passing through this first gate, Alain took his own keys out of his pocket and locked it behind him. He then walked another few steps through a small garden to the bungalow's thick wooden front door, protected by a smaller iron-barred gate. This second gate was kept locked, and he had to search through his jumble of keys some more to find the right one to open the padlock. After it was open, he unlocked the door. Once he was in, he only put the keys back into his pocket after he had locked the smaller gate from the inside.

The house was quiet, as he always allowed Rebecca, who was of the Luhya tribe, Kenya's second-largest ethnic community, to leave at 6:00 p.m., even on the days he was late. Though some demagogues of Kenya's largest tribe, the Kikuyu, disparaged the Luhya as fit only to be "watchmen" or "cooks," Rebecca trumped the unfair stereotype. She shrewdly managed the household budget he entrusted to her in addition to preparing flavorful local dishes, long on chicken and strong on vegetables.

Wandering into the kitchen, he heated up the pot of rich Kenyan coffee Rebecca had left him and took a bite of one of the sandwiches neatly laid out for him on a plate accompanied by a mound of *ugali* paste made from maize. He then added some banana and papaya slices and took his meal into his study to eat while he worked. The article he was supposed to have finished by the end of the week was still only in its draft phase. He was probably going to have to stay up much too late again, but he wasn't worried about it. He could get by with only a few hours of sleep when he had to.

The sandwiches were satisfying. The thick slices of cooked ham were fresh and the unsalted butter lacing the roughly textured whole-grain bread was sweet. When he was finished, he took the empty plate and coffee cup back to the kitchen and returned to his writing.

Two hours later, a little after 10, Alain was still sitting at his desk in his study. He removed his glasses, rubbed his eyes, and peered out the window into the murky night. Squinting through the branches of the honeysuckle tree outside, he could see no stars or moon to illuminate the darkness except for the flickering of a solitary street lamp two blocks away. The bulbs of all the other lamps in the vicinity had long since burned out and still hadn't been replaced.

The article he was writing was going badly. He couldn't seem to put his heart into his work as his thoughts would periodically take off on a rambling jaunt in search of the right words or phrases, which never seemed to come. How was he supposed to describe all the changes this country had gone through since achieving independence from the British in 1963 in only a few thousand words? Yet that was what his editors wanted: a feature article compressing 34 years into one tightly-constructed article.

The round black keys of his classic 1938 Hermes green portable typewriter, with the letters of the alphabet stamped on them in crisp white characters, stared back at him. They made it seem so easy to write. All one had to do was type letters to make up just one word, with another word following it, and then another until a sentence was formed that laid out an idea, described an event, or recounted some dialogue. That was what it boiled down to, so there was really no reason for getting stuck as long as you could begin with just one word. In fact, not only was there no good reason, there was no excuse for getting stuck, at least not for long, since some kind of word would always come with a little conscious effort, and then the next one would always follow.

Getting stuck really meant quitting. It meant giving up on finding the right word or waiting until it slipped into one's consciousness on its own. And that might not happen for quite a while – that is, if it ever would without the nudge of beginning with some other word, any word at all really.

But putting the first word down on paper depended, of course, on figuring out what he wanted to write about and understanding it. Once he achieved that, words would start flowing as surely as night followed day. He thought of a reporter from another news organization who didn't let not knowing what he was writing about stop him from writing, and writing plenty. Why couldn't he be like that? After all, in the end who really cared what he would leave out in any article he wrote? Who would notice? Did very many people care to remember what they read in this newspaper or in that magazine during the past week, much less what they heard on the radio or saw on television?

No matter, he should be grateful for his job, not the least because he was being paid well. He could thank his mother for his fluency in French, but it was his British father who also taught him English from childhood and made this assignment possible, which was into its fourth month now. And if the first month here was an adventure, the following three were a widening window of his initial glimpses into this land and its people.

Nairobi was a good place to do reporting. Nestled in Kenya's highlands at some 1,660 meters above sea level, it was one of the African continent's largest cities between Johannesburg in the south and Cairo in the north. From here one could cover not only the political and economic issues of the immediate region but a good part of the rest of Africa as well.

As with so many of the capital cities of Africa, Nairobi was also marked by stark contrasts. Within walking distance of the hustle and bustle of the city center was the sprawling slum of Kibera, home to close to one million impoverished people. Alain was shaken when he had first seen it for himself. The sight of its teeming shanties bereft of sewers and running water, riddled with squalor and disease, and surrounded by immense piles of garbage, weighed heavily on him for some time. He had never seen hunger and desperation on such a scale before.

It was a nice thing to be a tourist and be whisked from the airport to comfortable quarters in a picturesque travel lodge. It was a fine thing to dine on generous portions of mouthwatering meats accompanied by imported wines in one of Kenya's noted game parks. It was another thing entirely, however, to visit Kibera and remain unaffected by it. The happy trajectory from airport to lodge to park, back to lodge and then back to airport, offered only a passing, oblique look into the heart of this country. And now he had to describe life in this land as it really was.

Out of the corner of his left eye, he caught a slight movement in the light of his desk lamp. Looking closer, he saw an ant struggling to free itself from the snares of a cobweb under the far edge of the windowsill. Ensnared next to the ant in the web was a small beetle that had already given up the fight and was now motionless. He looked more carefully at the web and then the windowsill. He didn't see the spider anywhere. Maybe it was busy spinning another web somewhere.

He considered the ant and its struggle. All he had to do was flick his finger at the web and it would be free. As he began to move his hand toward the web his gaze caught his dog-eared copy of *Considering Poverty in the Developing World,* which he had been reading on and off the past few weeks.

He flipped over to the page he had bookmarked. It began: "Absolute poverty is defined according to a fixed scale of resources that are judged necessary to meet a minimal standard of living. In developing societies where absolute poverty prevails, there is generally little economic growth when measured against the rate of growth in industrial societies. Some scholars hold that in the case of Africa, for example, original natural advantages, such as the ample plant and animal stock amenable to domestication enjoyed by Eurasia, were lacking and substantially held back its economic development."

He read further down the page. "Other scholars believe that Africa's slower development has been in no small part due to its warm climate and abundant wild life, which led to a comfortable accommodation with nature. In contrast, a confrontational encounter with the environment was required in the colder regions of Eurasia, resulting in the building of lasting and complex infrastructure as protection against the elements. While colonialism eventually brought technologically advanced infrastructure to the African continent, at the same time it fostered a culture of dependency in native Africans at odds with the entrepreneurial attitudes associated with robust economic development.

"Still other scholars allude to the economic benefits of the cohesive, homogeneous social texture of the newly industrialized nations of Asia and compare it to the mutual suspicion generated by extensive tribal heterogeneity in the run of African nation-states, which can limit the cooperation necessary for economic progress on a significant scale."

Alain then skimmed through to the last page of the chapter, where he read: "Relative poverty is poverty perceived in the eyes of the beholder. A society may be poor by one set of standards but not feel poor in its own collective subjective judgment. Furthermore, what is considered poverty in one place at one given time may not be considered poverty in a different historical context."

His eyes blurred as he closed the book, which had even more theories of poverty that he wasn't about to wade into now. He was too tired to reflect on what he had just read, much less read any further. He set it aside.

His gaze caught the web at the edge of the windowsill again. The ant was still there, but moving a little more slowly now. He extended his left hand to the web and flicked it with his index finger. The ant landed on the floor, and after licking the remnants of the cobweb off his body with oily saliva, it wobbled toward the hallway.

He tried to refocus on finding the right approach for his article but could not overcome the unease that was now gripping him. The mob scene and then the office dispute had pretty much ruined his mood. Restless, he got up to turn on the table radio at the opposite end of the room, tuned in to a local station, and caught the lively rhythms of a round of East African dance music.

Suddenly, sounds of thunder boomed in the distance. He walked over to the living room to look out on the road through its large picture window, and through the flashes of lightning

17

he could just make out the gnarled, wooden telephone poles extending out into the distance in a neat, single file, some of their wires dangling dangerously close to the ground in long, swaying loops. During the day, he had noted that all a passerby had to do was grab one of the power lines or maybe stumble into one to be electrocuted to death.

He listened to the slow, pulsating rhythms of the dance music playing background to the violent sounds of the storm until after only a few minutes, as quickly as it had arrived, the pouring rain abated.

After he walked back to his desk and started thinking once again about what to write, he was diverted this time by the fluttering, noxious sound of swarms of flying termites. Their wings flailing against the window of his study, they were burrowing their way inside through the spaces where the glass panes did not fit closely enough to the window frame.

As they squeezed in between the frame and the panes, some shearing off their wings in the process, Alain tore pages of a newspaper into shreds and stuffed them into all the gaps he could. But as soon as he closed off one gap, the swarm would pour in through another.

When Alain finally sealed off all the gaps, he was startled by the sound of frenzied pounding against the main door. Running into the hall and turning on the light, he saw fresh columns of termites burrowing through the crack between the door and the floor. The ones still with wings were now whirring above his head while the ones without wings were scurrying around his feet.

These termites, as big as dragonflies, were much larger and stronger than any he had ever seen before. He knew they were prized as food in some places once they were caught and dried in the sun, their wings removed, and their bodies crushed into a nutritious paste. But the last thing he wanted to do was to sample any of these pests now as he struggled to keep them from forcing their way in through the crack, swatting as many as he could with a rolled-up newspaper in one hand while stuffing more paper under the door with the other.

Once he had managed to stop the invasion, he left the ones that had already forced their way in just as they were, whether dead or barely alive, scattered all over the hallway. He returned to his study, where he brushed mounds of dying termites off his desk onto the floor and turned off the radio. He had had enough music and enough of the termites and would ask Rebecca to clean up the mess the next morning.

As his fingers eased onto the smooth keys of the Hermes once again, he thought that he heard the iron gate to the entrance clanging once. He wondered if it might have been a gust of wind from the storm and returned to his writing. In a minute or two, the clanging resumed, only much louder. This time he stood up from his chair and went to the foyer peering outside through one of the small glass windows on both sides of the door to try to see the wall outside, but there was nothing to be seen. When this wall had first been erected, the owners had apparently not thought of setting up lights on it.

His anxiety grew. He recalled what had happened a few weeks ago to a diplomat from Asia posted here. A gang of over a dozen intruders had shown up one night at his residence, ripping into it with crowbars and hammers and stripping it clean of its valuables in a matter of minutes.

Intrusions like this into the wealthier residential sections of Nairobi, from the banks of the polluted Nairobi river dotted with spacious whitewashed, orange-tiled homes to the more modest area where he resided, had become all too common in "the green city in the sun," as it used to be called in popular travel books.

One police official was now referring to these kinds of incidents as "normal crimes," the term he used to describe the morning shooting-death of an expatriate mother by carjackers as she was dropping her daughter off at primary school.

Alain walked slowly and deliberately back to his desk and once again tried to concentrate on his writing, but couldn't; he was worried, debating whether or not he should go out and check with the night guard at the driveway entrance. Before he could decide, the clanging resumed, this time more loudly, more insistently.

He fumbled in the closet to find a flashlight, went back to the main door in the lobby, and shone the light out through the right window. The rain had left a fine mist in the air, and it was not easy to see more than a few meters.

The beam of his flashlight just reached the wall outside and brought into view a pair of large hands shaking two of the entrance gate's inner iron bars. The hands were wrapped so tightly around the bars that the knuckles were white, the blood drained out of them. Alain focused the flashlight above the hands, squinted sharply, and made out the face of his night guard, Okoth.

This was against the rules. All the guards had been specifically instructed by the security company to disturb tenants only in case of emergency and to signal the alarm first. He had heard no alarm. Now Alain was beginning to get as annoyed as he was worried. Still, he had no choice but to see what the guard wanted.

He unlocked the door, then loosened the metal pegs on the top and bottom of the door pinning it to the floor and to the wall rising to the ceiling. Once the door was open, he signaled to Okoth that he was coming while he unlocked the gate just in front of it. He then walked to the wall and its gate supported by two main pillars at each side. The wall itself was topped all around by broken glass. He spoke to Okoth through the gate's bars.

"Okoth, what is it? Is there something wrong?"

Face to face with Alain, Okoth assumed an apologetic look. It was hard for Alain to imagine that this subdued man was behind all the violent clanging he had just heard. This tall

20

figure of a man clad in a yellow rubber raincoat, who had been so vigorously shaking the bars of his gate, was now looking at him with almost pleading eyes.

"I'm sorry, sir, for bothering you," he stammered, "but I could see you through the window. I received some bad news earlier tonight."

"Well, tell me, what is it?" Alain asked. His anxiety was alleviated but not his annoyance. He could smell strong liquor on Okoth's breath. It reeked of *changaa*, cheap and potent and also the most deadly kind of illicit spirits to be had in Kenya. Prepared from maize, millet, or sugarcane, it was often laced with methanol by unscrupulous peddlers. From time to time it left several men and women blind, paralyzed, or dead in Nairobi's slums.

"Here, you can see for yourself, sir. Here is the telegram. My brother's house just burned down."

The guard thrust the telegram of crumpled paper into Alain's hand, leaving him no choice but to read its two-line message: "A fire burned our house down this morning. Please help, John."

"So, John is your brother?" Alain asked.

"Yes, sir."

"But what can I do?" Alain asked half-heartedly, already knowing that he was about to be asked for money.

"I need 6,000 shillings to give him to begin rebuilding the house, sir. Could you please loan it to me?"

"You know that you could be fired for asking me for a loan. The contract with the security company forbids your asking me for a loan. You know that don't you? And you wouldn't be able to repay it anyway, would you?"

"No, sir, I mean yes, sir." The words stumbled slowly out of Okoth's mouth.

"Can you ask your company for a loan? Won't they help?"

"No, sir."

"Are you sure? Have you tried before?"

"Yes, sir. They won't help."

"What about your relatives? I'm only a visitor here. Don't you have anybody at all you can turn to for help?"

"No, sir. My family and relatives are very poor."

"Then what about your tribe? What tribe are you?" Alain asked, knowing full well what his tribe was.

"I'm a Luhya, sir."

"Well, that's a very big tribe. Isn't there anybody in your community that will help you?"

"No one who has any money, sir. This is too much money for anyone I know."

Alain studied this strong and well-built man. They had no contact other than the perfunctory greetings they made to each other twice a day as Alain was leaving and returning to his residence. When a previous guard of another tribe had tried to borrow money from him, Alain had seen to it that he was fired even though he felt sorry for him. He thought that the message had gotten around and that this one knew better. Still, he valued this guard more for his vigilance and alertness. He had never caught him falling asleep or absent from his post.

"All right, Okoth. I'll think about this and talk to you tomorrow. Now go back to work."

"Thank you, sir. Thank you," Okoth replied gratefully, sensing that Alain had already crossed the gulf within a human being that separates pity from indifference.

Alain went back inside after locking the gates and main door and headed into the kitchen. He then opened the side door to go out into the small rear patio enclosed within its high, stone walls. Standing straight, he swallowed large gulps of the cool, wet air. As he felt a growing sense of peace, he walked around the patio and listened to the croaking of a frog and the chirping of crickets. In a few more hours, the Barred Wren Warbler that had made its home in the garden would begin its early morning trilling calls, the bright, rhythmical cadences flowing in perfect repetition one after another.

And then all the lights in the patio and in the house went out.

"These damn power outages again," Alain muttered under his breath.

He waited until his eyes became accustomed to the dark and groped his way to the house and into the kitchen, where he knew two candlesticks and matches were placed just for such times. After lighting the candles, he made his way to his bedroom to go to sleep. The next morning, he was to go with a Kenyan woman, a translator his editors had let him hire to do interviews for a section on ethnic clashes he was including in his article. They were going to visit a camp of displaced persons from those clashes in an area not far from the town of Molo in the Rift Valley. He would need to be fresh and he had stayed up far too long already.

Just as he was drifting off to much-needed sleep, the ringing of the phone on his bed stand startled him. He didn't want to pick it up but he did.

"Alain, is that you?" It was a soft, anxious voice on the other end. "It's me, Alexandra."

"Alexandra! Are you joking? What are you doing calling me now after two years? How did you find out where I was? Where are you?"

"I'm in Geneva. I'm living here now. We're only two hours behind you, so I know that this is a terrible hour to call since it's already approaching midnight here. But I knew that you liked to stay up late, and I just had to hear your voice again. Your news agency's office in Paris gave me your number."

"This is too much, Alexandra. Have you forgotten that you were the one who called it quits and left? You broke things off. I didn't. Don't you remember?"

"Oh, I know, Alain. I was so foolish, so much the child. I'm very sorry, but I never forgot you. I just had to hear your voice again. I always loved to hear your voice, to hear you talk."

"What are you doing now, Alexandra? You say you're living in Geneva. Are you still working for the European Commission?"

"Yes, Alain. I am. I transferred to the Geneva office from Paris because I married a Swiss man last month. I left him sleeping in the other room to call you."

"Are you saying you're married, Alexandra?" Alain exclaimed as the blood drained from his face and he felt weak and unsteady.

"Yes, Alain. I began seeing him after we broke up, and he was so attentive and so kind. He was not as exciting as you, my darling, but he made me feel special. I met him while attending a conference at the Lissandro Hotel where he was the maitre d'."

"So you are married?" Alain asked incredulously again. "Married?"

"Yes, in a Catholic ceremony here in Geneva. I'm sorry that you are taking this news badly, dear Alain. He's a good man. And I was sure that you would have married by now, also. Neither one of us was getting any younger. I'm already 29."

"This is why you call me, Alexandra, to tell me that you're married? Wasn't it enough when you broke off our relationship because you said you needed to find yourself?"

Alain's hands were now shaking. "Do you know how much I longed for you, how much I missed you, how I hoped that I would see you again? But I respected your wishes and never called you after you went your way. Now you call me after all this time to tell me that you're married. It's unbelievable. What are you trying to do to me?"

"Alain, my darling Alain. I'm so sorry, so sorry. I never thought you would take this so hard. I didn't know that you still loved me. I thought I was doing the right thing by marrying this man. But I realized afterwards that something was missing and that I needed to hear your voice."

"It's too late, Alexandra." Anger was creeping into Alain's voice. "You made your choice. I'm not going to let you make me suffer anymore."

"Alain, please don't hang up. I already feel so much better after talking to you. I needed to hear your voice so very much! Don't hang up. I'm so sorry."

"Goodbye, Alexandra!" Alain shouted as he slammed down the phone.

He stood up from the edge of the bed where he had been sitting while taking the call, hardly noticing that the power had returned. His hands still trembling, he walked slowly to the bathroom. After switching on the light, he turned on the faucet and splashed cold water on his face. He looked into the mirror. It seemed to him that he looked older than his 38 years.

He turned away and went back into the bedroom to the chest of drawers. Jerking the bottom drawer open, he began rummaging through the odds and ends until he found a green photo album embossed with golden swirls along its edges. He flipped through it until he found the picture he was looking for. It was the last one he had saved of Alexandra, both of them side by side, happily posing for the camera while on vacation in Athens, Greece. Having destroyed every other photo he had of her, he had resolved not to destroy this one until he was certain he would never see her again. He took it now in his hands and slowly crushed the glossy picture.

As the finality of it all began to sink in amid a rush of images coming back to him of her lovely, smiling face, waves of her soft, golden hair glistening as they graced her shoulders, and her bright green eyes sparkling, he bolted out of the room and ran toward the kitchen. Forgetting that he already had matches in his pocket, he clumsily groped in the pantry until he found another box and ignited the crumpled photo, watching it burn up into a sticky, charred mess. He then threw it into the garbage can under the sink.

Seeing a half-empty bottle of wine on the counter, he seized it and threw it crashing onto the kitchen wall. With tears burning his eyes, he then stared vacantly at the splattered wine dripping into the nooks and crannies of the pieces of glass that had scattered before his feet.

He watched until the last drop of wine settled into place and then walked slowly back to his bedroom. After opening the window, he pulled the chair standing in the corner to the window's ledge, sat down, and quietly folded his hands in his lap. Far off in the distance, he could hear the howling of a lone dog, rising and falling, and then not rising or falling so much until it turned into a whine and finally a whimper.

When he could hear the faint echoes no more, he returned to bed. He knew that he needed to rest. The translator he was to meet, a Wangetha Wachira, would be waiting for him at around 10:30 a.m. in the commercial district. He stared out into the darkness until he fell asleep.

CHAPTER 3
A MESSAGE FROM SIERRA LEONE

∽

The next day Alain awoke at half past eight. As he rubbed the sleep out of his eyes, he realized that he had forgotten his notes and directions for the trip to Molo. Luckily though, he would have enough time to drive to his office and get them before meeting his Kenyan translator. There would even be enough time to take breakfast in a nearby hotel. He quickly cleaned up the mess he had left in the kitchen, got dressed, and headed out the door.

As he slipped into his Subaru under the brightly rising sun, he waved to Rebecca, who had just arrived. The traffic was already heavy as Alain began the drive to his office. Japanese minivans known as *matatus*, crammed full of passengers, were careening in and out of traffic, while buses belching black and sooty smoke were jockeying for position with a relentless stream of cars of every size, shape, and condition on Nairobi's thinly-tarmacked roads.

Nearly three-quarters of an hour later, he pulled into the parking lot, the tires of his Subaru noisily crunching the gravel. He greeted the attendant and went straight to the main door of Chichester House. It was open so he didn't have to use his key.

After climbing the steps to the third floor, he noticed that the lights were on in the office down the hall from his. That was where the correspondent for the United American Wire Service hung out, an American by the name of Kenneth

Williams whom Alain had run into a few times while covering the local diplomatic scene. He guessed that Williams was about his age.

Since Williams had been gone for a while, Alain was curious as to his doings and wandered over to his office. Through the open door he saw him packing his effects into a large green duffel bag, the kind soldiers used. He knocked on the door frame.

Caught off guard, Williams looked up. "Alain Sardou, right? What can I do for you?"

"Oh, nothing. I just haven't seen you lately. I hope that I'm not intruding on you."

"No, not at all. I'm just a little busy right now, as you can see. But I'm in no hurry."

As Alain walked in, he saw that the walls were already bare.

"I thought you were going to be around longer. Is your assignment here over?"

"Yeah, I finally finished my tour. Five years in this part of the world has been interesting, but it's enough. I need to move on." Williams continued packing, throwing notebooks, files, and books into the duffel bag.

"Where are you going from here?"

"For right now I'm going back to the United States."

"I've spent a lot of time in England, but I've never been to the States," Alain said.

"It's the only place I want to be right now."

"You covered Rwanda at the height of the genocide in '94 didn't you? I was in Paris when it happened, but I read some of your stories off the wire. You turned in some good reporting."

"What was so good about it?" Williams snapped. "Because it came from me as a black man?"

"No, of course not," Alain said, taken aback. "Your reporting was good, period."

Williams stopped packing to take a good look at Alain, who was still standing in the door. "Thanks for putting it that way. It's just that so many of you white folks assume that because my ancestors were from this continent I have some kind of special access to it. But let me tell it to you straight. If I ever felt that before coming here, I don't feel it now that I've lived here for a while. If you could've seen what went on a few nights ago at the Jockey Pub in the Hilton Hotel, you would understand in a flash. But what am I saying? You were there. I remember seeing you. It was a couple of Fridays ago, around 5:00 p.m., when the pub's happy hour begins."

Alain thought hard for a minute. "Now that you mention it, I was there. I dropped in while I was waiting for a visitor to come down from his room. What about it?"

"You didn't see me in the left corner at a table, did you?"

"No, I didn't notice. I just went to the table closest to the bar and sat down. There isn't that much light in there. I didn't bother to look around. Why?"

"Well, I'd been sitting at that table for about 10 minutes. A server had passed by with a tray and said he would get back to me right away. I was waiting for him when you came in. Imagine how I felt when that same server, a local Kenyan darkie, then came out of the kitchen, sized you up on the spot, and took your order. I was still waiting, get the picture? You as a whitey are served at once, while I cool my black heels."

Alain looked at his watch. There was plenty of time. He walked over to a chair in Williams' office that was facing his desk and sat down. Williams continued staring at him.

"I had no idea," Alain said, shaking his head. "For sure, I didn't want to be served before you."

"You don't have to say anything. Just don't put all of us into the same box. I'm not saying that's what you do, Alain. But I hardly have to tell you that things are not always what they seem."

29

"How well I know," Alain nodded in agreement. "But on that point I also know that any decent reporter will do his damnedest to make people see things, especially disturbing things, not as they seem but just as they are. And believe me, that is exactly what your reporting on the blood fest in Rwanda did. Your accounts of the killing in all their gruesome details were hard on our feelings. But that's what it took to alarm the rest of the world and help stop the genocide. You..."

"Wait a minute," Williams interrupted. "I reported on the killing in Rwanda for over one month. One story even came complete with photos of some of the thousands of bodies flowing down the Kagera River into Lake Victoria like so many logs on a timber run. But the killing didn't stop then, not by a long shot. Get the pun, Alain?"

Alain managed a wry smile. "Yeah, I get it."

"Neither your country nor mine, much less the United Nations, hardly lifted a finger to stop it. Don't tell me that you don't know that it was an invading Tutsi army from neighboring Uganda that finally stopped the killing."

"Of course I know," Alain winced, embarrassed at his careless assessment of how the genocide had been halted. "It was a bad time for all of us," he said quietly. "We all should have done more."

Williams took a deep breath. "The numbers still stagger me. Nearly one million Rwandans, mostly Tutsis but also many Hutus, met a bullet or the blade of a machete. And we're on the cusp of the twenty-first century. We're supposed to be making social progress in this world."

He went back to his packing.

"Do you want to see something, Alain?"

"It depends. What is it?"

"You probably don't know that I just came back from Freetown in Sierra Leone. It's something that a Sierra Leonean man, a 45-year-old father of six children, gave me."

"So, what is it?" Alain asked, his interest piqued.

"Here, catch," Williams said, as he reached into his duffel bag and threw a jar of formaldehyde with a severed black hand floating in it right at Alain's stomach, forcing him to catch it before it dropped.

"Hey, what's the meaning of this?" Alain exclaimed, rising from his chair and clutching the jar.

"I'm glad you asked," Williams replied, "because I'm going to take your figure of speech at its word. What is the meaning of this – this hand? That should be the real question, shouldn't it? Not, what do I mean by throwing it at you. In fact, we should be talking about two hands. I didn't bring the other one, which was also chopped off. So, what is their meaning? We know what they meant to the father of the six children who lost them. They were his means of supporting his family. They were the daily tools of his manhood, of his husband-hood, of his fatherhood."

"This was part of the campaign of atrocities by the rebels, wasn't it?"

"That's right. I learned that the so-called rebels that did this had taken over some diamond mines. The bastards wanted to make an example of this man. They wanted to send a message. Look here, people: this is what will happen to anyone who won't dig up diamonds for us. It wasn't even a question of his refusing to do the work. It was just a matter of the rebels scaring hell out of anyone and everyone."

"And once again, these crimes were not exactly being carried out without anyone knowing about it," Alain acknowledged. "Plenty had been written and said about them."

"But little done."

"What about the family of this poor man in Sierra Leone?"

"Now it's his wife who is spoon-feeding him while his daughters fetch the wood for a fire to cook the food handouts they manage to get."

Williams paused to let his words sink in. "So we know what these hands meant to this man. But what do they mean to us, us bystanders? That's what I haven't figured out."

Williams paused again, as if reaching deeply back into his mind for more thoughts. "Now don't misunderstand me. I know that anyone with the least human feeling would feel sorry for this man and his family. But I also know that all the sympathy in the world cannot bring his hands back, just as I know that all the remorse expressed by politicians and diplomats over their inaction in Rwanda cannot give the victims their lives back."

"We can't change what has been done," Alain nodded.

"No, of course not," Williams responded, "but I can't get over the lack of balance in the equation coming out of tragedies such as Rwanda and Sierra Leone. On the one side is the brutal loss of life and limb. On the other side is our response in the form of feeling sorry about it. But can how we respond ever balance out an equation so heavily weighted on the side of suffering? Can the most exquisite expressions of remorse or sadness ever count as much as the pain on the other side?

"I know you must be thinking that I've set up an irrelevant proposition to begin with," Williams continued. "After all, why should there be such an equation in the first place? Well, I'll tell you why. It's because we, the bystanders, set it up when we gush out these words of regret in response to the horrors we've just seen. We create the equation right then and there. And it is woefully unbalanced."

"But the imbalance in your equation is not always our fault, Kenneth. In bloodbaths on the scale of a Rwanda, yes, no doubt. But in other places, what you would see as an imbalance is often the best that we bystanders can do. We can't possibly send armies into every place in the world where there is conflict, much less prevent every atrocity. To think we could is not being practical or realistic. And where we can't intervene or where we learn too late, our expressions of sorrow are to be commended, don't you think? They show our humanity, our solidarity with the victimized."

"Don't get me wrong, Alain. Of course they're commendable. But again, whatever the reasons, the imbalance in the basic equation keeps haunting me. On the one side, immeasurable suffering and irreplaceable losses. On the other side, our fine feelings, for which we even congratulate ourselves at times. These simply aren't enough to compensate for the pain and loss."

"And I suppose in your equation, even acts of charity to help the victims could not balance the equation."

"No, it wouldn't be enough, and it would be too late."

"So people should not try to help?"

"Again, please don't misunderstand me, Alain. Of course, we need to do everything possible to awaken the world to these kinds of atrocities. And we need to help the victims as much as we can. All this can make the equation less one-sided. But at the same time we need to see that unless our efforts can restore hands to as good as new, as with the father in Sierra Leone, they can't adequately compensate the victims."

"What more can we do then, Kenneth? Most of us in this world are going to be bystanders of one sort or another. That's our destiny, like it or not."

Williams turned his face away from Alain to look into his desk drawer and take out the last of the pens and pencils he kept there. After throwing them into his duffel bag, he looked at Alain again.

"Maybe there's something wrong with me, Alain. Why do I want to see my equation balance out? Why should it even exist in the first place? And yet it *exists* for me, and I want it balanced more than anything else in the world."

"You tell me," Alain said.

Williams furrowed his brow. "It was to force myself to come to grips with that equation that I saved this crumpled fist."

33

"In Rwanda," Williams continued, "I saw mostly the dead, but in Sierra Leone I saw mostly the maimed and disfigured. I was at a small town, close to the country's prized diamond fields a few hours from the capital, to get the atmospherics of this so-called civil war. My hope was to take some photos of the rebels, maybe even catch a brief firefight from a distance. You know the kind of stuff I'm talking about, what gets us journalists just close enough to the action without getting killed.

"I ran across this scene of about a dozen people running into the town screaming and yelling for help. All of them, men and women alike, had had at least one of their hands chopped off. The townspeople immediately rushed the victims to the small local clinic to stop their bleeding. As tourniquets and gauze were applied, I learned that the rebels had attacked them on the edge of town as they were looking for firewood. I risked going back to the scene with a couple of other townspeople who took a bucket to fetch whatever hands were still left there. We collected five hands and took them back to the clinic, where we laid them in front of the victims. The man I told you about identified two of them as his own. After he told me his dreadful story, I decided, with his permission, to keep one of them in this jar until I came to terms with it. I swore that I would throw it away once I did that, but I haven't figured out any kind of answer yet."

"Why do you need an answer?" Alain asked. "It happened. We feel badly about it. This is tragedy, Kenneth. Stare it in the face and accept it as part of life, as part of its brutal, inexplicable side. You couldn't do anything more about it than what you did. You wrote truly about what you saw. Why not feel encouraged that you faced it without turning your eyes away or flinching?"

"Something would still be missing for me, Alain. Doesn't it bother you that some of the very leaders of the gangs chopping off hands are going unpunished?"

"Of course. That to me is another tragedy."

"But of a different kind?" Williams asked.

"Of a different kind, yes. It's a matter of political injustice."

"OK. But then let's go back to what I asked you earlier. Considering all that we've said about them up to now, what do his hands mean?"

"You tell me," Alain frowned.

"They mean very little to us," Williams retorted.

"How can you say that? Is this an extrapolation from your equation?"

"It's so obvious," Williams elaborated. "Anything that means anything, anything that we value, we pay for in some way. But in this case there was no price exacted for his hands. Just as you said, it happened. It was a tragedy. A man's hands are chopped off, and there is no price that either the butchers or we the onlookers have had to pay. So for us there can't really be very much meaning to them. The meaning is all in that poor man's head, because he is paying a price hour on the hour as he tries to live without his hands. We can say nice words of pity. But they don't add up to very much. The butchers don't care, and some of them may even wind up in high offices in the government. There is no price paid there. So what did those hands mean? What were they worth?"

"What if the butchers had been arrested and punished and even had their own hands cut off?" Alain responded. "Or if they were executed after being tortured? They would have paid dearly for their crimes. Would that have balanced out your equation?"

"Ah, you think that you have found a way out, don't you?" William rejoined. "An eye for an eye, a tooth for a tooth, or let's even say two eyes for one eye. But tell me honestly, how does that restore our man's hands to wholeness? It doesn't restore anything at all. It may serve as a warning to others. It may bring some evil to heel and offer a level of justice. But this man's loss will haunt him until the day he dies."

35

"What if our man were to somehow forgive these criminals and bear his loss bravely, becoming a hero. Would you still say the equation was unbalanced?"

"His heroism would be a fine thing. It would draw our admiration. But it figures outside the equation since it can't restore his loss. He has to live with it forever."

"What about putting hooks in place of his hands? That would help, wouldn't it?"

"Somewhat, but not enough."

"By your very own terms then, there is no human way to balance out his loss. It remains irreplaceable."

"Now you see my dilemma," Williams said. "It's too bad for me that I just couldn't have walked away from that scene in Sierra Leone and forgotten about it."

"Actually, I admire you for not having forgotten about it," Alain responded.

Williams turned away from Alain to inspect the contents of his duffel bag. "Thanks for stopping by, but now I have to get out of here."

He picked up his duffel bag, grabbed the jar away from Alain, threw it in, and walked out the door.

"Goodbye, Kenneth," Alain called out as Williams paced down the hallway. "You're a good man."

Williams turned a quick glance back, said nothing, and went out into the street.

Alain stood looking at the bare desk Williams left behind – not even a paper clip was left on it. He closed the door behind him and walked out into the street. Williams was already nowhere to be seen. Alain checked his watch. There was plenty of time to have a good breakfast before he had to get to his appointment with Wangetha Wachira, but all he really wanted now was a simple cup of coffee.

CHAPTER 4
ON THE ROAD TO MOLO

∽

The Rift Valley in Kenya possessed some of the richest land in the country, coveted by pastoralists for the grazing of livestock and by farmers for growing maize and vegetables. But during the last few years, fighting had marred the relations among the three major tribes in the region: the Kikuyu, Kalenjin, and Masai.

The Kikuyu were convinced that hard-line elements of the ruling party, dominated by the Kalenjin tribe, were provoking the ethnic clashes to benefit the local Kalenjin and Masai communities.

But hard evidence of specific crimes was elusive in Kenya, with untainted facts as hard to come by as the older 100-shilling notes featuring the imposing visage of Jomo Kenyatta, Kenya's first president.

Even so, it was clear that the energetic Kikuyu, Kenya's largest tribe, were the main losers in the clashes. Enough of their people had been displaced, enough lives were lost, and enough property was destroyed to leave no doubt.

Many in the other smaller tribes remained unsympathetic, choosing to believe that it was the Kikuyu themselves who had instigated the violence, or at the very least had deservedly brought it upon themselves.

Most human rights workers, however, representing both international and local organizations, were ready to indict the government and pointed to the inflammatory statements made by a prominent cabinet minister, a member of the Masai tribe. He had earlier warned the Kikuyu in the affected areas to "lie low like an envelope," or they would be "cut down."

As he approached the city center driving his news agency's Land Cruiser, which he had earlier substituted for his Subaru in Chichester House's parking lot, Alain checked his wristwatch. He should have arrived at the television station where his translator worked some 10 minutes earlier, but he knew that it wouldn't matter. In Kenya it was understood that people would be late for appointments.

Then he saw a tall, statuesque woman standing in front of the building which housed the television station. Stylishly dressed in a lavender jacket, glistening white silk blouse, and a flowing yellow-print skirt dotted by large, orange-tinted sunflowers, she was glancing to the left, and then to the right. He could not help but notice how her proud, tautly sculptured face stood out in sharp relief against the blueness of the morning sky.

Could this be his appointment? He managed to find a parking place in a nearby street and approached the woman in the lavender jacket from her backside, welcoming the opportunity to touch her on the shoulder.

"Are you Wangetha Wachira?" he asked.

"Why, yes. Yes, I am," she said, quizzically, as she turned around, a little startled at the touch of his hand on her body.

He immediately recognized a pleasant Kenyan sound to her English, as opposed to the strictly British-accented variety.

"I'm Alain Sardou from the French press service. I was supposed to meet you at 10:30 a.m. in the lobby of this building. I'm sorry I'm late. The traffic was heavier than I expected."

"It's quite all right," she said softly, her face easing into a smile. "I thought I would come out here in front and wait, since I wasn't sure you knew how to find the station. We're on the seventh and eighth floors with no other floors above us."

"Oh, I think I could have found it, but it was nice of you to come out and wait for me anyway," Alain answered, smiling in turn. "Are you ready to leave for Molo?" he asked.

"Yes," she answered, her dark eyes shining and now fixed on him. She liked well-dressed men, and Alain looked every inch the part of the suave European traveler in his light beige khakis, red scarf, leather belt, and polished boots.

"Is something wrong?" Alain asked, feeling her gaze.

"Oh, no," she answered quickly. "It's just that it's nice to work with someone from France for a change. Usually, British or American journalists are the ones looking for translators."

"You see," she explained, "there really aren't very many Frenchmen working here in Kenya, just as there are few French tourists. It's only natural that they would prefer to visit or live and work in West Africa, where everyone speaks French, instead of here in East Africa, where so many people speak English."

Alain was beginning to feel a little self-conscious about standing on the sidewalk with this attractive black woman, while passersby were slowing down to take a good look at them. He put his hand behind her back and began nudging her in the direction of the Land Cruiser.

In a half-hour's time they had cleared congested Nairobi's outskirts with its ramshackle roadside stalls, makeshift shops, and gray cinder-block motels. After passing a number of road-side peddlers hawking baby rabbits, fruit and woven baskets, they were soon approaching the outer reaches of the ridge of the Great Rift Valley.

Winding down through the eastern side of the African continent, from the Dead Sea in the Jordan Valley, through the Red Sea, through the highlands of Ethiopia, through vast areas of Kenya and Tanzania, and ending in central Mozambique, the Great Rift Valley was the result of the massive tearing of the earth's surface when the tectonic plates of the continents of Eurasia and Africa violently collided and then separated millions of years ago.

As they continued on, passing occasional groups of zebras with their tails flicking as they grazed on the wild grass, and long-necked giraffes nibbling on thistle bushes, they could see Lake Naivasha in the distance – a bluish-green, mirage-like invitation to descend into the valley.

Wangetha's voice interrupted his fascination with the beckoning oasis. "Did you notice the zebras back there?"

"Yes, why?"

"I was asked about them once by a visitor whom I was accompanying here. I was wondering if you would ask the same kind of question that he did."

"What did he want to know?"

"Well, his question was that since zebras had the same kind of physical characteristics as horses and were also grass eaters, why hadn't we tamed them and put them to work, just like horses, instead of letting them all run free? He seemed to think it was an awful waste and perhaps not very smart. What would you say?"

"I would suppose that people here have tried to do that, much as Hannibal used elephants in his army, but didn't have any success."

"And what would you say as to why we didn't have success?"

"There must be something about the zebra that makes it difficult, if not impossible, to domesticate them. So, how did you answer your visitor?"

"I told him just what you said. But he made it seem as though it were somehow our fault, also. Yet nothing could be further from the truth."

"I can imagine that people here tried very hard to make good use of them. It would certainly be to their advantage."

"Yes, but what is not so well known about the zebra, in spite of its charming appearance, is that it will bite without letting go once it gets close enough to anyone. It's simply unchangeable in this respect," she said with a laugh.

Alain joined in the laughter. "Remind me not to get too close to one."

After a few more kilometers had passed, Alain looked to his right to read a road sign, when his eyes caught Wangetha in a fresh view that made him swallow hard. As the coolness of the morning was yielding to the warmth of the late morning sun, she had removed her jacket exposing her white silk blouse, which, loose-fitting that it was, nonetheless left little doubt about the fullness of her womanly assets.

"Is it getting too warm for you?" queried Alain, feigning only passing interest in her appearance.

"No, not really," Wangetha answered. "As you can imagine, I'm very used to the weather, having spent all my life here. I just wanted to be a little more comfortable, a little less encumbered. Sometimes I feel so dragged down, especially when I think about the things we're going to see. To tell you the truth, I didn't really want to go today, but I needed the fee that your news agency is going to pay me."

"How is it that you can speak all these languages?" Alain inquired. "I mean, you speak excellent English, and I'm told Swahili, the Maa language of the Masai, Kikuyu, and the Nandi dialect spoken by the Kalenjin as well. I know Kenyans who speak three of those, but to speak all five is extremely unusual."

"My mother spoke Kikuyu with me from my early childhood until I left home," Wangetha responded. "I studied English and Swahili at school and learned Nandi from my father. I picked up Maa from friends. I was very close to my mother, and when she died, her language stayed with me. Every word of Kikuyu that I hear or speak carries with it the presence of my mother. I can say a word in English properly and understand everything there is to know about it as a fact. But when I say the same word in Kikuyu, it is as if my mother and her being, everything that she was and everything connected to her, come to life.

"Ours was a large, extended family, but my mother always made me feel special. She could speak to me in the lively tones of water rippling in the stream during the day, or the calming sounds of the wind passing through the tall grass in the evening. And when she spoke, her words went straight through every wall of indifference or anger that I might have built up inside my heart. Then they either stirred my soul or soothed it, whichever it was I needed most.

"I remember all of her words, even the plain ones, about eating our fruits and vegetables, keeping our rooms clean, and studying hard at school. Then there were the grander ones about the importance of sharing the love we had received from her and my father with others. They all live in me even now, and will be with me forever.

"You see, when I hear words in Kikuyu, my mother's tongue, I get something deeper than any understanding or image. I get the flavor of the thing itself. Yes, that's it: the flavor, the full flavor. For me, speaking and hearing her language brings a taste to things that cannot be put into words."

Wangetha stopped and looked at Alain. "I'm getting carried away. What I'm saying must sound so simple to someone as well educated as you are. I'm sure others have that experience with their own mother tongue."

Alain thought before answering. "I really wouldn't know. But I do know that I'm only moved by the French chansons, especially as they serenade the ebbs and flows of love. Whenever I hear one of those songs translated into another language, much of the emotional meaning is lost for me, even though I may understand the literal meaning of the words perfectly. You are associating the word with your mother, while I am associating it with my culture."

Wangetha looked at Alain even more intently. "I don't know what it is about you, Alain, but you make me want to talk, to express my feelings. Ah, but that is probably the effect that you have on all the women you meet."

She was smiling again.

Embarrassed, Alain concentrated on driving. Soon, they were well into their descent down from the mountain ridge and could begin to see the murky, blue-green features of Lake Naivasha come into view more clearly. As they drew closer, Alain suggested they stop for lunch at the country club on its shores.

Fifteen minutes later, after navigating the craters and remnants of what seemed to have once been a respectable road, they drove up to the club's main building entrance area, lined by purple and red bougainvillea vines. Sauntering along the brick walkway, they were flanked by dainty white cottages with rust-red tiled roofs, set among numerous flower-bearing bushes, large, yellow-barked acacia trees with mushroom-like canopies, and spreading fever trees. When they reached the sculptured mahogany and glass door of the colonial-era property, a porter in a white shirt and black trousers greeted them.

"*Jambo,* welcome to the Lake Naivasha Country Club," he announced cheerfully, as he waved them inside. Large bay windows revealed the green gardens in the back adjoining the lake's papyrus-tufted shore, which was speckled with blue water lilies.

They walked slowly over to the expansive green lawn where lunch was being served, while Wangetha impulsively tucked her left hand into Alain's right arm. As they sat down in two finely made wicker chairs, they could catch a full view of the bluish-green hues of the rippling lake.

"It's pleasant here, isn't it?" Alain remarked as he helped Wangetha into her chair. "I've heard so much about this place and wanted to see it first-hand. Though I do think that allowing the peacocks to roam here in the garden and walk among us seems a little too fantastic."

"Oh, no. You shouldn't think that at all," Wangetha demurred. "That's only because you foreigners are used to seeing them in the zoo. They were brought here from abroad and are a common sight now in some of our lodges.

"Of course, we're very proud of the richness of our own wildlife. There are several hundred bird species around the lake. Just look over there at that fish eagle with its white head and tail and the pink-backed pelicans in the distance.

"In Lake Nakuru, which is not too far away, there can be hundreds of thousands of flamingos at times, making the whole lake appear pink. If we were to go out on a boat here, we could also see the heads of a school of hippopotami bobbing in the waves. And if we were lucky, we could see one open its cavernous jaws and scare us half to death. In the meanwhile, look at that shaggy colobus monkey there on the roof of the club. Doesn't he look splendid in his black, long-haired suit with the white trim? I mean, I couldn't have designed a better monkey if I tried," she laughed.

She suddenly stopped laughing when she noted that Alain was gazing at her left shoulder.

"Alain, what is it? What is it that you are looking at that is so interesting?"

Alain looked back at her face. "I just watched a butterfly alight on your shoulder, adorning you as no jewelry ever could. Please don't move your head or it will leave."

Wangetha's eyes looked down in embarrassment. "How do you know what jewelry would look like on me?" she asked as she looked back at him. "Aren't you being a little forward?"

"What if I am? Do you mind?"

She turned her eyes downward again.

"Is the butterfly still there?" she asked.

"Yes."

"Could you please tell me what it looks like?"

"It's very hard to do justice to this butterfly with words."

"Oh, please try."

"All right, I'll try. The butterfly is about eight centimeters high and a little more than that length across, with delicate wings stretched wide that are fluttering slightly in the gusts of wind from the lake. They have been painted with every color of the rainbow, and I can see them all – red, orange, yellow, green, blue, indigo, and violet – on a backdrop of black that looks as soft as velvet. Two crescents of emerald green on each wing, laced with traces of turquoise, frame the butterfly's sliver of a body from which a pair of finely curved antennae extends upward to the sky."

"I like that, Alain. I like that very much. Is it still there?"

"No, it has just flown away, but you should be happy."

"Why, because I am with you?" she smiled.

"I hope so, but also because, as you must know, the butterfly represents hope, and a butterfly with such an exquisite blend of colors as this one must mean a special kind of hope."

"That's very nice, Alain, but why would I need hope?"

"I don't know, Wangetha. I just know that this is what the butterfly means to many people."

"Do you know that I saw a butterfly land on an elephant once? How did that help the elephant, when they are being slaughtered by poachers for their ivory tusks all over the continent?"

"The butterfly only landed on one elephant," Alain responded. "Correct?"

"Yes."

"Do you know what happened to that elephant?"

"No."

"Well, maybe that one elephant is still alive and well. They live for many years, don't they?"

"Yes, of course, Alain. You are right. But do you know what especially struck me about that day?"

"Tell me."

"It was the remarkable contrast between that tiny, fragile butterfly, preening its thin, red-and-blue wings against the backdrop of this massive elephant's heap of thick, gray skin, lined by endless creases and wrinkles. And then I thought how much stranger still that I even existed, and could be aware of standing there in this world and taking in this sight. How could all this have happened, I asked myself? Have you ever had such an experience?"

"Not with butterflies and elephants."

"Then with what?"

"Maybe on an outing to a lake where a lovely woman made me forget all about time and place and everything else except her."

Wangetha smiled and did not look away as she did before.

When the waiter came, they both ordered the fish specialty of the day, which was the pan-fried tilapia, freshly caught from the lake, accompanied by wild rice and a light mushroom sauce.

"I feel guilty being here," Alain said after the waiter had left. "Most of the population can't enjoy a day like this."

"I wouldn't worry about it too much, Alain. You are what you are. And besides, I'm part of the population and I'm enjoying myself."

"*Touché,*" Alain responded happily. "Sometimes I hate this balancing act that we Europeans often have to play in Africa – being ourselves, but not being too conspicuous in the process. I only wish that I had it in my power to make your country rich and prosperous. I know that sounds ridiculous, but I really do wish that."

Wangetha turned her head, as if distracted by something in the distance. When she turned her head back, she caught Alain's gaze with her own eyes that had become as luminous as black onyx. A shiver ran down his spine as he felt them probing the desires of his heart. He was now looking deeper into these two glistening pools which were beckoning him, drawing him in as they receded before him, inviting him to fall further and further into what was no longer blackness, but a mosaic of the lush hues of the same colors of the rainbow he had seen in the butterfly, when the waiter's voice startled him.

"Here is your order, sir," the waiter said as he placed the dishes before him.

After Alain thanked the waiter and turned again to Wangetha, her smoldering stare was no more.

"Is there something wrong, Alain?" Wangetha asked. "You seem suddenly preoccupied."

"Oh, no. Everything is fine," he replied, as he invited her to begin eating. "This looks terrific. Please, let's start. We still have a long drive ahead of us. From what I was told, it will take us well over half an hour to reach Nakuru, and then at least that much time to Molo, since we first must pass through Njoro and Elburgon."

A half-hour later they had finished their pleasant lunch and were well on their way to Nakuru, the capital city of Rift Valley province. Once on its outskirts, Alain eased the Land Cruiser into the Agip petrol station that had appeared on the side of the road.

"I think I had better tank up and check the tires before we get into Molo. Care for a soft drink or anything? I've brought bottled water and a thermos of tea, but even so, it's going to be well into the afternoon before we're back this way."

"I'll have a stony, thanks."

After Alain had brought back the cold soda and handed it over to her, he leaned back on his seat to watch her as she drank it down, her long svelte neck arching back to take some unhurried swallows.

"Are you sure there's nothing else that I can get for you?" he found himself saying, when what he really wanted to say was, "I think you're the most beautiful woman I've ever seen in my life."

CHAPTER 5
THE OLD KIKUYU

෧෨

On the road leading to Molo, the green countryside provided the only distraction from the rough ride.

"I can see why there is such a fierce struggle over this land," Alain noted, holding the steering wheel firmly in his two hands. "It appears very fertile. Everywhere I look I see plots of maize or some kind of vegetables along with the grassland and grazing cows. Both animals and agriculture seem to thrive here."

"That's exactly it. You've seen the dilemma," responded Wangetha. "The land in our Rift Valley serves the purposes of three distinct cultures, the Kikuyu, the Kalenjin, and the Masai. As I'm sure you know, the Kikuyu, our largest tribe, are skilled farmers. They can take the last scrap of arable land to grow a variety of vegetables, from peas, beans, and lentils to cabbage, tomatoes, onions, and carrots. That's in addition to the standbys of maize and millet.

"The Kalenjin, our fourth-largest tribe, are adept at both animal husbandry and farming. In addition to raising cows, the crops they grow include tea and sorghum as well as millet and maize. They are somewhat related to the Masai, who are our true cattlemen.

"The Masai are only one and a half percent of the population, but some would say they are our most distinct ethnic group. For many centuries they have depended on their herds of cows for basic nutrition, which for them means drinking their milk and blood. They revere their cows and consider the land on which they graze to be sacred. Traditionally, they've believed that cultivating it with tools, even to dig wells, would be dishonorable to the land."

"But who has the most legitimate claim to all this land that we see?"

"Ah, Alain. For a journalist, I thought that you were more perceptive than that. You make it seem there can be a clear answer."

"But isn't it true that the Masai lived in the Rift Valley originally and the Kikuyu are largely latecomers? Weren't they granted much of this land by your first president, Jomo Kenyatta? And wasn't he also a Kikuyu?"

"Yes, yes, yes, everything you say is true, Alain. The Kikuyu did receive most of the land redistributed by Kenyatta's government after we gained independence from the British. But it's a little more complicated than that."

"What do you mean?"

"Well, when the British gave us our independence they advanced a large loan to the new government to buy back the land the settlers had taken. The government was to sell parcels of the land to any Kenyan who wanted to buy it. The Kikuyus bought a great deal of the land then, at very low prices."

"And the Masai?"

"They didn't have the finances to buy the land."

"But the Kikuyu did?"

"The Kikuyu were able to find financing, yes, through loans and so forth."

"Would some say they had the inside track to get the land?"

"Yes, some would say that; in fact, many do say that. Another reason the Masai did not try to buy the land back was because of what they considered to be the principle involved. Much of this land had belonged to them before the English settlers first came in the nineteenth century and began to appropriate it. Some reasoned that once the settlers left, the land should be restored to them. They saw it as unjust that they would have to be forced to buy back what had originally been theirs."

"So in the end, they lost the land anyway."

"Just think of what would have happened if the Masai had regained the land. They used so much of it for grazing their herds of cattle, including land that could grow food. At one time, this didn't pose a problem. But today, with our rapidly-growing population, it does."

"Is it fair to deny the Masai the right to regain their own land?" Alain asked.

"They could have bought it back, just as the Kikuyu did."

"But as you admit, they probably didn't have the same access to financing as the Kikuyu did."

"They still could have organized and bought quite a bit of the land if they wanted to," Wangetha responded.

"If they had started buying it, however, they would have been implicitly giving up their claim, correct?"

"Yes, Alain, I'm afraid there's a lot of truth to what you say, though I wish it weren't so. Yet, the world changes, time changes. I go back to what I just said. Our population has grown dramatically since the land was all theirs and used only for grazing."

"Even so, does that make taking away their land just?" Alain asked.

"Is one small group of nomads entitled to occupy huge areas of land with little to show for it when so many other people need food?" Wangetha responded. "Shouldn't they share?"

"Your Kikuyu blood is showing. You're taking their side and not answering my question."

"Please, Alain, you are not answering *my* question," Wangetha countered. "Should this small group of nomads be allowed to monopolize many tens of thousands of acres of arable land, land that could produce wheat for bread, cotton for clothes, and vegetables and fruit for a wholesome diet? Is it right that they can have it all just for their few heads of cattle? What about the farms, ranches, wildlife preserves, and other economic projects that have since been created from that land?

"In the meanwhile, the Masai have a homeland and continue to graze their cattle," Wangetha added. "It's not like it was before. That's true. But it's not as though they have lost everything either. Not at all."

"That's good to know."

"I'm glad that you are pleased," Wangetha said, somewhat sullenly. "It's so easy for you to look at us with a critical eye. It's not an issue of life and death for you or your country, but it is for us. I wish that there were enough land for everyone, but there isn't. And so much of what is available is marginal quality, subject to droughts every few years, and so on."

"I can see that this is an issue for you that goes beyond any bias on your part for the Kikuyu," Alain said in a conciliatory tone. "For a moment I almost thought that you might be hundred percent Kikuyu."

"I never told you what I am," Wangetha responded, a little irritated, forgetting what she had said earlier about her mother. "But I do have some Kalenjin blood, so your argument doesn't hold water since I should then also take the side of the Kalenjin, who have been in step with the Masai on these land issues. But as it happens, I am trying very hard to be neutral."

Alain fell silent. As they continued driving, the signs of the ethnic clashes began to come into view. On one side of the road they could see the burned remains of what had been wooden shacks, with their collapsed tin roofs smudged black from flames.

"This was once a village teeming with activity," noted Wangetha, with emotion in her voice. "Now you can see for yourself how it has been razed to the ground with not the slightest infrastructure left. All the people have fled. There is nothing now."

Alain nodded in assent.

Occasionally, they would see villagers from a few remaining shacks that had not been destroyed lined up on the side of the road waving as they drove by.

"Why are they waving?" Alain asked.

"It's part of our Kenyan hospitality to visitors and especially to members of donor organizations. They can tell from our Land Cruiser that we are potential contributors. They're hoping that we will stop and give them something. They feel they have to find help wherever they can."

After another few kilometers, they saw a school sign and pulled off to a dirt road. Soon, the outlines of the gutted stone shell of an old schoolhouse appeared on the horizon. Outside the building, smoke was spiraling up into the sky from a large cooking fire, with several pots and pans dangling from a long iron rod propped up by stones over the flames. Over a dozen people, young and old, were gathered around the fire. Others were moving in and out of the schoolhouse.

"Is that our destination?" asked Alain.

"Yes," Wangetha replied. "This is where you wanted to go. We are at the camp that was set up by the relief organization of Dr. Victor Vinensky, the man you said you were scheduled to see. It's a temporary refugee center for displaced persons."

Alain parked the Land Cruiser near two older British Land Rovers, which he guessed belonged to Vinensky. As he and Wangetha walked toward the building, they could see the faces of men and women rising from squatting positions next to the fire to fetch more wood. But they didn't see anyone who might be Vinensky.

Wangetha went over to talk to one of the women, who immediately started tugging on her arm and trying to lead her over to a group of children huddled inside the schoolhouse. Then, a strong, upbeat voice, seeming to arise from nowhere, addressed Alain, who quickly turned around to see who it was.

"Are you Alain Sardou?" the friendly voice asked in an accent that Alain guessed to be Eastern European. A tall, tanned, slim, white-haired man, clad in faded-blue dungarees and a light-green, long-sleeved shirt open at the neck approached him, hand extended.

"Yes, I am."

"And you are Dr. Vinensky?" Alain asked, taking in his beaming face and shaking his hand equally firmly. He felt better immediately.

"Yes, that's me. Just call me Victor. I've been expecting you. We were worried you might lose your way."

"That's why I brought my friend, who knows this region well," Alain responded. "Her name is Wangetha Wachira. My editors asked her to accompany me, not only because she's been here before but because she can speak Masai and Kikuyu, as well as Kalenjin. They were afraid that English and Swahili would not be enough for me to get the full picture. There she is, next to those children. I'll go get her."

As Alain returned with Wangetha, Vinensky offered her his hand, which she readily accepted.

"Please join us, Miss Wachira."

"Please, call me Wangetha."

"Wangetha it is. And please call me Victor."

He smiled at Wangetha and Alain. "Let's go over there and sit down," he said, pointing to a shaded area under a nearby tree where four bamboo chairs were placed around a small table that appeared to have been made from some salvaged wood. As one of the nearby women came over to him, he whispered something quickly into her ear before she left to go back to the fire.

"She's going to bring us some tea," he explained.

In a few moments the tea was brought to them in an old pot from which the soot had been wiped clean. On the small board serving as a tray there were also three porcelain cups hand-decorated with red and green flowers.

"I brought these from Nairobi," Vinensky said as he handed Alain and Wangetha each a cup and poured them the steaming tea from the pot, which he then set down on the table. After pouring tea for himself, he thanked the woman and excused her.

"This tea is called Kenya Marinyn, an excellent black tea. It has its own sweetness and fragrance, so you can enjoy it as it is," he explained. "Tea-growing was introduced to East Africa's highlands by the British and the Germans, much later than other staples such as maize, which first arrived in Africa in the fifteenth century. And once the tea plants took root here, Kenya began growing the best varieties in the world. I don't know how much of this beautiful country you've had the chance to see. But until you've seen its lush tea plantations with their never-ending rows of green tea plants, waist-high and perfectly manicured, you haven't seen all its bounty."

He took a long sip. "I'm very glad you've come," he said.

Alain took a sip from his tea, admitting to himself that it was as good as Vinensky said it would be. He frowned nonetheless.

"But aren't the owners of these vast plantations that you talk about multinationals or large commodities firms?"

"Yes, some are. But most of the land being cultivated for tea is, in fact, owned by smallholder Kenyan farmers. And the tea they bring to market is considered the best quality."

"I didn't know that," Alain said. "Now maybe you can shed some light on some other matters as well," he continued as he looked at Wangetha sitting next to him. "I'm interested in knowing the real story behind the ethnic clashes that have scarred this area here. There are so many rumors, so many conflicting accounts. In my country, people still care very much about what takes place in Africa, and there will undoubtedly be a large readership for my story. The newspapers that carry my articles have hundreds of thousands of readers. So you won't be wasting your time talking to us."

"I wouldn't care if only 10 people read your story," Vinensky smiled. "I would spend just as much time with you. I'm just happy to talk to you and get the truth out.

"Even the government has realized that it can't keep this place cordoned off from public sight forever," he continued. "I'm glad the administration police let you through."

"They didn't really let us through," Alain rejoined. "There was no checkpoint anywhere on the road, from the beginning to here."

"Ah," exclaimed Vinensky. "That means they are losing interest. And if they're losing interest it means the clashes have accomplished their goal. Most of the Kikuyu farmers have been driven out. What you see here are the remnants of the displaced families."

"Why do you put yourself in such danger by staying here? Why don't you go back to your offices in Nairobi until the tension eases and..."

"You are too intelligent to even ask such a question," responded Vinensky, cutting Alain's question short. "Let's change the subject to what I'm sure you want to know more about, the violence. There's a dimension to this latest out-break of hostility that after all my years here even I don't understand."

"What do you mean?" queried Alain, somewhat surprised.

"I mean that the Kikuyu, the Kalenjin, and the Masai have no recent history of attacking one another with such brutality. They've managed to coexist peacefully for scores of years until this decade. The last conflict that we know of took place between small bands of them over some water rights, and that was resolved peacefully."

"But aren't these violent attacks against the Kikuyu pay-back for the advantages they obtained when Kenya freed itself from British colonialism?" Alain pressed. "Aren't the other tribes now settling scores? You know how the Kikuyu benefited from the land distribution under President Kenyatta. Isn't it understandable that the smaller tribes want their share of land also?"

"The fundamental problem does center on land," agreed Vinensky. "Sometimes, it seems that everyone wants land, even if it is someone else's."

He reached for the pot to pour more tea into Alain's and Wangetha's cups, which they had set down on the vacant chair between them.

"As you must know," Vinensky continued, "the Kikuyu paid for much of this land. They didn't just confiscate it. They have titles to it, though we have to acknowledge that they had the right connections and received very favorable financial terms."

"But for the Masai the issue has been the government's selling off land which belonged to them before the colonialists came," Alain interjected.

"Yes, they have often raised that issue," Vinensky concurred. "For them it is indeed a matter of justice. They believe the land should have reverted to them once the colonialists left."

"Wangetha believes the country had no choice but to spread the land out to other tribes," Alain said, "But tell me, what is to become of the Masai? Given their customs and their dependency on the land, how can their culture survive?"

"Don't forget that they still number around half a million and have their own Masailand, which is parceled now but still covers thousands of square kilometers," Vinensky responded. "Yet how right you are to ask such questions.

"You know, during my years at the United Nations I had the opportunity to travel to many of the countries of the developing world. While in Asia once, in that remote area caught between China and the Russian Federation known as Mongolia, I learned that the nomadic Mongol tribes were very possessive about the lands and routes they traversed. They not only claimed the vast areas they used as pastures for their herds as their own but the routes connecting them as well.

"The notion of land as a place to which they belonged was crucial to them. It was an integral part of their identity. To uproot them from their attachment to their historic soil and their routes of migration would have been tantamount to cultural genocide."

"As happened to the native Indians of North America," Alain added.

"You see the problem. I'll never forget the sorrow etched in the face of a Cherokee woman I once met in the States. Here is what she asked as she drew on the lines of that great poem, the *Lament of the Cherokee,* to mourn the dispossession of her people from their native lands: 'Can a tree that is torn from its root by the fountain flourish when it is removed to the rock of the mountain, unwarmed by the sun and unwatered by care?'

"She is part of a grand company. Place is inherent in the remembered historical narrative of every civilization, tying one generation to the next. That is a given. The significance of place holds true even for those of us constantly on the move. We cherish some places more than others and consider them our home, so to speak. In fact, the person who has no attachment at all to a place is a rarity. It takes a tremendous commitment to something else to supplant the need of attachment to a place."

"We French are an excellent case," Alain said. "We love our land and our sea coasts."

"Now," Vinensky continued, "just think for a moment of the dilemma created when in today's shrinking world the sense of place for one group of people continues to encompass large tracts of land which they mostly just traverse. In the past that was no problem. But with the growing human population, there is a problem, a very great problem. The land constituting the place for one population turns out to be necessary for the survival of other populations."

"As in Kenya with the Masai," Alain said, looking at Wangetha.

"Precisely. Now what can be done? If the Masai were a duly constituted nation recognized under international law that would be one thing. But they are drawn together with 40 other tribes into a nation whose boundaries were created by colonial powers from another continent."

"And the Kikuyu is the largest and some say the most energetic of those tribes," Alain observed.

"Yes. I won't go back to how the Masai have been losing their land. We have already discussed the controversy that exists around that. Only consider the underlying tragedy playing itself out here: that is, the loss of the sense of place."

"Now you sound as though you are favoring the Masai over the Kikuyu," Alain noted.

"I sympathize with them greatly, but that does not mean I now accept their claim to their place of the past, though I do believe they were treated unjustly. This is a paradox, I know. I have to acknowledge that and I don't pretend I can reconcile it.

"But a very basic question leads us relentlessly to this paradox. In order for me to have my sense of place intact, am I entitled to maintain under my control land that I use only occasionally for grazing or wandering? That was the crux of the dilemma underlying the conquest of America. While the native Indians had every right to the land constituting their place where they grew their crops and tended their animals, how much of the tens of thousands of square kilometers of the vast North American continent could they claim as rightfully theirs if they only traversed or hunted it from time to time, or worse, if they had no practical dominion over it and rarely or never set foot on it?"

"And in the process keep the settlers from creating a new sense of place for themselves on vast stretches of largely uninhabited land. Is that it?" Alain asked.

"Yes. And note that you said largely uninhabited land. Creating a sense of place for oneself on densely inhabited land that has long belonged to others is an entirely different question since it involves forcibly displacing people, confiscating their land, and depriving them of their legitimate sense of place. When this happens, violent resistance on the part of the dispossessed is often the result as we have seen throughout human history. In fact, as we well know, there can be violent resistance to newcomers even when the land is sparsely inhabited, though it is less justified."

Vinensky set down his cup of tea. "Let's face it. Whether there is a sparse or dense inhabitation, it is never easy for people to relinquish their sense of place because of the meaning they associate with it. Place engenders an emotional, even mystical hold over them. We can see that even with places that do not directly belong to us but are nearby. Consider the majestic Mount Kilimanjaro, nearly six kilometers high, in neighboring Tanzania. It is not part of territorial Kenya, but it belongs to the Kenyan people's sense of place almost as much as their own imposing Mount Kenya.

"Now for the native Indians, of course, letting in the settlers meant that they would have to reduce a sense of place that was immense. For centuries, the sweeping natural splendor of America constituted an integral sense of their place, regardless of how little of that panorama they actually inhabited. But that didn't mean they didn't have to pay a great cultural and spiritual cost in having to relinquish most of it."

"Let me see if I follow you," Alain said. "The way you see it, the dilemma is respecting a people's need for a place while understanding that the spread of humanity has entailed putting limits on the size and boundaries of that place."

"Exactly," answered Vinensky, "and that is why I cannot justify what happened to the Kikuyu here. It is time for the Masai to reconstitute their sense of place, as difficult as it might be. These are the pains of civilizations in transition. The problem is they sometimes collide with our notions of justice, and that is why I cannot condone what happened to the Masai either. I have major reservations about the way the land was sold after the colonialists left. Still, it is an internal issue, and while I believe it should be resolved with as much generosity as possible toward the Masai, we shouldn't try to interfere."

Vinensky paused. "You have your work cut out for you in writing about these problems, Alain. Just write about them here in Kenya as honestly as you can."

"I believe that Alain will do just that, Victor," Wangetha interjected quietly. "You don't have an axe to grind here do you, Alain?"

"Not yet," Alain responded good-naturedly.

As he took another sip of his tea, he began to feel uncomfortable, as if someone were staring at him. When he turned around to look, he noticed an elderly, wizened man rise up from his hunched position next to the fire. His face was a mosaic of crisscrossed wrinkles, with most of his front teeth missing, and he needed a walking stick to hold himself up.

Reeking of smoke, he approached the three of them and asked to be alone with Vinensky, who took him by the arm and led him to the side of the building. As they began talking quietly, Alain looked at Wangetha to see if she could make out what they were saying, which to him didn't sound like either English or Swahili. But she was giving no sign that she was following their conversation.

On returning, Vinensky addressed them bluntly. "He is the elder of one of the villages that was destroyed in the clashes. He wants to show you where the home of his son used to be. Do you want to go? We'll need someone to translate. He can only speak Kikuyu."

So Vinensky could speak Kikuyu, Alain realized. That was what they were speaking.

"Why not?" Alain answered. "Wangetha can come with us to translate. Or you can do the honors."

"No, I would prefer that Wangetha do it. I'm sure that her Kikuyu is better than mine. Though I will do the introduction."

Vinensky turned to the old man, addressing him in Kikuyu. *"My friend has agreed to go with you. Let me present Alain Sardou."*

"Ikinya ria mukuru rikinyaga muruna," the old Kikuyu said as he reached his hand out to shake Alain's.

"He says old people's walking teaches young ones to walk," Wangetha said. "By that he means in agreeing to go with him, you will learn something."

After walking for about 15 minutes along some winding, well-worn paths through grassy fields with the old man leading the way, the three entered a ravaged, burned area, with only charred wood remnants of the building once there. There were also several mounds of earth with simple white crosses, to which the old Kikuyu pointed as he began talking again.

"Alain, he is saying that these are graves of his son's wife and children, who were in their small house when raiders came and burned it to the ground. It happened while his son was taking vegetables to market. In his grief, his son has left this area."

"Why would the raiders attack your village?" Alain asked sympathetically, looking at the old man.

"He says that you must surely know the reason, Alain, because you British are so clever. He is mistaking you for an Englishman, by the way. He says the Masai allied themselves with the Kalenjin against the Kikuyu in a game of deadly politics. All the smaller tribes fear the Kikuyu because of their size and skill with the land. No one wants to see them grow strong again as under the days of Kenyatta."

Wangetha continued translating. "He sees a puzzled look in your eyes, Alain, but he asks you to consider whether the Kenyan tribes are really that different from people in your part of the world. Don't your political parties fear and mistrust one another? Once his daughter brought home one of her school history books. She translated for him some of the paragraphs about your second great war, and he learned that you Europeans killed one another in the tens of millions. He had an especially hard time comprehending the deaths of the millions of civilians not even involved in the fighting."

Alain frowned. "You can tell him it is hard for us to comprehend too. But does he forget that his beloved Mau Mau slaughtered their own fair share of people in their war against the British colonialists?"

"Please, Alain, remember it is *he* saying these things, not I. I am only the translator."

The Kikuyu's eyes began to narrow. "What is he saying now?" Alain asked.

"He is addressing you again as an Englishman. There is anger in his voice. He says, 'We can thank you for our problems because you deprived us of our own Kikuyu nation. We had our own language, ways, and history, but you thought nothing of suddenly throwing us together with all the other tribes into a big soup kettle to cook us into a porridge that you thought you could easily digest.

"'But after this mix proved indigestible, you spit it out and your soldiers departed. The sputum you left on the ground, all hopelessly swirled together, was no true porridge. Yes, you had simmered it in a fine and expensive pot and used strong, well-made steel spoons to stir it. But this porridge has not yet found its own natural texture and taste. We old Kikuyu still prefer our *ugali* paste. It is simple, made with the maize we grow and harvest ourselves, and has not been spoiled by the likes of you.'"

As Wangetha finished translating these last words, the Kikuyu elder turned his back on Alain with obvious disdain and began slowly walking with his stick, back along the long winding path toward the camp.

Vinensky looked at Alain somberly. "He doesn't know that you are French, and I'm glad that you didn't argue with him."

They walked back to the camp in silence, the old Kikuyu elder barely visible in the distance. Once there, Vinensky called for fresh cups of tea, which they sipped slowly and silently at their small table. After a few minutes, he rose and went over to one of the clusters of refugees, talked with them quietly, and then returned to sit next to Alain and Wangetha.

"Have you seen everything that you need to?" Vinensky asked.

"Not really," Alain answered evenly, "but it's enough for today. I'll come back to the area in the next few days to see if I can get interviews with some of the Masai and Kalenjin in the area."

"That's a good idea. You need to see all sides. I know what I think, but of course you need to find out for yourself. I hope that I was some help to you."

"Yes, you were, very much so."

Alain rose. "It was a pleasure meeting you, Victor. We must go now."

"Thank you for coming," Vinensky replied as he accompanied them to the Land Cruiser.

As Alain eased out onto the dirt road, he turned to Wangetha seated next to him. "Well, what do you think? Which of the tribes is at fault?"

"As I said before, I only wish it were that simple. Please, let's go."

Sensing that she was annoyed, Alain kept his silence. They were well along the dirt road back to the main highway before he broke the awkward silence.

"It's a beautiful view, there in the distance," Alain offered.

Reading contrition in this remark, she smiled at him and turned her head to look out at the distant ridges of the Rift

Valley's escarpment partially covered by wisps of cirrus clouds. As he caught a glance of her profile against the dark-blue backdrop of the late afternoon sky, he remembered how she appeared when he first saw her standing at the town center waiting for him, with the same proud look, the same finely-etched profile. He also couldn't help noticing once again how her white silk blouse clung softly to her body. He had to turn his head back quickly to avoid running off the road.

CHAPTER 6
PETROL AND DREADLOCKS

༄

It was not easy for Alain to get the sultry image of Wangetha out of his mind and concentrate on the road ahead, but he focused on his driving and after another half-hour and some more small talk, he announced it was time to stop.

"In a few minutes we'll be nearing the outskirts of Nakuru. I need to pull into the Agip station again to have the windshield cleaned before heading back toward Nairobi. We can get some soft drinks or bottled water, whatever you want."

"That's fine with me, Alain. The refreshments will be good, but I also have to make a quick call to Nairobi. Maybe they have a telephone there."

As they entered the driveway of the station, Alain slowed to a halt under the canopy next to the pumps. After summoning the attendant, he watched in fascination as Wangetha strolled toward the office and merged into the low-hanging, brilliant crimson sun, her gait flowing as smoothly and effortlessly as the tall grass he had seen on the Masai Mara's vast plains in the late afternoon wind.

He averted his gaze only after the attendant that came to the Land Cruiser had addressed him twice.

"Petrol, sir? Petrol, sir?"

"Yes. Right to the top."

While Alain waited inside the Land Cruiser, the attendant filled the tank in the back. He then came around to the front, washed the windshield with a sponge, and rubbed the glass with a towel until it sparkled.

"Could you please also check the tires?" Alain asked.

In a moment, the attendant returned shaking his head.

"The left rear tire is just a little low, sir. If you wish, you can drive to the end of the station. We have an air hose there."

"I'll take a look at it first."

Alain got out and kneeled down next to the tire. The attendant was right. It could use a little air. But just as he began to stand up, he saw Wangetha returning to the Land Cruiser. She was walking in a different way this time, her leisurely gait replaced by the kind of brisk, self-assured tempo he had seen fashion models exhibit on the choicest catwalks of Europe.

He began to wonder which walk pleased him more. Dancing alone with her, it would be the first Wangetha he wanted when the music was slow and easy and they wrapped their arms tightly around each other, becoming one solitary, gliding motion across the floor. Then, as the music took on an edge with pounding drums rending the air, they would break away with bold moves and dance for each other. Here, it was the second Wangetha he would want for the sheer pleasure of watching her.

But very soon he would want the first again, and then the second, until the two blended into one continuous rhythmical movement. Then it would no longer make any difference which Wangetha he had at any moment because the next moment would always bring back the other one.

He caught his breath, for now it was the second Wangetha, the second Wangetha only, moving toward him with the smoldering sunset gracing her every curve. It was no out-of-reach catwalk on which she was walking. She was walking directly toward him on the hot asphalt, coming closer and closer, her hips swaying in perfect rhythm to the rustling of her skirt, and she was staring right at him.

As his pulse quickened and his breathing deepened, he could not take his eyes off this feline presence approaching him. What was she thinking as she came nearer, he wondered. Did it matter to her that he was in this awkward position next to the tire? Did he seem defenseless to her? The fading but still potent African sun added to the weakness overtaking him, his legs unsteady as he rose to his feet, his eyes as riveted on her as her eyes were on him.

As she drew closer and he could see her smiling, he felt his strength return and extended his hand to hers, welcoming her back.

"Were you able to make your call?" he asked, feigning nonchalance.

Wangetha squeezed his hand. "Yes, it was really nothing. I just had to let someone know where I was. I hope that you didn't mind."

"Oh, no. I'm glad that your call went through. It's not always easy to reach Nairobi from here."

Alain was about to open the passenger door to let Wangetha in, when he was startled by the noise of an approaching car's roaring engine, then the sound of squealing brakes. He whirled around and saw an old Peugeot sedan screeching to a stop. The doors swung wide open. Four men wearing sunglasses leaped out and began running toward them. All had green canvas safari hats pulled low and tight over their heads. Two with dreadlocks protruding from under their hats were at the front and shouting.

"Police, police, we arrest you!" they screamed in the English of young men who had been schooled, as they pulled out revolvers and aimed them directly at Alain.

He caught the sight of the attendant rushing back into the station and slamming the door behind him. After that it became silent, with no other cars anywhere to be seen.

Beads of sweat formed on his forehead as he gripped the Land Cruiser's passenger door. He glanced at Wangetha. She had put her hands in front of her eyes, refusing to look at the men.

"Why aren't you in uniforms? Where are your badges?" Alain demanded, tension surging through his body.

"We're in our plainclothes," one of the pistol men retorted. "Turn around and get your hands up!"

Alain's chest heaved as he felt a gun press into his back. "What are you doing? We've done nothing to you!"

"Take the whore away," the pistol man snapped to his partner, who dragged Wangetha to the Peugeot, weeping and stumbling, her head in her hands, her blouse ripped open.

The pistol man then pushed Alain to the other side of the Land Crusier, forcing him into the driver's seat. He could hear two bodies sliding into the back seat, the barrel of the gun now boring into the back of his head.

"Who are you? Why are you doing this?"

"Shut up, shut up!" a voice yelled at him in English. "And stop looking at us in the rear-view mirror!"

Before he turned away from the mirror, Alain could see that the voice belonged to someone with wrap-around sun-glasses. He could also make out the traces of dreadlocks under his safari hat. But that was all he could see.

The voice continued yelling at him. "Where do you live? Don't lie or we'll kill you and then your precious Wangetha. Where do you live?"

"In the capital," he answered, catching a glimpse of the Peugeot speeding away with Wangetha and the other two men in-side. It had turned onto the highway and was headed toward Nairobi as it disappeared from view.

"Where are you taking her?" Alain asked angrily.

"Shut up, shut up!" the voice screamed again.

Then he heard the other voice, speaking words he couldn't understand but which sounded like Kikuyu to him.

"*He is a pain,*" the second voice said. "*Shouldn't we kill him now?*"

"*No, you fool, control yourself,*" the first voice answered in what also sounded like Kikuyu. "*Remember, he's money.*"

"Get going!" the first voice ordered in English.

"Where to?"

"To Nairobi, where else?"

Alain gunned the Land Cruiser back onto the highway, hoping that he could catch sight of the Peugeot.

"Not so fast. We're in no hurry," the first voice ordered. "Where in Nairobi do you live? On which street?"

"On Kilanji Drive, off of Karanja Road."

"The number. Which number?"

"620."

"The house, what kind of house? How big? What color?"

"I already told you the number. Why do you need to know what it looks like?"

"In case we forget the number," the first voice answered.

Alain sneaked a glance at the rear-view mirror, but still couldn't discern the face behind the wrap-around sunglasses. He couldn't see the other face at all.

"It's a white house, with one level," Alain answered, slowly and deliberately so they wouldn't harass him any more about it. "Brick tiles for the roof."

"You must be rich to live in such a house," the second voice snickered.

"It's not mine and I'm not rich. I'm only renting it."

"What kind of work do you do?" The first voice asked.

"I'm a writer."

"What do you write about?"

"Whatever I think is interesting."

"And this whore was helping you to translate what you thought was interesting. Is that it?"

"If you say so."

"*She always did like these Wazungu, didn't she,*" the other voice snickered in Kikuyu. "*Well, she'll have to like us now because our guys are going to have plenty of fun with her.*"

He turned to his partner. "*You bastard, why didn't you let me go with them?*"

"We'll be with them soon enough. Just be patient. You'll get what you want before we're finished with her."

Alain felt shut out and helpless as he heard the exchanges in Kikuyu but couldn't understand any of them. He tried to concentrate on the drive back to Nairobi, with slow-moving rickety buses and smoke-bellowing trucks to pass on the steep slopes going up and then carts and donkeys to avoid on the descent back down to the city limits. It would have been a pleasant trip, except for the thugs behind him.

Time passed quickly and it was silent now in the car. For most of the past half-hour not one word had been spoken by these backseat boys, not to him, nor to each other. He wondered if they were taking some dope or drinking *changaa*. But each time he sneaked a sideways glance into the rear-view mirror he could see no movement, nor could he smell the telltale odor of cheap alcohol.

This kind of silence, this absence of any motion or sound, was something that had always taken him aback in Africa when he encountered it. The ability to just sit and say and do nothing was alien to him. How was it that these guys could live in the silence seemingly with no problem, no problem at all?

"Hey, wake up," the first voice shouted. "You're going to get us all killed if you don't pay attention to the road."

Maybe they were silent, but they were still busy inside their heads, Alain realized. They could tell his mind was wandering away from the driving.

"Now that we're getting close to Nairobi, head for the area where you live!" the first voice ordered.

Alain complied, and they passed through upscale Westlands, joining the sluggish traffic on Uhuru highway before entering the noisy congestion of the roundabout leading to Kenyatta Avenue. From there it was on to Valley Road and then the rush of *matatus* and commercial traffic on Ngong Road. Going around the City Mortuary roundabout was the same ordeal it always was, with the *matatus* showing as little respect for traffic rules as they did other drivers.

Relieved to leave that madness behind, he turned off to join Kabarnet Road and headed toward Karanja Road with its street boys.

"Now drive to the street where you live. Drive there slowly, but not too slowly. We don't want the police to notice us."

"What do you mean you don't want to be noticed? You said you were the police."

"Shut up, you smart ass!" screamed the second voice pushing the barrel of his gun into the back of Alain's head again. "Now, drive."

Alain could see that they didn't know much about him. But what about Wangetha? They had called her by name and knew she was a translator. Her they knew.

"Tell me when we get within one kilometer of your house!"

As they closed in on his house, Alain cheerfully exclaimed, "We are about one kilometer away. But I can't tell you exactly."

Sensing the sarcasm in Alain's response, the second voice yelled, "Shut up again! As we said, stop one kilometer away from your house."

After another short burst of driving Alain mumbled, "My house is now less than one kilometer away."

"Speak up! We can't hear you." The first voice began yelling again.

"But you said to shut up."

"Very funny. Now how much further?"

"We're about half of a kilometer away now."

"Then stop here, and pull over," the second voice commanded.

The evening sun had faded out of sight, but there was enough moonlight for Alain to turn around to get a quick look at his two friends. But should he? Too dangerous, he decided in short order. What about making a run for it? Also too dangerous. Feeling cold steel against the back of his head had soured him on taking chances.

As Alain stopped the car in a secluded spot, the first voice barked sharply, "Don't look at us! You have 72 hours from this hour to get one million shillings together if you ever want to see your girlfriend alive again. We'll let you know where to leave the money."

"How?"

"We're going to contact you by telephone," the first voice answered. "Give us your number, and it better be the right number!"

"I know, I know," Alain muttered. "The number is 798-421."

He heard some paper being shuffled and some quick scrawling.

"You'll hear from us," the first voice said. "We'll tell you where to leave the money. Don't go to the police because it won't help your girlfriend. Don't even think about it. If you do, we'll kill her and then you later. We're not going to share this money with them, do you understand? 72 hours."

"That's not enough time," Alain said, continuing to face the windshield. "How can I possibly raise one million shillings in such a short time? I don't have that kind of money."

"You know how to get it. You have contacts."

"But this money is for a ransom," Alain countered. "I can't go to the bank and ask for a loan with that as a reason. This won't be easy. It will take time and you're not giving me enough of it."

He heard them talking in Kikuyu again. "*Maybe we should give him a little extra time. We need to make sure that he gets the money.*"

"*But the more time we give him, the more time it gives the police to find us.*"

"*He won't go to the police because he knows we'll kill her if he does.*"

"*What if he doesn't care if we kill her?*"

"*Did you get a good look at Wangetha, you fool? That should answer your question.*"

"All right," the first voice said to Alain. "We'll be generous and give you 10 days beginning tomorrow. If you don't give us the money when we tell you, we'll finish with her and then come looking for you. We'll find you. There won't be any place for you to hide. We'll let you know where to drop off the money and the exact time."

"What about my Land Cruiser?"

"What about it?"

"Am I going to get it back?"

The laughter was so loud he wondered how he could have asked such a stupid question. Of course they wouldn't give it back to him. In a few days it would be swallowed up in Tanzania somewhere. They had plenty of time to unload it since they knew he wouldn't report what had happened.

The next thing Alain knew he was picking himself up off the street watching the rear end of the Land Cruiser disappear into the distance. It was now dark, but there was enough light from the one street lamp for him to find his way home. He walked the several blocks to his house slowly, where Okoth opened the gate and let him in. Alain looked disheveled but it was not Okoth's way to ask questions. For his part, Alain said nothing to him.

When he entered the house and looked at the clock on the wall, he saw that it was nearly 8:00 p.m. Some nine hours had passed since he had picked up Wangetha that morning. What was he going to do? All he knew right now was that since he didn't have diplomatic status he was subject to all of Kenya's laws. That meant that he would have to be careful, whatever he did.

He also knew that he didn't want the French embassy involved. That would only complicate things. They would almost certainly inform the Kenyan police, and he didn't want to risk getting Wangetha killed. But whom could he talk to about his predicament? He would have to think of someone soon.

That would have to be tomorrow because he was too tired to think anymore. He went to his bedroom, crawled under the cover fully clothed, and fell asleep.

CHAPTER 7
DREAMTIME

∽

It was in the very early morning hours that Alain had a vivid dream. He found himself walking on the left bank of the Seine river in Paris at mid-afternoon when he heard a woman's high-pitched voice calling his name from a long distance away. "Alain, Alain," the voice called. At first faint, it became louder and louder – "Alain, Alain, Alain" – until he felt a presence behind him and turned around to see Alexandra standing there in a bright red dress, her green eyes sparkling.

"My darling Alain! You've come back. I've waited so long. I was bad to you, but I didn't mean it. Every day I hoped that you would see through my pride and stupidity and come back to me. Oh, my dear sweet darling, how I missed you. But now you are here, and we're together again. You've made me so very happy."

He stared at her entranced, as the loveliness of her face, her smile, her luxurious blond hair, and her expressive eyes became even more alluring against Paris' skyline with its grand monuments and fine buildings. How could he have stayed away so long? He moved toward her, longing to feel her once again in his arms, her lips clinging to his, her breasts tight against his chest.

But as he embraced her, to his horror her face began to slowly change, her eyes becoming the narrow slits of a salamander, her tongue flicking and grasping at flies.

The rest of her followed, her red dress turning into the body of a deformed toad while the monuments of Paris crumbled into ruins and sank into a putrid swamp.

The swamp was creeping up on him as he pushed the toad away, which began swimming with abandon in the muck, grunting loudly in pleasure, until it suddenly paddled back to him and placed a vise-like hold on his neck with its two stubby front legs. With the additional weight of the toad, Alain was sinking further into the slime, which was now working its way up closer and closer to his nostrils.

Terrified, he looked frantically around him for support, but all he could see were endless reaches of swamp with no shoreline. Just as he was about to make one last effort to wrench himself free of the toad's grip, he glanced upwards and saw the blinding, orange sun. Somehow he had not noticed it before, even though it now filled the entire sky.

To his amazement and relief, the sun's powerful, fiery rays began incinerating the toad while sparing him, turning it into ashes which scattered in thousands of small pieces, like so much confetti, over the swamp's surface. A strong, howling wind then dispersed the ashes even further away until they disappeared as the swamp began drying up and he felt himself on solid ground again. The vast stretches of the magnificent Masai Mara's sweeping grasslands then came into view, nourished green and plump by the second season of rains, dotted thickly by immense herds of wildebeest, antelope, and zebra.

On the far side of the Masai Mara, he could see a pack of hyenas encircling a black water buffalo, its huge antlers and massive body of no use against the sharp teeth tearing at the bones and sinews of its thin ankles and lean legs. Hurling its body round and round in futile lunges at the hyenas, its skin glistening with sweat and weakened from loss of blood, the buffalo had finally fallen to its knees. As they tore its body apart piece by piece, Alain could see the hyenas rising on their haunches, slapping each other on the shoulders with their paws, and laughing hysterically.

Startled by the sound of loud, mechanical noises, he turned his head and looked to the horizon where he saw a narrow stretch of highway emerging from the port of Mombasa on the Indian Ocean. Then, as suddenly as when he first heard the noises, he found himself standing directly next to the highway while trucks careened past him carrying huge loads hidden under heavy canvas. Some were so heavy and so wide that their wheels slipped off the highway's edge, which had no elevated soft shoulders to cushion the drop into the adjoining ravine.

With eyes recessed deep in their sockets, the skin on their faces stretched tight over protruding cheekbones, and their shirts and trousers hanging loose on wasted, emaciated bodies, the drivers flayed wildly at their jumping, jerking steering wheels with their bony hands.

The groaning trucks, coming in unending succession, were now drawing nearer to him on the edge of the highway, the violent gusts of their slipstreams almost blowing him over. He was saved only when at the last minute a gigantic tanker that had begun veering in his direction hit a gaping pothole, spun out of control, and careened into the ravine, spilling massive amounts of crude oil.

The truck following immediately behind it skidded in the oil slick and slammed into a huge acacia tree on the side of the road, strewing its cargo of diamonds, gold, cobalt, platinum, and uranium into the countryside, nearly blinding him with the intensity of their glitter.

Still more trucks came, one after another sliding into the ravine. Some were falling on their backs with their 16 wheels spinning in the air after spilling cargoes of bleached human bones across the desert. Others were lurching on their side while still others had their noses driven into the ground.

He managed to tear his gaze away from the spectacle of the crashing tractor-trailers, over to the other side of the road where there was a different procession. There he could see a continuous row of hooded figures in white robes, all holding burning candles, winding their way up a path on the green slopes of what appeared to him at first to be Mount Kiliman-jaro. Only, this was a mountain far greater and higher than any mountain he had ever seen before, dizzying his mind as his eyes tried to ascend to its peak against the backdrop of a sky that was as blue as the purest of cobalt.

As the procession neared the snow-white caps of this mas-sive mountain, one candle caught his attention as it seemed to be burning brighter than the others. As he looked more closely, he could see that it belonged to a man, whose dark face was beaming as he held onto his candle with two strong hands. Behind him was a woman with a large smile on her face, holding onto her candle, as six children followed along, laughing happily. But then he could no longer follow them as they disappeared one by one into the cloudy mists surround-ing the peak.

A huge roar diverted his attention and he looked back at the highway. One more truck, larger than all the rest, was now coming furiously at him. Somehow he knew that this one would not be deterred by the pothole. This one would not careen off the road into the ravine because of its huge wheels. This one could follow him even through the slick-est slime. He started running away but the immense truck kept coming after him, belching gusts of black smoke from its smokestack.

There were several drivers crammed into the cab, and he could hear them breaking out into hideous laughs. Then he saw their faces glaring at him, and though he could see every feature as if he had known them intimately for many years, they did not create the impression of complete faces. Just as he thought he could make out a white face it became a black face, and just as he thought he could make out a black face it became a white face.

Then one of the drivers, who appeared to have a black face, was reaching out toward him, right through the windshield, with huge, oversized hands. But they weren't black hands. To his astonishment they were white, opening and closing, changing before his eyes into a construction crane's jaws.

Suddenly a mirror was thrust into his hand. Shocked, he saw that his own face had turned black, but not just the brownish black common to many Africans. His face was as black as ebony, glistening in the reflection of the mirror, though his eyes remained the bluest of blue. The mirror was then abruptly taken away from him.

The truck kept coming at him with the outstretched mechanical jaws. Just as he thought it was going to crush him, it screeched to a halt and out of its bin jumped a growling lioness, her claws bared, heading with great speed directly at him. Her maw was wide open, her eyes ablaze with excitement.

Alain began to run as fast as his legs could carry him, but he was no match for the lioness and she was rapidly gaining on him. He could hear her loud panting coming nearer and nearer. Now he could feel her hot breath on the back of his head and neck. There was nothing to do but turn around and face his death like a man.

As he turned around and waited for the inevitable leap to his throat, to his amazement the lioness had changed into Wangetha and she was walking directly toward him, the same Wangetha that had walked toward him in the shimmering sunset at the Agip petrol station in Nakuru. Only, now as she was coming to him she was moving her hands to her blouse, to each button of her blouse. After she had opened her blouse and continued to walk toward him, her tongue rolling along her sensuous mouth, her hands moving up and down along her hips, he awoke abruptly in a cold sweat with his heart pounding wildly.

He pulled himself up in bed and peered nervously around the room, but could see that there was only silence and darkness. After breathing in and out slowly for several minutes, his heart calmed enough for him to lie down again and drift back to sleep.

CHAPTER 8
AT THE NGONG HILLS LODGE

୬

When Alain awoke the next morning, the rays of the burning Nairobi sun were already lighting up the room as they passed right through the thin window shade he had pulled down the night before. Racked with indecision about his course of action, he mulled over his options again and again. He had seen too many newspaper photos of dead robbers caught in shootouts with the police to risk going to them just now. Jeopardizing Wangetha's life in any way while she was being held by her abductors was out of the question. But what could he do? He needed to talk to someone, throw out ideas, and get some good advice. But with whom?

Why hadn't he taken the time to make some good Kenyan friends? How he could have used a good, trusted confidant now.

Wasn't there anyone he could get hold of, who knew how to navigate in Kenyan society in ways that went far beyond the superficial social whirl?

The more he thought about it, the more one name came to him: Joseph Regalo, a former U.S. Marine-turned-private security consultant with corporate clients in the region. Alain had never met him personally but had heard enough about him to bring him to mind now. He was invariably described as a moody, tough character whose talents as well as prickliness were honed while serving in Lebanon during its violent convulsions in the 1980s.

Not everyone thought he was just working for himself, though. Some of Alain's colleagues in the press wondered whether he was actually an undercover plant of the CIA. One telling sign, they said, was that when they would contact him for background information about some regional issue, he would often wind up turning the tables and become the interrogator. They found this quirk of his as bothersome as it was suspicious.

Even so, they had to admit that for all they knew, Regalo was only cultivating an image of himself cloaked in mystery for his own amusement. But wasn't it just this kind of guy who could sniff out the best information on things like corruption, crime, and terrorism?

While his reputation helped to bring in business, Regalo also gained an edge on the competition by setting up his own Internet Web page at a time when this was still something of a novelty. In addition, for a monthly fee Regalo provided subscriber clients with an electronic newsletter sizing up the security situation and business climate in various parts of Africa. His clients swore by him as his counsel was shrewd and candid in assessing the layers of corruption through which a deal would have to pass to stand any chance of success.

He was also one of the few expatriates in Kenya who managed to obtain a gun permit from the Kenyan authorities and carried an easy-to-conceal Colt M-1911A1 single-action .45 caliber semi-automatic pistol, an updated version of the M-1911 which had seen service in World War I, World War II, the Korean War, and the Vietnam War. It was the weapon with which he grew familiar during his military years and he would use no other, favoring it for its explosive power, short trigger, and wide front sight.

One distinctive fact about Regalo that Alain had learned was his insatiable appetite for nightlife and for liquor. He was a common fixture at the seedier nightspots in Nairobi where he would fill his bottomless cup with as much beer or whiskey that could be poured into it in one night and still show up in his office at 7:00 a.m. Apparently his clients knew about his shadow self, but were indifferent, in view of his uncanny ability to read situations and people to a T. After all, how much different was he from the hard-boiled, hard-drinking characters of Humphrey Bogart movies?

It was also widely believed that Regalo once found a way to embarrass a top government official without being thrown out of the country. The story was that during the last outbreak of ethnic violence in the Rift Valley, Regalo was angered by the role of the official in whipping up tensions through diatribes that were being duly printed in the press. Knowing his dining habits, Regalo accosted him at his favorite restaurant at noon, sat down next to him uninvited, and began whispering to him. After a short time, he suddenly bolted up, gagging on his food, his face drawn of its rich luster, and ran out into the street calling for his car and leaving his mistress at the table with Regalo.

It didn't take long for this tale to make the rounds, with most of the gossips figuring that Regalo had shamed the official with revelations of personal details about either his women or his corrupt business dealings. Whatever Regalo might have said to him, it was noteworthy that he engaged in no more inflammatory tribal rhetoric after that incident. What was also noteworthy was how Regalo's reputation grew by leaps and bounds.

As Alain considered his limited options, he began to warm to the idea of seeking Regalo out. His dilemma required nothing less than the kind of bold thinking and action that he sensed was second nature to Regalo. After a few more minutes pondering the matter while he was shaving, he decided to contact him.

When he called Regalo's number at his publicly listed office, a taped recording with Regalo's voice answered, noting that he was in town and asking that the caller leave a phone number. Alain left a message, in which he introduced himself and said he had very urgent business for him. He suggested that they meet at the popular Nyama Choma bar later that evening, around 9:00 p.m., and left his number. Alain hoped the invitation to meet at a bar that he had heard Regalo favored would put him in a receptive mood to agree to do what he was going to ask of him. Half an hour later, Regalo had returned his call and in a gruff voice agreed to meet him that evening.

Not sure of what to do until he saw Regalo, Alain's intuition told him it would not be wise to stay home. He threw on some clothes and headed for the kitchen to tell Rebecca that he was going away for a change of scenery to better concentrate on his writing. He would be gone for about a week, and she only needed to do routine housecleaning while he was away. He asked her to be sure to take down any messages as he would call her now and then from where he would be staying, which was at the Ngong Hills Lodge, a few kilometers out of Nairobi. She was not to tell anyone where he was.

He walked out to the gate to talk to Okoth before heading to the garage to get into his Subaru, warning him that there was a violent gang loose in the area and that he shouldn't take any chances if he saw strangers approaching.

"These criminals are serious, Okoth, and you don't have a gun. There is only one thing to do when they come. Sound the siren and run, run like crazy, run for your life. They'll kill you without a second thought."

Okoth nervously fingered the baton attached to his belt wishing it were a gun as he watched Alain speed away in his old Subaru.

A sense of dread began creeping over Alain as he headed for the outskirts of Nairobi. The foreboding was not as much about his own safety as it was about harm to Wangetha. She was in great danger and he felt powerless. He continued to agonize over his predicament, reconsidering his options. If he went to the police, not only was there the risk of a shootout later, there was also a chance someone would first tip off the kidnappers about what he had done. Then they would be after him just as they had promised. So there were two risks. That meant he couldn't go to the police, not yet.

But the French embassy, why not go to the French embassy he asked himself once again. He carried a French passport, and Kenyan officials favored the French ambassador. They especially liked to be invited to events at his elegant residence, where only the best food was served, including a variety of fine imported cheeses and wines. There was even the nice touch of a piglet slowly roasting on a spit over glowing charcoal embers that he remembered from the last time he was invited to a summer reception at the residence.

And then there was the ambassador's wife herself, her shapely legs put on display for all to see and enjoy in her ultra-miniskirts as she welcomed the guests in the receiving line next to her husband. This ambassador was not one of the angry group of diplomats always sounding off about the country's corruption, mismanagement, and deteriorating infrastructure. Not at all. This was an ambassador who knew how to squeeze a drop of pleasure from any kind of wineskin handed to him.

Still, the problem for Alain, aside from the risk that the embassy would contact the police, was that he had studiously avoided the French community ever since arriving in Kenya. It would be hypocritical of him to seek the help of the French embassy now.

No, the one thing he had to do was to try to get the one-million-shillings ransom while lying as low as possible and not nosing around anymore than he had to. In Kenya this was a huge sum though not exorbitant by Western standards, only about 20,000 U.S. dollars. But he didn't have nearly that much money in his savings account in Paris. He was going to have to think of a way to raise the cash and do it fast.

He had already put on the kind of loose, casual clothes that tourists wear when visiting Kenya and was sporting a wide-brimmed hat and dark sunglasses. He had had little choice in telling Rebecca that he was going away and that he would check in with her for phone messages. He couldn't take the chance that they would come after him at home, especially after he had told them exactly where he lived and what his house looked like. He felt relieved that they had not asked him where he worked. Maybe they knew that already and weren't letting on. Maybe they knew more about him than he first thought.

After guiding the Subaru through Ngong Road on to the heavy noonday traffic on Thika Road and driving for about another 20 minutes, he came to the turn-off for the road to the place he had in mind to hide out for the next few days, the Ngong Hills Lodge. He had seen it described in travelers' guides as a modest, nondescript hotel a few kilometers outside of Nairobi, off the well-beaten paths of the lodges featured in the general run of safari packages. It was owned by an elderly British expatriate widow, who catered to the budget-minded tourists, mostly students from Europe and the U.S.

As he drove up the dusty road, he saw to his satisfaction that only a few cars were in the parking lot adjacent to the one-story, whitewashed building with a row of cottages behind it. After being welcomed by the porter and giving him his one bag, he went to the reception desk where he was warmly greeted in English by the desk clerk, a friendly young man, and filled out the registration form.

Alain congratulated himself on his excellent choice of accommodations. It was exactly what he was looking for. Removed from the din of Nairobi, the Ngong Hills Lodge was unpretentious and clean. He could stay here for at least a week without anyone taking notice.

It began to dawn on him as he was being escorted to his room by the desk clerk with the porter in tow that he was acutely hungry. Once he checked into his room and washed his face and hands, he headed for the hotel's garden patio, where he ordered a local beer and sandwich and began to contemplate his surroundings. Early in his journalistic career, he had learned to study the people and settings around him wherever he was, as he never knew what he might need to flesh out his next story. It was a habit that also helped him to take his mind off himself whenever he was too worried about things, such as now.

Only one other person was in the patio. He was a digni-fied-looking, well-dressed white man with a full shock of gray hair parted neatly to the right side, who appeared to be in his early 60s, sitting at a table alone and sipping tea out of a fine china cup. He guessed from his appearance and his fussiness with his tea as he poured in just the right amount of milk that he might be British, but he couldn't be sure. Nor could he tell if the man was a local expatriate or a tourist.

While Alain was drinking his beer, he noticed what ap-peared to be a local artist wandering through the grounds car-rying two medium-sized, unframed paintings. Slim of build, dressed in shiny brown polyester pants too short for his legs, and a bluish tropical, short-sleeved shirt too long for his arms, Alain estimated him to be about 35 years old. But he knew that among the poorer Kenyans one had to be very careful in guessing how old they were, as many of them looked older than their true ages.

As the artist came closer, with his bare feet stepping gin-gerly on the grass surrounding the patio, he paused, surveying the area as he held out his paintings. Alain could see that both of them were of wildlife, done in oil on canvas. One was of a group of grazing zebras, with crisp black and white stripes, their tails flickering. The other was of a single, reclining lion with a huge mane at ease under the sun, his front paws visible under his chest, gazing serenely ahead.

Both had exacting scenery as backdrops to their sub-jects, including several acacia trees with their flattened tops and mushroom-like appearance set against a pale blue sky. He stretched out his neck to get a closer look. The quality of the rendering of the lion surprised him. He had only seen such clarity and vividness in paintings of wildlife in the most expensive galleries of Nairobi.

The artist then headed straight for the tea-drinking gentleman, stopped in front of him, and addressed him in pidgin English.

"Painting, sir? Buy painting, sir? Zebras or lion? Very good. I sell. My wife sick."

The artist held the two paintings before him for inspection, one in each outstretched hand, in an obviously awkward and uncomfortable position. As the tea man looked, he furrowed his brow and curled his lips into the suggestion of a sneer, though Alain could see that his eyes were avidly scrutinizing the paintings down to the last detail.

After a few minutes, the tea man snatched the canvases from the artist's hands, one at a time, further examining them and fingering their frameless edges, after which he abruptly thrust them back. Finally, the tea man exclaimed, "All right then, how much do you want for this one of the bloody lion? It's not that good really, but I might be willing to give you something for it."

Alain pretended not to hear and assumed that the tea man was only posturing for the sake of getting a bargain. He had seen several paintings of lions in his time, and this was clearly one of the finest he had ever seen. From where he sat he could clearly see the careful detail given to the rugged facial features, the glaring eyes, and the full mane.

To paint such defining contours of the lion's visage, not to mention the realism of the natural surroundings, down to a creek gurgling sparkling blue water, must have taken many days if not weeks of concentrated effort.

"I ask only 2,000 shillings," the artist blurted out. "I sell. My wife sick."

"2,000 shillings!" the tea man shot back, visibly annoyed. "That is impossible. Go away. I have no time for you."

Alain watched from the corner of his eye while continuing to pretend that he was not paying any attention. He knew that a painting of similar size and quality would easily get 10 times this asking price in one of the established galleries in Nairobi, if not even more. Didn't the tea man know what a bargain only 2,000 shillings would be? Didn't the painter know that also? If he did, why didn't he go to a gallery? Or had he already tried?

"Sir, sir," the artist pleaded. "Please, give me price. How much you give?"

The tea man peered even more closely at the two paintings, examining both from top to bottom, from side to side, and then from top to bottom again, repeating his ritual of fingering the rough edges of the canvas, but finally settling his gaze on the one of the lion.

"900 shillings. That's it. I won't give more. Take it or leave it."

"900 shillings! Please sir! A little more!"

"900 shillings. That's it."

"Please sir!"

"No, I won't give more!"

"But you can more. You rich!"

"Get away from me!"

"Please sir!"

"Will you take it or won't you?"

For just a moment, the artist looked over to where Alain was sitting, but Alain immediately turned his face away. He didn't want to meet his eyes. He wanted this pleading man with the beautiful paintings to go away. He wanted to shout to him, "Don't drag me into your pitiful world when my world is filled with enough trouble. What could I do anyway, to help you? Grab the tea man by the lapels of his seersucker jacket and the rear of his trousers, turn him upside down, and then shake him until the right number of shillings dropped out of his pocket?

"Isn't that that a pretty tall order for me to intervene, my artist friend, considering that your world and mine have only now just barely intersected? And if I did, how would the tea man take it? Would he slap us both on the back and say, 'Well done?' Or would you lose the sale altogether?"

He didn't know this artist from Adam any more than the artist knew him from Adam. But, of course, it didn't have to stay that way. There was something else he could do. He could step into the artist's world, bringing his world with him and making their two worlds a new world of its own. Then they could try to negotiate with the tea man together. Even if congratulating the painter and Alain for having brought him into the right was not likely, at least he might cough up a few more shillings.

But did he really want to go this far when all he really found himself wanting to do was to say, along with the tea man, "Just go away. Just go away and don't bother me." He had no time for paintings now. He had no time for this other's world. He had come and he had seen but he was not ready to do more. His hands were already full with a crisis not of his making. The last thing he wanted was to get involved in this squabble.

As Alain turned his head away, the artist slowly turned his head back to meet the expectant gaze of the tea man.

"Give 900 shillings. It's yours."

Not long after that, Alain went back to his room, leaving his bottle of beer on the table half full and the sandwich he had ordered untouched.

CHAPTER 9
ENCOUNTER WITH REGALO

☙

The Nyama Choma bar in downtown Nairobi was crawling as usual with customers. The combination of rich beer and strong whiskey, scantily-dressed waitresses and dancers, as well as the prostitutes with their come-hither looks and bright makeup was enough to pack it full every night. By the time Alain arrived a few minutes after 9:00 p.m., the action on the dance floor was in full swing, every table crowded with boozing, playful men and women. The smoke made his eyes smart, forcing him to squint at first to see his way through, but he was finally able to make his way over to the back corner. One of the waiters had let him know that Regalo was already seated and waiting for him there.

He was hard to miss. Hoisting a large bottle of Tusker Gold beer, appearing to be in his early 40s, he was the only *mzungu* to be seen. Alain observed him with interest as he slowly approached his table, noting his sharp, angular facial features, thick, dark-black hair and well-trimmed mustache, his shirt unbuttoned to his chest, and his lean, wiry hands revealing the kind of tanned complexion seen in Mediterranean or Mid-Eastern populations.

He was speaking spiritedly to two, younger African men leaning toward him, who didn't look as though they belonged to any of the local tribes.

As Alain neared them, Regalo paused only long enough to finish gulping down his Tusker before bellowing.

"No, no, no! It's not what I wanted. Take your so-called information and shove it. I could get better information from the nearest horse's ass. What you have to tell me is useless. You Nigerians are all the same, you swindlers, you bloodsuckers. You're all con artists. There is no deal! I'm not paying for any of this crap. Go take it and peddle it elsewhere. Go find some rich, retired person in America. To hell with you!"

He rose angrily from his chair and almost collided with Alain, who grabbed the chance to address him.

"Pardon me, are you Joseph Regalo?"

"Yeah, that's me," Regalo answered hurriedly. He was on his way to the bar and Alain was standing in his way.

"What do you want?" he scowled, casting a quick look at Alain to size him up.

"I'm Alain Sardou, the one who asked you to meet me here."

"So you're the guy."

"Yes. I'm a journalist recently assigned here."

"Oh, no! You didn't mention that in your voice-mail. Not another one of you! Aren't there enough of you hookers here in Nairobi already? Get out of my way. I don't have time for this."

"Wait, just wait a minute!" The words burst from Alain's mouth as he tried to keep up with Regalo who was by now deep in the crowd as he waded through the teeming bodies to the bar. "I'm not coming to you as a journalist. I don't want to interview you or anything like that. This is a personal matter. Please, let me explain what the problem is."

Regalo stopped his forward lurch in order to take a better look at Alain, catching him directly in the eyes with a probing stare.

"Why would it be worth my time to talk to you about your personal issues? What are they to me?"

"How will you know until you hear what they are?"

Regalo's brow furrowed, now looking at Alain as if he were really seeing him for the first time.

"OK, short and simple, but that's a good answer. Let's go back to my table. You want a beer?"

"Why not?"

After going to the bar and ordering two beers, they sat down at Regalo's table. The wall behind them, which had once been painted white, was now shot through with flecks of grey revealing its cinderblock makeup.

"So tell me what you have on your mind. But hurry up. I don't have much time, and I had better not see any of what we're going to talk about in the papers, on any level of attribution. And I mean any level, not on the record, not on background, not even as a so-called source. Is that clear?"

Alain disguised his surprise. Few people could speak about levels of attribution with such exactness. This bordered on house knowledge.

"Of course," Alain answered, now speaking less hurriedly. "As I said, this is personal. I'm not about to write about my own problems so there's not going to be an article and you can't be quoted in any way about anything."

"So tell me. What's the problem?"

"I'm coming to you for your readout of my options. I know your reputation. You know Kenya like few others..."

"Thanks for the compliment," Regalo interrupted in a sarcastic tone. "But continue. The problem. What's the problem?"

The waiter arrived with the bottles of Tusker and Regalo immediately took a long pull.

"I'm a witness to a kidnapping, and I'm being extorted to pay a ransom. I was on a fact-finding mission in the Rift Valley yesterday accompanied by a woman translator. We had left a camp of displaced people in Molo and stopped at a petrol station near Nakuru to get fuel. A few moments later an old Peugeot sedan came screeching in from nowhere. A gang of four piled out, guns waving..."

"What color was it?" Regalo interrupted.

"White, with a brown right fender."

"You say the Peugot was old. Does that mean the paint looked faded?"

"I can't say for sure."

"Well, was the paint bright then?"

"No."

"I mean the white paint."

"I understand. No, it wasn't bright or new-looking."

"What about the brown paint, faded or bright?"

"Somewhat new-looking, now that I think of it. But why is that important?"

"If the white paint was faded, it means that it wasn't re-painted to disguise a stolen car. The fresher brown paint on the fender means that it was probably a part from another newer Peugeot. This may or may not be helpful to know later on, but please go on."

"They claimed to be plainclothes police and seemed to recognize my translator, calling her by name. In no time they had forced her out of my car and into theirs while restraining me. Two of them took her in the direction of Nairobi while the other two forced me to drive them back at gunpoint."

"Also to Nairobi?"

"Yeah, but they wouldn't let me overtake the other two."

"What did they look like?"

"They all wore safari hats and sunglasses, though I saw dreadlocks hanging out from under the hat of two of them. They appeared to be in their late 20s or early 30s, and they spoke Kikuyu, that I'm sure of. I memorized a few of the words I overheard, at least the phonetic sounds of them. I have a good ear, so I could repeat them to you."

Regalo laughed. "That's good. That's very good. But let's save that for later. I don't speak Kikuyu."

"They're demanding one million shillings in ransom. I've been lying low since, except for meeting you here. I'm wary of going to the police, and I can't go to my own embassy. Don't ask me why, but I can't. Frankly, I don't know whom I can trust."

"I'll tell you. No one. You can trust absolutely no one." The answer from Regalo came forcefully and without hesitation.

"You included?" Alain asked just for effect. He knew what the answer would be.

"Me included. Now what about the attendants at the petrol station? What did they see?"

"There was only one, and he ran and hid as soon as the thugs got out of their car, waving their guns. He doesn't know anything."

Alain's voice became more urgent. "Listen, Joseph. It's not me that I'm concerned about. It's the woman. She's special…"

Regalo cut Alain short. "Don't give me that story that you're not concerned about yourself. Just tell me who she is."

"She's Wangetha Wachira, a beautiful black woman. Her father was a civil servant in the Kenyatta government. She speaks several of the local dialects fluently and has been working as a freelance interpreter. It's hard to say exactly what her tribal mix is because she won't talk about it, but there must be a lot of Kikuyu since she said that her mother spoke Kikuyu to her as a child."

"How about another beer?" Regalo asked, snapping his fingers for the waiter. "This time I'll be more patient and wait for him to come to us."

"Sure."

"Wangetha Wachira," Regalo enunciated the name slowly. "If that's the Wangetha Wachira I know, you're in a world of trouble my friend, and money may not be the way out of this mess. There are exceptions to the money rule you know, even in this part of the world. She is none other than the one-time mistress of the high commissioner of Zimugabwa, Robidi

Amimuga. And this is no ordinary emissary. He's a former minister of state in his home country. Time has crept up on him, and he's an old geezer now but still powerful in the politics of this continent. He has friends and well-wishers in high places everywhere, even where you would least expect it.

"He amazes me. He just amazes me," Regalo continued. "With his high-pitched voice, British accent, and horn-rimmed glasses, you would never think that this was a lady's man. But his revolutionary past coupled with his wealth and influence had Wangetha bamboozled. And he was thrilled, of course, that such a desirable woman could be interested in him."

"What happened to their affair?" Alain asked with some annoyance.

"She left him, is that what you wanted to hear?"

"Why did she leave him?"

"She realized that all she could ever be was a plaything for good old Robidi. And she also became aware of his wife's intense dislike for her. The truth is that the wife would normally have tolerated this affair as long as she was kept in the style to which she was accustomed. That would be a mansion filled with servants at her beck and call and regular shopping trips abroad. But Wangetha was different. She was too classy, not one of his average mistresses. She made Robidi's wife very jealous. With time, Wangetha began to feel very uncomfortable in this *ménage a trois* and got out."

"So it was Wangetha who left him?"

"Yeah, Wangetha. And she wasn't very discreet about letting people know what she really thought of him, which didn't help matters as word got back to Robidi. He was already enraged because she left him. But then he became worried as well because of what she knew about his corrupt dealings, which were plenty. He was involved in everything from land fraud to killings.

"You were with her when she was kidnapped?" Regalo mused. "That's rich, too rich."

"This is some story," Alain frowned.

"Believe it, friend. It's true."

As Alain took a long swallow of the fresh beer that had been set before him, he noticed a change in Regalo's demeanor. There was no more of his intense, probing look, with his eyebrows turning up, asking his questions in a way that made his interlocutor feel stupid for either not having thought of the question himself or for not knowing the answer. This earlier look of condescension had now switched to a look of bemusement with a slight, cruel smile beginning to form at the edges of his mouth while his lips remained closed. Was Regalo taking delight in seeing him in this dilemma? He had heard that Regalo was an embittered, sardonic man. Was he seeing some evidence of this now? He didn't know for sure, but it made him uneasy.

"There must be some way to rescue her."

"I think that we need a couple of more Tuskers first before we do that," Regalo grinned as he called the waiter over again.

"But we haven't finished the last two."

Regalo took his beer and downed it in one long swallow.

"Speak for yourself. I'm done."

Wiping his mouth with a napkin, he turned back to Alain, serious once again. "So you haven't gone to the police and don't plan to."

"That's right."

"Well then, let's use our heads and see what we can figure out."

"I'm with you."

"What we can be sure about is that these guys were after Wangetha, since you said they knew her name. That means they started following you at some point, even if you didn't notice."

"Makes sense."

"So what would be their motive? If they were your everyday criminals out on a carjacking jaunt, they wouldn't be tracking Wangetha and you specifically. Someone had to tell them where to find her, where she worked, where she would be, whom she was accompanying, and so on. What reason would they have had to figure that out for themselves? Why go to all this trouble for a carjacking when the streets of Nairobi are full of cars that are easier targets?"

"But there was someone for whom the trouble was worth it."

"Exactly, someone like our well-connected high commissioner. She knew too much, and once she left him she became dangerous. Of course, we can't know what precise instructions the goons were given, whether they were told to kill her or kidnap her. My bet, though, is that they were told to kill her."

"Go on."

"After all, why would Robidi want to keep her alive just to try to get a ransom for her? Whom would he ask for the money? You? You're a journalist, not some rich businessman. And why would he want to take the risk of being found out? Ten to one the kidnapping wasn't his idea. That had to be the goons' idea."

"I'm following you," Alain said, intently.

"And besides, he's filthy rich anyway. He doesn't need to stoop to kidnap a former mistress to try to make money. We also have to remember that hired killers come cheap on this continent. There's no reason to think that the thugs that kidnapped Wangetha were going to get more than a few thousand shillings apiece for killing her. That means they could have used some more money. The way they figured it, even a reporter like you is going to be able to raise a decent amount of ransom money."

Regalo leaned back, as if taking stock of the effect of his interpretation of events. Alain remained very focused on him.

"But what the hell do I know?"

Alain did not take the bait to praise Regalo's perceptive analysis. He knew that Regalo already knew how good it was. There was no need to tell him just now and feed his arrogance.

"By the way, in case you were wondering, that's also the easy answer to the question of why you weren't shot and eliminated as a witness to the kidnapping."

Regalo's eyes narrowed as he lowered his voice almost to a whisper, making it hard for Alain to hear him with all the background noise around them. "Pardon me. That was probably a little presumptuous of me to suggest that I know what you're thinking. But you must realize how easy it would have been for these guys to kill you in case you hadn't thought about it."

Now Alain could see the slight, cruel, downturn of Regalo's mouth once again. "Common criminals kill foreigners from time to time in this country, as you know."

"I understand that," Alain responded with some irritation. "Could we get back to Wangetha please?"

"Of course. Back to Wangetha. Now you should know there are rumors of her having had other affairs besides the one with our high commissioner. So could there have been someone else who might have had one reason or another to want her to disappear?"

Regalo leaned back again, letting the question sink in.

"Well, what about it? Could there have been?" Alain asked impatiently.

"I can't go into every rumor I've ever heard about her. But I think there's next to zero chance that there was another disgruntled lover behind this caper."

Regalo took a long pull from his Tusker.

"There's only one thing that puzzles me now," Alain said.

"Go ahead. What is it?"

"Do these guys really think they can get away with double-crossing their boss?"

"Come on, Alain. They must or they wouldn't be trying it. They've probably made up some story to tell Robidi about how they killed her and fed her body to the lions. He has no reason not to believe that they wouldn't follow through on his orders and finish her off. He's so full of himself that it wouldn't cross his mind that they would risk double-crossing him and maybe getting killed themselves once he caught up with them. The only thing he could ever wonder about is whether or not they were lying about having killed her because they botched the job.

"But in that case, if she was still alive and she escaped, some news about her would have to turn up somewhere. She hasn't escaped as far as we know, though, and there probably won't be any escape. So let's not comfort ourselves with that remote possibility. There won't be any news about her that could find its way back to Robidi.

"And with no news, he wouldn't know that he's been double-crossed and that his goons are trying to line their pockets with an extortion plot focused on you. As long as she stays disappeared, with no reports about her to the contrary, Robidi has to figure she is dead. He has no reason to think otherwise."

Regalo took another long swallow of his Tusker. "You've been here long enough. You've seen the destitution." He was enunciating slowly now, as a teacher talking to a student. "Having nothing can make you take chances you or I wouldn't even consider. The fact is, that is exactly the way these hoodlums see life. In their eyes, neither theirs nor anyone else's is worth that much in the first place. Besides, they wouldn't have to stay in Kenya once they got the money. They could slip over the border into Tanzania and try to blend in there. It happens all the time nowadays with carjackers. They all speak Swahili, the official language of Tanzania, so it isn't that hard to fit in, especially if you have money."

Regalo took still another good swallow. "The only chance they are really taking according to their twisted thinking is that you may not care enough about Wangetha to raise the ransom to free her. But what do they have to lose? If you don't pay off, they will go ahead and kill her as they were ordered to.

102

In fact, they may be planning to kill her even after you deliver the ransom to them. But you can worry about that later. In the meanwhile, you shouldn't waste too much time. The gang is no doubt taking turns raping her as we speak. Before long she won't be worth too much to any man if somebody doesn't find her soon."

Alain flinched as Regalo studied his face again.

"Just what is your interest in this Wangetha, anyway? Why are you so concerned about someone you hardly know? Rape is a fact of life in this continent and elsewhere. Do you think you're going to be able to do anything about it? Are you sure you don't just want to bed her yourself?"

Alain felt his temperature rising. The words poured out of him in a staccato burst. "Don't speculate on my motives, Joseph! There's been a crime committed, a very serious crime. I'm asking for your help in dealing with it, that's all."

Regalo sighed as his eyes dropped their quizzical look.

"You're going to have to blacken your face, neck, and hands as soon as you can. You won't last long like this. They know who you are. If they think you are nosing around where you shouldn't be, doing anything but getting them the money, they'll know about it and will find you. You probably wouldn't even be able to skip over the border, looking like this.

"Use the charcoal from natural wood that is burned here for cooking. You can buy a sack of it off the street. Get it on your hands and smudge it over your face and neck. Be careful not to get it into your eyes and wash it off regularly so that it doesn't poison your skin. It shouldn't hurt you if you do that. You'll be surprised that no one will notice except for the people that knew you in your other life.

"You should look good in black, though your blue eyes will be a problem," Regalo continued as he warmed to his subject. "So don't let any African get too close to you. Wear sunglasses all the time. With your French accent, you can pass yourself off as an African from the western Francophone coast. That's believable since there are a few of them here and there in the country.

"I take it that part of your job as a reporter requires speaking Swahili?"

"Yeah, it's decent enough."

"Good. Your Swahili will also have an accent, which will work for you as well. And always wear some kind of hat to cover your thin hair. There are plenty of Moslems here, so even wearing a *kofia* cap is plausible on your part."

"I doubt that I will do that."

"It's your choice."

"From everything you've told me so far, the assailants were Kikuyus," Regalo observed matter-of-factly. "You have to find a Kikuyu you can trust to find out if she's still alive and where she's being held. This should be someone who's not in the government or too strong into politics, but is still well-plugged into the Kikuyu community. That information will help you decide if you want to pay the ransom or go to the police."

He pulled out a scrap of paper from his wallet and a ballpoint pen from his rumpled shirt pocket. Scrawling two names on the paper, he gulped down the last of his beer and called for the check.

"These are the people you need to see," Regalo said as he shoved the note across the table to Alain. "The first is a good contact for you in the Kikuyu community, a guy by the name of Haran Nakaya. He is said to be Wangetha's brother, but you will notice they have different names. I've never asked him about it since it wasn't really my business. It's up to you if you want to ask him about it."

"What kind of relationship do they have?" Alain asked. "You say Wangetha's brother?"

"As far as I know he is her brother by blood, having the same mother, but they've been estranged."

"Why estranged?"

"I don't know the details, but from what I've heard she was disappointed in him because of his business failings and wanted to disown him. He'd taken the family inheritance and tried to start different enterprises with no success."

"What kind?"

"Construction and light manufacturing. But nothing panned out. He wound up losing all of the family's money. Because he was well educated and had a law degree, he set up a small legal services practice in a rundown building downtown. He also started drinking heavily. It's all such a waste."

"So why should I see him?"

"They may be estranged but he's still her brother. He may be willing to help her and try to redeem himself in her eyes. Then there is the fact that he's very well connected to the Kikuyu community, and because of the depths to which he's sunk he should be able to plug into the Kikuyu underworld as well. You've got nothing to lose and everything to gain by calling on him."

"How well do you know him?"

"Fairly well. I've met him a few times. He's very impressive looking, just like Wangetha. You'll see what I mean."

"Can you introduce me to him?"

"Sure, I'll ring him up to let him know you'll be paying a call."

"What about this other name?"

"This guy is an American business executive named Wayne Jefferson. Wangetha has done some publicity work in addition to interpreting for his company."

"What kind of company is it?"

"It specializes in marketing household wares imported from the USA. Wangetha did some advertising spots for them on TV and in the local newspapers. She's some looker, isn't she?"

"So he knows her," Alain noted, ignoring Regalo's comment.

"Righto. I've met the man, and he has an eye for the ladies. But there's no reason to think there has ever been any hanky-panky on his part with Wangetha. His wife follows his every move and would have killed him. He's also known to be a generous donor to various social causes here but has no fondness for Robidi's government."

"So why is he worth checking out?"

"Because he may be able to help get what you need for the ransom, if that's the route you decide to take. Though from what I understand, he's becoming more and more wary of whom he gives money to, having been burned a few times by conmen. And in your case, you'd be trying to get money to deal with a crime you haven't reported to the police. That might put him off, but then again it might not, since he's smart and would understand the nature of your dilemma."

"Can you let him know I'll be calling on him?"

"Sorry, but with Wayne you are on your own."

Alain wondered why Regalo would not introduce him to Wayne as well but didn't say anything. He wasn't going to press his luck with him any further this evening.

As the waiter approached their table, Alain called him to his side of the table and asked for the bill.

"What are you doing?" Regalo snapped. "The check is mine."

"I should pay for this, Joseph. I asked to meet you. You were my guest here."

When the waiter returned with the bill, Alain looked at it with surprise. "Could this be right? The bill is for eight beers. Did we drink that many beers together? Didn't we only order six beers? I'm sure that's all we had, but here it says eight."

Regalo glared at Alain and grabbed the check out of his hand.

"I'll take care of this. You don't have to. It will be my pleasure."

He motioned the waiter to his side of the table.

"There seems to be some mistake here," Regalo said to the waiter. "We didn't have eight beers. That was impossible."

The waiter looked at him.

"How could you make such a stupid mistake?" Regalo said angrily. "We had at least five beers apiece, which makes a total of 10. The beer that you served us wasn't Tusker Gold. These were watered-down beers that you brought to us in opened Tusker Gold bottles. If you had brought us eight of those good, hearty Tusker Golds, we would have had our fill. But you, the thief that you are, couldn't resist diluting the beers you brought us, could you? And so we wind up drinking 10. Didn't you take these bottles and pour out a good part of the beer in each bottle and then fill it back up with water before you brought it out here? And now aren't you giving us a check for only eight beers to ease your bad feelings?"

Alain could see puzzlement in the waiter's eyes.

"But do you know what?" Regalo smiled. "We're going to pay for 10 beers because that's how many we drank – even if they were watered down."

Alain could also see that Regalo was playing with the waiter. He had drunk enough beer in Kenya to know that these beers weren't watered down, but the waiter was not disagreeing with Regalo.

"So, do you hear? I am going to pay for the full 10 beers that we drank."

Regalo reached into his pocket, pulled out three 500-shilling notes and thrust them into the waiter's hand.

"There you are, my friend," Regalo said, laughing, as the waiter hurried away.

Regalo got up while Alain looked at him with quiet amazement. He had just played the waiter for a fool, kneading and massaging his guilt to draw him into the trap of questioning his own hold on reality. The waiter was now left to wonder how many beers he had actually brought, who might have brought more, and who might have watered them, when in fact all he had done was inflate the count of six Gold Tusker bottles to eight bottles on the tab. In the end, he might conclude that Regalo was crazy or drunk, but even then it would probably be only after he had done some worrying about what had happened.

"Why did you play that game with the waiter?"Alain questioned Regalo. "Couldn't you just have told him that the bill was in error and that you weren't going to pay all of it?"

"He wouldn't have acknowledged it."

"How can you be so sure?"

"You can never be one-hundred percent sure, but when they put the fraud in writing, as on this bill, they don't back down from it very often."

"I guess you should know," Alain responded. "I'm at the Ngong Hills Lodge, Room 111, if you have something for me you think I need to know."

Regalo didn't say anything and stood up to leave, leaving Alain at the table.

"Thanks, Joseph, for coming tonight," Alain said with emphasis.

"It's all right. Good luck."

Alain watched Regalo's back as he moved through the din of the noise and smoke and sidestepped the couples gripping one another on the dance floor. Alain didn't know whether to be repelled by what Regalo had done to the waiter, or admire him for his audacity.

He followed Regalo's figure sliding forward confidently, his shoulders ducking and weaving as he squeezed through the crowd toward the exit. The drums were pounding so loudly that he was surprised he had been oblivious to them until now. On the dance floor, he watched the skimpily-clad seductresses grinding out bumps and grinds as he searched his mind for any comparable images he might have stored away somewhere. There were none.

He could not imagine this dance number, with all its pounding noise, ever having a beginning. Nor did the flashes of red, yellow, blue, and green streams of light pouring out of the strobe light dangling from above the dance floor give any hint of ever stopping.

He forgot all about Regalo as he stared in fascination at the bodies crammed into this small space, glistening beads of sweat dripping down taut, sleek muscles or smooth, full curves. How could he have been so unaware of all this frenzied activity around him? Was Regalo that interesting?

Over to the right corner, he was diverted by the sight of a middle-aged, professional-looking man slipping some concoction into his female partner's drink as she got up to leave the table, presumably to go to the bathroom. Would she know or care what he had done once she returned and had started drinking the potion? He could see the drink in the cocktail glass which now showed chalky streaks. Was he going to stir the drink at least a little to hide his gift? Or did he not care whether she knew? Could it be that he knew that she would pretend that she didn't know even though she knew?

As he saw that the professional man was not going to stir his girl friend's drink, he turned his head away, and caught the sight of two men toward the left in a darkened corner, locked in each other's arms and exchanging deep, probing kisses.

He took a final sip of his beer and looked at the crumpled note Regalo had left for him on the table. It said, "Haran Nakaya, Biashara Street." Nothing else. For a moment, he felt like running after Regalo to demand the rest of the address, which he surely knew. But he thought better of it. He thought of the contemptuous eyes that would greet him, the quizzical arrogant look that would be questioning his own ingratitude. No, he would find this Haran Nakaya, even if he had to knock on the door of every building on Biashara Street.

CHAPTER 10
HARAN NAKAYA

෨

After flagging down a taxi which took him back to the Ngong Hills Lodge, Alain stumbled into his room and fell on his bed. Staring up at the ceiling in the dark, he began to take stock of what he had to do. He valued what Regalo had told him, and he had to admit to a grudging respect for his shrewd mind. Regalo was even right about his feelings for Wangetha. He found her irresistible and could hardly forget the sight of her in Nakuru, swaying her hips with the smoldering sun behind her as she catwalked her way to him. But he couldn't let himself think about her anymore if he were to get some much-needed sleep.

When he awoke eight hours later, he resolved to find Haran as soon as possible. For a moment he wondered if Wangetha's kidnappers would already be on the lookout for him, but decided not to worry about it. Their main interest was the ransom money, and they knew they had to wait for it. So there would be no reason for them to search for him just now.

Still, it made sense for him to stay away from his bungalow. He would follow Regalo's advice – blacken his appearance and play up his French accent, while posing as a visitor from West Africa.

Using the charcoal from the bag the porter had delivered to him for a generous tip, Alain smudged his face, neck, and hands. He was surprised at the effectiveness of this simple treatment as he considered his changed look in the mirror.

He felt ready now to go out on the street and look up Haran Nakaya.

As he got into the taxi that the porter had called for him, Alain was pleased that the driver didn't seem to notice anything amiss with his face. After he was dropped off at the intersection of Biashara Street and Moi Avenue, Alain got out and entered what looked like a department store with rows and racks of shirts, socks and underwear. Walking toward the cashier's station, elevated from the rest of the floor, he noticed a distinguished-looking man with a turban wrapped around his head standing nearby, staring at him. Alain approached him and asked if he knew where the office of Haran Nakaya was located.

"Is that why you have come into my store?" the man questioned with a scowl.

Alain immediately regretted that he had not purchased something first.

"Actually, no," he answered quickly. "I was looking for a nice pair of pajamas, but didn't see any here on display."

"Well, why don't you try looking over there?" he countered, pointing to the area far behind. "I'm sure that you will find something there to please you." He was no longer frowning.

"Are you the proprietor?" Alain ventured.

"Yes, along with two brothers. We own three other stores in the city."

After he had directed Alain to the shelves displaying the pajamas, he turned around and barked at a curtained area in the back. "Jomo, get out here! You need to show someone our fine pajamas."

A black face protruded from between the curtains.

"But you ordered me to finish stacking these boxes, sir. I'm not yet finished."

"It doesn't matter. Come out now!" The proprietor was waving his finger at him.

A tall, thin black Kenyan came out of the back area and hastened to the cashier's station.

"Over there," the proprietor ordered, gesturing with his right hand toward Alain and the pajama sets.

The clerk hurriedly approached Alain. "What size do you wear, good man? A medium? It looks as though that size would sit well on you, sir."

"That is my size, exactly," Alain answered appreciatively.

The clerk carefully lifted up a pair of blue-striped pajamas from the shelf and cradled them with his long fingers for Alain to inspect.

"This is what we have in your size, sir, this fine imported pair, made of pure cotton."

"You have no others?"

"No, this is all we have in your size."

Alain turned to the proprietor. "It seems strange to have to buy pajamas here in Kenya that have been imported."

"They are of excellent quality. Why should it seem strange?"

"Only because I know that you had a thriving textile industry here once."

"That might have been once. It is cheaper to bring in pajamas from abroad, even with the duties, than to invest in all the machinery to produce them here. Interest rates from the banks at some 25 percent are much too high to think about getting a business loan. We would have a hard time paying it back."

"But what about the jobs that would be created here with that investment?"

"More jobs would be good for the country, of course. But first we would have to weigh the high cost of gearing up the industry against the returns of the small domestic market we have. Right now, it doesn't look like a good investment. And then we could never compete with Asian mills in exporting

113

textile goods to other markets. Everything is much cheaper this way. Are you a businessman?"

"No," Alain answered quickly.

He turned back to the clerk. "I'll take the pajamas you showed me."

Jomo picked them up and carried them to the cash register.

As Alain reached into his wallet for the 800 shillings to pay for the pajamas, he looked up at the proprietor. "By the way, do you mind if I ask you again where the office of Haran Nakaya is?"

"I take it you mean the Haran Nakaya on this street who has a law practice."

"Yes, he is the one," Alain answered.

"He's in the fourth building down, on this same side of the street, third floor."

A few minutes later, Alain was climbing the rickety stairs leading to Haran's office. After reaching the third floor, he saw an unpainted, unvarnished, shabby-looking door with no formal sign, just the name "Haran Nakaya, Esquire," scrawled on it, probably with a dark-brown, felt-tip marker.

He knocked briskly and waited, surveying the water-stained plaster of the surrounding walls.

After waiting for what he judged was at least one full minute, Alain knocked again, this time a little harder.

Following another pause, but shorter this time, a rich, baritone voice rang out.

"Who is it?"

"My name is Alain Sardou. Your friend Joseph Regalo sent me. It's important that I see you. I need your help. Please let me in and I'll explain."

When the door creaked open, Alain saw a tall, lean, handsome man with broad shoulders and short-cropped hair standing before him. He had a close resemblance to Wangetha, as Regalo said. But unlike Wangetha, he was shabbily dressed, wearing a rumpled, white shirt and gray slacks that looked as if they hadn't been pressed in weeks.

As Haran ushered him in, Alain surveyed the dark, cramped room that apparently was meant to pass for an office. He couldn't help but note that the glass panes of the room's two windows were cracked in several places, with thick strips of masking tape holding the panes together, limiting the light from outside that could get through.

On one of the window sills sat a large crimson pot with an earlike handle on each side, filled with black earth, containing a tangled mess of unruly green vines. A wooden stake was thrust in the middle, around which the vines were supposed to grow, but he could see only two or three inching up. He was not surprised, considering how dry the dirt looked.

The only relief that Alain found in viewing the office's drab interior, with its peeling old wallpaper, was a painting that could grace any home or office and was in stark contrast to its bleak surroundings. Hanging in a plain, wooden frame, it was a beautiful rendering of a man and woman sitting peacefully on a bench in the shade under the sweeping branches of an acacia tree, holding hands as they gazed at a broad stretch of tall, green savannah.

Glancing upward, he saw a lone, bare bulb screwed into some kind of fixture on the cracked ceiling, but it was not burning.

Following Alain's upward gaze, Haran remarked, "Sorry it's so dark, but the electricity has been turned off for a few weeks now." He then motioned for Alain to be seated on a chair opposite his desk.

Alain could see that his chair was apparently the one place in the room for guests to sit. The only other furniture, besides the desk and the two chairs, were two bookcases fashioned out of planks and cinder blocks, holding what appeared to be thick law books. He noticed a law degree from Nairobi University, with the same kind of simple frame as the painting, hanging from the wall behind the desk. On the wall next to the door, he recognized the formal picture of President Moi that seemed to be everywhere in Nairobi. He had missed it when he first entered the room.

"I see that you are an admirer of our president, Mr. Sardou," Haran said half-smilingly. "Is that why you have blackened your face, to be more like him, or maybe more like all of us?"

Alain's face fell before he could respond. He had been wearing black on his face all this time and had forgotten about it.

As if reading Alain's chagrin in being found out, Haran instantly moved to set him at ease.

"You know, Regalo told me that you were a Frenchman. And, yes, he told me that you're in a very difficult situation. So I can understand why you darkened your skin. It's not a bad job really. It probably would have fooled me if Regalo hadn't told me who you were."

"So you found me out," Alain joked. He pointed to the picture of Moi. "I still haven't been able to decide how I feel about these pictures everywhere. I see both sides of the argument, the need for a unifying, paternal symbol versus the insinuations of a cult of personality. If these images were not everywhere, I think that I would lean to the former view."

"That's very charitable of you," Haran responded without pursuing the matter any further, while he sat down behind his desk and waved to the chair again. "Now, please sit down and tell me what I can do for you."

"I'm here for some good advice. I take it you have some time, which I'm not here to waste, by the way. I will pay you your fee, whatever it is," Alain emphasized as he sat down.

"We can discuss that later. Let's hear the case first," Haran said good-naturedly in his husky voice. He bent down to open the lower drawer of his desk and pulled out a bottle, which Alain recognized as a British gin.

"But before you tell me, can I pour you a drink? The colonialists were not all bad, you know. We absorbed their language, adopted their political, educational, and legal systems, and we learned how to drink tea, beer, and gin," Haran grinned.

"Don't mind if I do," Alain said. "Gin is really not my preferred drink, but why not."

"Good." Haran pulled out two small teacups from the same drawer, wiped them with a small towel he pulled out from another drawer, and poured enough gin into both cups to half fill them.

"To your health, Mr. Sardou."

"Alain. Please call me Alain."

"And just call me Haran."

As the two men drank deeply, Alain could see some of the ravages that drinking had brought to Haran. At first, he had thought his reddish eyes were from tiredness. Now he knew better.

"Before I begin, Haran," Alain said in a serious tone, "you need to know that I'm only here because I have no choice but to trust both you and Regalo. I don't know very much about you. I only know that Regalo told me you might be able to help me."

"Well, maybe I can. Maybe I can't. We'll have to see."

"Do you know the nature of the problem?" Alain asked.

"Only very generally. Regalo told me about a Kikuyu woman being kidnapped at gunpoint."

"So Regalo did not tell you who she was?" Alain asked.

"No."

"For what it's worth, she's part Kikuyu and part Kalenjin. I hope that doesn't make a difference to you." Alain wasn't yet ready to tell him it was his sister.

"She's the translator I was traveling with in the Molo region when she was kidnapped by four gunmen before my very eyes in Nakuru. I have good reason to think that they were Kikuyu, which is ironic because I was gathering information to write about their ordeal in the ethnic clashes."

Haran's eyebrows arched and deep furrows appeared in his forehead. "Why do you think that they were Kikuyu?"

"I had heard them speaking Swahili for a brief time, which I understand pretty well. But most of the time I heard them use words that sounded like Kikuyu."

"How could you tell?"

"I've heard it spoken a few times since I've been here in Kenya. Based on the phonetic way they sounded, I was able to memorize a phrase they used."

"Let's hear it."

"It sounded like this: *Hiti ciathii mbwe ciegangara.*"

"Those are Kikuyu words all right," Haran acknowledged with a bemused look. "Do you want to know what they mean?"

"Tell me, please."

"They were referring to themselves as jackals, who could eat once the hyenas had enough."

"So who are the hyenas?"

"That's something you'll have to figure out, my friend, though it shouldn't be too hard to do. Now, where did this abduction take place?"

"We had just returned from interviewing a Kikuyu elder in Molo," Alain continued. "We stopped for fuel at a petrol station on the outskirts of Nakuru when an older-model Peugeot sedan careened into the station. Four men poured out claiming to be policemen. One kept me at gunpoint while another grabbed my translator. They seemed to know who she was because they talked to her in English with profane familiarity, calling her a whore and so forth. Two of them then took her away in their Peugeot. The other two forced me to drive back to Nairobi, where they dumped me with a ransom demand for a million shillings."

Haran turned somber. "The Kikuyu can be bold, clever, and ruthless. I hate to have to say that, considering that I have more than a little Kikuyu blood flowing in my veins. I wish that I could only point to our crusading Kikuyu journalists, dedicated Kikuyu evangelists and priests, and ambitious but honest Kikuyu businessmen. Even so, when you see those bodies in the street after the police have mowed them down in a wild car chase, too often they are the bodies of Kikuyu. Then again, you have to remember that we make up the largest percentage of the population in this country."

Haran forced a smile. "That's enough of that. Tell me more about this woman."

"She is very beautiful."

"I see."

Not knowing what to make of Haran's apparent sincerity and fine manners, Alain felt his guard going up.

"You haven't told me who this woman is."

Alain weighed his thoughts. Why was he waiting to reveal who she was? Shouldn't he have done this much sooner? Was he worried about what Haran would say about his estranged sister? Would he be offended that he was trying to rescue her?

"It's Wangetha Wachira," Alain uttered the words slowly, wondering if Haran had already figured this out. "I'm told that she is your sister. Regalo thinks that the goons kidnapping her were hired by Robidi Amimuga, the high commissioner of Zimugabwa, to eliminate her after she jilted him. But instead of killing her, as they were instructed to do, they set up this ransom scene to get more money."

Haran turned his face away from Alain, drank the last of the gin in his teacup, and poured in more from the bottle which he had left on the desk. Alain waved his hand to show he had had enough.

"I should have known," he sighed loudly. "There is no escaping her. Wherever I go, whatever I do, she finds me. Even after I had taken another surname."

Now Alain understood why his name was not the same as Wangetha's. "She was not looking for you, Haran. I was the one looking for you."

"No matter. It's the same thing. Through you she is looking for me. Her being always finds a way to me."

119

"It's not my intention to pry into your personal life, Haran. Regalo suggested that you weren't on the best of terms with each other, but he also said that you knew the Kikuyu underground."

"I don't know whether to take that as a reproach or a compliment."

"I took it as an acknowledgment of your smarts. Can you help me?"

"Yes, I can tell you where to look. But you may get into trouble over your head, even killed, trying to find her. Is she really worth it to you? I can show you 10 more willing women, good ones, bad ones, easy ones, all attractive, all ready for the taking at your pleasure. Some can dance in ways that will leave you gasping. Others will make you feel that you are the cleverest, most splendid man on this earth. They will fulfill your every physical desire and magnify your manhood in ways that you couldn't have imagined. Are you sure you want to risk your own life over this one woman? What is she to you?" His large, dark eyes were probing Alain now.

"All I can say, Haran, is that this woman, your sister, has opened up an entirely new world for me, one that in some ways makes my old world seem dull in comparison. Oh, I know. It would be so easy to just call it one European man's fascination with the exotic. But it is so much more than that. She completes me in a way I never expected.

"Don't ask me to go into more detail about my feelings here, with you, Haran," Alain continued. "I hardly know you, and frankly I'm embarrassed to say this much because you are tied to her by blood. If this were only infatuation I wouldn't be here. As I said, call my feelings what you want, but I felt a bond growing between us. I know that she felt it, too, though she hadn't said so, yet. I hadn't said so either, but she knows my feelings for her as surely as I know her feelings for me. So let's leave it at that. You know that I need your assistance. Can you find out who the kidnappers are and where they are keeping her? Can you help me come up with a plan to ransom her safely? You must still care enough about her to want to see her freed."

Haran put his face into his hands. "Just look around here at my office, Alain. This is nothing to be proud of. The fact is that my sister is ashamed of me. You don't know my past."

"You don't have to tell me."

"I know. But you will find out sooner or later, if you don't know already. Our parents were prosperous, and they made certain that both of us received the best education available in Kenya. When they passed away a few years ago, Wangetha trusted me to manage the family's assets left to us in common receivership. Our parents didn't want to divide them among us because they feared that we would then go our separate ways. I was determined to keep her trust as well as earn her gratitude and looked for ways to multiply this inheritance as fast as possible. I don't mind saying it. I wanted to become rich.

"Soon, I had become involved in a number of construction projects, none of which succeeded. I lost all of our family's inheritance and came to the conclusion that I had no talent for business. With both of us ruined, Wangetha began taking up with the likes of Robidi."

"Your revealing your past doesn't make any difference to me, Haran," Alain responded softly. "I have no choice but to trust you."

"You may or may not regret that, Alain," Haran's face was serious. "In the meanwhile, have you thought all of this through? Do you want to play the ransom game with these criminals?"

"What else can I possibly do? The alternative is going to the police, and you know the risks that would entail."

"All right. I have a suggestion for you, but you're going to need more money than the one million shillings for the ransom. I will need at least 100,000 shillings to get some information about this gang that we can use to our advantage."

Alain hid his discomfort. So this was the basis of his uneasy inkling about him. "That's a tidy sum here."

"No, no, Alain!" Haran broke in as if sensing Alain's unease. "The money isn't for me. It's for informants. Money is all they understand. It's always welcome and never disappoints, buying the comforts of the day on the one hand, and the pleasures of the night on the other. With money we'll go far. Without it we'll be stuck in the starting block.

"Remember, getting information is only the first step, but it requires money, 100,000 shillings at the minimum. Find the money as soon as you can. The best would be cash or funds in your bank account ready to be drawn. Once you have the money, call me. Here is my private number at my apartment."

"Does your plan mean that we will also be paying the kidnappers off and trusting them to release Wangetha afterwards?" Alain asked, his annoyance showing. "I don't need your help for that."

"I didn't say anything about paying the ransom and then trusting the kidnappers to release her. We need information first before we do anything. We need the money to get information, and the more money we have the better our chance of getting good information. That should be obvious, Alain. With the money in hand, we'll have a measure of power that we wouldn't have otherwise. As word gets out that I have money and lots of it, I will attract informants as easily as bees to honey.

"It's so important that there is a nice amount of money in my hands. I can't pretend to have a lot of it and then dribble it out a little at a time to would-be informants stretching their hands out from the gutter. People here can sense if you have money or not, and they can sense how much you have, too. We can't be cute about this essential matter, Alain. And let's not discount the effect the money will have on us when we know that we have plenty of it backing us up. You see my point. The money will make us think and act more boldly."

"First of all, please don't say 'We,'" Alain said. "You will be the one that is identified with the money, not me. I'm going to be in the background, where I should be. Secondly, I don't know if I agree with you about the results of throwing this money around."

"You don't have to," Haran smiled. "But do you really have a better way? Don't think that what I have to do will be easy. I'll have to stick my nose into Nairobi's putrid sewers dangling shilling notes to find informants. But once we have the money, they will know it. They will savor its sweet fragrance in the air as surely as you and I are taking in the aroma of the gin in our teacups. I won't have to yell from the rooftops. The fact is I won't really need to tell anyone. The smell of money, the smell of shillings is that strong here. You will see."

"You needn't say any more. We'll try it your way. I don't know you very well yet, Haran. But I have no choice other than to rely on you and hope that you don't have designs on this money for yourself. I'm sorry that I have to be so blunt."

"That's fine, Alain. I understand. There's a lot at stake here. We need to work together to make matters right."

"I agree. I'll be calling you to set up a time to give you the money," Alain said as he reached for the piece of paper on which Haran had written his private number. "I should be calling you very soon."

"The sooner the better, Alain."

"I know, I know. You will get it, and you will get it soon." Alain rose from his chair ready to leave.

"Wait, Alain. Aren't you going to give me your number and address as well?"

Alain looked around at the room as if he wanted to remember exactly what it looked like for a long time. He caught the visage of Moi again, the man who called himself the father of the nation. What kind of nation? Was he any closer to knowing the answer than the first day he arrived?

And as for finding Wangetha, would trolling money in the underworld of Nairobi do any good?

"It's best that I call you, Haran. Please don't ask me to explain."

"As you wish, Alain. I'll wait for your call. Or you can just drop by. I'll be here all afternoon tomorrow."

"Right, Haran. Thanks for your help."

"It's nothing. Adieu, Alain."

"Adieu, Haran."

CHAPTER 11
A DAY IN THE LIFE OF REGALO

༝

When Regalo arrived at his town house in a well-guarded residential complex in the western quarter of Nairobi, he was coming home to a routine that marked the only happiness in his life. There, at the door, his demure housekeeper, Rachel, was waiting to let him in and lead him to his favorite place of rest on a large, overstuffed sofa next to his stereo. She had already begun playing a cassette for him with some light baroque chamber music from Bach.

The rippling, melodic lines of this music, often counterpointing but always in harmony, had gradually grown on Rachel. Her tribe, the Luo, the third-largest in Kenya, was known for its love of lyrical music-making, and she was no exception. A little old-fashioned, she was partial to the lively, traditional chants conveying a message accompanied by the *nyatiti*, a lyre-like instrument with eight strings that was plucked. She could easily imagine the classical guitars and violins that she heard in Regalo's collection as ornaments complementing the *nyatiti's* spirited riffs as they accompanied her favorite songs in Dholuo, her tribal tongue.

Rachel knew that setting the stereo at just the right levels for volume, bass, and treble was very important to Regalo. He never talked about it to her. But when she saw the way he once adjusted the knobs after she had accidentally touched them while cleaning, she realized that there were some settings he preferred to others. The volume could be neither too high nor too low. There couldn't be too much bass nor too much treble. She also noticed with time that most of the music to which he listened had a gentle touch.

It was several months after she had begun working for Regalo that she guessed something was wrong with his left ear. At first she thought his listening habits had to do with his moods and the music was to calm him. But seeing him night after night positioning himself with the speakers facing that one ear made her suspect there was another reason.

Eventually, she went to a wise, old, Asian doctor who knew of Regalo, to get his opinion regarding Regalo's hearing, given his peculiar habits. He listened to her patiently and with great concentration, weighing her words, as she described the way Regalo arranged his seating to always have the speakers send music to the left ear, always at a certain volume, and always with peaceful melodies.

He explained to her that to the best of his knowledge Regalo had a wartime condition that his father, also a doctor, had seen when they were still living in India. A soldier who had returned from the Second World War, when Indian troops fought alongside the British, had come to him complaining about ringing in one ear. He had been assigned to an artillery battalion, and after being exposed for some time to its exploding heavy guns he began hearing the sound of the roaring ocean in that ear. All his father could do for him was to prescribe a few drops of onion juice into his affected ear several times a week. Each time the juice was to be held in the ear for nearly half an hour with small cotton balls. The hope was that the healing effects of the onion droplets would soothe the inner ear. But while he knew this treatment had helped some sufferers with this condition, he never knew if the onion juice worked for that soldier since they never saw him again.

In the case of Regalo, he did not know what kind of noise he was hearing. But if he was directing music to the left ear, it must be doing him some good or he would not be doing it every evening. In his medical opinion, the music was calming his nerves while giving his mind some pleasant sounds to vie with the trouble in his ear. Perhaps, with time, he advised her, he would begin to hear it less and less because of this competition for his brain's attention. The neural pathways of the ringing sounds might even begin to wear out.

He said that he would be happy to see Regalo, but as a former military officer, he had probably already received the best treatment options available. He looked at Rachel kindly and told her not to worry too much about him since he seemed to be managing his ailment intelligently, which would gradually improve with time.

After she had laid out on a tray the roasted red snapper she had prepared for Regalo, with steamed green beans and rice on the side, she brought it to the small dining room and rang the serving bell. Regalo soon entered, sitting down so that his left ear faced the entrance to the living room from which the music on the stereo continued to play. He smiled at her. She was happy to see him in good spirits.

She had lit two candles to light the room and placed a bottle of dry Kenyan papaya wine, freshly opened, on the middle of the table. Regalo poured himself a glass and savored its musky, unique fragrance. Made from Kenya's own papaya fruit, few foreigners could tolerate its strong taste, almost overpowering the palate with an odor some likened to spoiled fruit. But Regalo found the scent and flavor of this wine more appealing than the skimpy bouquets of the South African whites that the expatriates in Nairobi bought in five-liter paper boxes. Rachel was secretly pleased that Regalo preferred it to the imported wines and put candles in the empty green bottles to use as lights during power outages.

After finishing the healthful supper, delicately-seasoned with cloves and nutmeg, and drinking two generous glasses of the papaya wine, Regalo returned to the living room and eased himself into the sofa once again. As Rachel brought him his customary evening vodka tonic, he considered the three newspapers that had been delivered by courier and were now neatly laid out before him on the coffee table. Two were from the U.S. and one from England.

Scanning the papers, he saw that there was an item by a columnist complaining that he didn't like readers making snap judgments about his real personality, which he wanted everyone to know was much more complex than what was revealed in his columns. His brows knit into an even tighter furrow as he thought for a moment. Wasn't this the same gentleman who never missed an opportunity to tag the purveyor of this or that idea as out of the mainstream, whatever that meant?

The more he considered the matter, the more disgruntled he became. Didn't and shouldn't ideas speak for themselves? Was it asking too much to discuss issues on their own merits without mindless name-calling?

But he knew that was asking too much, far too much. It would mean having to shove all of one's biases and petty hatreds out of the way and letting ideas have center stage. And that would mean giving up quite a bit. After all, who would want to miss out on all the fun of running down someone's name and reputation?

The real journalist didn't try to run your mind for you. But these pretenders wanted to be perched on your shoulder, their tails all curled up and their hands waving in your face to make sure you paid attention while their little jaws chattered on and on.

Sometimes they would even grab your ear with both of those tiny hands and shake it to make sure that you, the poor schoolboy that you were, understood that they were in charge of showing you what the world was really like, just in case you were looking at it the wrong way. After all, you might not have understood what the lies of this or that politician really meant.

He crumpled the offending page of the newspaper into a tight little ball and aimed it at the dustbin off to the corner. It dropped right in. That was nicely done, even if way too late. He had already played right into the hands of this masher of language and character. It was the reader on whom he depended to maintain his perch, from where he could look out over the world and pass judgment. But if there were no reader, what good would the perch be? He could jabber all he wanted, not just from one perch but all the perches in the world, and no one would be paying attention. Then where would he be?

Small comfort that kind of wishful thinking was now. The words of the column, with all their smugness and pretension to true knowledge, had already slithered through his eyeballs and wormed their way into his brain. So what could he do? There they were and that was that. He would just have to try to think about something else and forget about the bad taste that had crept into his mouth as well. Maybe gulping down the rest of the vodka tonic would help.

After swallowing the last drop, Regalo set aside the papers and went to the bedroom. There he would change and then shower in the bathroom in preparation for his evening massage.

Rachel was waiting for him in the second bedroom of the apartment, which had been converted into a salon of sorts. There in the middle of the room was a massage table imported from Sweden and an ultraviolet warming lamp from Germany. Soon, he would come in and lie down on the table with a towel wrapped around his waist and buttocks. She knew which points around his neck and back to knead because she had seen him once slouched in his chair in his office, which she deduced must have been his typical sitting position.

It was when she had run short on money for household expenses that she had dropped in on him unexpectedly. He was talking on the telephone, so she seated herself in one of the two chairs he reserved for his guests, and waited patiently for him to finish. As she looked around, she was nearly overwhelmed by all the modern electronic equipment he had there, including a television set, a bulky radio, a computer, and two telephones on his desk. In addition, one entire wall of his office was neatly lined with books from floor to ceiling. On another wall were photos of Regalo with people she didn't recognize, some black faces, but mostly white. One photo especially caught her eye. It was of Regalo in a military uniform, looking very commanding.

On the wall immediately behind his desk was a large, aluminum-framed color print of a racing car with the emblem of a galloping horse on its grille. It was bright red, sitting high on its wheels and heading down a long, black ribbon of asphalt. To her it seemed to exude so much strength and energy that it was ready to pounce out of its frame and begin roaring around the world.

In some ways, it reminded her of the Jeep Cherokee that Regalo drove, which he would spend hours working on with tools from a steel box he kept in the garage. Every time he started it, the engine would growl and make her think of a lion. He would polish the Jeep until its blue paint shone in the sun, and when the least nick would appear in the finish, he would pull out a small bottle of paint and touch it up with so much attention and care that she could never see it again, no matter how hard she looked.

She had become so impressed with his mechanical abilities, that one day while he was outside working on his Jeep, she decided to ask him for some help with a small matter bothering her. She was sitting in the kitchen with one of her cleaning gloves in her lap that had a tear she wanted to mend. But the nylon thread that she was holding in her right hand would not go through the eye of the needle that she was holding in her left.

When she tried to make the thread go through, it would become frayed, so she would reach over to the table for the scissors lying there, cut the thread to a fresh edge, and try threading it once again. But each time, the thread would fray again and not go through. Just as she was ready to give up, she wondered if Regalo could do something with it. She ran out to the driveway in front of the garage where he had his head stuck underneath the hood of the Jeep and pulled at his shirt.

After she had caught his attention and explained the problem to him, he took the spool of thread gently from her hand and reached into his tool box, taking out what she recognized as a magnifying glass. He held the magnifying glass in front of him, catching the rays of the noon-day sun, until she could see a bright single beam emerging from under the glass. Focusing the beam on the end of the thread, he held it until it smoldered slightly. After he saw that it had become solid, Regalo asked Rachel to give him the needle, through which he easily passed the thread.

She remembered how grateful she was. She also remembered how her feelings of admiration for this man were growing and beginning to touch her heart.

While Rachel sat and waited in Regalo's office, the phones rang non-stop. Before one call was even finished, the other phone rang, with Regalo putting the caller on hold to finish the first call before taking it. This pattern went on for so long she was afraid she might be interfering in some important business. As she got up and began waving goodbye to him, he abruptly told the caller he would call back, set the phone down, and told her not to go. "It's all right, Rachel," he said gently. "You weren't interrupting. This is how it usually is."

"Who are all those people on the phone?" she asked, feeling both curious and apprehensive. Because Regalo was so seriously involved in each one of his conversations, she wondered if a war or catastrophe was breaking out somewhere.

"These people are contacts from around Africa and Europe," Regalo answered, smiling for the first time since she came in. "I deal with everyone."

Rachel's reverie was interrupted as Regalo walked into the salon and laid down on the table. Soon, she was kneading and massaging his aching muscles and joints in the expert manner she had learned from the local oriental masseuses to whom Regalo had sent her for training.

After she had finished massaging Regalo and gone to the kitchen, he returned to the bedroom. There he slipped on a Japanese kimono and bamboo sandals and went back to the living room to sit and read, choosing from one of several books from the bookshelf. Rachel stuck her head in to say goodnight and began the long walk to the bus stop.

Regalo walked over to the liquor cabinet and opened it, staring at the bottle of vodka. He had already had his allotted one vodka tonic and two papaya wines. If he stuck to this regimen, he would be fine tomorrow. But the night was still young and so what if he wanted to kick back with another one of his vodka delights?

The only trouble was that it had not always been just one more. And then Rachel would arrive early in the morning to see him sprawled out on the sofa still in his kimono. She would take away the glasses, wash them out, and throw the empty vodka bottle in the trash as if nothing had happened, God bless her soul. But he didn't want her to see him like that again, so that was enough for happy hour tonight.

As he slowly closed the cabinet and sat back down on the sofa, his eye caught a slight irregularity in the way the painting of some elephants drinking at a water hole was hanging on the wall over the bookshelf. The bottom of the frame was off maybe 15 degrees from being perfectly parallel to the slope of the top shelf.

But why should he care? This town house, much less this room, held no special interest for him. He had lived in worse quarters. He had lived in better ones. Nor did he care how many paintings were on the wall or for that matter what kind they were. Still, this painting's alignment was wrong, and it rankled him.

But why? What was driving him now? Why couldn't he let it be? But he couldn't just let it be.

He got up, walked over to the painting, righted it to line up parallel to the top of the shelf and returned to the sofa.

He looked at it expectantly, but it remained slightly off. Muttering to himself, he got up to align the painting again. Back on the sofa, he studied the painting still once more, and this time he stayed where he was. It was lined up right.

After trying unsuccessfully to concentrate on his reading for the next quarter-hour or so, Regalo got up from the sofa and went to the bathroom to wash his face. The splashes of water felt cool on his forehead and cheeks. He looked in the mirror to examine the condition of his eyes. It was astonishing, he thought to himself, that in spite of how much he had drunk since joining the army some 20 years before, there were no traces of redness.

He proceeded to inspect his nose and again noted with some satisfaction the lack of any red veins. He knew that he had a strong constitution, which he owed to a lucky draw from the gene pool. The circles under his eyes now caught his attention. He was not so lucky here. Whether he drank or not, they were always there. When he was well rested, they were somewhat less noticeable, but even then they were there.

During his college days, a girlfriend had once told him that he had certain Mid-Eastern characteristics. She listed them as his prominent nose, the circles under his eyes, his black hair and darkly-tanned skin, and the leanness of his body. She asked who his parents were, and when he told her that his parents were Italian, she just smiled. Before they broke up, he finally admitted to her that he had been adopted and that he had no idea who his biological parents were. Her reaction was to give him her knowing smile again.

The truth was that he was afraid of finding out who his real parents were. He didn't want to feel under any obligation to a past that locked him out of any group through no fault or choice of his own. He believed that it was better not to know to whom he belonged if it also meant knowing to whom he didn't belong.

He had learned to make the best use of the ambiguity his physiognomy afforded him. After he graduated from college, he enlisted in the army and enrolled in the intelligence unit, where he took tests that showed he had an unusual aptitude for languages. With his quasi-Semitic features and the shortage of Arabic speakers, he was sent to the Defense Language Institute in Monterey, California, where he developed fluency in Arabic in a period of two years, drawing the praise of his instructors.

He was subsequently sent to Beirut, Lebanon, in the early 1980s and assigned the task of interviewing informants for what they knew about the various terrorist groups in the region. Someone had tipped a gang of Islamic militants, who grabbed him as he was leaving a local bistro one night and dragged him away to a hideout.

After they tied him to a chair, one of them would come in around the clock with a snub-nosed six-shooter, which he would hold behind his head and fire. Each time he expected that the ensuing blast would be the last thing he ever heard until the gunman's laughter filled the room because the cartridge had been a blank.

"Who are you?" they would shout at him in Arabic. "How did you learn to speak our language this well? Are you the CIA?"

When he would give them his name, rank, and serial number, but nothing else, they would become enraged and take turns knocking him around until his head spun. With his ears ringing and head pounding from the blasts of the gun, he finally broke down and sputtered out some words about how he had learned Arabic. He also spewed out names of some of the informants he had questioned, but didn't feel badly about it since he knew they were actually pseudonyms. In his role, he had never dealt with their real names for good reason.

The militants then brought in a rival militiaman captured from the Phalangist forces operating in East Beirut. They offered Regalo a deal. They would let him go if he delivered the coup de grâce to the prisoner, whom they accused of participating in the killings of Palestinian civilians. But if he didn't comply, he would be executed along with the Phalangist.

They gave him one day to consider. The next evening, they took him to the cell of the prisoner, who was tied up in a chair, still wearing his Phalangist militia uniform.

"Were you there at the Sabra and Shatila refugee camps when you Phalangists were killing innocent Palestinians?" they barked at the prisoner.

"So what if I was," the soldier retorted. "Yet I swear that I had nothing to do with the killing."

"How could you have been there and had nothing to do with the killing?"

"I was outside the camps. I didn't know what was going on inside."

"Did you hear any shooting?"

"Yes."

"What did you think it meant?"

"How should I know? There is shooting of one kind or another almost every day in Beirut."

"Did you hear any screams? Did you hear the screams of any of the hundreds of women, children, and men as they were being shot?"

"I didn't know people screamed as they were being shot."

One of the militants slapped him across the face. "You will pay for this insolence! You were seen entering the camp. Let's kill him now! Death is all that he deserves!"

Another one took out a roll of thick duct tape and fastened an M-16 assault rifle to a chair so that it pointed at the

Phalangist's head. After checking the weapon's line of sight, he nailed the chair tightly to the wooden floor with a hammer so it couldn't move in any direction. He then took a piece of wire and formed a loop at one end, into which he inserted the trigger. He taped it together with the wire and cycled the rifle's action.

They forced Regalo into another chair behind the M-16, putting the other end of the wire into his hand. "You have your choice now. You can pull this and send a murderer of women and children to hell, or be executed yourself."

"Why are you putting me in this position?" Regalo protested, taking care not to move the wire in his hand in any way while noting that the firing mode of the M-16 was selected to single shot with one trigger squeeze.

"We want to have the satisfaction of seeing you, an American, render justice on behalf of your country to us for once. It will be that much more satisfying seeing you use an American weapon."

"How did you get it?"

"We have our ways. The important thing is that you will be serving justice with it."

"I won't be rendering justice on behalf of America or anyone," Regalo responded sarcastically. "What kind of trial is this?"

"The best that we can cobble together," the militant man snapped. "Your conscience should not trouble you in the slightest for driving a bullet to this killer's brain. Do you think that we also have no consciences? To whom can we turn him over for trial? To the Lebanese authorities?" they laughed.

"The lives of our Palestinian people under occupation mean next to nothing to you Americans," the militant man continued angrily. "We can have our land taken from us right before your eyes, but there won't be even a shrug of concern from your leaders. Our communities can be torn apart by concrete walls and highways we can never use, but there won't be a word about our human rights. Our water can be sucked away, our orchards razed, our homes demolished, and our children cut down over and over again for throwing rocks, but there won't be any mournful expressions of sympathy. Then, when we react in subhuman ways, you are shocked. But aren't we just living out your expectations? When you are treated as subhuman, don't you wind up acting as a subhuman?

"Please educate me and my friends. Tell us about our rights. We are such poor learners. We only see what we see and hear what we hear. Oh, I know. We keep complaining about the vomit of our wretched lives. Why can't we just be quiet instead of always going back and sniffing it and then howling at the moon? Do we have to behave like dogs? And if we do, if that's what we are, why can't we swallow whatever scraps are thrown to us and wag our tails in gratitude? Isn't that it?"

"There's never an excuse for acting as a subhuman, much less as a dog, regardless of how you may be treated or what your circumstances are," Regalo answered slowly. "You can say what you will, but I am not going to pull the wire and shoot him."

"Why not? What is he to you?"

"I am not going to pull the wire."

"This is no game! That means we have to kill you as well as him."

As Regalo felt the barrel of a gun pushing into the back of his head, he looked at the Phalangist tied to his chair across from him. For a moment, he saw what seemed to be a knowing look taking shape in the man's eyes. What that look meant, he didn't know exactly, but he couldn't mistake the air of superiority it conveyed. Did he feel that he had achieved some kind of psychological victory in this godforsaken place by virtue of Regalo's refusal to act as his executioner?

Infuriated by this small gesture of defiance by someone who was at his mercy, Regalo clenched his teeth while his hands began to twitch nervously as he held the wire.

"You must pull the wire now! This is your last chance."

Regalo didn't move.

"You have had your chance. Now let's shoot the American!"

At the same moment that Regalo heard the explosion, he felt the hot blast searing the back of his head. Not knowing if he was alive or dead, his hand inadvertently squeezed the wire as his body's reflexes jarred his chair. He watched, sickened, as the Phalangist crumpled forward into his chair, blood splattered across his chest. But he himself was not crumpling. It was a blank again, and he was alive.

"What did you do?" a voice yelled. "You forgot to put real bullets in the pistol this time!"

"It doesn't matter," another militant shouted back. "We've achieved our purpose. He killed him, and that's what we wanted."

Two days later, Regalo was released and found his way back to the base. But he never told anyone about his shooting the Phalangist man. He felt that no human being could ever understand what he had endured.

In fact, it was not only the peculiar circumstances of his ordeal that made Regalo keep his silence. It was wondering whether the blank in the pistol was put there accidentally or deliberately. Had they really intended to kill him? Had this scenario been staged from the beginning? Had it all been planned to make sure that he would remain alive and be forever implicated in the killing for whatever reasons they had?

He was certain that the Phalangist man had been shot, because he saw the blood. But there was another question that he turned over and over in his mind. Was it actually the M-16 connected to the wire he was holding that executed him? Did it add up that they would rely on the shock of a blank to make him jerk the wire? That was no sure thing, not with him, not with anybody. Bodies, arms, hands can respond in different ways to that kind of shock.

He could only remember feeling that he had squeezed the wire, not tugged it, when the blank went off behind his head.

It was possible, of course, that when squeezing the wire he had also jerked it slightly and not noticed. But would that have been enough to make the rifle go off?

Was it too farfetched to imagine another scenario, one in which there were two sets of blanks? One set in the pistol fired at his head and another set in the M-16 aimed at the Phalangist? In that case, there would have been another third weapon fired behind him to ensure the execution, going off simultaneously with the blank exploding next to his head.

They could have figured that with the sound of the explosion and its reverberations, he would not have noticed that a different gun was actually doing the firing. This meant that even if he had tugged the wire connected to the trigger of the M-16, it was not the weapon that killed the man.

He was relieved to know there was this chance that he did not actually shoot the Phalangist man. But he would never know for certain, even when he took out the vodka bottle to help him figure it all out.

Two years later, he left the army and contracted his services to a multinational firm with offices on the African continent. He enjoyed the travel, but didn't last long due to repeated clashes with management. In 1990, he set up his own security consulting office in Nairobi. Here, because he was on his own, he had lasted. So far, at any rate.

He headed toward the bedroom. It was time to go to sleep.

෨

It was mid-morning when Alain, following up on Regalo's suggestion, set out for his meeting with Wayne Jefferson. He had called Jefferson's secretary the day before to tell her that he was planning a feature article on successful business executives in Kenya for a high-profile French magazine. His pitch was that he needed to see her boss for just a few minutes to do a brief interview and make arrangements for a photo shoot. He emphasized the photo shoot.

The strategy had worked, and the secretary found a slot for Alain this very morning.

Wearing sunglasses and a hat but not his black face, Alain showed up at Jefferson's spacious offices in Barclay's Plaza, Kenya's most prestigious high-rise building, at 10:30 a.m. After he checked in with the secretary, she motioned him to sit down on a large, modern sofa under a framed color photograph of the Grand Canyon.

"Mr. Jefferson has another appointment that is running longer than I expected, but it shouldn't take too much more time," she said politely.

As Alain sat down he could hear voices coming from Jefferson's office, whose door was halfway open.

"No, please don't say that we don't want to help you. Our company's foundation has helped many development organizations in Kenya."

"Then why aren't you willing to help me?"

"As I explained to you, sir, your project still sounds vague to me. You say that you want to raise the consciousness of the population?"

"Exactly. We are in a new world, and Kenya has to adjust to it. That means people's attitudes have to change."

"Yes, but could you please be a little more specific?"

"As I tried to explain to you earlier, Mr. Jefferson, by holding seminars and conferences we can challenge people to think in new ways to advance the country socially and economically."

"That is still not specific enough for me to understand."

"People in Kenya are still living in the past. They need to think in the present."

"You can't be any more specific?"

"The world is changing, and we have to adapt to it. The seminars will show people how to do that."

"But what exactly will you show them?"

"As I said, to think in new ways."

"You can't be any more specific?"

"I just told you, the world is changing and we need to adapt. That's the message."

Jefferson paused as if to mull over what he would say. "And I assume you will be the principal speaker at these seminars?"

"In most cases. I will also invite other speakers from time to time, but I will always be the host."

"And what is it that you said you needed again?"

"I will need a four-wheel drive vehicle to travel around the country, an office, a computer, telephone, and two or three staff persons."

"And so you're asking for a donation from us to get you started and to finance your activities for the first year?"

"Yes. Your company is doing well and this is an important project. It will change Kenya."

"What town are you from?"

"I am from upcountry, from the area around Embu."

"Do all the children from your community go to school?"

"No."

"Many families cannot afford the school fees, right?"

"Yes, that is a major problem."

"Have you thought about ways to solve this problem?"

"What do you mean?"

"I mean ways to help more children go to school."

"I have no money, sir. That is why I'm here."

"I know, but have you thought of some ways that maybe you and others who care about education in your community could raise some money to help them?"

"We are all poor."

"I know, but have you thought of a way that all of you together could raise enough money to give one child enough money to go to school for one year?"

"Oh, you mean a *harambee*?"

"No, I don't mean just a one-time event when people gather to give money for a cause. Those are good, but that's not what I mean. You need to make your own money."

"But I just told you that we don't have any money. Besides, we have too many children that need school fees. That is why we need new ways of thinking."

"Let's just talk about helping one child first. What if you started your own tomato farm? Tomatoes here sell for an average price of 30 shillings or so a kilo. Just think of the money you could make if you raised 2,000 kilos of tomatoes a year. There would be plenty of money to pay the tuition of one child, wouldn't you agree?"

"Of course, more than enough for one child, enough for a number of children. But we have no water for irrigation and very little land to begin with. We can't raise tomatoes."

"What if I gave you a small loan of $1,000 or 50,000 shillings in your money, so that you could rent the equipment to bore your own well?"

"That would be good, but we have very little land. I have a plot which is only about 12 meters by 12 meters."

"What if you made several long trays out of wire and lined them with plastic sheeting? You could tie them to bamboo poles and stack them on top of each other. Then you could fill them with compost and plant tomato seeds in them."

"We would need a pump from the well and at least a several thousand liter water tower from which we could sprinkle water on the tomato plants with a hose."

"You're getting the idea. The pump, the water tower, the hose, the bamboo posts, the wire, the plastic sheeting, and the seeds could all be bought with the loan we would give you. We would also show you how to make the compost from chicken manure, cow dung, and other agricultural residues. You do have cows and chickens in your community?"

"Yes."

"Now, just from this small plot you could grow 2,000 kilos of tomatoes from harvests throughout the year thanks to our warm climate. All that is required of you is to first set up this system, which shouldn't be very hard. After that you would just let the sun shine on the growing tomatoes, water them, pick the crop, and take it to market. And as you know, there is always a good demand for fresh tomatoes here in Kenya."

"But what about my seminars and my travel around the country?"

"That is up to you and your schedule, of course. I wouldn't want to say anything about that."

"But what about the four-wheel drive vehicle and the computer equipment?"

"We can talk about that later once you begin your tomato farm and master the cultivation system. Then maybe you could go around the country showing other communities how it works, not just with tomatoes but other vegetables as well."

"And how would I need to pay this loan back?"

"Only as a small percentage from your sales of each tomato harvest."

"I understand. Well, I will think about what you've suggested."

"I hope that you will come back soon with your plan on how you want to begin. At that time we will grant you your loan. We will also guide you every step of the way in setting up your first tomato farm."

"I will be back. You can count on it."

"Good. I'm looking forward to it."

As the man left, Jefferson himself, tall with a ruddy complexion and silver hair, came out and beamed at Alain, waving him into his office.

"Come in, come in, Mr. Sardou. Good to see you. Have a chair."

Alain seated himself in front of Jefferson's desk while Jefferson sat down in his high back executive chair.

"Just call me Alain."

"And just call me Wayne."

"I've been looking forward to talking to you as you have the reputation of being one of the most successful businessmen in East Africa. Thank you for making the time to see me on such short notice."

"Think nothing of it, Alain," Jefferson responded. "But maybe we could speak to each other in French. *J'aimarais parler Francais avec vous parce que j'ai peu de occasions de converser en cette langue magnifique.*"

Alain was surprised by the smooth French that Jefferson spoke. Still, he knew that if he accepted his opening gambit to conduct their meeting in French, he would be letting him set the terms of their interview. This smacked of one-upmanship. Even so, Jefferson seemed to be playing this first move with genuine goodwill. Maybe he should give him the benefit of the doubt. Maybe Jefferson was just trying to show respect for his native language. It was true after all, that in France there was no surer way to ingratiate yourself with the people than to speak their language, no matter how badly. But whatever Jefferson's motives were, Alain felt that he could not yield.

"Thanks, Wayne. I must compliment you on your French, but I would prefer to continue in English. I will take notes, and my editors will put the quotations they want to use into French. They will then be made available for your review, as your French is clearly very good. I hope that's all right with you."

"But wouldn't it be much easier to go ahead and do the interview in French now and save all that time?"

"Easier perhaps, but please remember that while your French is good, your mother tongue is English, I take it, and we need complete accuracy in the interview."

"Does that mean that your editors can translate from English to French better than I can in my own head?"

"I didn't say that, and of course I mean no such thing," Alain responded. "Yet surely you would agree that you can express your thinking most exactly in your mother tongue?"

Alain paused, but Jefferson did not say anything.

"If you were to express your thoughts originally in French, there is a chance we might miss something."

Alain paused again.

"How did you learn English so well?" Jefferson asked, changing the subject. "From birth on?"

"Almost. My father was from England, and I went to an international school from early childhood, where the entire curriculum was taught in both French and English."

"Impressive."

"Can we go ahead and do the interview in English then?" Alain asked. "My job is to make it go as smoothly as possible, that's all."

Jefferson was now smiling broadly. "*Touché,* Alain. You win. I don't necessarily agree, but that's OK. Your points are well made, and we'll do the interview in English. Now what is it that we're going to talk about?"

Alain breathed an inward sigh of relief. He hadn't yielded, and at the same time he was confident that he had established himself in Jefferson's eyes as an interlocutor worthy of his time and attention.

"I would like your views on the pluses and minuses of investing in a developing country like Kenya," Alain said as he took out his notebook and began writing.

"Well, you've been here for a while now and have seen what this country is like. With its per capita income of less than a dollar a day, this is one of the poorest countries in the world."

"Hasn't all the development aid from the donors done any good? From what I've learned, Africa has received over 400 billion dollars in foreign aid since 1960, with Kenya receiving its own fair share."

"Of course it's done some good."

"How much good, if the continent is still racked by widespread poverty? Hasn't the aid, for the large part, only enriched the post-colonial ruling class of big men and would-be big men just as the critics maintain? As an unwelcome side-effect, hasn't it bred dependency as well?"

"Those are all questions that a good journalist should ask. Why don't you find the answers? One thing is for sure. The aid has not resulted in enough development. This country, for instance, has very little purchasing power."

"So why bother to try to do business in a place like this?"

"You've seen Africa's natural resources, abounding with vast mineral and petroleum deposits, breathtaking scenery, and spectacular wild life. Now even though the quality of the soil can be uneven, there is a temperate climate in much of the region, such as here in Kenya. It allows for the successful cultivation of fine black tea and full-bodied, acidic arabica coffee, the main plantation cash crops of the area. The climate is also suitable for year-round production of produce and fruit in the highlands.

"But most importantly, there is the energetic population, a vast, inexpensive labor pool waiting to be tapped – Africa's potentially greatest resource."

"I've heard a UN official suggest that this country is on the verge of becoming a newly-industrialized nation," Alain said.

"That's what we would like to think. If the textile sector can regroup, for example, and duties were reduced abroad for Kenyan exports, light manufacturing could regain a foothold here. It's all a matter of getting a market economy and good governance well in place for the economic take-off that we all want for this country."

"Hasn't the donor community been saying that for years now? Why isn't it happening? In Asia, economic take-offs have already taken place in countries that were also formerly ruled by colonialists."

"Those countries don't have dozens of tribes speaking different languages. But all that is irrelevant now. We believe Kenya is set to take off."

"And if it doesn't?"

"We believe it will."

"Has corruption been a drawback?"

"Of course it has. It's been a major drag. It doesn't do anything to attract investment, and it enriches a few at the expense of the many."

"What are you doing about it?"

"For our part, we refuse to pay bribes or kickbacks to get business."

"Your company has been accused of doing just that in places like the Congo."

"That may have been in the past when we were competing with the Soviet Union for influence on this continent. We've since learned our lesson."

"But aren't some other companies still making payoffs?"

"That may be."

"What about the failure to maintain the infrastructure? Just look at the sagging telephone and power lines, the crumbling roads, and the mounds of garbage piled up throughout the city."

"There's a chronic shortage of public funds to attend to these things."

"That's the only reason?"

"No."

"Many say corruption is another reason," Alain pressed.

"True."

"Others say there are also cultural factors going back in time."

"I've heard of those theories and others, but they're irrelevant as far as I'm concerned."

"Why?"

"We have to deal with the present, not the past."

"But just to look at the past for a moment, nonetheless," Alain continued. "When the British colonialists first arrived, they brought advanced farming methods and created physical and institutional infrastructure. They built modern roads, schools, and hospitals and started an industrial base."

"Again, all true. But remember, they were exploiting cheap native labor and bringing with them a preexisting agro/industrial culture, which had been developed in Europe over the course of centuries. It was brought over lock, stock, and barrel. But it was all new to the locals. The adaptation to it has been slow, no doubt. Many continue to cling to old ways and attitudes that don't work in the world we find ourselves in now. In that sense, the visitor I just had was right. But how to effectively change those ways, on both a small scale and large scale, is the question."

Alain set aside his notebook to look up at Jefferson. "May I ask you something that is a little off the subject?"

He was finally getting to the real point of his visit.

"Sure. What is it?"

"It's with regard to another story I may write, about a woman named Wangetha Wachira."

Jefferson gave a long whistle. "You certainly have good taste in women, Alain, if you know Wangetha. She is one fine lady. All you have to do is see her walking down the street. That's enough. It doesn't matter what she's wearing. Of course, the less the better, if you know what I mean," Jefferson winked.

"Are you seeing her?" Jefferson asked, grinning mischievously.

"No, I'm not," Alain replied casually, "I mean not now, though she did accompany me as a translator on a field trip recently. I understand that she used to work for your company, is that right?"

Jefferson smiled. "You must be referring to that time I was seen around town occasionally with Wangetha when she was doing some public relations work for our company. Man, that was great publicity she brought us, and I guess we did cut a pretty couple in those photo ops that appeared in the press. But did I catch hell from my wife!

"You know how women can be, Alain. Once they become wives they expect you to toe the line. There can't be any more fooling around."

"Oh, yes. I know what you mean," Alain laughed, feeling more comfortable now in talking to Jefferson. "Whatever they say about us French, most of the wives in our country are not that different from wives anywhere else.

"On a more serious note, there is something that I must tell you since you knew Wangetha and thought well of her.

Something disastrous has happened. Did you know that she was kidnapped?"

Jefferson's brows knit tightly. His voice was soft. "No, no. Of course, I didn't know. This is terrible. How was she kidnapped?"

"It happened out of the clear blue sky when we were on our field trip in the Rift Valley. We were at a petrol station when four toughs poured out of an old Peugeot and seized her at gunpoint."

"It was her they wanted, I take it?"

"Yes, not me. They took off with her to Nairobi and are hiding her away somewhere there."

"What about you, what did they do with you?"

"Dumped me back at my home after demanding a ransom for Wangetha."

"Are the police involved?"

"Not yet."

"You are telling me about a kidnapping but not telling the police. Isn't that a little odd?"

Alain had little doubt that Jefferson understood why he hadn't gone to the police, but answered pro forma anyway. "I can see how it would look that way, but there are reasons..."

"I know," Jefferson interrupted. "Do you have any idea who's behind the kidnapping or what motivated it?"

Alain weighed going into greater detail, but decided against it. He didn't know conclusively that it was Robidi yet and wouldn't want to get Jefferson involved any deeper than he had to. Things were already complicated enough.

"I can't tell you any more than I have. Again, there are reasons..."

"I know," Jefferson responded again, only more curtly. "Well, I won't probe any further. I trust that you know what you are doing."

"I hope so."

"What you've told me is safe with me." Jefferson looked at his watch. "How time flies. I have another appointment waiting for me. Would you please excuse me?"

Alain was caught by surprise at the abruptness with which Jefferson cut off the discussion. Did Jefferson sense that the conservation was about to turn to money? Probably. Given who he was, no doubt he had the sharpest antenna in town when it came to being hit up for money.

"Of course," Alain said. "I've taken up too much of your time already. May I just ask you one more thing before I go?"

"Sure. What is it? Just make it quick."

"I hesitate to ask this, but would you be willing to contribute 700,000 shillings toward the one million-shilling ransom demanded by the kidnappers to free her? That would only be 14,000 dollars in your money. I have 300,000 shillings of my own money to put up, which would be another 6,000 dollars. Your contribution and mine would add up to 20,000 dollars, which is then equivalent to one million-shillings. You're widely known to be generous. Can you be generous now? Her life depends on our help."

Alain did not say anything about the additional 100,000 shillings he would be passing on to Haran.

Jefferson clasped his hands together and looked up at the ceiling. "This is very sudden, and that is a lot of money. I hardly know you. How do I know your story is true?"

Alain pulled out his French passport and reporter's identification card and showed them to Jefferson. "These confirm who I am. I'm well known in Paris. All you would have to do is call my news service's offices there to confirm my professional bona fides, though I hope you would say nothing about this situation. I'm not planning on filing a story on it until we're looking at it in the rear-view mirror, and even then I may not file one for personal reasons."

"I'm sure that you are who you say you are," Jefferson conceded, "but how do I know that the money won't be used for something else?"

"You have my word."

"Your word? That's all? You have no collateral to put up? This is a lot of money."

"Just my word, unless you want an old Subaru sedan."

"Let me go back to what I said. I've only just met you."

"And let me go back to what I said. You can check me out. Call my editors in Paris."

Jefferson turned to look out the window in his office.

"You know, it's not always easy to do business in this region. We're questioned about our intentions, and many think that even our donations to the needy have a self-serving interest. But that's not the case. The poverty I see troubles me a great deal. Of course, if this country could ever get on its feet economically speaking, it would mean more sales for my company. But that's not all there is to it. It bothers me to leave this office and get into my nice car and go home to my nice house and be served by all the nice help, knowing day in and day out that not far me so many others barely have enough to eat and are prey to one disease after another.

"But do you know how often a good amount of the money we donate winds up in the wrong hands never to be seen again? Do you know how disappointing that is? And when you see that happen over and over again your enthusiasm to continue donating wanes, and not just a little bit."

Jefferson turned back from the window. "Now you tell me that Wangetha is in serious trouble and you need money. But do you have any idea how many requests for money our foundation gets? They're in our mailbox, they slip under the door, or they drop right into our lap when we least expect it. Of course we try to pick out the most deserving ones, but we can't respond to them all. No one can."

"I understand," Alain responded. "And I also understand that I have no claim on your generosity. All I know is that Wangetha represents the future of this country as no other person I've met here. She's special. Isn't that enough for you to take another chance on helping someone?"

"As I said, this is very sudden, very sudden indeed, and I may be a fool for doing this. But you've managed to persuade me her life is at stake. So I'll help you. But if this is a game, believe me, I'll take you up on your offer to contact your people back in France. And I mean that."

"I understand," Alain responded calmly. "You would have every right to do that and more."

Jefferson slowly opened the top drawer of his desk and pulled out his checkbook. He began writing.

"Did you say 700,000 shillings?"

"Yes, 700,000 shillings exactly. I'm putting up the rest of the ransom, as I said."

After Jefferson wrote out the check, he handed it to Alain carefully.

"I made this out to you. The bank can call me when you try to cash it. It won't be easy to redeem a check like this here, but I will try to make it as easy for you as possible. I don't keep that kind of money around here."

"I can't thank you enough," Alain mumbled as Jefferson handed him the check.

"Oh, and one more thing. This doesn't have anything to do with your article. Write exactly what you want. Or to avoid even the appearance of conflict, it might be better that you don't write anything about me at all."

"As you wish. Again, thank you. Thank you very much."

"Let me know how all this works out." Jefferson smiled. "And don't get in over your head."

"I'll let you know. Goodbye, Wayne."

"Goodbye."

After they shook hands, Jefferson led him out through the door of his office. As Alain passed through the reception room, he didn't see anyone waiting.

Walking out onto the street, he wondered what to make of Jefferson. Was his generosity really from the heart? It seemed so. He would hate to think that he was playing some angle here that he hadn't thought of. His donor fatigue took him back a little. That was a side to Jefferson he didn't expect to see and actually found endearing. It meant that Jefferson took charity seriously and agonized over where it would do the most good. But it also meant that he could still have second thoughts about the check he had written. If he wanted to, he could order his bank to stop payment on it before Alain could get there. Anything was possible on this continent when it came to money. Nevertheless, he didn't want to doubt Jefferson in the least. The check would be good. He was sure of it. His intuition told him so, and his intuition was seldom wrong. And if it was wrong, he would know soon enough.

CHAPTER 13
IN THE SERVANT'S ROOM

∿

Wangetha clutched her shoulders with both hands to cover herself as she cringed, shivering in the corner of the one-room servant's cottage behind the main house. Staring blankly into space, all she could do was wonder if they were coming back. Would they finally leave her alone for the night, this longest night of her life? Was there no pity in them, no pity at all?

She allowed her left hand to move from her shoulder to her face and then slowly downward, to feel the swelling and bruises that had left her body throbbing with pain. What a mess they had made of her, she thought, as she clutched her shoulders together again to try to warm her naked body. She knew she should crawl over to the simple, frame bed that was in the room, get in, pull the sheets and blanket over her, and rest. But during her struggles earlier, the bedding had become so much filthy rags to her. She didn't want to even touch the spoiled sheets, much less lie between them. Better to go to sleep huddled into a ball in the corner on the bare concrete floor. They could have the bed, but they would never have her, even if they thought they did.

She felt that the darkness of the room was suffocating her, even though she knew that there was nothing in it that she could taste, touch, or smell. Darkness was not the same as the humidity in the air after a heavy rain, making it harder to breathe. It was not the dust thrown up from the road by a strong wind that worked its way down into your windpipe and lungs. It was only the absence of light. In that case, how could the absence of something have such an oppressive effect? It didn't make sense to her, but it made sense to others, whom she knew, others who believed that darkness represented a world unto itself in which evil often made its home. But that meant it was not the darkness itself that was oppressing her, and on realizing that, she felt better for a moment. It was the evil in this darkness, the evil that was being concealed from the light, that made the darkness weigh so heavily upon her.

She recalled the horror of being dragged into this cell and her captors' inability to get the light switch to work. At first, they cursed when they saw that they would be in the dark, but then they began laughing hilariously as they brutally began taking turns with her. She shuddered. No, it was not from the darkness she had anything to fear, only from the evil that made its home there.

What was she thinking anyway, when Robidi had first approached her at that garden reception in Karen on the outskirts of Nairobi? He had walked up to her so confidently, asking her who she was and hadn't they met somewhere before? It was such a worthless, stupid line, but he had delivered it in just the right way, with boldness, capturing her interest, in spite of his age and high-pitched voice. When he had then revealed to her that he was the high commissioner of Zimugabwa, she felt flattered because she, like everyone else, knew of his much-heralded revolutionary past.

She warmed to him as he paid her one compliment after another, extolling her beauty and charm, and before long they were sitting at the edge of the lawn in two wicker chairs, side by side, as she hung onto his every word. She also hadn't failed to notice that each time the smartly-dressed waiter brought them a fresh round of drinks, he pulled a roll of bills out of his pocket with which to tip him that seemed to grow fatter each time he did it. She wondered if this were some kind of magical trick. Did he have a secret stash somewhere deep in his pocket? Was he flaunting his wealth purposely for her benefit?

However he was doing this trick, if it was a trick, it had its effect on her and soon she felt herself desiring this powerful man, who only had to nod his head this way or that to make other strong men come running to do his bidding. One time he had nodded and his chauffeur came running with a fresh pack of cigarettes. Another time he nodded and one of his bodyguards came with his appointment book and a pen. It was amazing how they knew what he wanted just through his nods. It was just as amazing that they were so focused on him that they never missed one of them.

Later on, when he walked over to the patio, where a podium had been set up for him to make some remarks to the group assembled there, she almost had to laugh as she heard the long-winded introduction from the host. It was almost comical the way he managed to refer to Robidi as either his excellent high commissioner or prince of his country, every 15 seconds or so, each time looking obsequiously in his direction.

But she was not laughing when she felt Robidi's kiss on her forehead as he returned to sit down next to her. His presence exuded power and wealth. And when he then opened his appointment book, taking his long, bony finger and running it down the page he had just turned to, she paid attention.

"I have time for you this next Thursday," he had said in perfectly-schooled British English.

"Time for what?" she had asked with feigned naiveté. The last thing she wanted him to assume was that she was easy, even though behind her polite manners she had already given in much earlier in the evening. He knew it and she knew it.

"For dinner," he had said.

He had looked at her with amusement then, a look that made her feel almost worthless, but she had responded, "Dinner would be nice," knowing full well what he expected and what she would have to give him.

What would her mother have said about this? Wasn't it her mother who had always warned her about the kind of false men that would come into her life, the men who would use her for her body and then discard her as casually as a banana peel? Wangetha had laughed, then, at the colorful image her mother had used to make her point, in the same way she was inwardly laughing at the slavish pomp and circumstance being constantly doled out to Robidi. But she realized now that while she had gotten it right in being amused by the inane idolatry offered Robidi, she had been wrong to discount the clumsy but sincere warnings offered by her mother. Her words had come from the goodness of her heart, and such words could never be anything but fine and pure.

Why hadn't she listened to her mother and learned from her example? She had been happily married to her father, a modest man, who never boasted of his many good works in public service. If only she could feel her mother's love now in this godforsaken place. If only she could see her mother smile at her once again, just as she used to when she was still very little and would run into the kitchen to tug at the hem of her mother's long, flowing dress and then feel her arms reach down for her, lifting her up to her warm bosom and giving her the best and biggest hugs in the entire world. It never mattered how many cousins or uncles or aunts were in the house – and usually there were many – or how busy she was. Her mother could always sense that little tug at the hem of her dress and knew exactly what it meant.

She would feel the warmth and strength of those hugs for the rest of the day and night, regardless of where she went or what she did. They made her feel safe when she was in the garden after dusk and looked up into the sky, feeling so small, wondering how many stars there were. Or when she was alone in her bed at night and heard the sounds of wild dogs barking.

There were also the times when she noticed her mother smiling at her, for no apparent reason, with the kind of smile that she never received from anyone else. It was neither the smile of laughter, nor the smile of happiness. It was a different kind of smile altogether, and it was only as she was older, after her mother had died and she had never seen that smile again, that she understood what it meant. Behind that special smile was her mother's delight in her just for being her daughter with no strings attached. It was not even the quiet smile of pride that comes when a parent basks in her child's accomplishments, beauty, handsomeness, strength, or skill. It was instead the smile of a selfless, unconditional love that knew no limits or bounds, and to see it was the best feeling that she ever experienced in her life because she knew then that she was loved for herself and for herself alone.

How then could she have disappointed her mother by taking up with the likes of Robidi? What value did the fancy hotel suites, the fine clothes, the jewelry, and the expensive car she received from him have, if her mother would not have approved of him? What good were the feelings of importance she experienced at his side if she were living in the shadowlands of her mother's shame over her choice in men?

And even more shame would be coming if she became pregnant from one of these rapists who had their way with her during these last two days. What would she do with the child? Would she find a way to do away with it before it saw the light of day, or would she keep it? What would her mother say? It would not be that difficult to choose the first course, even if not popular with the women in this part of the world. She had received enough money from Robidi to do whatever she wanted. But if she kept the child, could she love it, knowing a criminal rapist was the father?

Yes, she had already decided, since the child was innocent of the rape, as innocent as she was. They would be two kindred spirits.

Longing for some fresh air, she slowly got herself up from the floor, feeling along the wall with her hands until she made

161

out the contours of a window. From there she could at last see some light. It was not much, only a sliver of the moon in the distance, but enough to allow her to notice something odd about the window. There were no bars on the outside of it. That was strange. All the colonial-era houses she had seen had bars on the windows. Why didn't this one?

She didn't find any kind of lock on this window either which would open to the outside. There was a lock on the gate to the cottage all right, and it was fastened, but the window was another matter. All she had to do was lift the two handles in the middle and the two glass partitions would let in all the fresh air she wanted.

Would they let her out as well, she wondered? She lifted the two handles and pushed the glass gently. She shivered as the two partitions separated a little and cool air began coming into the room. She pushed a little more and the crack widened. All she had to do now was push all the way and there would be a space large enough for her to crawl through and escape this vile place.

But could her captors really have been so careless as to leave her in a room with a window that opened to the outside with no bars? Or were they completely disdainful of her as a lowly, weak woman, not even bothering to worry about her getting away? Or, perhaps, they were so twisted and full of themselves that they couldn't believe that she would really want to escape from under their control. She had a surprise for them. Maybe they knew her body by now, but they didn't know the spirit that was inside her.

Whatever the reason, she had her chance now and she would take it. It would even be better to be shot dead as she tried to escape than to submit to them any more. She had also noticed that there were no dogs on the property, not even one. The thugs were probably afraid of dogs. That increased her chances. At least she wouldn't be mauled to death if they caught her. Maybe shot, but not mauled by dogs.

As she stood in front of the window, she thought of her brother Haran who was so strong in both mind and body. He would not be afraid to take the chance she had now, that was for sure. She was angry with him for squandering their family inheritance, but she never questioned his fortitude or courage. Nothing would stop him from beating these gangsters to death with his bare hands once he learned what they had done to her. In the meanwhile, all she had to do was get away somehow. That is what he would want her to do. Escape and run to him for protection.

But what about Alain? She knew he was as taken with her as much as she was with him. Still, did his feelings have any depth? For that matter, did her own feelings for him have any depth to them? What attracted her to him, she wondered? Was it the man himself, or the fantasy of life in Paris? She had always wanted to go there since visiting England for a few days with her father years before. She had loved London, with its watchful towers, sturdy bridges, and solid cobblestone streets. Yet Paris, she had been told, with its lush scenery, artistic treasures, and exquisite food, was to London what champagne was to wine, and ever since she had wanted not only to sample a taste but to take her fill of it.

Alain was the closest thing to Paris she could imagine. She was irresistibly drawn to his fine style and polish the moment she turned around and saw him after he had tapped her on the shoulder in downtown Nairobi. Even the way he first touched her – so reserved but so insistent at the same time – had appealed to the woman in her. She had never before wanted so much to both possess someone and be possessed.

How happy she would be if he were trying to find her. And how much happier still if her brother had not forgotten her, in spite of their having exchanged cross words with each other, which now seemed an eternity ago and no longer held any importance.

What was she going to do? Was she going to just stand there naked in front of the window until one of these poor excuses for men had the bright idea to come back and take another turn with her? She tiptoed to the other side of the room, where they had thrown her clothing, and quietly dressed, putting on her underwear and blouse but leaving her shoes and skirt. It was very late. The house was quiet now and she would have to be very quiet herself.

She tiptoed back to the window and pushed the glass gently until the two wings unfolded completely, exposing an open space before her. She slipped one leg over the windowsill and then pulled the other leg along bracing herself with her left arm until she was sitting on it. After listening for any sounds from the inside of the house and not hearing any, she jumped a few feet down onto the grass below with a soft thud, catching herself with her hands, and then slowly righted herself.

She felt encouraged now that she was outside. It was even darker than she had imagined, with the moon yielding only the thinnest sliver of light. If she crouched low she could reach the back fence and crawl over it without anyone seeing her. When they had first brought her here, she had seen only one guard at the main entrance gate. The little bit of moonlight was just enough for her to see the bare outlines of the fence and to begin crawling toward it on her hands and knees, keeping as low as possible to the ground. She knew that the fence would in all likelihood be topped by a row of barbed wire, as were most of the fences around homes like this one, and that her hands would be cut, possibly cut badly as she grabbed it to pull herself over. But that was a price well worth paying to escape from being touched ever again by these cruel lowlifes.

After she had crawled about half the distance to the fence, she stopped to catch her breath, alarmed that such a short distance had already exhausted her. Where was the Wangetha brimming with energy who could walk all day in the wilds with a knapsack on her shoulders and not feel the least bit tired? Where was the Wangetha who could dance to the driving rhythms of drums and guitars the whole night long? Had so much life already been battered and drained from her these past days? How could she possibly pull herself up and over the fence and all its barbed wire?

She resumed inching toward the fence when suddenly a beam of light flashed nearby on the ground and then formed quick circles around her. She froze in her position but the encircling light was now accompanied by a voice she knew all too well. It was the voice of the man who had been the first to force himself upon her as if it were his right, shoving the others aside contemptuously.

He was yelling in Swahili, "*So there you are, you bitch. I was looking for you.*"

As she felt his heavy footsteps thumping the ground and coming closer, she drew on the last bit of strength that was in her, springing up and running to the fence with a power and fury that she didn't know existed in her. She ran hard and fast on her long, graceful legs when, with the fence just a few meters away, her right foot caught a small hole, causing her to tumble face down onto the grass.

In a moment he was on her, straddling her back, grabbing her hair from behind and forcing her head so deeply into the grass that she could feel the dirt creeping into her nostrils.

"*I should kill you now, you whore,*" he shouted at her back. "*But that will have to wait a little while.*"

Still clutching onto her hair, he jerked her head up so violently she thought her neck would break as he forced her to stand. Pushing her to the house, with his right hand on her head and his left hand squeezing her arm, she stumbled and grimaced in pain, but had no more strength to resist.

She was trembling because she knew what was coming next.

CHAPTER 14
A VISITOR FROM ABROAD

∾

Now that it was Saturday, Alain hoped he could wind down a little bit. He had to scramble – and scramble hard – the previous day to navigate all the red tape involved in getting Jefferson's check cashed and his own funds wired to his account from Paris. Earlier today, he had dropped off 100,000 shillings to Haran and now there was nothing more he could do for the time being.

As Alain returned to his room at the Ngong Hills Lodge, he took stock of things. Three of the precious days that he had to raise the ransom money had passed. Thank God, Jefferson's check had been good. Now he had enough money to pay the ransom for Wangetha, even if he couldn't be sure it would wind up buying her freedom. After putting on his robe, he called the night porter for a cup of tea and sat down in front of the window facing the garden to reflect on his next move. He would have gone out to sit on the patio, but it was a little too cool tonight, and besides, he wasn't in the mood.

When the knock came on the door he quickly got up to open it, expecting to see the porter with his tea. But to his shock, it was not the porter facing him, but Alexandra, of all people, looking as beautiful as ever. He absorbed her in an instant. Her glowing blond hair was still parted in the middle and floated down to her cheeks. Her large, green eyes were as sparkling and fascinating as the first time he saw her. Her lips were just as full and ruby-red, while her figure was no less svelte. And even now, in a simple, blue skirt with a snugly-fitting, white knit top, she looked as if she had walked right out of the pages of *Mademoiselle* magazine.

The sound of her soft voice, once again up close and in person, had not changed at all either.

"Hello, Alain. I know you must be very surprised to see me," she said awkwardly. "Please forgive me for coming to you like this, but after we talked last week over the telephone I very much needed to see you. So I flew over here. It's only a few hours from Geneva by plane nowadays, so I thought, why not? After hearing your voice, I just couldn't wait to see you again."

She looked down at her feet. "You have every right to slam the door and throw me out. I've behaved in a despicable manner toward you."

Dazed, all Alain could do was mumble, "How did you find me? Why did you come?"

Slowly she looked up, intently, into Alain's eyes. "Is that all you have to say? Aren't you glad to see me, my darling? It wasn't easy locating you. But once I learned from your housekeeper that you were away on assignment, I called every hotel in Kenya that was outside of Nairobi to inquire about a man with your description. This was the eleventh hotel that I tried. When the reception desk matched you to it, I was elated. Even then I almost didn't come when I saw how close it was to Nairobi. I couldn't imagine that you would be here, knowing your adventurous spirit and how much you love to be in the countryside. But I so very much wanted to see you that I came, just to be sure, and now here I am and here you are."

"So my housekeeper didn't tell you where I was?"

"No, Alain. She didn't. She just said that you were away for a few days. I figured out the rest. You should see my telephone bill at my hotel. It's quite expensive to make long distance calls all over Kenya."

"Are you telling me the truth, Alexandra?"

"Of course I am, Alain."

"You haven't always been candid with me in the past."

"Oh, Alain, let's not visit the past and why I might have said stupid, silly things back then. Are you going to make me stand out here on the doorstep all night? Won't you invite me in? I promise that I won't bite you. Please let me try to explain why I came. It's cold out here."

With the door wide open and Alain still not making any gesture to welcome her inside, she glided through the space between Alain and the left side of the door frame. He didn't stop her. Seating herself on one of the two bamboo chairs around the table in the small drawing room, she crossed her legs and let one of her red, leather high heels slip to the floor, exposing her perfectly-manicured left foot. Though Alain was perturbed by Alexandra's audacious entry back into his life, he couldn't help but pause and let his eyes take in how the smooth white skin of her ankles contrasted with the loose, dark-blue skirt whose hem she was slowly, casually pulling down below her knees. After she tucked herself into the chair, she turned her body toward Alain, who was still standing, locking eyes with him.

After a few moments of gazing into each other's eyes, he suddenly collected himself, pulled his bathrobe tight around him, and exclaimed harshly, "Your coming to me like this is really incredible. What are you trying to do? You told me over the phone that you had married!"

"But I am still married."

"Still married? Then why did you seek me out? What is the point?"

"Alain, I need your help to get out of this marriage. I feel so trapped, so powerless, so unhappy. You must help me find my way out of the maze in which I find myself. Marrying Alberto was a big mistake, and I have regretted it terribly. It was always you that I wanted. Please believe that."

As she looked at him imploringly, with her expressive green eyes, Alain could see again how little she had changed over the past two years. Her cheekbones were set exquisitely high in her oval face, while her pouting lips were made to be kissed, and kissed, and then kissed again. In spite of himself, he felt himself being drawn back to her, his desire for her as a woman rekindling in him. How could this gorgeous creature have evaded him, he kept asking himself, as he looked at her, unable to avert his eyes.

"Alain, please say something – anything. I'm so sorry. Please forgive me."

When Alexandra began crying, all Alain could do was continue staring at her. His initial anger was dissipating as surely as his feelings of desire were growing in him.

"What can I say?" Alain asked pointedly, fighting his resurgent feelings as he began pacing around the room. "You destroyed the world of love we were once creating together and replaced it with another world more conducive to you. You should live in what you created. You wanted it. Now you have it."

"Oh, Alain, please don't be so distant," she whispered. "I suddenly feel a chill." She began to rub her arms and shoulders with her hands.

While she shivered in the chair, Alain couldn't help noting how vulnerable and helpless she now seemed. He still couldn't grasp that she had come all the way to Africa to see him. And now she was cold and in need of some warmth. He could no longer endure seeing her like this.

"Alexandra, come here," he said in a low, gentle voice.

As she rose from her chair and came to him, he took her two hands in his and pulled her strongly to himself. She threw her arms around his neck while he locked his arms around her waist and began gently kissing her on every part of her face, first her lips, then her cheeks, then her forehead, and then back to her lips, with his kisses growing in passion, probing more deeply, asking more and more of her.

Abruptly, Alexandra pulled away from him and looked at him almost defiantly.

"Alain! Please stop it. I can't, I just can't."

"What do you mean you can't? I thought you wanted me to kiss you. I thought you wanted me. What are you saying?"

"I can't, Alain, not now. As much as I want to, I can't be with you until I am free of my husband. I don't know what he will do if he finds out I came to see you. He doesn't know you are here in East Africa but he knows about you. He knows what we had, and he's very jealous. He said he would do terrible things if I left him for you. He thinks I've stopped over here in Nairobi for consultations at the UN Mission on the way to visiting my parents who are vacationing in the Côte d'Ivoire. I had my meetings yesterday, and I'm leaving for Abidjan tomorrow so he won't think anything is amiss."

"Then why did you come to see me, Alexandra? This isn't fair. You're going to drive me crazy like this."

Alain's mind was reeling, and as he looked at Alexandra more closely he remembered his grotesque dream of her in Paris. Was she really that much of a prize? How much of her carefully crafted appearance was genuine and how much of it was false? Images of Wangetha that he had crowded out of his consciousness under Alexandra's artful spell were coming back to him now: Wangetha and her love of family, native people, and nature's creatures; Wangetha and her quiet reverence for the simple, descriptive power of words; and, to be sure, Wangetha and her rhythmic sensuality, as smoldering as the hot African sun drenching her in its afternoon rays in the Rift Valley.

How he wished he could be with her now, but it was Alexandra who was speaking to him, not Wangetha.

"Please don't take this the wrong way, Alain," Alexandra said evenly in answering Alain's question as to why she came.

"It was so that we can think this through together. I need you. I just don't know how to get out of this mess by myself. I never would have married him if I had thought you were still unmarried yourself."

"First of all, let's keep the record straight, Alexandra. There was more to your succumbing to the attentions of this man than just the man himself. There was that way of life you were so keen on in the comfort of Europe. You know how much you liked the social whirl there, the hobnobbing with the diplomatic set, the literary salons, the cinema, the arts, the leisurely strolls along leafy boulevards, the chic restaurants, the long vacations on the Côte d'Azure. Is there anything that I left out?"

"We could have shared all that together, my love. That was always my dream."

"Ah, your dream. Yet I was being called away to foreign assignments. You knew that. You didn't want that kind of life."

"Part of what you say is true; I can't deny it. But I was immature. I didn't know what was important. I also thought you had already married. That was the main reason I married this other man."

"But the fact is I was unmarried. What made you think that I was married?"

"I just assumed it, Alain. You are such a handsome man. I know you've always had plenty of women around you."

"Did you also presume that my love for you was that shallow, that I would forget you so quickly?"

"Yes, Alain, I'm afraid so. I see now how wrong I was. But that's what I thought. Why was I to think that you would be different from so many other men?"

"I thought that you were too intelligent to make categorical judgments about men, Alexandra. How could you stereotype me like that?"

"I don't know. I guess that I just wasn't thinking clearly when I left you. Since then I've had a great deal of time to reflect, and now I know the price of leaving you. It's a price that's proven too high, my darling. But we don't have to pay the price forever if we don't want to."

Alain's voice was slowly rising, along with his frustration. "Alexandra, I don't see how I can help you. Go back to the priest that married the two of you. Didn't you say that you were married in the church when you called me earlier? Maybe he can tell you what to do."

"No, Alain. He can't tell me, because I know what he will say. I married my husband, and now I must stay with him, unless he has been brutal to me or been unfaithful. He's an uncomplicated man, who has been both kind and true to me. I can't fault him in any way. That's just the problem, Alain. He'd do anything for me. He loves me with complete devotion."

"That makes it even more wrong, Alexandra. You shouldn't have come."

"But only *you* can help me, Alain. Only you, maybe by taking me by force away somewhere, as I yield my will to the inevitable."

"Oh, I see. I take you by force and relieve you of your responsibility for your actions. Then whatever your husband does, I'm to blame. I have to live with the consequences. Is that the way you would have it?"

"Alain, you've always been stronger than me."

"What do you mean by that? Do you mean that I'm stronger than you are to wear the cross of his suffering around my neck? Is that what you see in me, the capacity to wear another man's pain with enough agility to make its memory fade away for both of us? I don't have that kind of strength if strength is what that is. I pity your husband, Alexandra. I pity any man that clutches onto a woman as he does to you, even if she is as attractive as you are."

"It's nice of you to say that about me, Alain. I am so happy that you still think I'm attractive. I once felt that way about myself. Now I just think that I'm ugly. I avoid looking at myself in the mirror whenever possible these days. I don't like what I see. I'm in the process of ruining the lives of two men, two very different men, but two men nonetheless."

"No. You're wrong, Alexandra. You will never ruin my life. Slowly, surely, I've come to realize that you're not worth it." He moved away from her and stood next to the door.

"Alain, what are you talking about? You just embraced me and kissed me. Of course you shouldn't let your life be spoiled by someone as pathetic as me. Don't misunderstand me. I'm sure you think now that I was being presumptuous when I said that. Please don't misunderstand."

"Alexandra, you really should go. There just isn't any future for us," Alain said, too keenly aware of the pleasures of sight and touch that he was turning aside.

"Don't say that, Alain. I came to ask for your support, to show me the way."

"There is no way with me any longer, Alexandra. You said you had to go. Now, please go."

"You're serious, aren't you?"

"Yes. I'll call a taxi for you. Please go to the reception desk and wait there."

"You won't even wait with me?"

"No. It wouldn't do any good."

Alain opened the door and Alexandra walked out slowly, looking back at him one more time.

"Is this really what you want, Alain? Are you sure? We could meet in Geneva, soon, after you had some more time to think things through."

"I have thought things through, Alexandra. And I'm not going to go to Geneva. This is goodbye. Now please go to the lobby."

"You won't at least see me to my hotel?"

"No."

"I'll always love you, Alain. There can never be anyone like you."

"Goodbye, Alexandra."

As Alexandra walked out of the room, she left the door open. Alain made no effort to close it as the cool breezes of the African night entered. Even after he called for the taxi to take her away, he left the door as it was. He sat down in one of the bamboo chairs and waited to see its arrival from the front window of the drawing room. In about 20 minutes – though it seemed much, much longer – he could hear a car pull up and then the sound of its door opening and then closing shut.

He had half-expected to hear the door being slammed after Alexandra got in as a fitting end to this scene, but he knew better. For a single European woman the driver would be opening the door to let her in, and out of deference would not slam the door in closing it. But would she have slammed the door if the driver had not closed it for her?

No, he didn't think so, as he considered it. The door would have closed even more slowly than the respectful way this taxi driver had closed it. Weren't forlorn lovers of two minds after all? They were sometimes sad and sometimes angry. The door slams when there is anger. But this was a time of sadness, when there was little energy left to expend on the world, including the doors of departing taxis in Africa.

He stepped out into the yard, not minding the cool air, and watched the car as it pulled away on the dirt road leading from the Ngong Hills Lodge back to the highway. His eyes followed it until all he could see was the settling cloud of dust left in its wake. Then he walked slowly back to his room, not forgetting to close the door behind him. He closed it softly and locked it securely. The porter hadn't come with the tea after all, and he would have no other guests this evening.

CHAPTER 15
A DAY IN THE LIFE OF HARAN

∿

It was well into the afternoon when Haran looked outside onto Biashara Street through the cracked panes of his office window. It was around 3:30 p.m., he guessed. Time to close shop early since it was Saturday, after all. No one would come calling now. He didn't like having to work Saturdays, but he needed all the business he could drum up.

Ever since he hocked his wristwatch, he had become fairly adept at telling the time by the rising and setting of the sun. He congratulated himself. Even if it was the old way to tell time, he was good at something, at least.

He walked back to his desk on the other side of the room and slumped down into its worn leather chair. If only he were as good at business as he was at telling the time of day. He let his gaze fall on the painting of the peaceful man and woman sitting under the acacia tree. It made him feel a little better.

This had not been a good week for his law practice. There had been only one new client. Yesterday, a man of little means had come to see him and that was it. He wanted advice about a piece of property some city official was trying to grab from him. It was a one-acre plot, bordering the desirable area of Westlands, and the grabber wanted to build an apartment complex on it. As they pored over his deeds and documents, Haran advised him that all his papers were in order and he would be willing to represent him in court, but he warned him it would be a long-drawn-out process with no guarantees. The merits of the case were one thing. The judge hearing the case was the other, more decisive factor. And who that judge might be, he had no way of knowing beforehand.

The man had thanked him for his advice and said he would think over his options. He also thanked Haran for charging him only 500 shillings for the consultation, which he knew was far less than what most attorneys would have charged.

Haran had seen this kind of caller all too often lately. Now that word had spread about his being down on his luck, he was being pegged as an easy touch for cheap legal advice.

His hand began to reach down to the drawer where he kept his gin. Why not, he asked himself. It had been a long day. On the plus side, he had found out where the kidnappers were keeping Wangetha. He had also learned that they had once received money from Robidi, the Zimugabwa high commissioner. He hadn't been able to find out for what, though he suspected it was for knocking her off.

Didn't he, therefore, deserve a little something now to lift his spirits, to put him in a better mood? Of course, Wangetha wouldn't understand, but what of it? If Regalo and Alain managed to free her, all of them, Wangetha included, would have him to thank. They didn't have a clue where she was being held, but he had nosed around in the muck of Nairobi's underground and found out in only one day.

It was true, abundantly true, that the money Alain had given him had helped to make informants out of people who normally were too scared to do anything other than mind their own business. But in the end, his connections were what had counted. Who else could have navigated through the tangled maze of the Kikuyu community so effortlessly and then reached down into its dregs to pluck out these gems of information? So, perhaps all that time he had spent in Nairobi's bars was not completely wasted.

"Do you understand that, Wangetha?" he found himself yelling to the peeling walls. "It is not always that simple.

Success comes in different forms, my dear sister. It can take strange, convoluted paths."

She was the last one who should lecture him on the meaning of success and failure. He had warned her about Robidi long ago when he had heard about his pursuing her.

"Stay away from him," he had told her. "This bloodsucking ghost will draw the life out of you and leave you feeling empty and ashamed of yourself. In the end, he will discard you as casually as a bottle of gin drawn down to the last drop, or the Mercedes Benz in his fleet with too much rust and too many kilometers."

But she had not listened and kept going back to him. Robidi represented influence and a way out of their marginalized state. And feted by many he was, Haran had to admit. Robidi's revolutionary past lent him status and credibility throughout the continent, even if in the end it had become clear that whatever ideals he once had were long since replaced by his shameless grabbing for money, status, and power. Wangetha was the cute little doll he kept on hand to play with once the serious work of strong-arming anything that stood in his way was done. And there was plenty that Robidi needed to strong-arm into submission, not the least being the restive workers on his own plantation back in Zimugabwa, many of whom he knew had less to eat than the dogs foraging for scraps in the slums of Nairobi.

Wangetha was as clever as she was pretty and had managed to finagle some very expensive presents out of the tightwad. Haran had seen her once from a distance at a reception at the Grand Regency Hotel. She was wearing a full complement of the jewelry she had received from Robidi, including a tennis bracelet made of diamonds shining more brightly on her wrist than the crystal chandeliers hanging from the ceiling. He didn't know then whether to feel proud of his sister or to detest her, though she seemed as radiant as he had ever seen her.

It had been a real surprise to Haran when Wangetha had turned the tables on the old hyena and left him before he was through with her. How happy he had been to hear the news, even though he knew there would be complications since there was no reason to think Robidi would go quietly. Not this autocrat. He believed that her will should have been subjected to his as a matter of course, just as with the staff at his residence and plantation. Even so, Haran hadn't expected that he would go so far as to try to have her killed.

He pulled his hand back from the drawer, rose from his chair, and walked over to inspect his law diploma hanging from the wall. "I know, dear Wangetha, what hopes you once held for me," he muttered to the wall as if it were her. "I mastered everything the colonialists had taught us. I was first in my class, and I saw the look of pride and respect in your eyes each time you looked at me. Nothing could stop me. I was sure of it. And when I pooled together our family inheritance and invested everything in that construction project in Eastlands, I was confident of success. I know our critics said that I had picked the wrong part of town and that I should have brought more foreigners on board. But I honestly didn't see how it could fail.

"Then when the main building collapsed due to the poor grade of concrete used for the foundation, I couldn't believe it. I had ordered high-quality stuff, not junk. This wasn't my fault, do you hear, Wangetha? It wasn't my fault! How could I know that my suppliers would thin out the concrete's strength with too much sand?"

He settled back down in his chair, emotionally spent, and opened up the drawer, this time pulling out the bottle of Beefeater which was still almost full. The night before he had been bar-crawling and hadn't needed to pull any sucks of consolation from this bottle. There had been plenty everywhere he went. He eyed the bottle carefully. There was more than enough for a few good pulls now.

He swallowed deeply and felt the warm fluid trickle down his throat into his stomach. Then he took a second swallow and leaned back in his chair. Once again, his gaze caught the painting of the couple sitting under the acacia tree. He stared at it almost spellbound. Then he noticed that the cord from which the painting hung was fraying. The painting would soon fall to the ground, he realized, but not just yet.

He took his eyes away to look at the bottle of Beefeater. He had already had two good, long swallows. Did he really need one more? Did he really need that one more long swallow, or would it be two, three, or four more until the bottle was empty? And then would that be enough? Or would he be out on the street headed for the nearest *changaa* bar for even more, risking blindness or death by drinking the methyl alcohol–laced poison served there?

He looked again at the painting with the fraying cord, and as he studied it even more, it became absorbed in the wall, blending into it until they were one.

He jerked himself back to the present. What about Wangetha? She was in serious trouble, and here he was staring at a picture and contemplating getting drunk. Didn't he owe his sister more than that?

He opened the drawer and slowly put the bottle back into its place. He had had enough. He would go out for a sandwich, come back, and sleep in the office tonight. Who knew whom he would meet tomorrow? It wouldn't do any good to be hung over then. That was not who he was or what he was.

CHAPTER 16
THE HIGH COMMISSIONER OF ZIMUGABWA

∽

On Sunday morning, Alain was roused from his sleep by loud and vigorous pounding at his door. After throwing on his bathrobe and opening it, two armed, uniformed guardsters confronted him. One was somewhat taller than the other.

"Are you Alain Sardou?" the taller one asked gruffly.

"Yes, I am. What can I do for you?" Alain asked, trying not to let his anxiety show.

"The high commissioner wants to see you. We are here to take you to him."

"The high commissioner of what?"

"The high commissioner of Zimugabwa," the taller one snapped.

"I didn't realize that the high commissioner sends armed guardsters to grab people in a country that's not his own," Alain glared.

"Get dressed. We'll wait outside the door," the shorter one said angrily, opening his jacket and fondling a holstered gun.

"Fine, I'll get dressed," Alain muttered, starting to close the door.

The tall guardster put his right shoe in the doorway, blocking Alain from closing it.

"Leave the door open. Don't use the telephone to call anyone."

"And hurry. The high commissioner is impatient to see you," the shorter one added.

How could Robidi have found me, Alain wondered as he slipped on a pair of jeans, white polo shirt, and blue cotton blazer in the bathroom, all the time wishing he had time to call Regalo. He could understand how the kidnappers had found out that he was going to be with Wangetha in Nakuru. As Regalo had figured it at the Nyama Choma bar, Robidi's people probably tipped them as to where both Wangetha and he were going to be that day.

But Rebecca and Regalo were the only people on the face of this earth in whom he confided about staying at the Ngong Hills Lodge. Which one would have informed Robidi, under what circumstances, and why?

Alain continued to puzzle over who might have given his whereabouts away as he was led toward a black Mercedes sedan waiting outside. Before he knew it, he was sandwiched in between the two guardsters in the rear seat. The driver stepped on it and within minutes the sedan was hurtling into Nairobi's Sunday morning traffic. When they arrived at the high commissioner's compound in a tony section of Westlands, the taller guardster pushed him hard out of the car while the shorter one ran around to his side of the door and poked a gun in his back.

Alain could see four gardeners busily tending to the vast assortment of flowers and plants surrounding the residence. Off to one side, he could also see what looked like three laundrywomen carrying bundles of wet clothes. Parked in the driveway were two other late-model Mercedes sedans with at least five men in uniform stationed around them. Five more men were positioned along the perimeter of the grounds, which were densely lined by a tall, green hedge.

Noting how Alain was surveying the grounds, the shorter guardster prodded him forward with the barrel of his gun toward a plain door at the side entrance. The taller one noisily sounded the knocker. The door opened almost immediately, and Alain found himself abruptly pushed down onto the brightly-polished, hardwood floor. He was barely able to get his hands out in time to break his fall and keep his face from being smashed.

While the taller one put his boot on Alain's back, pinning him to the floor, the shorter one ran down the hall. As Alain squirmed, the guardster returned.

"We can bring him. His excellency will see him now!"

The taller guardster lifted his boot from Alain's back. "Get up!" he barked. His partner studied Alain with contempt as he slowly pushed himself up from the floor.

"None of this was necessary," Alain muttered as he rose to his feet.

"His excellency will decide what is necessary, not you!" the shorter guardster snarled, as he shoved Alain down the long, dark hall. Alain could barely see ahead of him, but as he stumbled along he could still make out large portraits hanging askance, in worn, chipped, gold-leafed frames, of the high commissioner standing in various stately poses.

By the time they reached the end of the hall, Alain was feeling very warm and uncomfortable. He couldn't understand why there were no windows to let in the light and fresh air. This must be an alternate route to his office, he guessed, not the official one. The paintings were probably older vintage that Robidi used to hang in his office.

The shorter guardster knocked on what sounded to Alain as a metal door. That would make sense, he thought, if the door were to provide maximum security.

"Who is it?" yelled a high-pitched voice through the door.

"We are here, sir. We've brought him."

"Bring him in," the voice commanded.

As Alain was pushed into the room he saw a tall, thin, elderly black man, wearing thick, horn-rimmed glasses, standing behind a large desk covered with miniature replicas of hyenas, water buffalos, giraffes, zebras, rhinoceroses, and lions. The high commissioner was scowling at him and eyeing him pointedly as he spoke to the guardsters.

"Stay here," he ordered. "And don't let anyone in, no matter what."

The "no matter what part" drew Alain's attention.

"Why did you bring me here?" he asked sharply, hoping that the rough edge to his voice would cloak the fear creeping up on him.

"Ah, Mr. Sardou. You should know better than anyone in all of Kenya why we have brought you here," the high commissioner replied in careful, measured tones of British English. Alain could tell immediately that this man was not lacking education.

As to the high commissioner's tribe, Alain had no clue. If anything, his physical appearance resembled that of the dictator of Robidi's home country, whose name he could not recall just now.

"Did you hear me, Mr. Sardou? You should know better than anyone why you are here!"

The shrill voice jolted Alain out of his wandering thoughts as the high commissioner moved from behind his desk to stand right in front of him, face to face.

"May I commend you for your excellent taste in women, Mr. Sardou? They don't come any more attractive than Wangetha. She is quite a treasure. But you are French, isn't that right? So maybe that is to be expected."

"I will take that as a compliment," Alain said.

"Tell me, Mr. Sardou, how did you meet her?"

"I met her by accident."

"Oh, I see, by accident. But isn't that how we all meet our women, quite by accident as the English would say. So let me see if I understand this correctly. Once you saw her, once you laid your eyes on this Wangetha Wachira, you became enamored of her, just like that?"

186

"Is that why I'm here, Mr. High Commissioner? Because I took a liking to an African woman? I was hoping that you brought me here because you wanted to give me your personal insights into the economic and social disaster that is unfolding in your home country."

"I will pretend that I did not hear that insult, Mr. Sardou. I know that you would love to change the subject. Of course, you would rather talk politics, a fascinating subject at which you, as a journalist, I am sure excel. But it is of considerably more importance to me when a white man would rob us of one of our most beautiful treasures."

The intercom on the high commissioner's large desk buzzed loudly, jarring Alain into remembering the high commissioner's last name, Amimuga. Robidi Amimuga, the autocratic politician described by Regalo over several Tusker beers. "Don't interrupt me!" Robidi yelled at the intercom. "I'm busy."

He turned his attention back to Alain. "I'm sorry about that interruption, Mr. Sardou. I was educated to have better manners than that. Manners are important. I wish you had shown better manners in your choice of women."

The blow from Robidi's fist came so quickly that he had no time to collect himself and deflect the punch. He fell backwards on the thick Indian rug covering most of the floor, his mouth and jaw turning numb while his head throbbed with pain. He was astounded at the power of this lanky man's punch, even as he took some personal satisfaction in knowing that he had not been knocked out.

"Pick him up!" Robidi ordered the two guardsters.

After they set Alain on his feet in front of Robidi and released him, his legs buckled and he found himself on the rug again, this time face down, directly confronting its large flowery patterns. The man favored fine rugs as well as fine women, Alain thought as he sought to catch his breath. But given what Robidi saw in Wangetha, what could she have seen in this decrepit bully? Maybe, when he was younger and full of revolutionary zeal and promise. But now?

Robidi laughed, not knowing Alain's thoughts.

"An Englishman would have stayed on his feet after being helped up once."

"But it was a Frenchman that took your woman," Alain sneered, spitting out blood as he slowly stood up.

As Robidi nodded, one of the guardsters moved in. Alain just caught the sight of his uplifted knee before it drove into his groin and his body exploded in pain. He fell backward again, in slow motion, his head gliding to the rug. As he was passing out, he could see in the swimming, glittering blackness that had replaced the finely-wallpapered walls of Robidi's office, the same angry crowd on Moi Avenue, joined this time by the young thief. Just as they were raising their fists in unison to pummel him, Alain came to and saw the taller guardster pouring a pitcher of water on his face while Robidi was hovering next to him.

"Pick him up and this time set him down in that chair."

As the guardsters lifted Alain up and dragged him to the chair, Robidi reached for a tangerine from the bowl of fruit on his desk. Holding it in his right hand, he put it in his mouth and bit into it, taking out a piece of its skin. Alain's attention shifted for a moment from the throbbing pain in his head to the tangerine. The ones he had eaten in Europe were lighter in color than this one.

He watched as Robidi then took the tangerine into his left hand and held it there with his fingers while his thumb from the right hand picked away at its surrounding skin. When only the inner fruit was left, Robidi took both of his thumbs to separate it into two even halves, which he popped into his mouth one after the other.

"That looks like a very fine tangerine," Alain mumbled to Robidi. "But it doesn't look like the tangerines that I know."

"There are many things that you don't know, Mr. Sardou. This is actually a minneola tangelo grown in South Africa, a hybrid of the grapefruit and tangerine that was developed in, of all places, the good old USA. It is, of course, larger than the small clementines from Spain that you have probably sampled. Or, for all I know, you may have in mind the mandarins from the Mediterranean region. The minneola in my hand has a deeper orange color than that variety, but I will wager that it is much more succulent. I see a look of doubt in your eyes. Here, why don't you try one?" he offered as he took another piece of the fruit out of the bowl, fished a knife out his pocket, and cut it into two halves. "It's from my own private stock so you know it must be of the best quality."

Robidi walked over to Alain and stood in front of him holding one half of the tangerine in his hand. The shorter guardster, as if on cue, moved behind Alain's chair and pulled his two arms behind it, holding them fast. "Here, have a bite," Robidi snickered, as he pressed the fruit into Alain's mouth and kept it there until he gagged. "How does it taste?"

After the guardster let his arms go, Alain wiped the citrus fruit from his face, which was stinging the cuts on his mouth. Robidi was laughing so hard that he put his hand on the shoulder of the guardster to steady himself.

"Have we hurt your tiny feelings, Mr. Sardou, by not showing you the deference to which I am sure you believe you are entitled by virtue of your heritage and the color of your skin? What a pity," Robidi sneered, "that there is no respect coming your way today."

Alain could barely contain his anger, but he knew there was nothing he could do. Robidi was holding all the cards and doing with them as he pleased. All he could do was watch him as he sauntered back to his desk and sat down.

"Now, let us get back to the subject of Wangetha. Where is she?"

Alain did not answer.

"Did you hear me, Mr. Sardou? Where is Wangetha?"

"I thought she was supposed to be dead," Alain answered.

Robidi raised his voice. "Let's not be funny, Mr. Sardou. You and I both know that she's not dead and that she's being held somewhere."

"How do you know that, when you are the one who ordered her killed?"

Robidi said nothing, only nodding to the two guardsters. The taller one went to the front of Alain's chair, lifted him up, and turned him around to face the shorter one, who proceeded to deliver his clenched fist deep into Alain's stomach. As he winced with more pain, ready to collapse on the floor again, the taller one continued to hold him from behind, at first preventing him from falling and then dumping him into his chair.

"You are probably wondering how I intend to get away with beating you to a bloody pulp. You are probably thinking that you will report me to the local authorities. But think a little more about it. What can any of them do, or better yet, what would they want to do? You show up all beaten up and a bloody mess, but how can you ever prove it was done by my boys or by me? I will just deny that I ever saw you. No one knows that you are here.

"And don't count on the staff at the Ngong Hills Lodge to take your side if they should be questioned. I have seen after them handsomely with plenty of shillings. But even without any payoff, do you suppose that they, the authorities, or anyone else on this continent for that matter would take your side against me? This is my continent, Mr. Sardou. Not yours. Mine. Always remember that. The days when you could rule the roost here are long over. And that goes for all of you from abroad. You are all the same. You would try to rule the roost again if you could. But we will never let you lord it over us again. Do you hear? Never again! So let's be serious. What are your accusations against my explanations? You're too smart not to know that you won't have a case, not in this pretty part of the world. Go back, Mr. Sardou. Go back from where you came. We don't want you and we don't need you."

He nodded toward the shorter guardster standing in front of Alain, who this time hit him in the face with a full fist. He would have fallen from the chair without the other guardster holding him in place. Even so, his head fell down upon his chest as he fought to overcome the vertigo gripping him.

Robidi grabbed Alain's head by the hair and forced him to look directly into his face.

"No, don't worry, Mr. Sardou, we are not going to kill you. Though if we did, nobody could do anything about it."

He released Alain's head, which slumped back onto his chest.

He nodded to the guardsters again, who this time let Alain fall to the floor.

"I'm going to give you a couple of days to think about what I've asked you, and then we'll come calling again, Mr. Sardou."

"You bastard," Alain voiced the words slowly and clearly through his bloody mouth as he carefully lifted himself up. "You low-class bastard," he repeated, targeting his words at Robidi's vanity.

"You tempt me sorely to give you the back of my hand and see you bleed one more time," Robidi shouted at Alain. "But I've had enough of you!"

He pointed to the bathroom at the far end of his office, and the shorter guardster fetched a basin of water and a towel. The other one then washed and dried his face. Robidi motioned to the door.

"The pleasure was mine, Mr. Sardou," Robidi said as the guardsters dragged him staggering out of the office, down the long dark hallway again, and into the same black Mercedes Benz sedan.

He was hardly aware of the car moving, how much time went by, or where he was, when he was pushed out into what he could see was a dirt alley.

With jelly legs that could barely hold him up, Alain looked around to get his bearings in the glare of the morning sun.

He felt weak and he felt strange. His legs began moving him toward the left, following the alley, until after a few minutes he saw traffic. Stepping out onto a sidewalk that seemed to appear from nowhere, he stumbled through the light flow of pedestrians and began looking for a taxi.

As he neared the next intersection, he saw an old, banged-up sedan with a taxi sign on its roof parked next to a bus stop. He reached for his wallet in the rear pocket of his trousers and pulled out a 1,000-shilling note, double the average fare for going a good distance within Nairobi's city limits.

"Hey, I need to go to Karanja Road," Alain blurted to the driver standing next to his taxi as he fought to compose himself.

"I'm sorry, sir, but I'm waiting for someone. He promised to return in a few minutes."

"Forget about him. How do you know he's coming back? You don't know, do you? In the meanwhile, here is a sure 1,000 shillings if you take me to where I need to go."

The driver stared at the 1,000-shilling note. "You pay me first."

"Only once I get in the car and you start driving."

Alain squeezed into the creaky rear seat while the driver started up the motor. As the car began moving, the driver extended his right hand to Alain while keeping his left hand on the wheel. Alain thrust the 1,000-shilling note into his hand and leaned back on the grainy-beige vinyl, completely exhausted.

His eyes closed as the taxi bounced along the potholed road headed toward Langata and would have stayed closed had the driver not yelled at him.

"Mister, who are you? Why are we being followed?"

Alain turned around to look through the rear window and could see a white, late-model Mercedes sedan with four men inside. It was hard to tell for sure from this distance, but two of them looked like the guardsters who had just beaten him up at Robidi's. Since he hadn't given Wangetha's whereabouts away, he guessed that they were going to follow him wherever he went. The white Mercedes was to throw him off and must have been behind the black one that dumped him in the alley. Robidi's suggestion that they would wait to contact him was nonsense.

"Lose them any way you can, and I'll give you another 1,000 shillings, maybe 2,000 to 3,000 shillings if you are good. I don't care what you do. Just lose them."

"I can't lose them. This is a slow, old car."

"Go as fast as you can anyway. I'll pay for any repairs. Go!"

As the rickety car accelerated, its rattles became so loud that Alain could hardly hear the sound of the traffic around them. But he could still think, and it all came together for him now. Of course, there was good reason why they had not beaten him more badly or even killed him. What good would it have done Robidi? He clearly didn't know where Wangetha was, though he had learned that she had been taken away somewhere and wasn't dead.

Robidi had slipped right through Regalo's tight analysis. What had he said at the Nyama Choma bar? Wasn't it some-thing to the effect that Robidi's hired-killers-turned double-crossing kidnappers wouldn't be letting any news get out about their caper that could find its way back to Robidi?

That sounded plausible at the time. But now it was clear that some news did leak out anyway. Alain didn't know just how much, but it was enough to wisen up Robidi to the fact that Wangetha had been kidnapped and that he was with her at the time. Even so, whoever tipped Robidi on that score couldn't have known he was staying at the Ngong Hills Lodge. Only Regalo and Rebecca knew that.

And now Robidi was on to him and his boys were tailing him. He probably figured that as banged up as he was, he wouldn't notice that he was being followed and so would un-wittingly lead them to Wangetha sooner or later. In that case, they would be tailing him until he was ready to deal with the kidnappers, which would be some time yet.

The driver was pushing the old junk heap for all it was worth, passing cars whenever he could or driving off the road onto the sidewalk and scaring hell out of the pedestrians. But Alain could see that the Mercedes was using the same reckless tactics and was keeping up with them.

With no hope of outdistancing the Mercedes, Alain decided he would have to make a run for it. When the taxi slowed as it approached the next intersection, he suddenly swung open the door, said thank you to the driver as he slipped him another 1,000-shilling note and bolted out on to the street, running as fast as his tired legs could carry him to the nearby sidewalk jammed with people.

Once he was on the sidewalk, he heard the screeching of tires, a stream of curses in Swahili, and the slamming of car doors. He glanced back over his shoulder to see Robidi's men running in his direction, pointing and yelling at him.

Didn't they realize that chasing him was stupid? What was the point? What would they do once they caught up with him? They dared not kill him since they needed him to find Wangetha. So wouldn't they have done better by following him in the background and shadowing his moves?

On the other hand, maybe Robidi had second thoughts on letting him go and instructed his goons to take care of him after all. Maybe he figured he could find her without him. What was it they said about Robidi? That you never knew what he would do next and that it wasn't always rational.

What Alain did know was that if he were going to help Wangetha, he had to shake Robidi's boys and shake them fast.

He took a few deep breaths and began to zigzag through the briskly-moving pedestrians before him, doing all he could do to avoid colliding with anyone.

After running like this for a few minutes, he looked back and saw them stop to huddle. When he glanced back again a few moments later, they were gone.

They must have realized their mistake in being too visible and were now following him from a distance. So what should he do? What could he do? Waves of exhaustion rolled over him. He had to sit down somewhere and rest.

Just then he noticed a narrow side street jutting off to the right and ran in. About 10 houses down, he came to what looked to be a simple, storefront building with a plaque in the window reading Rock and Foundation Church. Hearing loud, singing voices, he pulled open the entrance door, crouched down, and made a dash for the last bench in the back where only an old lady was sitting and clapping her hands.

At first, she didn't seem to even notice him, not even while he reached into his pocket for the small tin of charcoal he had been carrying during the past three days, and not even while he was rubbing it all over his face, neck, and hands. It was only when he pulled out his large, blue handkerchief and wrapped it bandana style around his head to cover his hair that she turned to see what he was doing. But then she went right back to her clapping and singing.

Alain breathed a sigh of relief. She hadn't paid attention to the charcoal routine, or had she? And had any others? In fact, now that he thought about it, there was really nothing to stop the choir members standing at the front of the congregation from observing him either. He couldn't be sure. All he was sure of was that all of the two hundred or so worshippers sitting on the wooden benches in this hall were singing with such enthusiasm that the walls seemed to be weaving in and out in rhythm to the music before his tired, swollen eyes.

The sounds of the music, with all the energetic singing, clapping, swaying, and praising, made him forget about how fatigued he was. He sat quietly on the bench and gathered his strength.

CHAPTER 17
THE MURDER BOARD

୭

Regalo was in a hurry. He had to be at the Stanley Hotel by 11:00 a.m. but it was already 10:45 a.m. and he was still stuck on Kenyatta Avenue in heavy traffic. Normally, he wouldn't have cared how late he would be for a meeting. But when his attorney had called him from the States earlier in the week to tell him that the firm wanted to settle with him out of court, he felt the first stirrings of well-being in months. It had been worth the wait to get this hopeful news.

He jerked the steering wheel of his Jeep hard to the right when he saw the first opening in the lane next to him and cut into the nearest side street, drawing to a halt in front of a Chinese restaurant he knew well. After clambering out and locking the doors, he rushed into the dining room, approached the waiter who was setting the dishes and utensils, and crammed a 200-shilling note into his hands.

"Watch my car. I'll be back in an hour."

Regalo did not wait to see the startled reaction of the waiter, who was alternately staring at Regalo's back fading into the distance and the crumpled 200-shilling note in his hand. Regalo ran back to Kenyatta Avenue, clambered into a noisy *matatu*, and headed toward the hotel.

The *matatu* swerved back into the bustling, chaotic traffic that was Kenyatta Avenue at this time of day. Hordes of other *matatus* crammed full of passengers were winding in and out of loading areas at breakneck speeds, blaring ear-splitting rock music, but Regalo didn't let any of the commotion faze him.

This was the chance he had been waiting for. By filing the lawsuit over his discharge, he had put the firm on notice. They were going to have to deal with him. Now it would be their turn to squirm.

He had smarted for well over a year about the terms of his discharge. His contacting the rebels in the Angolan bush was the excuse they used for getting rid of him. But the real cause, Regalo believed, was that he had sown doubts in the minds of some higher-ups about his loyalty and usefulness. Regalo knew that he had it coming for other reasons as well, since he had never mastered the helpful art of kissing the various behinds in front of him as he tried to climb up the career ladder.

Even so, his real problems began during a policy session at the firm's headquarters two years back when he had the temerity to suggest that the regime ensconced in Angola's capital, Luanda, was as corrupt as the rebel fighters in the bush were brutal. It was then that he saw the eyebrows in the room rise. He knew how irritating his views must have sounded at a time when the firm was trying to work out a big oil deal with the Luanda regime. But didn't money-grabbing ever have any limits? Did no one notice or did no one care that Luanda's corruption had reached the point of siphoning off not just hundreds of millions of dollars in oil revenues, but billions?

In his breach of contract lawsuit following his termination, he maintained that he had sent an email to his supervisors about meeting the rebels well in advance. This was not true. He had sent no such email. He had come up with this ruse on the spur of the moment while he was arguing with the firm over the terms of his dismissal. Laying it out with a straight face hadn't helped him. Without the email itself to adduce as proof, his account was flatly rejected. The one month of administrative leave he received to find another job, as well as full retirement benefits, were inducements to shut him up as far as Regalo was concerned. His case was closed, or so it seemed.

But once out on his own, he had hit upon a way to simulate an email message sent on the firm's computer network. He remembered enough about the models and specifications of the hard drives used in the network to locate a drive identical to what he used there. He was then able to take formatting features from the computer files he had downloaded before he left Angola, integrate them into the same version of the interoffice email program used at corporate headquarters, and create an email message that had similar embedded characteristics of emails sent from there two years ago.

Once he was satisfied that the email to his supervisor about his trip looked genuine, replete with a seemingly plausible time and date of transmission, he had flown back to Washington, D.C. There he retained Aaron Warner, one of the beltway's most tenacious attorneys dealing with personnel issues.

Creating this email was dishonest, that Regalo well knew. But as far as he was concerned, he was at war with the firm. And in wars didn't anything go, including lies, especially lies?

As for Warner, Regalo felt no obligation to tell him that the email was counterfeit since he never asked.

On the face of it, the email constituted enough of a basis to file a lawsuit over the merits of his dismissal. And both Warner and Regalo knew that once the judicial proceedings went forward, they could get enough sensitive, internal information about the nature of the firm's dealings with Luanda out into the open to damage its image. But just as they had expected, it had not come to this. Representatives of the firm's front office were ready to talk.

But this time it would be a little more serious than before. This time he wouldn't be on the defensive as he was when they canned him. This was going to be a set of negotiations on an entirely different level. Warner wasn't going to be with him, but he had learned enough about his rights to feel confident.

Regalo felt energized as he sauntered up to the lobby of the Stanley Hotel, but he put on a calm front. He didn't want anyone to see how anxious he was to turn the tables on his detractors.

He had to compliment the firm on its taste in hotels. He knew the Stanley and had spent more than a few hours at its fine bar, taking a drink while sitting below its electric fans that looked just like palm leaves.

But when he entered the room set aside for the meeting and saw the faces of the two people sitting at the small round table, he took a deep breath. They were the faces of his former supervisors.

Sitting at the left of the table he could see Steven Kacey, who had written the evaluation recommending his dismissal. That was to be expected. But if all this were going to be a form of psychological intimidation, as he immediately suspected, why was Harvey Boward included as the second man, the man who had mentored him and sang his praises? Why was he here?

"Sit down, relax, Joseph," Kacey beamed at him. "I know you must be surprised to see us here today. You must be wondering about our intentions, but we are here merely doing our duty. These are serious negotiations we're about to enter, and the front office wanted to make sure that you conducted them with colleagues you know well." Kacey's mouth tightened before finishing. "And who know you well."

Regalo showed no emotion, knowing he had to be careful. He had forced them into a negotiating mode. But he also knew that to be in the same room for any length of time with these people could precipitate some kind of angry blunder on his part.

He could walk out, but then he would lose his chance to force a settlement. He had no more interest in following through with his lawsuit than they had in responding to it. He couldn't offer the huge legal expenses and he would just as soon pass on dredging up memories he would rather forget.

"Joseph," Kacey continued in a low, measured tone. "As I just said, we understand that you may be surprised to see the two of us here. And you're right if you are surmising that it's no accident that we were asked to meet with you. We're here voluntarily. We were given a choice to serve. I agreed, because – and this may surprise you – I actually admire you.

"I also have good news for you. The front office sent us here to make a deal with you. So in a way, you've won already. This kind of negotiation doesn't take place very often, does it, Harvey?"

"Very rarely, if ever," Boward nodded in agreement.

"You see, Joseph," Kacey intoned, "we know that you're smart. Very smart. That's why we're here. You filed a very clever lawsuit. You knew very well that to go to court we might have to let out some information which we weren't ready to disclose. And for what? Just so you can have your job back? That doesn't make very much sense to us. As far as we're concerned, you can have your job back."

Regalo could not believe what he was hearing. "What are you saying? My lawsuit was not about being reinstated. I would never work with you again if my life depended on it! I sued to reverse the spurious, vindictive disciplinary finding against me, which resulted in my being forced out. You have to be aware of that distinction."

Boward smiled at Regalo. "You know that I always liked you, Joseph. Have you forgotten the evaluation I gave you? That was an extraordinary rating you received from me. I have never given anyone anything like that before or after. Did you hear me? It was the best of the best! Never before and never after! I thought the world of you.

"Just remember," Boward continued, now in an accusatory tone, "when that adverse personnel action was filed against you, it was not from my panel. Even so, panels have to follow the guidelines given them, and you had made bad choices in your contacts. You did what suited you without considering what your supervisors might have thought. In retrospect, wasn't that pretty selfish, Joseph?"

Regalo frowned bitterly. It was evident that Boward had sold out. It was two against one. "You know very well that I met with those rebels in Angola at their initiative. I didn't go searching for them. But they opened my eyes to all the rot in Luanda, and I shared my findings accordingly."

"We understand that," Kacey chimed in. "We're only human." He put together his hands in supplication to the ceiling. "But Harvey and I want to make it up to you. We will reinstate you with full privileges if you drop the lawsuit."

By now Regalo was on the verge of screaming. He had just told them he wasn't seeking reinstatement. That was the last thing in the world that he wanted, and he had no doubt that they had known that all along. Was the offer planned ahead of time to bait and rile him, knowing full well that he would decline?

"You have every reason to hate me, Joseph," Kacey said. "But you must understand that it was precisely because we shared the same Italian heritage that I couldn't let it appear as if I were showing favoritism to you. Wasn't it always you who placed such a high value on professionalism? Isn't that the ethical basis of your lawsuit? That you violated no established company policy or practice?"

Regalo was now ready to explode. Kacey had been close enough to him to know that his true background was not known even though his adoptive parents were Italian. Why play on this chord?

Kacey smiled. "You have every reason to be disappointed in us. You probably even think we are secretly taping this session."

"Oh no, I would never think that," Regalo responded with the slightest of a sarcastic tone. "Let's cut out all this small talk. You know that I don't want to be reinstated. I want the disciplinary finding removed from my file, a letter of apology, and $175,000 in back pay."

Boward looked quickly at Kacey, caught his breath, and as he stared intently at Regalo he was barely able to contain his anger and frustration.

"You are ungrateful, Joseph! We came in a conciliatory spirit, and we offered you full reinstatement. We were right about you in the first place. You don't deserve our reaching out to you. There will be no change in the disciplinary finding, no apology, no financial settlement. You can proceed with your lawsuit."

"So, that's it?" Regalo sputtered, wondering how he could have been so optimistic about this meeting.

"That's it," Boward answered indignantly. "And I'd be careful if I were you. I'm saying this as fatherly advice."

"Is that a threat? Why should I be careful?"

"We were so right about you," Kacey said, avoiding the question. "We knew you would find a way to sabotage yourself."

"Oh, is that another threat? Just how am I going to sabotage myself?" By now Regalo's voice was oozing sarcasm.

"If anybody can find a way, it will be you, Joseph. You'll find a way to show us," Kacey said solemnly. "You know, Joseph, it's a real shame things turned out like this. You actually weren't that bad with words, if I do say so myself. I've always thought of myself as a wordsmith, and so I don't say that lightly. But you never did understand that you didn't have to be so brutal with language. You never seemed to understand that once spoken or written, words create their own reality. Even now, just listen to yourself, Joseph. No polish, no easy movement or flow. Just those harsh words that keep ringing in my ears now that you've said them, actually in both our ears, right Harvey? 'Just how am I going to sabotage myself?' Isn't that what you said? 'Just how am I going to sabotage myself?'

"These words sound much too uncivil. And by implication you are associating us with them, because this meeting, which we helped to set up for you, seems to be bringing them out from you. Is that the kind of world we represent to you, Joseph? Look at us, Joseph. Take a close look. Aren't we being civil with you? Aren't we trying to be understanding of you? Aren't we explaining things to you as best as we can?"

The fact that they weren't using profanities, as they often had with him, convinced Regalo, if he hadn't been convinced already, that this meeting was a set up and was secretly being taped. But he was sure that he hadn't given them anything that they could use. For all their talk about his sabotaging himself, it was they who introduced that notion, not he. He stood up straight and began walking to the door.

"See you in court, fellows. Thanks for nothing."

Just then Kacey spoke out to him softly. "Before you go, Joseph, I have something here which I'm sure will be of interest to you."

Kacey pulled out a memorandum from a folder on the table. "You're quite an expert with computers so you'll appreciate what we've done here. This is the electronic mail that you sent from your home computer in Angola to a retired colleague after you'd been reprimanded. Here is what you wrote.

"'I can't take seriously what they have done to me,' you stated. 'After all, consider who or what made that assessment of my performance. Supposedly the firm made it, but what is the firm? Certainly not its main building. There would still be a so-called firm if the people inside it moved to another building or even if they moved into a tent. So does that then mean the firm constitutes the people in the building or their employees in branches around the world? No, because they change every day, coming, staying for a while, and then going for good. With this ongoing flow of staff entering and leaving the so-called firm's ranks, which set of people is actually the firm? The set there now? The set that left? The set yet to come? Do you get it? There is no fixed set.

'Is the firm, then, its stated mission and regulations? How could that be? Those are abstract concepts that can't exist without people. There have to be individuals who implement them, but as I just noted, we can't define which ones comprise the firm. This means that the firm as something fixed, concrete, and real is nothing but an illusion. All we can say for certainty is that the staff with whom we are dealing at any moment can in some kind of temporary way be called the firm.

'A few of those people made a judgment about my performance, and they failed to fully consider motivations and circumstances. Why should I take that seriously, even if their judgment comes on the stationery of the firm with its official imprint? Imperial Rome had a seal once. What do its documents mean now? Nazi Germany had a seal once. What do its documents mean now? Do you see? In the end, the firm is a man-made illusion of no substance. The seal is the most superficial manifestation of this illusion. And those who judged me in the so-called firm are...'

"I won't read anymore, Joseph. I think we've made our point. You see, we found it odd that having written something like this, you would still want to correct the record about your performance. By your own words, this record doesn't mean anything."

"Were you drunk when you wrote this electronic mail?" Boward asked in a serious tone.

"Or were you drunk when you filed the lawsuit?" Kacey smirked. "But at bottom, there is something else you need to consider, Joseph. The real problem between us is that we never knew you and don't know you now. Oh, yes, we know how conflicted you are, but more fundamentally there is a way of thinking, of feeling, of seeing the world that is natural to us but unnatural to you. So quit clanging at the gate trying to get back in, do you hear? Pry your hands off of it and do it now! There was good reason to shut you out and now to keep you out.

"We're not comfortable with you and you're not comfortable with us. I don't know how you slipped in past the gate to mingle with us. The personnel department should have been able to smell the mangy dog that you are from the very start. In any event, it's too late for that now. You were so proud of never wagging your tail. Well, why don't you just tuck it between your legs and go home where you can lick your sores to your heart's content?"

His mocking eyes took in Regalo, not just knowingly but brazenly. Kacey then started singing in Italian, playing on their supposed common heritage.

"*O mio babbino caro*," Kacey sang in a mocking tone, beginning in Italian and switching to English. "You were always a fool, my dear sweet Joe, and you always will be."

By now Regalo felt the whole world closing in on him. And as his mind and senses worked feverishly to find a way out, he was catapulted back to that old, hated scene in Lebanon where another desperate man was also trapped. Tied up and facing execution from the barrel of the M-16, all that the Phalangist could do in the end was make a face. He could make a face too, and even snarl if he had to, but why leave it at that meaningless level? He might be trapped like the Phalangist, but at least he wasn't tied up like him. He would rise up to show them what he was made of!

His mind spinning with rage, Regalo lunged at Kacey, grabbed him by the collar, and threw him up against the wall. As he began to shake him, he glanced over at Boward, ready to let Kacey go to fight him off. But Boward was just standing passively with his arms folded, watching him rough up Kacey, who was offering no resistance. There was no expression on either of their faces.

Regalo caught himself and backed off. A shiver ran through him. His hands now felt cold. His scalp was tingling as the blood receded from his head and his heart slowed down. Feeling drained and empty, he rubbed his face with his two hands and looked listlessly ahead of him, barely aware of his surroundings, which suddenly seemed as strange as the memorandum they had just read back to him. He would never know how they had obtained it, nor how much of it was really his own. He had written something like that once. But whether it was word for word the same, he couldn't remember now.

Real or fake, it wasn't important any more, just as it finally didn't matter that the email he used to get this far was made up. What they read to him was close enough to his thoughts at the time, which he hadn't kept secret. They had succeeded in provoking him, and they had it all on tape. That was all that counted.

There was dead silence in the room as Regalo's two interlocutors continued to stand, fixated on his every movement and gesture. Without saying a word, Regalo turned and walked out of the room to the lobby and then out to the street where he kept on walking.

CHAPTER 18
A SAVING GRACE

❦

Just as Alain was beginning to catch his breath, he heard the door being kicked in behind him. He knew what that meant. They were still looking for him.

For a moment he thought that the pastor, seated to the side of the choir, would stop the service, but the singing continued as if nothing had happened. As the gang started down the aisle toward the pulpit, he heard a young man invite them to join in the praise and worship.

Laughing, they ignored the invitation and stormed to the front, where they stood four abreast and faced the congregation. As the pastor stood up and waved the choir to stop singing, the church became eerily quiet.

The shortest one of the four sneered, "The service is interrupted!"

The tallest one then yelled out, "Did anyone see a *mzungu* come in? He might have stopped here to rest. Speak up! Did anyone see him?"

Alain squirmed in the back row as he kept his blackened face at an angle to the front to keep the intruders from recognizing him.

"Speak up!" the tall one demanded again. "Did anyone see him?"

With no one answering, including the old woman sitting next to Alain, the pastor turned to the short intruder.

"You can see that no one has seen him," he said, calmly but resolutely. "Now you are welcome to join us. Otherwise, please go."

One of the other intruders caught the eye of the tall one. "Let's get out of this weird place. He's not here and we're losing time."

"You're right. He can't be hiding in here. Let's go."

After they were out the door, Alain looked over at the woman next to him to thank her. But she was already facing ahead joining the renewed singing. The light coming in from the windows on each side of the room illuminated every line and wrinkle in her face, and he wondered how old she was.

Whatever age she was, he could tell it didn't matter to her as she raised her arms and sang her song with all the feeling that was in her. To his weary eyes, which were now capable of seeing or not seeing almost anything, the entire group of worshippers seemed to be moving in sync right along with her. Waving their arms up and down in unison, their voices joined together in a cascade of alleluias that seemed to roll up the walls, to the uncovered rafters, and back down the walls again in a rhythm that kept perfect time with their swaying bodies. As tired as he was, it was still all he could do to keep from throwing his arms up in the air and begin moving to the rhythm of the singing himself.

When the hymn ended and the congregation sat down, he began taking a long series of deep breaths, exhaling slowly each time to recoup his energy. He then tried to catch the attention of the old woman next to him once again, whom he noticed was wearing a long yellow, cotton-print dress stamped with the images of different flowers. But looking more closely at some of the flowers, he could see that they were actually finely-shaped patches, in different colors, that she must have sewn onto the dress to cover up worn spots and tears. He was ready to feel sorry for her, but his feelings of gratitude were stronger.

He wanted to thank her for helping him, but before he could get the words out, she gave him a quick smile and turned away, pointing to the pastor who was beginning to address the congregation.

Alain smiled back, crouched down, and began hurrying to the door. But the booming voice of the preacher stopped him. He realized that it would be impolite to leave just as he was beginning his sermon. He couldn't appear to be ungrateful now.

Dressed in a flowing black robe, the preacher stood out against the dozen or so singers in their frocks, now seated behind him. For a moment, this tall, imposing man reminded Alain of the preacher he had seen earlier wielding the whip against the mob. Except now that he began to consider him more carefully, he realized to his astonishment that the preacher's face and hands were white, albino white! The intruders must have noticed too and decided they didn't want to stick around.

"Brothers and sisters," he beamed brightly. "I'm so glad that you are in high spirits today, because I'm going to raise them even higher."

As Alain watched the pastor, he saw the old woman from the corner of his left eye, beckoning to him with her hymn book to come back to the bench and sit next to her. He pretended he didn't see her, but he didn't leave either and remained standing in the back next to the door.

"Yes, I'm so glad that you are in high spirits today because I have a special word for you that will bring you even greater joy!"

"You always say that, pastor," a voice shot out from a bench somewhere in the middle.

"Praise the Lord that he does," rang another voice.

"Amen, amen, amen," went a round of voices.

"My dearly beloved, are you ready for today's word?"

"Yes, yes, yes!" cried the entire congregation, now rising to their feet and clapping their hands.

The preacher's hands reached over to the large, well-worn Bible on top of his podium and leafed through it until he found his reference. He then held the book up in both of his hands and began preaching from it in a booming voice.

"We have to go way back for today's word, all the way back to Genesis 25, for the story of the brothers Jacob and Esau. Since most of you should know that story, I'm going to ask you a few questions."

"Good, ask us!"

"Who was cooking a pot of stew one day?"

"It was Jacob, the son of Isaac."

"That's right, and who had just come in from the field tired and hungry?"

"His brother Esau!"

"Right again. Well, we know what happened after that, don't we? Esau sold him his birthright for some of that stew.

"We can see that was a very poor bargain. How can you sell your entire life's inheritance for one meager meal of a pot of stew? But do you know what? That story applies to us today as surely as it applied to Esau way back then. Each and every day we're faced with the temptation of squandering our birthright."

The preacher wiped the sweat off his brow.

"Now do you know what belongs to that birthright? I will bet some of you here don't even know."

"Tell us! Tell it to us!"

"All right! Let's turn to the first chapter of Genesis. It says here that we were created in God's image and were given dominion over all the earth.

"There it is, dearly beloved. Do you see it? It couldn't be any clearer, yet how often we miss it. Our birthright includes having dominion over the things of this world. But instead don't we sometimes act as if they have dominion over us?"

"Amen!"

"And every time we let that happen, we trade away our birthright for something as trivial as a pot of stew. In other words, we throw that birthright right back into the face of our creator."

"Yes, that's what we do! Amen! Amen! Amen!"

Alain almost felt like putting his hands over his ears, the shouting had become so loud.

"Is there anywhere in this blessed book where the Lord says these words don't apply to us in this part of the world?"

"No, no, no!"

"Are we going to take our rightful place at God's table, or are we going to beg for crumbs? Which one is it?"

"God's table!"

"I didn't hear you."

"God's table!" the congregation cried out even louder.

"No one can deny us our birthright!" the preacher thundered. No one! We can only deny it to ourselves. Did you hear me?"

"Yes, yes, yes!"

"It doesn't matter how poor our circumstances or how heavy our burden. I will say it again. No one can deny us our birthright. Not when we get up before dawn to go to jobs that blister our hands or break our backs; not when the noise and congestion of the city begin to pound our heads and frazzle our nerves; not when we are robbed; not when we are cheated; not when we are abused; not when our minds go blank from the monotony of our tasks; not when we can hardly stand up anymore from picking too much produce off the ground or carrying too many water jugs; and not even when we are so weary that we want to lie down, curl up into a ball, and roll away into the nearest pit.

"The prophet calls to us, 'Rise and shine for your light has come.' So lay down your burden today, dearly beloved, and lay it down every day as the evening sun sets. Then, when you pick it up again in the light of the morning sun, you won't be picking it up alone. There, beside you, the Lord will make a path through all the day's temptations and worries. Hold fast to that path, children. Don't lose sight of it. It's there for you and it's there for me. It's there for one and all."

By now the preacher had begun striding with long, powerful steps back and forth in front of the congregation, his robe unfurled, his hands punctuating the air for emphasis, and his brow shiny with sweat.

"Somebody help me! Somebody please help me! I'm a man of such poor words. But I proclaim it nonetheless!

"This path doesn't lead to the *changaa* house," he roared. "It doesn't lead to the whorehouse. And it doesn't lead to the house of stolen goods. It leads to glory! Did you hear me? It leads to glory! Winding surely through the cares and tribulations of this world, it is too narrow for the faithless but wide enough for those who seek the bright and morning star."

"Glory, glory, glory!" the congregation, now fully roused, shouted over and over in unison, with the clapping and singing reaching such deafening proportions that Alain thought the walls would burst.

"We are the children of the promise," the preacher continued, his voice ringing through the rafters. "So, let's deliver our message to all who have ears to hear. We may have to raise our voices to be heard above the din of the marketplace and public square. We may have to slap the hand back that would line our pockets with wrongly-begotten gain for a wrongly-begotten purpose. And we may have to slip the noose of hate that would strangle us. But do it we can, and do it we must."

As the preacher raised his arms to give the benediction, Alain darted out of the church and into the alley, his fatigue gone. The midday sun was scorching in its power, and he shielded his eyes as he looked ahead and all around him. There were no signs of Robidi's men, and he headed back in exactly the same direction from which he came.

CHAPTER 19
THE ALBINO

After the last worshipper left the hall, the preacher took the collection plate into the small office in the back. He set the plate with its coins and rumpled notes down on the desk in the corner while he hung up his robe on the hook on the backside of the door. He wished his wife had been with him to shake the hands of the worshippers as they filed out into the street after the service, but she had to stay home with their youngest child who had developed some kind of fever. She had it for several days now, and he was becoming more and more worried about her.

She was such a lively, happy girl, but lately she had been playing with some new friends, and nowadays one never knew what kind of sickness you could pick up from people. Perhaps it was from the water she drank at a neighbor's house. You had to be very careful with the water. Or maybe she ate something she shouldn't have. You had to be careful with food, too. But he wasn't going to take any chances. Tomorrow, for sure, he would take her to the national hospital so a doctor could see her.

He sat down on the folding chair next to the desk to begin counting the coins and the money with his gnarled hands, already touched by arthritis though he was only 41 years old. It wouldn't hurt these hands this afternoon, since there wasn't that much to handle. But it would have been better to have more pain if it meant more shilling notes in the offering. These were hard times, he knew, but he had hoped for a little more. There was just enough to pay the rent and provide for his salary for the week. And there was a small amount remaining for the emergency fund.

It was usually the treasurer that added up the money in his presence, reporting the total amount collected to him before the money was deposited in the bank. But the treasurer had contracted some kind of parasitical infection and dealing with the money now depended solely on him.

As he counted the money for the second time, he thought about how the service had gone. What about that handsome man in the back with the blue bandana? He had noticed him, all right, just as he was putting black on his face. If he hadn't seen him do that, he would have guessed that he was one of those black people from America that came to visit from time to time. He had also realized from the start that the stranger was in some kind of trouble from the way he went to the back after the service had begun and then tried to keep his face down. It wasn't his business as the pastor to wonder just what was wrong in the middle of a service, but the smell of trouble that he brought in with him was strong. And it became stronger still when those men came in looking for him. It was good that they missed him and didn't disrupt the service any more than they had.

But since the church had saved him, couldn't he have put something special into the plate? Well, maybe not. Maybe when you are on the run you don't have time to think about things like that. No, of course not. He would give him the benefit of the doubt. Maybe he would come back later to show his appreciation. One more thing to pray about. One more thing to add to a list that he could hardly keep track of any more.

He couldn't help but note the way the stranger looked at him when he did lift his head. And he did it more than once, staring even. "He hadn't missed my appearance, had he?" the preacher mused, as he stretched his hands before him to consider their harsh white pigment. He saw me for the albino that I am. How strange that he was putting on the very same color I wish I had for my own skin.

After he finished counting, the preacher stood up and went to the bathroom to wash his hands, catching a look at his face in the mirror above the basin. There was no getting around it. Anyone could see, even if they were half-blind, that his face was white, albino white to be sure, but white nonetheless. His congregation seemed to have gotten used to it, since they knew he was just like them except for this different pigment he was born with. Yet strangers were always taken aback. How could a preacher be an albino? Most of them didn't know that he wasn't the only albino around and that there were several thousand of them in East Africa. Even so, he knew it struck people as odd that an albino could be found in the pulpit of an African church. In fact, it struck him as odd from time to time as well.

How much easier his life would have been if he had the same blackness as that stranger sitting in the back appeared to have with his darkened face. But that wasn't his genetic draw, and he had to accept it and make the best of it. It hadn't stopped him from responding to the call he felt as a young man to preach the word, and it hadn't stopped him from going to Bible college and gradually building up this small congregation. When he had first felt the call years ago, he had wondered about it for months before yielding to it. Why him? Why an albino in a country where almost everybody was black? What would people think? But the call wouldn't go away, and it was only after he had yielded to it that he felt any peace. Then, when anyone asked him how he could be certain he was called, he always answered in the same way. That he knew it from the heart. That is what he said, and few ever asked him about it again.

In fact, nobody who knew him seemed to care about the color of his skin. It was only when he encountered strangers or stepped out onto the street that he received stares, with some people gawking, pointing, and even jeering.

It was worse now that witch doctors in Tanzania were paying nice sums of money for the body parts of albinos, which were supposed to have some kind of magical powers to attract riches and success. A fully dismembered body – with all the parts, including limbs, ears, nose, and tongue – could fetch over three million shillings. As a result, he knew that he had to be especially careful these days with whomever he met. But that wasn't going to stop him from doing his pastoral duties. His calling ruled out cowardice of any kind right from the beginning, and there was no getting around it.

He hadn't felt the least fear when those four men had stormed the service, and he considered the sermon he had preached one of his best. The congregation might have been distracted for a short while. But before long the worship service had taken on a momentum of its own, a power that carried them along on wave after wave of joyful noise, which he knew owed as much to their enthusiastic singing and clapping as it did to his spoken word. These were special moments when they all felt as one in the Lord's presence. And it was these moments that could carry him through a whole week's worth of travail that was sure to come, whether it was dealing with sickness or death, of which there was too much, or with the church's finances, of which there was too little.

He returned to the desk and put the money into a large manila envelope that the treasurer kept in one of the drawers and closed it. He then put it into a canvas tote bag, which he would take home until he could go to the bank tomorrow. The plainer the bag, the less chance someone would try to steal it from him on the bus.

The knock on the door startled him. Everyone had gone, so who could it be?

"Papa, it's me, Sheba," his eldest daughter answered through the door.

He rose quickly to let her in. "What is it, Sheba?" he asked, taking her hands in his and bringing a chair for her to sit down while he stood before her. "I thought you were going home to be with your mother," he said, as he noted how her fine black hands contrasted with his pale ones.

"I was, dear papa, but I am so worried about this upcoming semester at my school. You know how expensive the school fees are, and I didn't want mama to see how worried I was. I thought maybe we could talk about it further. Remember, you said that before Christmas comes, you would have enough saved to pay the fees so that I could continue with my studies there. Time is passing, dear papa. Will we have the money? And if we won't have it, what are we going to do?"

The preacher looked at the tote bag on the desk. He had taken the shillings due him, but there were a few thousand more shillings in it, shillings that belonged to the church, not only for rent, but also for emergencies. For the briefest of moments he wondered whether the need of his daughter could qualify as an emergency, and just as quickly, he dismissed the thought.

But then another thought came. Who would find out anyway that he borrowed two or three thousand shillings to help pay for her education? This could be a private transaction between him and the collection plate. No one would need to know, and God would be his witness that he would gradually pay it back with little additions to the collection plate in the coming months. What would be wrong with that? Surely that would not be stealing, just a little borrowing with his promise to the Lord that he would eventually pay.

"What are you thinking, papa? You're not talking at all, just standing there like a statue. Please tell me." Her big, brown eyes looked at him almost plaintively, not knowing if she should feel encouraged by the care her father seemed to be taking in thinking over the matter, or discouraged by the pained look on his face.

"You will have the money, Sheba. I will find a way. Now please go home and help your mother prepare the evening dinner."

"As you say, papa. A fine dinner of chicken with the sauce and rice that you like will be waiting for you. Goodbye, papa."

The thought of the dinner waiting for him made him feel a little better, and he opened the tote bag and began counting the money in the manila envelope again for the third time, running the shilling notes through his hands until they floated down onto the desk in a scattered pile. Should he or shouldn't he? He slowly gathered up all the coins and notes, studying each one as he put them back into the envelope. No, it wouldn't be right to borrow from here without telling anyone, even if he would pay it back in secret. Stealing was stealing, and he put the envelope back into the bag and closed it.

But after a few minutes of wringing his hands, he took the manila envelope out of the bag again, telling himself he needed to count the money for a fourth time just to be sure his tally was correct. As he counted, he kept asking himself what he could do for his daughter. Couldn't he borrow from the collection plate just once? His pale hands tightened around one of the bills. Just once! Why not just once? It would only be borrowing, and it would only be between him and the Lord, who knew his heart.

But his hand slowly opened and let the crumpled bill fall back onto the desk, where he smoothed it out with his two thumbs. No, he just couldn't do it.

What then about selling one's possessions? There was that big demand in neighboring Tanzania among the witch doctors for albino body parts. They were paying well, very well for every major part. At his age, was one leg or one arm that important to him any longer? Maybe the white color of his skin was actually a blessing by which he could help his daughter.

After all, it wouldn't be that much of an ordeal to do what had to be done. Sure, there would be pain and a time of adjustment, but he was of a strong constitution and he could find the right sort of doctor who would do it for a small percentage of what he would get. Hadn't all the suffering he had seen and experienced already inured him to it? Wasn't it time to squeeze some worldly value out of a worldly curse?

He studied the pictures of black-faced President Moi on the shilling notes spread out before him. Moi couldn't have achieved what he did had he looked albino. Moi's blessing was as undeserved as his own albinic curse. Did that make him less than Moi? Of course not. No more than it made Moi less than him.

But if that were the case, why would his body parts fetch such a high price in sorcerers' dens, while those the color of Moi's were in no demand at all?

He got up and went to the mirror, and after staring at the pale face staring back at him, he could contain himself no longer. Suddenly, he took his fist and smashed the mirror, sending bloody, broken pieces of glass into the washbasin below. Startled by the depth of his own anger, he instinctively touched his face everywhere to see if any shards of glass had flown close to his eyes.

Finding none, he turned to a large piece of glass in the mirror that hadn't been knocked out for a better look. But as he began to inspect his face, a face that was now covered with the smears of blood that his injured hand had left, a strange calm came over him. For it was no longer just his own blood-stained face looking back at him. There seemed to be another bloodied face there looking at him too, only with eyes of such compassion that they pierced straight through him until he was burning in his breast.

Was he seeing things? Was he feeling things? If not his eyes, then whose were they? He went back to his desk to sit down for a moment and collect himself. No, he knew whose eyes they were, and he felt ashamed, very ashamed.

Holding his head in his hands, he began to consider anew the thought that had kept clamoring for his attention after he had seen that white stranger blacken his face with such good effect. Why not do the same thing, the thought had insisted. And each time after he had brushed it off, it had come back even more insistently. Why not? It wouldn't be that inconvenient to rub some black stuff on his face and hands every morning and then wash it off at night. Then there would be no more stares, no more gawkers, no more worries about being kidnapped and sent cut up in a body bag to witch doctors somewhere.

But the thought had lost its power since he had looked in the mirror. He couldn't conjure it up even if he wanted to. It had slipped out through the backdoor of his mind, and he was certain it would never come back again. Even so, he was thankful the stranger had come to the worship service. Now he knew that he could have gotten out of his white face if he ever really needed to.

He stood up and put all the bills and coins back into the manila envelope, making sure it was sealed tight before he put it into his tote bag and headed to the door. The counting was over, the school fees would need more prayer, and it was time to go home.

CHAPTER 20
QUESTIONS

෨

Late the next afternoon, Alain flagged down a cab and gave the driver the address of Haran's office on Biashara Street. As he sat in the back of the cab, he began thinking. Though his anger at the beating he received from Robidi and his thugs had abated somewhat, he was still perplexed as to how Robidi had found him.

Haran opened the door, startled to see it was Alain who had been knocking insistently. Haran quickly let him into his office.

"Alain? What happened to you? You don't look very pretty with your swollen eyes and bruised mouth."

As Alain sunk into the chair next to Haran's desk, dropping his head into his hands for support, the realization sank in that he could thank his black face in the church for keeping Robidi's boys from noticing that too.

"So tell me what happened," Haran pressed, as he sat down behind his desk.

"I don't want to talk about it just yet. I want to know, first, if the money I gave you did any good."

"It worked like magic," Haran beamed. "We've got some information now that we can work with. I didn't expect to see you this soon, but now that you're here, I'll tell you what we found out. It will make you feel better. Then I want to hear your story."

"Just bring me up to date. Don't worry about how bad I look or how tired I sound."

"Wangetha is still alive, and I have the street address where she's being held. In fact, I know that house. I've seen it before."

"Bingo! That's more than I dared expect, on both counts. But are you certain about this? I'm not going to ask how you did it or who your sources were. I don't need to know and I don't want to know. Just tell me that you are sure."

"You always have to wonder in these parts. But in this case, I have a well connected cousin who actually checked things out."

"That's impressive work, Haran," Alain said wearily. "I can see that you were worth every shilling. I know that I should be enthusiastic about this news, but the truth is I feel pretty dejected right now. I've been sifted pretty good, to the point where I don't know any longer what I'm doing here with you, much less here on this continent."

"All right, Alain, get it out."

"You won't believe what I've been through."

"Let me guess. You had a falling out with someone from your community."

"I know you're being facetious. Journalists don't usually beat each other half to death."

"No, but when you *wazungu* have issues, regardless of your communities, settling them with fists is not that uncommon. Or have I watched too many action films from abroad?"

Alain tried to smile with his bruised mouth. "I had a falling out, all right, but it wasn't with a colleague. It was with a guy named Robidi."

"Not Robidi Amimuga."

"None other than the high commissioner of Zimugabwa himself. His bodyguards did one good number on me. The only reason they didn't mess me up any worse or kill me is because they don't know where Wangetha is and need me to lead them to her. But I got lucky and managed to shake them."

"I'm sorry Robidi got a hold of you, Alain," Haran sympathized.

"Somebody must have tipped him off to my whereabouts," Alain said, directing his gaze away from the floor to Haran. "I haven't been able to figure out who could have done it. It's a puzzle to me."

Haran listened quietly.

"What is it about your continent, Haran?" Alain continued. "Who are you people? What are you people?"

"So you're equating me with Robidi now, is that it?"

"No, no, Haran, of course not. But I've had it now with this region."

"Does that include Wangetha?"

"I don't know whom it includes or excludes right now. All I know is that I'm beat, Haran. You can take it from here, alone. You have all the right connections. You don't need me. She's your blood. You do it. You go get her."

"It won't be the same without you, Alain."

"What do you mean, 'It won't be the same?'"

"As her brother I want nothing more than to free her, but you add a quality of emotion to our venture that only a lover can."

Alain lifted his head up from his lap. "It doesn't matter right now. I can't go on."

"You're always going to hate yourself if you quit now, and I'm speaking to you as one man to another. You'll never know what it is to experience her love."

"She should see me now, tired, broken, trampled upon by her own people."

"Stop it, Alain. You're lumping the good and the bad together. Robidi and his goons don't speak for all of us. Only bigots could think that way, and you're not one of them."

Alain caught himself. "I'm sorry. Of course, you're right. I just can't think straight right now. You know there are times that I'm even suspicious of you. I still don't know who could have tipped off Robidi that I was staying at the Ngong Hills Lodge. There were only two people who knew that I was there – Regalo, and my housekeeper, Rebecca.

"So, let's think this thing through, Haran," Alain continued. "Regalo had no reason that I can think of to tip Robidi, because he has nothing but contempt for him. That leaves Rebecca. Robidi must have learned my whereabouts from her."

"You're the one saying that, Alain, not me. But in her defense, have you ever thought about the kind of pressures people like her deal with day in day out?"

"By now I think that I have heard enough about their daily grind. I pay Rebecca better than the going rate."

"She's no doubt supporting several people with the money she gets from you. What if Robidi's people offered her a lot of money just to share what seemed to her an innocent piece of information? How much of your dilemma had you explained to her? Very little, if any, I'll bet. And what if they claimed they needed to locate you because they had a news tip? What if they said that they knew you were working on an important story and were looking for just this information?"

"She should have known something was not right when they offered her money."

"But what if they told her the money was in appreciation for her helping them, and she was to use it to help her own family?"

"Then why didn't she call me first?"

"What if she was afraid to, because you had told her that she shouldn't talk to anyone about where you were? What if she was afraid you would misconstrue her contact with these people?"

"She had no reason to be afraid of me."

"Maybe not, yet. But do you know how hard it is for people like her to get a job working for Europeans? She sees things a little different than someone like you."

"So, she should have been that much more careful."

"Ah, yes, but what if she really wanted to be of help and steer you the information that you needed to make your story a success?"

"She had her instructions. It's not for her to decide what I need or don't need."

Alain fixed his gaze on Haran. "By the way, did Regalo ever mention my whereabouts to you? Did he tell you that I would be staying at the Ngong Hills Lodge?"

"No, why would he?"

"I don't know. Just wondering."

"I didn't appreciate that question," Haran responded with some irritation.

"I'm sorry, Haran. I didn't mean anything by it."

"Let's re-focus on what's important, Alain. I'm only asking you not to give up on Wangetha."

"Wait a minute. Now that I think about it, there was one more person who knew where I was staying."

"Who?"

"A former girl friend from Europe who came here to Nairobi and managed to find me somehow. As she explained it to me, when Rebecca told her over the phone that I wasn't in town, she assumed that I was around the country somewhere covering a story. Believe it or not, she called one hotel in Kenya after the other, giving my description until she connected with the Ngong Hills Lodge."

"What happened after she found you?"

"I sent her away. Whatever there had been between us was over. She took a flight back to Geneva."

"Now then," Alain continued, "if she had to call all these hotels looking for me, it means Rebecca didn't give away my whereabouts to her."

"No, not to her," Haran said. "But I go back to what I said about Rebecca earlier. What if she thought she was actually trying to help you by divulging some information to Robidi's people?"

"As I said, she had her instructions. It wasn't for her to decide what I needed or didn't need."

"And you've never acted on someone else's behalf without their knowing about it?" Haran's voice was rising. "Is it because you think an African housekeeper isn't capable of thinking of her employer in anything but selfish, materialistic terms?"

Haran left his chair and walked to the window to peer out through one of the cracked panes. Turning around to face Alain again, he pleaded. "Please, let me say it again, don't give up on Wangetha, for your own sake as much as hers."

"Here we go again. You're actually thinking about what is good for me. But what if I get killed in the process of helping to free Wangetha?"

Haran glared at Alain. "Have you forgotten that we are in this together now? Do you suppose that there is any less risk for me? My blackness doesn't exactly make me immune from being tracked down and hacked to death on this continent. Yes, I know, we have all heard the garbage spewing out of the mouth of the likes of Robidi about how much he respects his own kind. But do you know what the color of his own kind really is, Alain? It's not the color of Wangetha, or me, or the laborers on his grounds, as some would think. It's not even a human color. It's the color of whatever money he has crammed into his pockets at the moment. And the easier it is to get, whether you have had to rob your so-called own kind to get it or strip your country bare of the last resources it has, the sweeter it is because there is more time to eat and eat well."

As Haran stood in front of the window, the sound of the traffic of Biashara Street was audible in the background.

"Do you really think that he cares about the day-to-day lives of the people he represents? How can he, when he is too worried that he will wind up exactly like them?"

Haran pointed to the people on the sidewalk below. "There are millions upon millions of them in this continent living on less than a dollar a day, going home tonight to the slums where their huts are patched together from rusty tin and scraps of wood and plastic, with fraying gunny sacks for doors and windows. Robidi's type spends his days running, constantly looking over his shoulder to see if this beggar army is gaining on him. But he can never feel safe from them, even within the walls of lavish estates built to keep them at arm's length. And do you know why? It's because he knows too well that their discontent can grow out of control and bring these walls tumbling down."

"It sounds as though you know Robidi well, Haran. Have you ever met him personally?"

"What do you mean?"

"You know, talked to him at some social occasion?"

"No. I've never done that."

Alain looked up at the ceiling. "What are we going to do, Haran? Where do we go from here?"

"We're going to find her together."

"So, you are committed to helping Wangetha, and you want to prove yourself to her. That's very commendable."

"You give me no choice but to get more involved, now that I see what you've gone through. Sleep here on the floor tonight. There's a blanket over there in the sack in the corner. It won't be the most comfortable way to sleep, but it's not safe for you to go out onto the street right now. Let's talk some more tomorrow morning. I'm going home for the night. Here's the key to the office. Lock it from the inside after I leave. There's a washroom down the corridor. I'll have some sandwiches sent up."

"When will I see you tomorrow?"

"Later in the morning, right here, after I visit one of my clients being held in Athi River Prison in the city."

"Can't it wait?"

"I wish it could, but he's HIV-positive and not being treated very well. I promised I would bring his case to the attention of the higher-ups in the prison tomorrow, and I'm going to follow through on that promise. But as soon as I get back to the office, we'll figure out what to do next. Until tomorrow, Alain."

"Right, Haran."

CHAPTER 21
FLIGHT TO NOWHERE

∽

Rachel was tense. It was well past time for her to leave, and there were no more buses at this hour. Regalo would typically let her depart by 7:00 p.m. after first serving him dinner and giving him his evening massage. But now it was already 7:30 p.m. and he hadn't yet arrived or called.

She knew that she didn't have to wait if she didn't want to. Regalo had told her more than once that if he wasn't home by 7:00 p.m. she could go. Still, there had been a time when something deep inside her had told her to stay, just like now. She had curled up on the sofa and fallen asleep when she was abruptly wakened by the commotion of him staggering through the front door reeking of gin.

She had helped him to the sofa and taken him into her arms as he fell asleep on her lap, gradually extricating herself to cover him with a blanket. She had then set a pitcher of water on the coffee table next to the sofa and had gone out to the street to walk the two to three kilometers to the nearest taxi stand. At this hour there was no bus heading to the far corner of the city where she lived.

Paying for the taxi was a severe strain on the monthly salary of 7,500 shillings that Regalo gave her. She knew that it was a good amount by Kenyan standards, but it still barely covered the cost of sustaining her and her old parents, both of whom could no longer work and depended on her to take care of them.

But Regalo had remembered the following day that she had worked past her normal hours and would have had to take a taxi to get home. He had given her a 1,000-shilling note then, almost twice what the taxi fare actually cost, and she accepted it gratefully. Even so, he never said anything about his condition and she never brought it up either.

She was puzzled about the protective feelings that welled up in her when she first saw him walk unsteadily through the front door. He seemed then to be such a contrast to the strong, assertive man who spoke on the phone to the people calling him, providing information and counsel with such authority. This was the man that always walked tall and straight on the occasions she saw him in public. He always seemed to know exactly where he wanted to go, what he wanted to do, and what he wanted to say.

What was it about this *mzungu* that affected her so deeply, she wondered? She was not one to think about the reasons for her feelings, but she knew that she didn't see him as the average white man. She had worked for other families and had met a number of other American and European men, including those she briefly encountered at some social events where she was serving appetizers and drinks. But she had never before met a man of such fearlessness as Regalo.

If there was one thing that she had learned to do in the hard urban world of Nairobi, it was to smell fear, because fear all too often preceded aggression. She had never forgotten what she had seen in a man's eyes when she was once attacked on a side street in Nairobi. In broad daylight he tried to drag her to a nearby automobile while groping her body. She had managed to escape his grasp, but had never forgotten the wild look of excitement on his face, combined with the strangest traces of fear. She still shuddered every time she thought about this evil look.

When Regalo first interviewed her after she had responded to his newspaper ad, she immediately sensed the total absence of fear in the man. And she felt completely safe around him ever since.

He was also unlike some of the other men she had worked for, including men with wives and families, in that he never made any advances toward her. This is what surprised her the most. She had long ago resigned herself to the possibility that she might have to hand over her body to the men in the households willing to hire her as a housekeeper.

But even when Regalo had been drinking, he wouldn't approach her and touch her. She thought that maybe during one of the back massages she gave him every evening he would try something, but he never did. She wondered if he would ever remove more of his clothes before the massage than just his shirt and undershirt. But he never did.

There was a time, however, when she had noticed him eyeing her as she came out of the bathroom of her quarters next to the kitchen, wrapped carelessly in a skimpy towel that showed some of her breasts. He had stared at her intently then and she still remembered how flushed her face had become and the tingling that went through her body. No man, white or black, had ever looked at her that way before. It was as if he had the ability to see right into her very being, right into her womanly soul. It was not the hungry expression of lust, such as seen in the eyes of men in the bars of Nairobi's outskirts. It was the look of a man sure of himself, showing a strong but controlled desire for her. She liked that look. She liked it very much. But she never saw it again.

Once, while she was waiting for Regalo to come home from work, having already finished her chores and prepared his dinner, she felt the urge to articulate the feelings that had been growing inside her. She picked up a scrap of paper and started writing. The words flowed from her, and as simple as they were, they expressed what was in her heart. She then carefully folded the paper and tucked it away under a vase of flowers.

The walk of a bold man is sweet to my sight.
Unbroken by the weight of the day,
Unafraid of the terrors of the night,
He gives me the courage to love.

The gaze of an upright man lifts my spirit.
There are no lies or deceit in him,
His words are sincere,
He gives me the hope to love.

The touch of a kind man warms my heart.
His hands are gentle,
They are never rough,
He gives me the desire to love.

My man walks tall among men.
He speaks clearly and truly,
He makes his way to me softly,
And finds my love waiting and glowing in the sun.

She knew that she should have torn it up and thrown it away instead of placing it under the vase in the living room. But she also knew that in her heart of hearts she was hoping that he would one day find it.

The heavy clanging of the gate outside meant that he was here. Any moment now he would be at the door and would let himself in. He would have no reason to think she was here, so she just waited until he came in.

She was shocked by what she saw. Reeking of gin once again, he staggered in through the door.

"Why are you here?" Regalo asked gruffly.

"Because I thought you might need me," answered Rachel, guiding him slowly to the couch.

"How nice," Regalo sneered. "If you think that you're going to get any taxi money from me, think again. That's a cute trick of yours to get more moolah out of me."

Rachel grimaced. He had never spoken to her in such an angry tone before. She felt that there was something wrong tonight in a way that had not been wrong before.

Choosing to ignore his harsh words, she went to the kitchen and brought back a pitcher of cold water and a glass, which she filled for him. After he gulped down a few swallows, he rose from the sofa and stood in front of the large patio-door windows of the living room, staring out into the night.

"They got me, Rachel. They trapped me in my own hate and ambition. They made a fool of me," he cried as he spun around to glare at her face.

Startled, she knew she should be feeling fear, but even now she felt safe with him. Somehow, deep within, she knew that this man, who now seemed so angry and upset, would never strike her.

She didn't have any idea who the "they" were. All she knew was that a man as strong in his mind and will as Regalo would have to have enemies.

"No one could make a fool of you, sir," she whispered. "I could never believe that about you."

Regalo glared at her again. "You're right. I correct myself. I made a fool of myself. I defeated myself. Now go home. I don't need you tonight."

"Can't I do anything for you, sir? Maybe a massage," she offered, haltingly. Somehow she wanted to comfort him, but she didn't know how, given her shyness and the barrier of his consuming anger.

"No, nothing," he barked. "Now go home. That's an order. And you don't have to come to work all week. I won't be here. But don't worry. You'll still be paid."

Rachel knew from one of his previous disappearances what that meant.

"So you're going to Mombasa again, sir?"

"Yes, and you know where. It's the same place. They know me there and you have the number. Call me only in case of an emergency. I don't want to be disturbed under any other circumstances. Is that clear?"

"Yes, I understand, sir. Is it all right if I still come to the house every day so that I can catch up on some cleaning? I have so many things to do."

"If you want to. It's up to you."

Regalo became silent and walked slowly back to the couch and lay down. She watched him as he fell asleep, suddenly so quiet, suddenly so innocent. She ran into the bedroom and brought back a blanket, which she placed over him, and a pillow, which she gently put under his head. She set the volume on his stereo system to low and inserted one of his favorite cassettes. Then she took her plastic bag of leftover food to take home and slipped out of the house. It would take her close to an hour to walk the long distance to find a taxi. It was dark and it was late, but she didn't care.

The night felt cool on her cheeks as she stepped out onto the street. The street lamps were not working again, but somehow she did not feel alone as she followed the lights in the houses along the way to guide her to the main road. She knew that there were families finishing their dinners and enjoying the evening time together in those homes. The distance to the taxi stand did not seem so long now, and the time went by quickly.

CHAPTER 22
A PLAN UNFOLDS

∾

When Haran returned to the office mid-morning the following day, he found Alain sitting at his desk writing something by hand. Haran sat down in the chair across from him.

"You look a lot better, Alain. I can see that you got some sleep, even if it was on the floor. How's the mouth?"

"Much better, I suppose. May I use the phone? I need to call Rebecca. By now the kidnappers should have left some kind of message about how to pay the ransom."

"Sure, go ahead. Make your call. And help yourself to the pen and paper there," Haran said with a smile, noting that Alain had already done so.

"Thanks," Alain said in a serious tone, his attention focused on the old-fashioned British phone, as he dialed his home number.

Alain gestured toward the phone to indicate to Haran that she was on. "Hello, Rebecca. How are you? Good...I'm glad to hear that. Has anyone called for me or left a message?"

"Yes, I know about that woman looking for me. Anyone else?"

Alain listened intently before answering again, his voice urgent.

"Just a moment, Rebecca. A little slower, please. I need to write this down.

"A man's voice, you say. He said that I would know what this was about. I have to bring the package with me to the main entrance of the Sarit Centre. I should just stand and wait there. He would find me. Friday at 3:00 p.m.

"Don't be worried, Rebecca. It's going to turn out all right.

"What? He was asking questions about me? What kind of questions? About my personal life, whether I was married and so forth? And how did you answer?

"Don't be afraid to tell me. You didn't do anything wrong. You had to say something. It's all right. Just tell me exactly what you told him."

Alain listened carefully. "That was fine, Rebecca. If you just said that I was here from France for business and pleasure and you didn't think that I was married...

"No, you didn't cause me any problems. I hope to see you in a few days. If someone calls me again, just do what you did this time. Write down all the information that you receive and wait for me to call you.

"No. I don't know yet when I'll be back. I hope not too long. You didn't tell anyone that I was at the Ngong Hills Lodge, did you?

"Good, that's very good. Just so you know, I'm not there any longer. I'll tell you later where I am. Adieu for now, Rebecca. Take care of yourself."

Alain turned toward Haran. "Well, there it is. Rebecca said that she didn't tell anyone where I was staying. I can't believe that she was lying to me just now."

"So, then you are saying it was Regalo who revealed your whereabouts, is that it?"

"No, I'm not saying that either, Haran."

"Well, you can't have it both ways, you know. It had to be one or the other."

"All I know is that I don't believe that Regalo did it either. But I'm not going to worry about it now. Let's talk about something more important. As you heard, the kidnappers left me a message. I have to deliver the ransom by Friday afternoon, exactly three days from now. They didn't have to remind me that Wangetha would be killed if they don't get it at the designated time and place."

"We just have to hope, and hope very hard, that they haven't killed her already," Haran said.

"Without that hope there's no point in dealing with them, is there?" Alain responded.

"No. No point at all."

"One thing's for sure. They're not worried about my going to the police. If they were, they wouldn't have picked such a well-known place for the drop-off point, the busiest shopping center in East Africa."

"Maybe, maybe not," Haran said. "The fact is that any drop-off point could be monitored by the police, and they have to be aware of that. For all we know, this little scenario at the Sarit Centre will just be a test to see if you, or anyone who looks suspicious to them, shows up.

"But if it's the real deal," Haran continued, "they couldn't have picked a better place. With all the people going in and out you won't have the faintest idea which one of them is your contact until he approaches you. They will be watching all the time from a safe distance. When they think things look right, one of them will grab the package out of your hand, probably wearing some kind of disguise. It will happen fast. You won't be able to identify him. It's a good ploy on their part."

"I should do just fine then, don't you think? Just look at all the experience I have in being followed," Alain chuckled.

"Don't you think that it's odd that they've waited six days to contact you since dumping you on the road?"

"Wait a second. How did you know that I was dumped on the road?"

"What's wrong with you, Alain?" Haran shot back. "Don't you remember telling me that earlier, when you first came by to see me?"

Alain waited before answering. "All right, all right, Haran. I take the point. I just wonder why the kidnappers didn't tell me where to deliver the money right from the beginning."

"It must be just as Regalo had it figured, Alain. They pulled off the kidnapping on their own as a spontaneous double-cross of the high commissioner who had hired them to put away Wangetha for good. So they wouldn't have thought things through completely. They may also be fighting among themselves about who is calling the shots, how to divide up the money, things like that."

"That sounds plausible enough. But how about all the time they are giving me? I know I insisted on it, but they went along with it. Why would they be giving me leeway which I could use to work with the police to find them?"

"Are you kidding me, Alain?" Haran responded. "You know the answer as well as I do. They want the money so badly that they don't want to force the situation and risk your coming up empty-handed. They're not that stupid. They know that most people, you foreigners included, can't come up with that much ransom money overnight.

"We just can't forget how badly they want money, Alain, and a lot of it. Kidnapping Wangetha was the means to get it through you. There is nothing for them to gain in killing her now. Yes, they know they're giving you an opening. But they're betting you don't take it. They know that if you were to go to the police to push for a rescue attempt, you would risk getting Wangetha killed in the process."

"That's pretty good, Haran. That's awfully good. You certainly know your people, don't you?" Alain's voice was tinged with a hint of sarcasm.

"Please don't be like that, Alain. It's important to be realistic at a time like this. She's still alive and we know where she's being held. All we need is a plan to rescue her."

"I didn't press you yesterday as to how you found out the location of the safehouse. But I'd be more interested in knowing now," Alain asked Haran. "How did you do it?"

"The way information often gets passed around here, from the relative of a friend to another friend, to another relative and so on. Our money greased the grapevine pretty good and led us to someone who lives near the safehouse and knows the people living in it."

"Did anyone actually go into the safehouse and talk to Wangetha?" Alain asked.

"What is this all about, Alain? Don't you believe that I have the address? Do you think I just took your money to mislead you?"

"No, no, of course not," Alain rejoined quickly.

"My cousin also saw a guy with dreadlocks standing guard in front of the house and the Peugeot in the backyard where you couldn't see it from the street."

"How did you know it was the right Peugeot?"

"Regalo told me what the car looked like. He said it was white with a brown, right fender that had been replaced and hadn't yet been painted to match the rest of the car. There can't be too many Peugeots like that in Nairobi. Hey, why the third degree? Isn't that what you told Regalo?"

"More or less. It's nothing, Haran," Alain said as his voice brightened a little. "I just wanted to be sure that it was the right address."

"Trust me. It is."

"Well, now we're presented with the dilemma that we always knew we'd have to face once we were sure that she was alive. If we give them the ransom money, they will probably still go ahead and kill her. After all, they'd be getting rid of a witness who saw their faces."

"Assuming that they didn't continue wearing their hats and sunglasses after they nabbed her. That's just enough of a disguise to keep from making a clean identification."

"Right. But your cousin didn't say the guard he saw out-side the safehouse was wearing either one."

"He didn't say he wasn't wearing a hat or sunglasses ei-ther. I didn't ask him. I could call him. There is more that he told me, how the house looked and who he thinks are inside, besides the kidnappers and Wangetha."

"No, don't call him. It doesn't matter now."

"You're right, it doesn't. Sunglasses or no sunglasses, hat or no hat, their chances of getting caught go way down if they kill her after getting the ransom. We need to come up with our own plan of action, and we need to come up with it pretty damn quickly."

"Any ideas?" Alain asked.

"There is only one person I'm familiar with in all of Kenya that would know how to get Wangetha out of this mess with-out getting her killed in the process."

"Wait, let me guess. Not Regalo by any chance?"

"Who else has had his kind of training and experience in dealing with violent characters?" Haran said matter-of-factly.

"But from what I have heard he can be pretty violent him-self," Alain responded. "Do we want to take a chance on get-ting him involved in this any further? So far, he's only been on the margins. And why would he agree to get involved anyway? What's in it for him?"

"Maybe adventure, setting a wrong right, the thrill of life-and-death stakes," Haran speculated. "The truth is I don't really know. But there has to be a way to convince him to help us."

"Let's just call him and lay out our case. It's worth a try. Of course, we could always go to the police with the informa-tion we now have and not appeal to Regalo. But let's face it. Can you imagine that Wangetha would not be caught in the firefight when they charged the safehouse. What do you often see when the police go after carjackers in Nairobi? I'll tell you. Blazing shootouts and dead bodies sprawled on the street. That's what you see..."

"I know, Alain," Haran interrupted. "You don't have to convince me. With Regalo, our chances of getting her out alive would be much better."

"Time is short. Who's going to call Regalo?"

"I will," responded Haran. "I know him better than you do. I'll call him at his office now."

Haran reached across the desk to pick up his phone and dialed.

"No one answered," Haran said as he then began dialing Regalo's home number.

"Hello, this is Haran Nakaya. May I please speak to Joseph Regalo?"

"He's not here. Who are you? I don't recognize your name," Rachel answered warily.

"I'm a friend of his. What's your name?"

"I'm Rachel, but I don't know you."

"Miss Rachel, please listen to me. It's very important that I speak to Mr. Regalo. It's a matter of life and death."

"Whose life or death, sir? Is it Joseph's?" Haran was a little surprised to hear her refer to Regalo so personally. Most housekeepers in Kenya would never refer to their employers in that way to strangers.

"Well, since you ask, Miss Rachel, there is a life that is in danger. The life of an innocent Kenyan woman. He could help us save her."

"What kind of danger?" she asked, becoming concerned.

"Unfortunately, I can't give you all the details over the telephone. But I can tell you that he knows her. Please, let me speak to him."

"He's not here."

"When is he coming home?"

"I don't know."

"But surely you know where he is?"

"I cannot tell you."

Haran covered the phone's mouthpiece with his hand and looked at Alain. "He's not there and she won't tell me where he is."

"You've got to think of something. Find a way to win her trust."

"All right. I'll try."

"Miss Rachel. As I said, this is a matter of life and death. I hesitate to tell you this, but it involves someone you probably know."

"Someone I know? Who?"

"Let me explain. The person whose life is in danger is a woman named Wangetha Wachira."

"Who?"

"Wangetha Wachira. Don't you recognize that name?"

"I think that I might have seen or heard it somewhere."

"Do you follow the news?"

"Yes, every day in the *Taifa Leo* newspaper. Why?"

"She gave an interview in Swahili about the investments that an American corporation was making here."

"Oh, you mean that Wangetha Wachira? I think I saw a photo of her. She is beautiful and well-spoken, isn't she?"

"Yes, that's Wangetha Wachira."

"She must have many admirers and friends. What could she have done to put herself in such danger?"

"Listen to me, Miss Rachel. I can't tell you everything, but I can tell you that some very bad men have kidnapped her and will kill her if we don't help her first."

"To take the life of such a beautiful, talented African woman would be a great loss to us," Rachel said slowly.

"Yes, especially for me, since she is much closer to me than to you. She is my sister."

"Your sister? How terrible."

"Yes, but Joseph could help." Haran began to feel he was turning the corner with Rachel.

"Tell me one thing about him that will prove you know him well," Rachel challenged.

Haran thought for a moment. "Even when drinking he doesn't look at other women."

Rachel was silent. This was an unexpected answer. "How did you know that?" she asked slowly.

Knowing that this was exactly what she wanted to hear, Haran pushed his hand further. "I have heard him talk about you. I have heard him say some wonderful things about you. He told me once how lucky he was to have found you and that he couldn't imagine anyone comparable to you in all of Nairobi."

There was another silence. This time Haran felt he had hit his mark.

"I see that you know him, sir. You must know him better than many others. I can only tell you that he went to Mombasa. His spirit was very heavy, sir. He goes to Mombasa on the coast to forget his problems in the warm rays of the sun and the soothing sounds of the ocean's waves. That is what he tells me."

"When did he leave?"

"Early yesterday morning. I don't have anything else to tell you."

"Can you at least tell me where he will be staying?"

"No, No. That I won't tell you. I can't tell you. He made me promise, and I would never break a promise to him."

"Even to save a life? Even to save the life of Wangetha Wachira? Surely her life is worth saving."

"Yes, of course. But I still have to trust that you are telling me the truth about her. I only have your words."

"Trust not only the words, trust my voice. Do I sound like a liar? Would I lie about the life of a woman at risk, a woman who is my own sister?"

"Here, some people lie about everything."

"But I'm not one of those people. Will you at least call him on the telephone for me? That involves very little risk. Tell him what the problem is. He knows me and will understand the message. Please ask him to get on the last train scheduled to depart from Mombasa."

"When is that?"

"In the next few hours, this evening at 7:00 p.m. If he leaves then, he could be here by the morning."

"This is very difficult for me, but I will phone him and tell him you called and what the problem is. I still don't know whether I can believe everything you said, but I don't want anything to happen to Wangetha Wachira. So, I will give him your message and your telephone number and ask him to call you. That's the best I can do."

"Good. Here is my number: 768-954. I'm sure he knows the area code of Nairobi. Would you please call me after you talk with him to let me know what he said and if he plans to call me?"

"Yes, I will. If you hear nothing, it means that he doesn't want to talk to you."

"I know that this will not be easy for you, Miss Rachel. Joseph is a difficult and complicated man."

"Yes, he can be difficult, but he is not always so complicated." Rachel felt strange, finding herself explaining Regalo. But she couldn't help herself.

"Thank you, Miss Rachel. I will wait to hear from you."

"I will call as quickly as I can."

CHAPTER 23
THE LAST TRAIN FROM MOMBASA

∾

It was not yet noon, and Regalo was hunched over the billiards table in the nearly empty barroom of the Mombasa Palm Hotel, lining up a shot with the cue stick he had earlier picked from the rack. It was the least warped of the lot, and he decided he would have to make do with it. After straightening up, chalking the tip for the second time, and walking around the table to survey its layout for at least the third time, he leaned down again and took careful aim on the white cue ball. It was sitting pretty, about nine inches from the near rail of the table and another two feet from the white object ball.

With his right hand loosely wrapped around the butt of the cue stick, he drew it back and forth slowly through the line of sight formed by the thumb and forefinger of his left hand, its other three fingers sprawled out on the felt green for support. In an instant, Regalo's grip tightened as the full force of his right arm drove the cue stick into the cue ball, the blue-chalked tip of the stick catching it on its top half and driving it forward with enough speed and top-spin to make the onlooking bartender blink.

The cue ball caught one-third of the white object ball's left side, slamming into the left cushion from where it careened sharply off to the right, catching the far rail at its middle, rebounding from there to the next rail on the right from where it crossed the entire length of the table to ricochet from the near rail to the left side again, catching the second red object ball with a direct kiss.

As the two balls rolled to a stop after the hit, Regalo glanced up at the bartender, who had stepped out from behind the bar to get close to the billiard table for a better look at the action.

"Was that all right?" he asked the bartender while grinning broadly.

"Very few people I have seen over the years could hit a shot like that," the bartender replied with admiration showing on his face. "I like the way you impose your will on the ball. You make it go through such a complicated path, but exactly where you intend it to go. Can this skill come naturally to someone?"

"No, it does not happen naturally to anyone," Regalo answered matter-of-factly.

"Oh."

"But it is a skill you can acquire, if you want to," Regalo said good-naturedly.

"Is it hard to learn?"

"Much practice is required, but it will come to you if you always plan in your head first exactly the way you want the ball to go."

"Right. Well, I know one thing. You deserve a drink on the house for that superb shot. What will it be? Gin, whiskey, rum, whatever you want."

Regalo frowned. "None of that stuff while I'm shooting, man. Just coffee, that's all. Some good, strong coffee from the highlands."

"That will take time to make."

"Then make it, man. Make it."

"As you say."

"But before you go to the kitchen, there is a second skill that I can also show you."

"What is that?"

Regalo pointed to a mosquito flying lazily around the room, circling the light fixture on the ceiling. "See that mosquito?"

"Yes, I see it now. It shouldn't have gotten in."

"Chances are it is carrying malaria, right?"

"Yes, good chance unfortunately."

Regalo suddenly thrust out his arm in the direction of the mosquito, grabbed it in his fist, and then shook it violently. "That is so the bloodsucker's wings get banged up and he can't get his bearings to bite me while it is in my hand."

After shaking his hand vigorously for nearly a minute he opened it up and dropped the mosquito on the floor, where it crawled erratically from left to right unable to fly.

Regalo then took the butt of his cue stick, and lining it up in the direction of the mosquito, he drove it onto the insect, crushing it into a plastered mess.

"That was a perfect blow," the bartender noted approvingly. "You were far away with the cue stick. Still, you hit the mosquito just once, the very first time you struck."

"You don't have to try to kill it with just one blow. You can get much closer, and then you can hit it again and again and again until it is dead."

Regalo then pointed to a deck of playing cards on the corner table. "Could you bring those cards to me, please?"

After the bartender put the deck into his hands, Regalo spread the cards out on the green felt of the billiards table and began to build them up wall by wall, layer by layer, until he had fashioned them into a house of cards.

"Now, watch this," Regalo said, as he took a deep breath and proceeded to blow a gust of air from his lungs onto the house of cards, which immediately tumbled into a heap on the felt.

"That is also something you can learn to do," he said, smiling at the bartender. "Now please get me my coffee."

As the bartender started to leave, he noticed the reception clerk entering the room and scowled. Whenever he came, he knew it could mean that there was a call or message that would take a customer away for the day.

"What the bloody hell is it?" the bartender snapped at the approaching clerk.

"Someone left a telephone message for you, sir," the clerk announced to Regalo, ignoring the bartender.

"Oh no!" Regalo, moaned loudly. "Just when I was beginning to enjoy myself. Who was it?" he demanded.

The one patron sitting at the long bar turned around as the sound of Regalo's booming voice rippled around the barroom's hardwood walls.

Startled, the clerk stammered, "The caller was a she, sir. She said her name was Rachel and that you would know who she was. She said it was important you talk to her."

"Did she say anything else?" Regalo asked impatiently.

"No, sir. She said nothing else, only that she was waiting for you to call her."

"Wait a second," Regalo muttered angrily. "You said that she said nothing else but then you said that she was waiting for my call. Now, which is it? Damn it, man! Which is it?"

"Sir, when I said that she was waiting for you to call her it is almost the same as saying that it was important that you talk to her," the clerk answered nervously, wondering if the bulge under Regalo's light tropical blazer was a handgun.

"No, it isn't almost the same. They are different statements," Regalo responded testily. "Why didn't you deliver the message the right way the first time?"

"Sir, I only work here," the clerk answered, his voice rising as he began to find his courage. "I was just trying to relay the basic information. I wasn't paying attention to the details. But I see now how important the exact message was to you. I'm sorry if I offended you. We try to serve our guests well here. That is how we are trained."

Regalo reached into his pocket and pulled out a hundred-shilling note. "Here, take that for your trouble," he said in a more conciliatory voice. "Now, where is the telephone?"

"Just come with me, sir. I will take you there."

After putting his cue stick in the rack on the wall, Regalo followed the clerk through the small lobby of the hotel and into a cramped back office.

As he picked up the phone and began to dial his home number, he turned to the clerk watching him. "You don't need to stay. I want to be alone."

As the clerk left, Regalo finished dialing and waited for Rachel to answer. When she did, he spoke slowly into the telephone.

"Rachel, what is it? Why did you call me? You know that when I go away like this I don't want to be disturbed. You know the rules."

"Yes, of course I know, sir, but..."

"Well, please explain."

"If you remember sir, you did say in case of an emergency that I could call you in Mombasa."

Regalo waited before answering. "Yes, that's right, I did say that you could call me if there were an emergency. So what is it? Is the house burning down or have you been attacked by intruders?"

"No, sir. There is nothing like that. But there is danger."

"Danger to you?"

"No, not to me directly, sir, but to someone I promised to help."

"Someone you promised to help?" Regalo's voice betrayed his annoyance.

"Please, don't be angry, sir. I need your help for a friend, a friend who will be killed if you do not help. She has suffered so much already."

Regalo said nothing.

"Do you hear me, Joseph?" she persisted, as she directly addressed Regalo by his first name for the first time since she had known him. "She will be killed if we do not help."

"But who am I to help, Rachel?" Regalo asked almost plaintively. "Why must it be me? I came here to rest, to get away from everything for a while. You understand that, don't you?"

Sensing a change in Regalo's voice, Rachel's spirits rose. "Oh, yes, I understand it very well, Joseph. You work so hard and you deserve this rest. But you are a man with special skills. You can help. I know that you can help."

"What happened to your friend?"

"Some criminals kidnapped her, and if the ransom is not paid by Friday, she will be killed. That gives us just three days to rescue her."

"Why not just pay the ransom?" Regalo asked, as he realized this was about Wangetha.

As Rachel searched for words to answer, Regalo's annoyance grew. Sardou must be behind this, he concluded. Apparently, it was not enough to point him in the right direction by referring him to Haran. They were supposed to find out if she were still alive and then go ahead and pay the ransom if they wanted to. It was their choice to make. They could have also gone to the police. That was their choice to make as well. Why drag him into this any further?

"I think they are afraid that the kidnappers will take the money and kill her just the same," Rachel said. "At least, that is how I understood it."

"Who told you this? Who called you?" Regalo pressed, wondering why he had not asked this question at the very beginning. Rachel had caught him by surprise and he was not thinking fast enough.

"It was a man by the name of Haran Nakaya."

"Not someone by the name of Sardou?"

"No."

"It would mean so much to me if you could help Mr. Nakaya. You, Joseph, you can help to find a way to rescue her. I know you can."

"Thank you, Rachel. That's very kind of you." There was no more edge to Regalo's voice.

Rachel sensed that she had made a breakthrough.

"I checked the train schedule from Mombasa for you. The last train from Mombasa leaves at 7:00 p.m., giving you plenty of time to finish your business, pack, and get to the station in time."

"Don't you think that I know that, Rachel?" Regalo said, raising his voice. "It always leaves around that hour, and it arrives in Nairobi the next morning at close to 9:00 a.m., give or take a bunch of minutes."

"Forgive me, sir," Rachel said as she addressed him more formally once again. "Of course you know the schedule. I just called the train station to make sure that it was still leaving at that hour. Sometimes schedules change because of the weather or accidents. I just wanted to be helpful to you."

Regalo immediately regretted his impatience and lowered his voice. "Thanks for checking, Rachel."

"You will still be able to get some rest, sir," Rachel continued enthusiastically, "because you will be able to sleep the whole night in one of the sleeping compartments on the train if you wish. That would be very good for you. You will be fresh when you arrive."

"I am only coming because of you, Rachel. I just want you to know that."

Rachel's heart began beating faster. "I feel so happy to hear you say that."

"Call Haran and tell him that I will meet him in his office in the morning. I don't want to talk to him just now. Tell him that I don't want him to come to the train station for me either. I will get to his office on my own."

"I will tell him. Be very careful, Joseph."

"You be careful, too, Rachel. Goodbye for now."

"Goodbye, Joseph."

When she called Haran a few minutes later to tell him Regalo was coming, his face broke into a smile. "You did very well, Miss Rachel. You reached him and that is what matters."

"Yes, Haran," Rachel answered. "That is what matters."

CHAPTER 24
STRANGERS IN THE NIGHT

∽

Black smoke, tinged with gray wisps, was pouring out of the Kenya Railways diesel-powered locomotive, snaking and winding and bellowing upwards in the full face of the moon, as it pulled the night train from Mombasa toward Nairobi. Regalo was sleeping on the right-hand berth and a Kenyan man was lying on the left-hand berth in a first-class compartment on the tenth wagon behind the locomotive. But since the evening was cool on this stretch of the railway, both of them, though fully dressed, had their blankets thrown over them.

Regalo considered himself fortunate to be able to occupy a berth, since he knew that some of the train's other wagons were packed with people squeezed together, sitting on sacks and sacks of farm produce, with their restive chickens at their feet. Unlike those unlucky passengers, he would be able to arrive in Nairobi in the morning fairly rested.

With its smooth, steel wheels clicking away on the rails for a good four hours since leaving Mombasa, the train began to decelerate, nearing its first stop at Voi. This was a small town poised on the outer perimeter of Tsavo National Park, a vast reserve known for its thousands of elephants and numerous lions.

Regalo awoke. He looked out the window and then down at his wristwatch. It read 11:35 p.m. Reaching Voi meant that they had already covered some 160 kilometers and were making slow but decent progress. Oblivious to his cabin-mate, he rolled down the window for some fresh air.

As the train approached the station, which was about a kilometer from Voi town itself, his attention was drawn to the sight of two uniformed policemen who were standing outside his wagon among other travelers waiting to board. When the train stopped, he saw them get on. Before long, he heard them talking to the wagon's steward a few compartments down. He could make out the steward saying, *"He looks like an Arab. He might be one of the men you are seeking."*

The policemen walked briskly down the passageway, peering into each cabin. When they reached Regalo's compartment and looked inside, they came to an immediate stop. Regalo winced.

"Who are you? Show us your identification!" one of the policemen ordered Regalo, ignoring the other passenger, who was staring out the window.

"What's the problem?" Regalo asked calmly, as he showed him his Kenyan driver's license.

"There was a bomb threat called in earlier today. We are searching for all likely suspects."

"Where was it called in?"

"Why should we tell you? You may be the one who called it in."

"I've been on this train for the last four hours."

"Well, we will tell you that it was called in shortly before you got on the train in Mombasa," the second policeman said, as he inspected the ticket Regalo handed over to him. Regalo could see that the officer was very serious about what he was saying.

"What or who was the target of the bomb threat?"

"You don't know that, either?"

"No."

"It was a ship. An American ship, preparing to unload cargo in Mombasa Harbor."

"Is that right?"

"Yes. We have reason to believe that the caller belonged to an Islamist terrorist group."

The first policeman added, "They may have members in Kenya."

"What is your nationality?" he asked, noting his facial features.

"What difference does it make? I'm self-employed and have a permit to work in this country."

"Where is it?"

"I don't have it with me. Am I supposed to carry it with me everywhere? I showed you my driver's license."

"We have no way of knowing if it's genuine. It may be a forgery, and it will take time to check it out. Where is your passport?"

"I don't usually carry that with me, either, when I am traveling for pleasure in this country."

"That's a big mistake. How are the authorities supposed to know who you are?"

"I'm not used to being questioned by authorities."

"The train is preparing to depart," the second policeman interjected. "You'll have to come with us."

"Wait a minute!" Regalo was beginning to feel as angry as he felt trapped. "I'm an American citizen. Where do you suppose that I learned English?"

"Many Kenyans and Arabs speak excellent English. What is your original nationality?"

"I was born in the United States."

"That is not what we want to know. We want to know your original nationality."

"I am an American."

"You do not look American. Some here on the train say that you look like an Arab to them."

Now Regalo was becoming as exasperated as he was angry. "I don't know my racial origin, if that is what you want to know. I was adopted."

As the two policemen looked at each other, wondering what he meant, their suspicions rising, Regalo saw his chance and bolted through the space between them, leaving his backpack in the cabin With the police yelling for the passengers to stop him, he forced his way down the aisle, pushing people left and right, until he reached the door to the wagon. He could not believe his good luck that they had not searched him and found his Colt .45 in his shoulder holster under his jacket.

Clambering down the steps from the wagon, he noticed that the police car parked outside, in which the two policemen must have arrived, was empty. That meant no other policemen were waiting outside that could grab him. As he ran crouched down from the wagon to the station, bumping into people left and right, he knew they could still try to take a shot at him through the compartment windows. But that would risk hitting someone else if they didn't get him – and so far there were no shots.

"Get the terrorist before he escapes!" he heard the policemen shouting, who had gotten off the train and were taking a bead on him. But still no shots rang out.

As he ran around the station building and then out into the nearly empty street, he breathed a sigh of relief that they had not brought a dog with them. This was another break. With a dog they could have kept trailing him, even without seeing him.

He kept running in the direction of the town, counting on the topography and tree cover along the way to keep him out of sight of the policemen. Once in the town, he weaved in and out of the streets to further evade them, drawing little attention, until he finally broke out into the scrubland on the town's outskirts, where running with any kind of speed was no longer possible. Bending his legs and keeping his head down, he began zigzagging through the brush, always moving parallel in the general direction of the railroad tracks, but at a good distance.

By now the lights of the town had faded to distant flickers and he was enveloped in darkness. It was only then that he stopped to rest against a nearby acacia tree. The moon provided him just enough light to see where he was and where he was going.

After a brief respite, he worked his way through the rough terrain for another good while, at times stumbling in holes coming out of nowhere or getting caught short by a bush, but always swirling, driving, and powering himself further, until he became so winded that he had to sit down on the ground to rest again. He was now far away enough from the train station so that he could risk crossing the rail line to reach the highway to Nairobi which ran alongside the train tracks. Once he could make out the road, he stopped to fashion a plan.

He didn't think for long. Soon he found a big, fallen tree branch, dragged it over to the shoulder of the highway lane going to Nairobi, and waited.

When no headlights were shining from any oncoming vehicles on either side of the highway, he dragged the branch right up onto the Nairobi lane for a roadblock and stood behind it. He knew that if he were to stand in the road alone, even fully visible in the headlights, there was every chance the oncoming vehicle would run right over him. But with the large branch on the road, there would be few drivers willing to risk damaging their cars or losing control on such an isolated stretch of road. If it were a tractor trailer headed in his direction, that would be another story and he was prepared to get out of its way.

It was not long before he saw a pair of headlights approaching at a fast clip from the direction of Mombasa. He jumped out from behind the branch and waved his white handkerchief until a car came to a screeching halt directly in front of the road block. It was a silver, four-door, Mercedes-Benz sedan.

Pulling out his Colt pistol, Regalo walked over to its driver's side and motioned authoritatively for the driver to pull over to the side of the road. Regalo could see that sitting behind the driver's wheel was a middle-aged, portly man. After the car pulled over, Regalo waved his Colt again at the driver, signaling him to roll down the window.

Once the terrified man had rolled down the window, Regalo pointed the gun directly at his forehead.

"Don't kill me, please don't kill me. I will give you anything you want. I will give you all the money that I have, anything. Just please, don't kill me!"

"Relax," Regalo muttered, as he opened the door and reached in, lifting up the man's shirt to expose his midriff and make sure that there was no knife stashed there. He was not expecting to find a gun, since if the driver had one, he would have, or should have, used it on him already. As his quivering plump belly came into view, Regalo could see that here was a man who ate well.

"I have no intention of killing you. I need you to drive me to Nairobi. Now get out and help me move this branch before any more cars or trucks come along. We need to be on our way."

After clearing the branch and starting up the motor with Regalo seated next to him, the portly man soon had the Mercedes humming along on the highway. Relieved that he was still alive, he took his eyes off the road to glance at Regalo.

"Do you have to point that at me? It makes it hard to concentrate on my driving."

"Tell me where you are from first," Regalo replied.

"I'm from Nairobi. I deal in automobile parts, all kinds. There is a big need for my business since new cars have such high duties and are very expensive. Most people would rather try to keep an old car in repair."

As he caught the sight of Regalo slipping the gun under his belt, he felt a little more emboldened.

"And who are you, if I might ask?"

"It doesn't matter, but if you want to know, my name is Joseph Regalo. And I am not a criminal. I am not going to kill you or rob you. Circumstances left me no choice but to make you take me to Nairobi. Don't ask me what kind of circumstances. When we get to Nairobi, I intend to pay you fully for your gasoline and the inconvenience to you. If you want to turn my name in to the police then, that will be up to you."

"Your business in Nairobi is so urgent that you needed to commandeer a car at gunpoint?"

"If not your car it was going to be someone else's. It just so happens it was yours. Call it fate. Call it your bad luck."

"How do I know that you are just using me to get to Nairobi, and that you won't kill me as soon as we arrive?"

"Your question is completely irrelevant. What will happen to you will happen regardless of what you think will happen, hope will happen, or fear will happen. All you should do is trust me and quit worrying about what is going to happen."

"Why should I trust you?" He caught himself. "Wait, forget what I just said. That was a dumb question. You are right. I don't really have a choice but to trust you."

"That's right. It's all up to you. It would be easier on you to trust me."

"And if you are telling the truth that you won't kill me but I still call the police and tell them what you have done?"

"As I said, that's up to you."

"Ah, but you are very clever. You know that it will only be my word against yours."

"If you say so." Regalo was beginning to feel entertained by the line the conservation was taking. All this talk would keep him from falling asleep.

"After all, what proof would I have that you commandeered my car at gunpoint?"

"Look, just drive."

"Ah, you are clever, aren't you? You must be Jewish. They are very clever, and you look Semitic."

"Now, that is interesting," Regalo responded with amusement. "Some say that I look Arabic."

"Well, I did also say Semitic, didn't I? I meant you could be either one. Isn't that what the word means? Maybe you could be an Arab. Only you are too smart to be an Arab."

"What a stupid thing to say. There have been plenty of smart Arabs. Have you ever seen the pyramids of Egypt? They are among the greatest wonders of the world and were built by Arabs. But closer to home, do you follow the stock exchange at all in Nairobi?"

The corpulent man fidgeted in his seat.

"Well, do you? Speak up!"

"As a matter of fact I do, just like quite a few others."

"Well, you may have noticed that the prices of the stocks are listed in numbers with decimal fractions."

"Uh, yes I have noticed that. So what of it? They're listed like that in many places so far as I know."

"Well, it just so happens that the decimal numeral system was refined to include fractions by an Arabian mathematician in the tenth century. I even know his name – Abu'l-Hasan al-Uqlidisi. Have you heard of him?"

"Uh, no...I haven't. But that's very good to know. So maybe you are an Arab, or you wouldn't be getting angry. I am very sorry if I offended you."

"You didn't offend me. You irritated me. Now just drive."

The corpulent man remained quiet for a minute. "What was this terrorist's intent," he kept wondering. He didn't believe for a second that he would not be killed as soon as he was no longer useful. Maybe if he could just keep quiet. But he was too nervous and couldn't help it. Maybe, on the other hand, by keeping some kind of conversation going with him, he would appear more worthy and human to him. But

262

he knew he had blundered by what he had said about Arabs, especially since he appeared to be one. All he had wanted to do was goad him. But to what end, he didn't really know. Maybe just to find out more about him. Maybe just to change the atmosphere. Maybe just because he was afraid and wasn't thinking too clearly.

Then another thought came to him. What if he suddenly slammed on the brakes and veered the car to the side of the road? He had heard about a carjacking victim doing that in Nairobi. There, too, the carjacker was sitting next to the driver, brandishing a gun. When the driver brought the car to a screeching halt off to the side of the road, the carjacker's head had flown into the windshield, shaking him up so badly he couldn't follow the driver as he bolted out of the car. It was true that the carjacker then collected himself and drove off in the expensive sport utility vehicle, which was never to be recovered. As a result, the owner was out three million shillings since he had failed to buy anti-theft insurance. But he had saved his own life! And now here on this dark Mombasa Road, seated next to a criminal, he was faced with the same choice.

How could he have been so stupid to undertake this long drive so late at night? But business was business, and he couldn't disappoint his partners, who were waiting for him in Nairobi.

"Doesn't this Arab ever sleep?" he wondered. If only he dozed off. Then he could crush his face with his elbow and make a run for it.

But what if he couldn't run fast enough and the Arab recovered from the blow and ran after him to kill him out of anger? What good would it do for him to escape from the Arab, anyway? There were lions and hyenas and God knows what else out there in this wilderness. What would happen to him alone in this place even if he escaped from the Arab's clutches? Which was better? To be mauled to death by a lion, torn to pieces by a pack of hyenas with the vultures picking over what was left of his corpse, or have the Arab lodge a bullet into his brain on some side-street in Nairobi?

"Ah, but this Arab is clever," the corpulent man concluded in his mind. "He must have considered all these options. That is why he is resting so peacefully next to me. He's not worried. But wait! Wouldn't my odds be better, after all, with the lions and the hyenas? If I could just survive a few hours until daylight comes. Then I could step out to the side of the road and try to wave down a driver to stop for me. Only I wouldn't use a tree branch or anything like that.

"Maybe someone I know from Nairobi would come along and recognize me. But even if I didn't have that kind of luck, I could still flag down one of the many trucks driving during the day along this miserable stretch of highway, carrying goods to Nairobi. In the daylight, the truck drivers would notice me in my excellent suit that I had made expressly for me by a fine Asian tailor and they would know that I was someone of means. At least they would have good reason to think so because of my appearance. They would then make the obvious deduction that I probably have money, giving them all the more reason to stop.

"But what if the truck driver were filled with envy and hate? What if he were one of those citizens that burn down our shops every time there is a riot, whatever the reason for the riot in the first place? What if he were one of those who are bitter over our success in business and our wealth? Then it might not be so good. Then if he had the chance, he would even try to run over me to leave me to die on the road.

"Oh, is this Arab clever. He had probably thought about this, also. Otherwise, why is he so calm? Why did he tuck his pistol into his trouser? How can he be so smug? He didn't even check the glove compartment of the car for weapons. He didn't even frisk me. What if I had hidden a Berretta in my trousers? One thing is for sure. If I get out of this alive, I will always carry a Berretta in my trousers. Maybe I'm thinking too much. If I lose control of this car, we will both be killed. But that could be better than waiting until Nairobi. On the other hand, I haven't tried the money angle yet."

The corpulent man turned his attention to Regalo, who was looking straight ahead. "You know, whatever your name is..."

"My name is Regalo."

"Uh, yes, Mr. Regalo. Sorry, I forgot."

"No, just Regalo."

"Oh, I see. Well, I was just thinking. You see, I can make it worth your while if you let me go in Nairobi."

"I already said that I would let you go once we reach Nairobi. Then you can go to the police and report me, if you want to."

"Oh, I know that is what you said. But what if I offered you 500,000 shillings to make sure that you wouldn't change your mind?"

"I'm not going to change my mind."

"But, how do I know? How do I know?"

"Because I said so." Regalo's voice was now deep and edgy.

"So you're saying that I have to trust you."

"That is exactly what I'm saying and what I have been saying." There was exasperation in Regalo's voice.

"But think of my position. You have commandeered my car."

"I said I was sorry but that I had no other choice. Now, I'm going to tell you something and then I want you to shut up and concentrate on your driving before you get both of us killed. There is a life at stake. There is a woman in Nairobi whose life is in grave danger. I have been asked to help her. I need your help to get me there."

"But you are not giving me a choice to help or not to help. You have taken away my freedom."

"So why don't we just assume that you would have wanted to help. That way you don't have to worry about having lost your precious freedom."

"That is a cute trick with words to justify yourself."

"You can call it what you want. It will be up to you to decide later if what I have done to you is right or wrong."

The corpulent man sat quietly for the next half-hour thinking, ruminating about his situation while Regalo was half-dozing.

Suddenly, Regalo roused himself and glanced at the instrument panel. "I see that we are running low on petrol and we have another 100 kilometers to go before we reach Nairobi," he said testily. "How much gas do you keep in cans in the trunk?"

He was startled. How could the Arab know that he had petrol in the trunk? Of course, he kept petrol in the trunk for long trips like this in Kenya. But how would he know?

"What do you mean, how much petrol do I have in the trunk?"

"Just what I said. How much?"

"Why don't you look?"

"No. Let's both look. Pull the car over at the nearest available spot off to the side of the road."

After about another 10 kilometers, the Mercedes rolled to a stop where a dirt road intersected with the main Mombasa highway. After they got out of the car, opened the trunk, and looked in, Regalo grinned.

"I see that you have a good 20 liters here. That should be more than enough. Go ahead and put it into the tank."

After the corpulent man poured the gasoline into the tank and resumed driving, he started thinking some more. "This could not be an Arab. He is too confident that he will escape punishment for what he has done to me. He has Semitic features all right, but that does not mean he is the Arab that I thought he was. He is probably Jewish after all, and he is most likely an agent for the Mossad. Didn't the Israelis support Kenyatta in his struggle to wrest Kenya from the colonialists, and don't they have excellent relations with the government now? Wouldn't they want to keep an occasional eye on things in this part of the world since the terrorists are after them no matter where they are? This guy simply knows too much and he is too sure of himself. He must be schooled in the martial arts as well. That is why he is unafraid to put his gun back into his trousers. He knows that he can kill me in an instant with his bare hands if I try anything.

"Now I understand why he says that I can report my abduction to the Kenyan police when we get back to Nairobi. They would just go through the motions if I went to report him and then snicker behind my back once I left. They would probably even call him afterwards and then go out together and get drunk, laughing at my expense. At least now I feel better. He really has no reason to kill me. And I don't have to go through the humiliation of going to the police."

The unending potholes, constantly jarring the Mercedes, would normally make him think of the damage being done to its suspension and the chassis and all the resultant repair costs. But this did not concern him as much now, either. He glanced with relief at the Mossad agent who now seemed to be fully dozing. It would be less than an hour that they would be in Nairobi and nothing bad would happen to him.

CHAPTER 25
THE PLOTTERS

 ∿

Regalo wasted no time with pleasantries as he strode into Haran's office Wednesday morning without knocking. Unshaved, with his clothes smelling of desert dust, only his clean hands and fingernails suggested he had stopped somewhere to first wash up. Alain was sitting on a chair next to the window. Haran was seated at the desk with the telephone in his hand, beginning to dial. He stopped abruptly as he saw Regalo.

"All right, where are they holding her?" Regalo asked as he surveyed the room.

"Joseph. It's good to see you!" Haran exclaimed, rising and stretching out his hand. "How was your train ride? You look like you came in on horseback."

Regalo broke into a broad grin. "I had to take a little trip on the side, leading to some great entertainment on the way up."

"Thanks, Joseph. Thanks for coming. I hope that you're not too tired," Alain said as he stretched out his hand after Haran's.

"No, I'm fine and glad to be here."

Regalo took a look at Alain's bruised face. "What happened to you?"

"Robidi and his goons waylaid me."

"Sorry to hear that. How did they find out where you were?"

"We don't know. Haran and I have been trying to figure that out."

Regalo glanced at Haran but didn't say anything.

"The good thing is that I shook them off." Alain continued, "The bad thing is that they know Wangetha has been kidnapped."

"Man, have we got our work cut out for us," Regalo said, pointing to his wristwatch. "Time is running out. I know the ransom is due day after tomorrow, Alain. What time did they give you and where are you supposed to be?"

"3:00 p.m. in front of the Sarit Centre. The way we figure it, they can't be too worried about our going to the police or they wouldn't be making that kind of arrangement. Of course, we have no idea whom they will be sending to meet me. But we can assume I'll be watched the entire time."

"I wouldn't disagree with any of that."

"Do you want my chair?" Alain asked.

Regalo waved his hand. "No thanks. You can stay there. There's very little time. We have to do something to rescue her, not only to beat the ransom due date, but more importantly, to get to her before Robidi does. Now where is she being held?"

"145 East Woodside Drive," Haran replied, "in an area bordering a seedy part of the far outskirts of eastern Nairobi. It's quite a large home in the old colonial style, complete with a gabled roof line. I saw it once and learned that it used to be owned by a European expatriate family. But that was long ago. It's pretty rundown now as it hasn't been kept up very well. A good-sized Kikuyu family bought it, though I'm not really sure who owns it now. It's on a cul-de-sac, with no pavement, surrounded by a high wire fence with shrubs woven into it. There are no other houses nearby. Close to a dozen people are in there now, when you add up the children and the adults. The four kidnappers, some of whom could be relatives, took

Wangetha there and they've taken over. The family members are scared to death and pretty much keep to their rooms."

"How do you know all that?" Regalo asked as he began walking back and forth in front of the desk with his back to Alain.

"It took a while," Haran answered, "but I have my sources, just as you have yours."

"In the Kikuyu community, I take it."

"Of course. The best information money can buy."

"Reliable?"

"A cousin of mine checked it out."

"Cousins can lie, can't they, or are these saints?" Regalo snapped.

"He is a first cousin. He wouldn't lie to me. This information is as good as you can get in Kenya."

"All right, I won't pry. If you say that's the right address, we'll go with it."

Regalo stopped, as if a new idea had come to him. "Something's not clear to me, though. I thought about this on and off on the way here from Mombasa. Why couldn't she have made a break for it?" He looked impatiently, first at Haran, then at Alain.

"That's one hell of a question, Joseph," Alain answered. "You know that she's being held by force. What can she do?"

Regalo listened without any change of expression. He then looked at Haran.

"For all I know she could have tried to escape," Haran said. "My sister is a resourceful woman. We'll have to ask her."

Regalo's face broke into a half-smile as he took in Haran's response. "I was just blowing off some steam. Forget what I just said."

Haran turned to face Regalo. "Listen to this, Joseph. What I learned from my cousin is that they've put her in the servant's room behind the main house. The gate in front of the door is locked and one of the women of the house brings her food by first unlocking the gate under the watchful eye of one of the kidnappers. With the gate open, the woman places a tray before the door and knocks to let Wangetha know the food is there, who then opens the door and stoops down to pick it up."

"Do they know why she's there?"

"They can't help knowing that she's a kidnap victim, but no one seems to care, or if they do, they're too afraid to do anything. No one ever asked any questions, even when they heard Wangetha screaming."

"You mean one of them admitted that to your cousin?"

"Yes, from what he told me. Now you're going to ask me how my cousin could know that, aren't you?"

"How did you guess?"

"He called the house and spoke with one of the family members, the grandmother."

"She must have been watched as she was talking."

"Of course, but they had to let her answer the phone so that it would seem as if everything were normal."

"I understand that, but how could she have let on that there was screaming?"

"She started out in Kikuyu and then switched to Masai for a couple of minutes before they cut her off. My cousin is part Masai and so is she. A mixed heritage like that is not so uncommon here, you know."

"These gangsters are going to be more suspicious now," Regalo frowned.

"Probably," Haran nodded.

"Anything else?"

"They alternate as sentries posted outside. The one on duty is either walking back and forth in front of the house or stands right inside the gate. That leaves three to account for at any time."

Regalo clapped his hands. "That's good, Haran. We can't expect that all four are going to be there all the time. At least one of them has to go out for food and supplies. This is a scenario that can work for us or against us."

"Exactly," Haran added. "The fewer in the house the better for us. But the more inside, the worse for us."

"We'll have to prepare for both contingencies," Regalo said.

"We're lucky to know where they are," Alain noted.

"That may be, Alain, but there's not much to count as luck beyond that. Here, we are dealing with criminals who have no regard for human life, who without a doubt have been raping Wangetha repeatedly since they abducted her. You can bet your last dime that they won't give her up without trying to kill anyone who so much as tries to come close to her, much less rescue her. Please note that I didn't say 'probably raped' here. You can take it to the bank that they've been taking turns with her every chance they get."

Alain winced, turning his head away.

"Does that bother you, Alain? Then I'm very sorry, but that's how these thugs are."

"Can we get back to the point?" Haran insisted. "What do you suggest we do, assuming the scene is the way I described it to you? You're the expert in dealing with terrorists."

"First of all, these aren't terrorists. Let's get that straight. They're users. They're not driven by a cause as most terrorists are. And that's why we have a better chance here. They're not going to be as fanatical and disciplined, and they're impatient to get their money. That gives us an opening."

"What kind of opening?" Alain asked.

"An opening based on distraction. We would have a hard time distracting terrorists. But here we have a chance, for the reasons I just gave you. The very first thing we're going to have to do is sidetrack the sentry on duty outside. Then we'll have to neutralize the two or three that will be inside. Taking two out will be difficult. Three will be very difficult. We'll have to plan for both scenes and assume three will be there."

"It would certainly be easier if there were only two inside," Alain said.

"But we can't count on it," Regalo responded tartly. "As much as I would like to, we just can't assume that one of them will always be away somewhere."

"Do you have something to write on?" he asked Haran.

Haran reached into one of the drawers of the desk and retrieved a clean sheet of white paper. He then reached into his shirt pocket for a ballpoint pen.

"Since you say you've seen the house before, Haran, can you give us a rough sketch of it and the grounds?"

"Sure," Haran answered as he began drawing the outline of the yard, a rectangular box to represent the house, and a smaller box behind it to represent the servant's quarters.

"There it is," Haran said after he had finished. "Not that pretty, but it shows where everything is and the space involved as well."

"This is fine, Haran. Just what we need." Regalo picked up the pen and pointed to the X Haran had drawn to represent the sentry outside the house.

"Here is the plan," Regalo said, the enthusiasm in his voice growing. "You, Haran, will have to approach the sentry on duty, circling the block, and say that you are looking for a good *changaa* bar. Do it when he is at the farthest point from the gate. Tell him that you were told that there were some good ones nearby. Act like you are half drunk. Get some liquor on your breath to play the part. Make him think that you are a low-life just like he is.

"You've got to be convincing," Regalo emphasized as he clenched his fist. "Show him a chunk of cash to focus his attention. Peel off a nice bill and give it to him as you tell him that you need his help in finding a hot place."

"What if the guy sees through the ruse?" Alain asked.

"Don't worry, Alain," Haran responded, warming to the scheme. "He won't. I'll do whatever is needed to make it believable. Let me see if I can guess the next part. As I get his attention, Regalo will have gotten out of our Jeep, sneaked up on him from behind, and taken him out."

"Does that mean you're going to kill him?" Alain asked.

"I don't want to kill him if I don't have to," Regalo said. "But here killing will probably be necessary. Otherwise, if I only knock him unconscious he can revive and come after us or notify his pals. It's too big a risk not to kill him. Remember, he's a criminal involved in a kidnapping. That's already a capital crime. We will only be carrying out a sentence that he richly deserves."

"We're not legally constituted executioners," countered Haran.

"What do you propose we do then, Haran?" Regalo's eyes were blazing. "Call the police and take a chance on them? Do you want to risk Wangetha's life on hoping the right ones show up? Is that what you want?"

"No. That's not what I want," Haran answered testily. "I just don't want to see any unnecessary taking of life. You can tape the sentry's mouth shut and then tape his hands and feet together."

Regalo did not respond.

"What else is going to happen?" Haran pressed.

"To stun these guys and take out as many as we can before storming the servant's quarters, we will have to throw a grenade or two into the house, but not just anywhere, only into the rooms that we know for sure don't contain Wangetha."

"Grenades?" Alain asked incredulously. "Are you serious? How on earth are we going to get grenades?"

"You don't know, Alain? You don't know that there's a black market here in weapons? You can buy an AK-47 and grenades too, if the price is right."

"How so?"

"The spillover from the two wars north of the country, in Somalia and Ethiopia."

"You mean weapons from those wars that have made their way down here?"

"That's right."

"As absurd as using them sounds, I believe you when you say you can get a couple of grenades," Haran said. "But putting aside the legality of it for a minute, wouldn't using them risk injuring or killing some of the family members who are in the house?"

"Yes, there is that chance," Regalo admitted. "We wouldn't be hitting them intentionally, but they might be in the wrong place at the wrong time."

"That bothers me, Joseph."

"It bothers me, too, Haran," Regalo answered, "but in freeing Wangetha there are going to be these attendant risks. It's not what I want. But you get the picture. The exploding grenades will either take out one or two of the kidnappers, or drive them out of the house into the open yard where we can pick them off."

"Once again, Joseph, what about the other ones, the ones not involved in the crime, the ones who could be killed or maimed as the grenades explode?"

"I don't know how many of them will be hurt, Haran. I hope none. Certainly, we won't be aiming at innocent people running out of the house, either."

Regalo's voice was slower, more measured now. "There is no other choice if we are going to free Wangetha. We have to get those thugs out of the house. Maybe you have a better idea, Haran? Tear gas maybe? But before you propose that, remember that it would not take out any of the guys we want. It would only serve to drive them out into the yard, angry, ready to fire at anything."

"But you'd be ready to fire too, wouldn't you?" Haran interjected.

"Once they're out there, crouched down and hiding behind trees, it would be very difficult to take them all on at once. I'm not saying that it couldn't work, only that the risks are high that they could get away or even kill Wangetha in the confusion. What we need to do is disable as many as we can first, and that means wounding or killing at least one of the three that may be in there."

"Your method involves some risk to Wangetha as well, doesn't it?" Haran countered.

"Very little," Regalo responded. "Since we'll be throwing the grenades into the house and not into the servant's quarters, there's not much chance that any shrapnel could get to her. Remember, from what you said, this is one of those old colonial era houses. They were built strong with thick, brick walls."

"And if one of them makes a dash for the servant's room and runs out, holding Wangetha in front of him?" Alain asked.

"Good question. Haran and I will have made it to each side of the lawn close to the house after the grenade is thrown. One of us can then jump on him from the back. We won't be able to take a shot at him for risk of the bullet going through his body into Wangetha."

"I'm glad that you thought of that, Joseph," Haran said testily. "But I still don't like the first part of your plan, which could involve maiming or killing several innocent people. I've seen too much bloodshed and suffering, Joseph. The fact that we already inflict so much killing on one another in this bruised and bleeding part of the world doesn't give you carte blanche to do the same. Do you understand that, Joseph? I have had enough of it. What happened in Rwanda is enough. There have been enough villages dripping in their own blood and enough rows upon rows of bleached skulls lined up neatly for inspection by gawkers from abroad."

"Freedom is costly, Haran. It doesn't come cheap," Regalo retorted.

"That's just what I am talking about here, Joseph, the cost. Your notion and my notion of cost are a little different.

I think exacting the price of even one child's life for freedom is too high a cost."

"Freedom for Wangetha?"

"Not just Wangetha. Freedom for all of Africa or freedom for anywhere in the world. I don't care if it's 500,000 children in a place like Iraq or one child here. It's not worth it. It's not worth it whatever people say. It's never, ever worth it."

"That's very extreme, Haran. Freedom is never achieved without some sacrifice."

"Let it be your sacrifice then, but not that of one child or mother in that safehouse."

"We can't make those guarantees, Haran. You must know that. As I said already, no one wants to deliberately harm them or take their lives."

"I understand that, but you're ready to risk expending their lives..."

"Only for the greater good of her freedom," interrupted Regalo.

"Only for those who are still alive after the bloodletting it takes to achieve it. What good is freedom for those who are dead, Joseph?"

"So we can never liberate people, is that it, Haran? We leave them in their oppression?"

"Don't you think we should first find out if they would still want their freedom if they knew that a number of their fathers, mothers, wives, or children would be maimed or butchered in the process?"

"It's impossible to know that."

"How can you be sure? And even if we can't ask them, shouldn't we err on the side of respecting their lives? In the case of my own sister, I know that she wouldn't enjoy her freedom if she knew the price would be the life of even one of the children in that house."

"I appreciate your idealism, Haran. But everything is ultimately a trade-off. What is the price that you're willing to pay in liberating your sister? If you have a better plan, let's hear it. I imagine that you have a wealth of experience from which to draw."

"You're not even considering the legal issues here, Joseph. For us to throw grenades in there and injure someone would be a criminal act. We could be prosecuted, even if we were involved in a rescue attempt. We're already circumventing the police. That's bad enough."

"We would be out of there. No one would be able to report us. Besides, I'm not worried about any legal system. How much respect for the law is there to begin with in this part of the world? Everything has to be considered in its broader context."

"There is more respect for it than you think, Joseph. Can't you be open to other alternatives? You are so strong in this one way. And it seems to blind you from seeing that it's one thing to choose to put your own life on the line for freedom and that it's another thing to make that choice for others.

"You see, as far as I'm concerned," Haran continued, "you're the one who needs more idealism in pursuing the advance of freedom, especially when you pursue it for others. Have we really thought this through, Joseph? Can't we come up with another way that doesn't risk killing any innocent people?"

"I didn't say with certainty that the grenades would kill this or that woman or child."

"But we have to be ready for it."

"That's right."

"Do you know how this looks, you a white man, prepared to kill women and children of a different color?"

"You mean prepared to risk some fallout to rescue one innocent woman, held against her will?" Regalo responded curtly.

"A black woman who had no say in whether she agreed to that price for her liberation," Haran snapped back.

Regalo looked away.

"Haran's right, Joseph. We can't do it the way you are suggesting," Alain interjected.

"Oh, so lover boy is willing to act noble now, too," Regalo shot back. "I thought you wanted to see Wangetha alive. I never said that we were going to deliberately kill any of the family members there."

"But your strategy practically guarantees it."

"If we don't do it this way, we might not succeed. Is that what you want, Alain?"

"No, that's not what I want. But, as Haran said, there must be another way."

Haran was becoming visibly angry. "These are my brothers and sisters that you want to kill."

"So all of these people are now your brothers and sisters? I thought Wangetha was your one blood relative. Listen to me, carefully. I don't want to kill them. I don't even want to injure them. I never said that I did."

"Yet it's all so casual to you," rejoined Haran. "You rationalize their deaths so easily. How wonderful for you! I don't want any part of your plan. Do you understand? And I don't believe that Wangetha would. Now get out of here!"

Regalo didn't move. "Haran, we have to work together. Let's not issue ultimatums to each other. Have you forgotten that I came all the way from Mombasa for this? I didn't have to come."

"I know, Joseph. We appreciate that and we admire your resolve and expertise. We just have to find another way. That's all."

"Haran is right, Joseph," Alain nodded in agreement. "Surely, we can find another way."

Regalo began pacing back and forth running his hands through his hair. "Well and good. I understand how you feel, Haran. You have a right to your views, especially in the case of your own sister and your own people. There is another way to rescue your sister, but it will be very risky for us, and for Wangetha."

"What is it?" Alain asked.

"We're going to have to trick the kidnappers into coming out of the house. We can do it with a fake ransom package. We can do it this very afternoon. I've seen it tried before, but it will only work if the smell of money clouds their reason."

"Explain this, Joseph," Alain said. "They've already given us a time and place to drop off the ransom money. How could the cash be delivered to them sooner as you suggest? It would be a huge surprise."

"Exactly. It would be something totally unexpected. The success of the tactic would depend on how they react, on how they handle the prospect of suddenly coming into big money under such odd circumstances. The way we set things up will require them to make one quick decision after another. We'll be betting that they make the wrong ones."

"So where is the risk?" Haran asked.

"The risk is in their seeing through the tactic immediately and then threatening to kill Wangetha if we don't hand ourselves over," Regalo said.

"What do we do then?" Alain asked.

"They won't know how many of us are involved in the trickery," Regalo responded. "So one person handing himself over to them should be enough to save Wangetha's life for the moment. Then you, Alain, can still go ahead and take the ransom to the Sarit Centre with the hope that she's released."

"If one of us has to hand himself over in case the strategy doesn't work, it should be me," Haran said. "This is a price that I, alone, should pay. She and I are of the same land, of the same people, of the same blood. It's not for you, Joseph, or for you, Alain, to take this risk or pay this price."

"We could draw cards, Haran," Alain interjected.

Regalo nodded.

"No. It wouldn't be right," Haran said firmly.

Regalo looked at Alain. "Leave it alone, Alain. Haran has a point, and that's the way it will be, the way Haran wants it. If we have any kind of luck, this will work. As I said, I've seen a similar kind of ploy work once, and it's something else to behold."

Regalo rubbed his hands together. "Now, how about ordering some good Kenyan coffee to lift us up a little bit, Haran, as we go through everything step by step, down to the last detail."

Reaching under his jacket, Regalo then pulled out his Colt. "We may be outnumbered, but I do have one powerful equalizer that I'll use when and if I have to. Haran, what have you got?"

Haran reached into the bottom drawer of his desk. "Just this old knife. You have a permit for your firearm, but you know very well that without one, it's illegal in Kenya to have guns. Even if we're dealing with criminals, the police will still go after us for having them."

"So, you don't have a gun?"

"No. I think that you have enough firepower for us," Haran said.

Regalo turned to Alain. "What about you, Alain?"

"I agree with Haran. Your firepower should be plenty. I'm not too bad with a knife. Have you got another one, Haran?"

"I can find you something, Alain."

"That's good, Haran," Regalo said. "Now, the first thing we're going to have do is..."

CHAPTER 26
RACHEL AND THE MOUNTAIN

∽

After she had finished talking to Regalo over the telephone, Rachel could not put her heart into preparing the house for him in the way she usually did. As she walked through the rooms looking for dust to wipe away, she was at first content to know that she meant enough to him to leave Mombasa and return to Nairobi. But her quiet happiness was giving way to a gnawing concern that she had now exposed him to new dangers. Though she didn't know what these dangers were, she couldn't quell the anxiety that she felt.

She knew there had been no choice other than to call him and use what little influence she possessed to persuade him to help this woman, whom she had never even met personally. But she was aware of Wangetha's beauty and sensuality and knew she was the kind of woman that men desired and even fought over. It seemed strange that she would be the one trying to find help for her now. After all, who was she, a mere housemaid, in comparison with someone like her?

At 29 years, she was not too old yet and not too plain, either, to find a man. But she knew that she was not nearly as attractive or exciting as Wangetha.

Only two men in her life had ever really taken an interest in her for herself. One was her father and the other was the older of her two brothers, who was married and lived with his wife in a small village not far from Kisumu on the shores of Lake Victoria. The first time that she visited him, she was immediately struck by the immense size of this lake, with its waves of water, more greenish than blue, stretching out as far as the eye could see. Seeing it directly was much more impressive than reading about it in school, where she had learned that it was the second-largest freshwater lake in the world. It made her proud to learn that. It made her even prouder when she saw the lake first-hand.

The fine fish that her brother regularly caught there from his homemade canoe with its triangular sails were mostly Nile tilapia, with plump, shimmering, green-silvery bodies tapering down to short, pointed heads and small reddish eyes. Her brother had taken a few of his catch of the day, gutted them, smothered them with butter, then roasted them over a fire for the three of them the first evening she was there. He had served each one of them a whole blackened fish, complete with its crisply-singed skin, and she had savored hers slowly, carefully peeling off the white flesh from the fish's spine with her fork in tender flakes, taking much pleasure in eating the tilapia's delicious meat with its mildly sweet taste.

She was grateful to her brother for feeding her well, but she had also hoped that he would introduce her to an acceptable man, maybe a fisherman. She wasn't that particular. He didn't have to be big, or strong, or well-to-do. She was looking for a man with a good heart who would be honest and true to her. If he were poor, she would labor by his side. They could even go to work at one of the tea plantations in the highlands of the Rift Valley, if he didn't care to fish any more. The hours were long, yet they were regular and the pay was enough to live on.

But her brother never introduced her to such a man. And so she returned to Nairobi and continued to do housekeeping for the expatriate community. She was very fortunate in that she had been able to go to school long enough to learn English fairly well and could read the *Nation* and was always able to find some kind of work.

She was especially grateful for this job and never complained to anyone about her work schedule, which meant walking three kilometers every morning from her small flat above a restaurant on the east side of the city, often in the rain, followed by a one-hour ride, usually standing, in a crowded, stinking *matatu*, where she would have to clutch her purse with both hands to protect it from grabbing hands. After getting off the *matatu* and catching her breath, there would be another walk of some two kilometers to Regalo's house and her daily chores of washing, cooking, and cleaning. When her workday was over, she faced the same, long trek back in the darkness of the night, until she finally came home to the tired eyes that she saw staring back at her in her tiny bathroom mirror before falling into bed exhausted.

Nor did she complain about the helplessness she felt when her younger brother up-country would call asking for money to pay for the medicine he needed to treat his slim disease. In recent weeks, it had been this brother's sickness that had been the biggest strain on her finances. In addition to helping support her parents, she now had to pay for his medical treatment at a clinic within a bus ride of his village. The treatment consisted of some very expensive medicines. But, they didn't seem to be helping him, from what he told her when they talked over the telephone the past week.

Regalo allowed her to call her brother on a regular basis from his home telephone, even though, as sorry as she felt for him, there were times when she just couldn't bring herself to talk to him. Not only was his sickness getting worse and more expensive to treat, but she could still hardly contain the anger she felt when she thought about his marrying the widow of one of their cousins who had died last year. She knew that he had done this to follow their tribal custom of taking care of widows, rooted in their concern that a widow not be left alone, especially if she had children. And this woman had four.

Even so, he should have put the well-being of the widow and her children above whatever responsibility he felt toward his deceased cousin, assuming that is what it was and not just plain lust to add to himself a second wife. When she asked him why he was really marrying her since he was so sick and could transmit his disease to her, he became angry. No one could catch his disease, he insisted, which he didn't believe was really slim disease anyway, throwing back at her that the village elders approved of what he was doing.

"But did you tell the elders of your sickness?" she almost screamed at him. When he said that it was none of their business and then refused to answer her question if he had forced himself on the widow, she hung up on him. The next week, though, she called him again and sent more money. What else could she do, she asked herself. He didn't have enough money for the treatment he needed, and he was her brother.

His wasting away disease only added to her feelings of loneliness, since there was no one with whom she could discuss her brother's condition. But she also knew that she wouldn't want to discuss it with anyone that she knew anyway, her elderly parents included, who didn't know how sick he really was. She was ashamed to talk about it and felt that no one would want to listen. It was a disease that was everywhere but nowhere at the same time, often finishing its deadly business in the silence of hospital rooms few wanted to visit.

There were occasions when she had yielded to the temptation of going to a bar with some other housekeepers in the vicinity and regretted it each time. It was not that she did not feel secretly gladdened by the advances that the men made to her. Though their words were crude and their groping offensive, they at least reminded her that she had some womanly charms, and for a little while she did not feel so plain.

Still, she could never respond to their advances. The example of her father and the way he lived were too strong in her. His quiet dignity, his respectful way with her mother, his strong but gentle hands, and his taste for hard work had all formed in her an image of the kind of man she would forever seek. Few measured up. Now and then she would recognize one, but he would be married.

She recognized these qualities in a man almost instantly, regardless of his tribe or even race. That was how it was when she had been interviewed by Regalo, who was seeking a house-keeper. He was by all appearances a hard man, who kept his feelings to himself. The interview was very formal, very practi-cal, all about the details of maintaining a house in good order. But as he talked to her and she looked into his eyes, those very brown eyes surrounded by his tanned, olive skin and topped off by his high forehead, she had the strangest feeling that this man was similar to her father and that she could trust him. She could not explain to herself why she had those feelings, but she was sure of them.

It was only after she had been working for him for a few months that she understood the basis for those feelings. Re-gardless of the seeming gruffness with which he sometimes spoke to her, she saw that he kept his word and that she could count on whatever he told her he would do, from not bur-dening her with more duties, to paying her for the least bit of overtime. Neither did he ever approach her for sexual favors, as the men in the bars did. Nor did he use vulgar words in her presence. But most of all it was the sense of security she felt with him. He made her feel protected, and it was a wonder-ful feeling, one that soon began to accompany her not only throughout the day but deep into the night as well.

There were days when to know that this man was her protection was especially important to her. There were days when the ride to work from her small room on top of the little eatery, which was next to a cheap motel of unpainted cinder blocks frequented by truck drivers, was almost more than she could bear. It was one thing to sometimes lie awake half the night having to hear the noisy patrons drinking and eating below and then to listen to them going off to the motel with its open windows, where they made different kinds of noises.

She had gradually learned to find sleep in spite of these distractions. But she could never get used to the shoving, the pushing, the struggle for just a small space to stand in the *matatu* bringing her to within walking distance of Regalo's house in the morning. And when the driver would play the music loudly in the *matatu's* powerful sound system as it was winding crazily in and out of the flow of traffic, sometimes almost tipping over, she wanted to cry in frustration. She felt so small, so helpless, just a rag doll being thrown back and forth against the elbows and chests and backs of the sweating bodies crowded around her.

It was then that she would try to concentrate hard on the image of her deceased grandfather who had been the chief of her village for many years. She had always tried to please him when she was a little girl, fetching him his hot tea the way he liked it, with a good deal of milk, a custom he had acquired from the colonialists. As she would concentrate on the picture of him in her mind, she hoped that she had done nothing to displease him as he watched her from the spirit world. She was not so concerned about other deceased ancestors who might be watching her, because she could not visualize them.

But she could visualize her grandfather, and she knew that when she was living as she should, he was happy with her and that would make her happy too. And now she asked him to be good to her, to not be displeased with her, and to make sure that she could get off the *matatu* in one piece, without having her purse wrested out of her hands or having some man push himself against her in a vulgar way, or having someone elbow her in the face.

Once when her purse was stolen even after she had appealed to her grandfather, she was convinced that she had earlier displeased him in some way and thought for many days about what she could have done wrong. But try as hard as she might, she was not able to put her finger on it. Then, after many weeks of riding the *matatus* without being pushed or shoved too hard and without having anything stolen, she was sure that her grandfather must have become pleased with her once again. She was sure that it was because she was now sending nearly half of her wages home to her parents, in addition to sending money to her younger brother.

Sending this much money to them meant that she could not buy new shoes or the television she wanted for her room so that she would have a distraction from the noises around her. But she was still very grateful for all that she had. She didn't have to beg for money or sell her body. She didn't have slim disease. And she was protected by Regalo, to whose house she was sure that her grandfather had led her.

She returned to thinking about what was worrying her now. She had a bad feeling that Regalo was heading into some kind of danger, and there was nothing she could do about it. It weighed on her heart that she had called him in Mombasa and led him into these troubles she sensed he was now facing. But she knew that her grandfather would have been very unhappy if she had turned her back on this other woman, this Wangetha.

People here did not always do enough to help each other. She knew that was true. But sometimes there was only so much of life and energy left in people like her, after fighting the entire day just to live and make a few shillings. There was so little of one's own strength to then give to another. But her grandfather had always said to give what you could, so she wanted to help this woman, no matter how tired she was and how afraid she was for Regalo.

She slowly walked into the living room and searched among Regalo's collection of cassettes for the Italian name she associated with the music she had learned to love so much. After poring through the scores of cassettes, she located the name Alessandro Stradella on the one entitled *Musique de*

Chambre pour Trompette. She turned on the receiver, pushed the button that she knew would slide out the receptacle for the cassette and slipped it in.

This was the music that she had seen Regalo listen to over and over again during those nights when he came home with what she sensed was a heavy spirit. Now that her heart was burdened too, filled with worry and uncertainty, she would apply the same tonic to herself. In a few seconds, the soaring notes of the trumpet began to fill the room, making her fall in love with its pure and majestic melody all over again. Each time she heard these notes, the same feelings welled up in her that she experienced as a child when she once traveled to the Tanzanian border with her grandfather to the foot of Mount Kilimanjaro and saw for the first time its snow-shrouded peak gradually come into view as the morning mist was giving way to the light of the sun.

The sight of this immense mountain, formed from three volcanoes that had come together into one broad summit, topped with the whitest of snow and standing completely alone with no other mountains around it as far as the eye could see, had at first filled her with terror, as she tried to fathom the size of the hands that had formed it. But the more she gazed at this mighty force rising into the sky, which her grandfather told her approached 6,000 meters in height, the less fear she felt, until she sensed a warm glow rising inside her that gradually turned into a quiet inner peace.

It was good to know something so high and so commanding, that was far beyond anything to be found in the ordinary, evil-ridden world around her. She understood that the mountain, in all its power and glory, had simply been waiting patiently for her to recognize its splendor. Once she did that, it became her friend. She had paid her respects and now there was nothing to fear. The mountain belonged to her world, or better said, she now belonged to the world of the mountain.

As she thought some more about Kilimanjaro, she could imagine the lifting, arching notes coming out of Stradella's trumpet floating in the air, gliding gently into the sky, until they were lost in the mountain's white crest.

Her mind turned to Regalo. I am with you, she whispered in accompaniment to Stradella's music. My thoughts tonight will soar like the notes of this trumpet, taking wings to fly to you.

CHAPTER 27
AT THE SAFEHOUSE

∽

It was 3:25 p.m. on Thursday when Alain parked Regalo's Jeep two streets removed from the safehouse near some trees. His face was thoroughly smudged with charcoal. Regalo was dressed in black, making his dark olive skin look a little lighter than it was. Haran was still wearing the rumpled sports coat he had on earlier. The three got out of the vehicle.

"Now remember," Regalo said to Haran as they stood by its driver's side. "As soon as you have the sentry guy bought off and he thinks he is going to lead you to the *changaa* den, cough loudly into your walkie-talkie two times. These are compact, high-quality talkies, made in Japan that I've used before."

"Do they have enough range?" Haran asked.

"More than enough, and they're good at picking up voices. Keep yours in your inside breast pocket with the jacket open so I can hear some of your chatter. Your coughs will be the signal that it's time for me to make my approach. I'll sneak up, grab him from behind, and put a hold on him while you tie him up and gag him. Then we'll make him draw his buddies out to the street with talk of the ransom money having arrived."

"Sounds good," Alain nodded.

"OK, Haran. It's up to you now," Regalo said. "You lead. I'm never going to be more than a hundred meters behind you, and I'll have the fake ransom packet in my knapsack on my back. As soon as I get your signal, I'm moving in."

"*Hakuna matata,* no worries. Wish me luck!"

"You got it, partner."

Regalo turned to Alain. "Stay behind me, but not too close. We need to keep an eye out for anyone who might be driving up. Once we have the sentry disabled, we'll let you know on your walkie-talkie. By then we'll be into the second phase of our plan."

"I'll be ready, Joseph."

Regalo and Alain watched Haran until he disappeared into the distance. Within a few minutes, he had reached the vicinity of the safehouse and casually sauntered up to the sentry on duty at the gate entrance. Just as Regalo had predicted, Haran's talk of *changaa* and the roll of shillings that he flashed diverted his attention. When Haran then coughed twice, Regalo wasted no time in sneaking up to a tree closer to the gate. As the sentry was talking to Haran, Regalo made his move.

Gliding forward with lightning speed, he caught the sentry's mouth from behind with his right hand and then choked his neck with the left, forcing him to kneel on the ground. Haran then quickly pulled out a small roll of heavy-duty tape from his pocket, taped his mouth shut, and then taped his hands together. The entire maneuver could not have taken more than a minute.

While Regalo kept his pistol trained on the bound sentry's head, Haran helped him to his feet and shoved him closer to the gate but not directly in front of it where he could be seen from the house.

Regalo spoke in a low voice directly into the sentry's ear. "If you make the slightest move to escape, I'll blow your head off. You have a chance to live, but only if you do exactly as I say. When my friend removes the tape from your mouth, you must shout toward the house that a package has been dropped off by a speeding car. You must say that it has 'Ransom Money' written on it, and you must ask if you can leave your post to bring it to them. Do you understand?"

As the sentry nodded his head vigorously, Haran removed the tape from his mouth. He then pushed him step by step until he was standing at the far left of the driveway entrance. Regalo, concealed by the bushes, kept his gun trained on his head.

"Hold this package," Haran ordered as he thrust into his hands the cardboard box with 'Ransom Money' written on it in large black letters. "Now get started and show them the box."

Immediately, the sentry began yelling in the direction of the house. "Hey! Hey! A package has arrived. Listen to me!"

The front door opened and a lean, medium-height man with dreadlocks emerged.

"What is it? What are you talking about?"

"A package has arrived. I have it here in my hands. You can see it from there. It has 'Ransom Money' written on it."

"That was just fine," Regalo whispered to the sentry. "Now, be quiet until I tell you what else to say."

Regalo looked at Haran. "Let's see if they will carry the ball for us from here."

"So far so good," Haran thought as he and Regalo stood off to the side of the gate. The first step in the sequence had been easy, and they had set the next step into play. It was a lucky break that the kidnappers had picked this home at the end of a long cul-de-sac as their safehouse. There were no passersby or other traffic to worry about.

His confidence growing, Regalo signaled Alain to join up with them. "All that we have to do now, once these guys start coming out, is to be ready and surprise them from behind. Just like we did with this punk. Shooting will be a last resort, as we agreed. Let's hope that there will be two or even three who come out. If three come out, all will be accounted for. If two come out, we'll just have to hope the third one is not coming back anytime soon."

"And if only one comes out, we'll have to play it by the seat of our pants, I take it," Alain said.

"We can do it," Haran said calmly. "It will just mean that we have to sneak into the house and take out whoever is still in there one by one. Not easy, but doable."

The dreadlocks man in front of the house was now shaking his finger at the detained sentry, who was still standing at the left edge of the driveway. The barrel of Regalo's gun was out of the line of sight from the house but less than a meter away from his head.

"Don't do anything with that package yet," the dreadlocks man ordered.

He then turned around toward the house. "Should I tell him to bring the package here?" he asked.

"Are you stupid?" a loud voice from the inside of the house immediately retorted. "We have no idea what's in that package. It could be a bomb for all we know. Have you already forgotten that they were supposed to drop off the ransom money at the Sarit Centre tomorrow? Something is funny here."

"But the package has 'Ransom Money' written on it."

"So what? How stupid are you? Any kind of package can have 'Ransom Money' written on it."

"Why don't we both go up and look at it?"

"No! I have to stay here close to the bitch Wangetha. She has already tried to escape once."

"What should we do, then? The package looks like it's about money."

"You tell Rufus, since he is there with the package, to open it up and tell us what's inside."

"But you just said that it might have a bomb in it. What if it explodes while he's opening it?"

"That will be his bad luck. It's not for you to worry about! Now you tell him to open it and tell us what's inside."

"As you say."

The dreadlocks man turned around and yelled at the sentry man. "Open it up and see what's inside. Be quick about it!"

"Do what he says and show him a handful of the shilling notes that we put in there," Regalo instructed. "Tell him the package is full of money, many 1,000-shilling notes. And make it convincing. Your life depends on it."

The sentry man set the package down on the driveway and began to open it slowly.

"What do you see?" the dreadlocks man yelled as he stood impatiently by the door and began waving his gun.

"Answer! What do you see?"

The sentry man rose from the package with both fists filled with 1,000-shilling notes. "Money! There is money! A lot of money! Do you hear? Do you see what's in my hands? The package is full of money! There's also an envelope."

"Is there anything written on the envelope?"

"It says 'Instructions for releasing Wangetha Wachira, from Alain Sardou'."

The dreadlocks man ran back into the house. "Money, he found money! The package is filled with 1,000-shilling notes and a letter from her boyfriend. What should we do now?"

"Tell him to bring the package to us immediately," the loud voice said.

"Wouldn't it be better if I went to get it?"

"No! This could be a set-up."

"A set-up? But I saw the money with my own eyes and money can't lie. Money is money! I could almost smell the money, it was so close."

"Use your head for once. They could be using the money as bait to get us out of the house. This could be a trap. You tell him to bring the money to us."

As the dreadlocks man emerged out of the house again, he didn't see the sentry man at the gate. "Rufus, where are you?" he yelled. "Rufus, you bastard. Bring the money! Answer! Answer!"

He turned around and shouted at the house. "He's not answering. He's left with the damned money. He's run away with the money! The double-crosser! I'm going after him."

"Shut up and stay where you are!" the voice rang out from inside the house. "You don't know that he ran off with the money. Something could have happened to him."

"But he's not coming. And he had shown us the money. He practically threw it in front of our noses. But once he felt the money in his hands, once he smelled it, he couldn't resist and ran off with it. I never did trust him or any other Luo."

"What do you mean 'Luo'? Rufus is a Kikuyu."

"No, my dear brother, Rufus is not the Kikuyu you thought he was. I warned you about him. I warned you about taking on a Luo, but you didn't believe me."

"How can you say that he's a Luo when he speaks Kikuyu as well as you and I?"

"I heard him speaking Dholuo once in his sleep."

"And how do you know that you weren't asleep, also, and dreaming this up?"

"I wasn't dreaming. I heard him. Besides, he never really looked like a Kikuyu to me. I know you thought he looked Kikuyu enough, and there might have been some of us in him. But I saw the Luo in him too, and it was stronger than the Kikuyu. So what did it matter what language he spoke? His heart was Luo all along. He didn't give a damn about us, and now you see the result."

"He was with us all the way."

"No, not all the way. He was only with us until the money arrived. And now what can we do? Another Kikuyu we could have controlled. He could never have found refuge anywhere in this country if he double-crossed us. But the Luos will protect him, especially after he shows up with all this money. So who is the stupid one, huh? After all this trouble, I could almost smell the money from here myself. Then he runs off with it. I'm going to go after him. And when I find him, he will wish he were never born. The double-crosser!"

"Shut up, you fool! You don't know what happened at the gate," the voice from inside the house yelled. "And don't go out there. We don't know what's going on outside the gate now that he's gone."

"But I do know! I knew that we could never trust that damned Luo. They partner with us to use us. And we Kikuyu are supposed to be the clever ones. No, no my dear Kikuyu brother. They are the clever ones. We are the fools."

"Listen to me for once. This has nothing to do with his being a Luo or anything else. Quit talking that rubbish. You don't know what happened to him. Maybe they came back to get him. Maybe they ambushed him. Maybe they're waiting for us."

"I don't know if anyone is waiting to get us. I only know that Rufus loves money even more than he loves his beer. And now he's gone. He's gone with our sweet money. I tell you that I could almost smell the money, it was so close."

"Stop and think for just one minute! Why would they bring the ransom money here when we had a time and place already all arranged? And how would they know where we are? This is very strange. This looks like a set-up to me."

"You say that I'm a fool. You're the fool! You think that you have brains, but Rufus, that cunning Luo has twice the brains that you do. Oh, are those Luos smart! The trick has already been played, and Rufus was the one tricking us. He was angry about all the guard duty we made him do. And he was even angrier about being allowed to touch the bitch Wangetha just once or twice. This is his revenge, his sweet revenge against the oppressive Kikuyu. Just think what our other brother would think. Oh, if only he were here now."

Regalo nudged Haran and Alain as they were listening to the exchange. "It's nice to know that there are only two inside."

"I'm sick to my stomach over the money that has been taken from us. Do I have to tell you once again that I could smell the money, it was that close?"

"Control yourself, you fool. I'm tired of listening to your blather. Quit telling me that you could smell the money. Don't provoke me anymore and use your head for a change. He could have been ambushed. Think about that. This could be a trap for us!"

"You're not listening to me. I tell you that I could smell..."

The loud-voiced man now leaped out of the house and grabbed his cohort by his shirt lapels, shaking him hard and then slapping him on both cheeks.

"I told you that I'm not going to listen to you blather about smelling money anymore!"

"You didn't have to do that."

"Yes I did. Now get a hold of yourself and tell me what you saw, not what you smelled. Just how much money did you say there was?"

"Both of his fists were full of 1,000-shilling notes. So there must have been at least 50 notes. That's 50,000 shillings just in his hands."

"Could you see the numbers on the bills?"

"No, but I saw their color. I could recognize that color a kilometer away. Besides, he would have no reason to lie about the bills."

"But you just said that you didn't trust Luos."

"I don't, usually. But I saw him open the package and take out the bills. That was the first time he saw them."

"Enough of this talk! We'll go take a look, but we'll do it the smart way. You go first while I cover you from behind."

"Why me first?"

"Because you said he had disappeared with the money. So, if you're right, there's nothing to fear. But if you're wrong, if someone is waiting for us, you'll be the first one to know."

"Ha, ha. That's very funny. But I'll go ahead. I'm not afraid. We have to find out what happened to our Luo friend. Let's hurry so that we can still track him and get our money."

"Wait until I go get my gun."

As the loud-voiced man headed back inside the house, Regalo whispered to Haran and then to Alain.

"All right. This is it. We may be able to take them without firing a shot by sneaking up on them from behind. But first of all we have to take the guy we've bound up back to the Jeep. Alain, that's your job."

"Got it."

"Then once you're close to the Jeep, release his gag and force him at the point of your knife to call for his buddies."

"The timing is going to have to be just right," Haran said.

"You know it. We're only going to have a few seconds to nab them from the time the guy begins yelling," Regalo added.

He turned again to Alain. "If the two get to you before we can grab them, you will have to defend yourself. They may start shooting if they catch sight of you. But Haran and I are not going to let it come to that, are we, Haran?"

"Not on your life, Joseph."

"OK, get a move on now, Alain."

Regalo grabbed Alain by the shoulder as he was leaving. "Just one other thing. Keep your eyes peeled for any approaching cars. We know that the fourth guy is gone somewhere. If someone suspicious approaches, do your best to get the hell out of there and take the one with you to the police. Haran and I will fend for ourselves."

As Alain hustled the sentry man at knifepoint toward the Jeep, Regalo turned to Haran. "You wait here nestled behind the shrubs and foliage covering the left section of the fence. I'll hide myself in the same stuff on the right side. Then we can grab them as they pass through the gate on their way out."

"All we have to do is stay low and be quiet. They shouldn't be able to see us."

"Right, Haran. So let's take our positions."

"We move at the same time."

"That's the idea."

"Good. Let's get down and out of sight."

As Regalo and Haran kneeled down behind the two sides of the outer fence, the dreadlocks man and the loud-voiced man began walking slowly to the gate.

"Don't stay too close to me!" the loud-voiced man barked. "Move along. We need to create some distance between us so they can't get both of us at once."

"You scum of the earth. You don't care about my life at all, do you?"

"Shut up and keep going. When you get close to the gate tell me what you see."

"I'm nearly here. The gate is completely open and I don't see anything or anyone. I told you that he left with the money. There's nothing. Only a vehicle parked further down by some trees."

"All right, I'm coming up to you."

"You can see from where you are. There's nothing. I told you. Now will you admit that you were wrong? The money, the money! I could cry."

"You idiot," the loud-voiced man snapped as he approached the gate. "There are hardly ever any vehicles parked on the dirt streets around here. Any vehicle close by is suspicious."

"Wait, I hear something!"

"I'm here, I'm here," the sentry man yelled from a distance. "They left me tied up here. Come get me. I'm in this Jeep."

"Do you have the money with you?" the dreadlocks man yelled back.

Alain poked his knife into the sentry man's back as he kept telling him what to say.

"No, but I know where it is. Get me out of here!"

"Now I understand," the loud-voiced man said. "This is a trap, but not the way I thought. I know what happened. He took the money and commandeered this Jeep from somebody driving by. Now he wants to kill us both."

"That's it. You're right! But we can still overpower him and get the money, just the two of us."

"For once, you have an idea that's not completely stupid."

CHAPTER 28
FINDING WANGETHA

ﾟﾟ

"Hurry up! Get me out of here!" the sentry man yelled, at Alain's prompting.

"We're coming. Just be patient!"

"I will strangle this lying Luo with my bare hands for plotting to kill us and leaving with the money," threatened the loud-voiced man.

As the two walked through the gate, Regalo signaled to Haran with his hand, waving it down sharply and pointing to the backs of the dreadlocks man and the loud-voiced man. They jumped forward, with Regalo moving toward the one on the right and Haran the one on the left.

"This is it, you punk," Regalo grunted, pushing the barrel of his gun into the dreadlocks man's back. Haran brandished his knife with his right hand in the loud-voiced man's face, his left arm keeping a stranglehold around his neck. With both men cursing loudly, Alain appeared on the scene with duct tape and secured their hands behind their backs. He then taped their mouths shut. Once they were tied up, Regalo and Haran pushed them to a nearby tree on the grounds, where they taped their bodies against the trunk, one on each side.

"Excellent job," Regalo beamed. "We did it, Haran. We did it. Everything worked out just as we hoped."

"Yeah, we did it," Haran responded soberly. "But now we need to see how Wangetha is." He looked at Alain.

"Why don't you go in and get her?" Haran urged. "In the meanwhile, I'll go get the Jeep and the other guy."

"I left him there taped up pretty good," Alain said. "We can fix him to this other tree."

"Then we quit this place, all four of us, the sooner the better," Regalo said firmly.

"We're just going to leave these criminals here?" Alain asked.

"For the time being. We'll call the police later to get them," Regalo answered.

As Alain started toward the house he felt the sun's rays for the first time that day and caught sight of the brilliant sky. The lawn was green, too, he noted, and the flowers were in full bloom. And the colonial era house didn't even appear as rundown as he once imagined. Why hadn't he noticed all this before, he wondered, as he made his way to the house.

But why was he walking when he should have been running? Why were his palms sweating? Why was his heart racing? Why did he suddenly feel that time had slowed to a crawl? It was taking forever for him to get there. The more steps he took, the more the entryway seemed to recede into the house. He stopped to get a reading of how far away it was. It couldn't have been more than 50 meters now. He started to run as hard as he could. The grounds, the trees, the flowers, the house ahead of him all became a blur until he was finally there, standing in front of the splintered, white door, his sides heaving, knocking on it furiously to be let in.

Why was he knocking? He tried the door knob. It wouldn't turn. Why was it locked? When the two guys left the house to chase after the money, would they have thought of locking the door behind them? Then he caught himself and slowed his racing thoughts. "Of course, there were the other people inside. They were afraid. They must have locked the door from within."

Knowing that, he brushed aside the temptation to kick in the door. He would continue knocking.

"Please open the door. We are friends. You don't have to be afraid," he shouted.

Slowly, an aged woman opened the door with a broom in her hand, wearing a plain, long, formless dress. Alain could see the thinness of her bent body, the whiteness of her hair, and the deep furrows and wrinkles in her face. He could also not help but see the sadness and fatigue in her eyes.

"I am so tired, so very tired," she said quietly as she let Alain in. "I am so glad that you came. All of us, my entire family, we are so glad that you came. Please forgive me for coming to the door with this broom. I was just trying to make myself useful, cleaning what I could. It has been so hard to do anything with these men here."

She pointed her finger to a door down the hall. "That leads to the servant's room in the back. She has been waiting for you. Go to her."

"You know me?" Alain asked.

"I know about you," the woman answered.

Alain smiled at her and began walking down the hallway. On one side there were two windows facing out into the yard from which he could see a large magnolia tree, its trunk winding up out of sight. On the other side were three old prints. One was of a young African woman carrying her child on her back. Another was a print of an African cargo vessel docking at the port of Mombasa. He recognized the figure on the last print – Kenya's first president, *Mzee* Jomo Kenyatta in full regal garb.

As he passed through the door at the end of the hallway and entered the patio area before the servant's room, he tried to collect his thoughts. How would he react once he saw her? What if she had changed too much? What if her ordeal had disfigured her? What would he feel?

He went through the open gate wondering who had opened it and knocked gently on the door.

After waiting a few moments and not hearing any response, he tapped on the door lightly again.

"Wangetha, it's me, Alain. May I come in?"

"Is it really you, Alain?" he heard her say on the other side of the door. "Is it really you?"

"Yes, Wangetha. It's really me. You are free now. The men are gone. They can't hurt you anymore. Please open the door. We can go. We can leave this place."

"Oh, Alain," she sobbed. "I don't know if I should open the door. I don't want you to see me like this. You don't know what they've put me through. It's been terrible, just terrible."

"It doesn't matter," Alain found himself saying. "You are still Wangetha. Please open the door."

"You don't know. You don't know what they've done. I don't want you to know. I want to forget everything as soon as possible."

"It doesn't matter now. It's over. Please open the door so we can go. You can tell me everything then. We need to go. Everything will be all right. They're gone for now but we don't know who will come back. It's dangerous to stay here."

"I understand."

As the door began to creak open Alain could hardly recognize the person facing him. The beautiful woman, whose proud profile against the blue, morning sky was forever etched in his mind, was now standing before him in torn clothes with a face so bruised and swollen that he could hardly recognize it.

"So it is you, Alain, even with that black face," she said haltingly and then fell trembling into his arms. "Somehow I knew that you would come."

Alain held her tightly and brushed her mangled hair with his right hand. "Of course, I would come. Two others whom you will meet are with me."

Wangetha found his other hand and clutched it.

"There's a car waiting for us," Alain said, "and we have to hurry."

As they went back through the house, Wangetha stopped to kiss the woman with the broom on the cheek.

"She's been just wonderful," Wangetha murmured. "I couldn't have survived without her notes of encouragement tucked under the dishes on the trays of food she left for me."

As Alain grabbed her hand, they ran out of the faded house into the yard and out to the gate where the Jeep was waiting with the motor running.

"We have to get out of here," Haran said from the driver's seat. "Please get in the back seat, Wangetha."

"Haran, is that you?" Wangetha asked, choking back more tears. "You came for me also?"

"Yes, sister, I came for you."

৵

In the time it took Haran to put the safehouse well behind them, he noticed a car in the rear-view mirror.

"Somebody may be following us," he said. "I'll try to shake them by veering off to this road on the right. There was always that question about the fourth guy who was not at the house. It might be him. We can't take any chances."

As soon as Haran turned and had gone about half a kilometer, he saw that the car was still in the rear-view mirror. "They turned right also. We're definitely being followed!"

He floored the accelerator.

"Careful, Haran," Regalo warned. "This road is unpaved and in bad shape."

Regalo grabbed a set of binoculars from the glove box to get a look at the car behind them. "It's a Mercedes. They're driving like hell. Wait, now I can see who they are. There are three of them. One is a guy with dreadlocks who seems to be telling the driver where to go. And I can't believe it. Robidi is in the back!"

"Did you say dreadlocks?" Haran asked.

"Yeah, dreadlocks," Regalo answered.

"Then that must be the fourth guy," Alain chimed in. "There were two of them that I saw at Nakuru with dreadlocks. One of them we just left tied up. This is the other one. He must have told Robidi where Wangetha was being held, and Robidi was probably coming to finish the job himself. Why else would he be in the car with them?"

"That's it!" Regalo exclaimed, as Wangetha huddled in her blanket in the back seat. "The double-crossers get double-crossed. This fourth guy must have been getting impatient to get his share of the ransom. So he left his buddies to hook up with Robidi to squeeze some money out of him.

"And that explains why he wasn't in the safehouse and is now with Robidi," Regalo continued. "But what timing! What a coincidence that they were on their way back to take out Wangetha just as we were making our getaway! It's just too perfect. It makes more sense that someone tipped them off that we had appeared on the scene."

"So they were coming back not only to finish the job on Wangetha, but to get us too," Alain added.

"Right you are."

"But who could have tipped them?" Alain asked.

"It had to be someone from inside the safehouse," Regalo responded. "My guess is that Robidi and his new pal were waiting for the cover of the night to make their move on Wangetha when they got the word."

"So they pushed ahead their timetable when they heard we were here. But who inside the safehouse could have been the informant? I only saw the old lady who let me in," Alain noted. "And Wangetha was so grateful for the help she received from her."

"We know that there were others in the house from the information Haran's cousin gave us," Regalo responded. "It could have been one of them."

"What difference does all that make?" Wangetha asked in a raspy voice. "I'm the one to blame for this mess. I never should have gotten involved with him in the first place. I could see what kind of man he was. I wasn't blind."

She looked at Alain worriedly. "I know what you must think of me..."

"That's enough of that blabber right now," Regalo interjected. "We can't allow Haran to be distracted by all this talk. We're on one of the worst roads you can find on the outskirts of Nairobi. But let's hope that it slows Robidi down a little bit."

By now the Jeep was going full blast, but the Mercedes was slowly gaining on them.

"You're driving damn good," Regalo said to Haran. "But at any moment they're going to start firing. Everybody needs to get down and stay down. Haran, you're going to have to drive slouched forward. You'll have a hard time seeing, but it shouldn't be for too long."

As shots rang out from the Mercedes and Regalo began to return the fire, Haran glanced into the rear-view mirror before lowering his head. "I can barely see ahead of me. I don't know how long I can do this."

"I'll keep trying to hold them off from this side." Regalo was now shouting to make his voice heard above the shooting and the roar of the cars.

"Haran, listen to me!" Regalo yelled. "When I tell you to, slam your brakes full force. They won't be able to tell you're going to stop. I smashed our rear tail lights before we sped away from the safehouse in case we were followed."

"So that's what you were doing back there."

"That's right. Now as we come sliding to a halt, we'll kick up a lot of dust. No one will be able to see at first. But as the dust settles, I can try to pick them off before they can get to us."

When the Mercedes drew closer, Regalo shouted, "Now, Haran, now! Slam the brakes for all you're worth!"

Shuddering from front to end, the Jeep skidded to a stop, sending a whirlwind of brown dirt and dust into the sky. As the Mercedes veered around its rear bumper on the right side, Regalo threw open the Jeep's door, catching the extended hand of the gunman on the Mercedes' left side.

"My hand! My hand! Stop, stop! For the love of God, stop!" the gunman yelled to the driver, who pulled the Mercedes to a halt. "Oh my God, my hand, my hand!"

Regalo closed the door quickly to keep any more dust from getting inside the Jeep. Haran and Alain had already rolled up its windows. But the windows of the Mercedes were still open while the outside panel of its left door was red with the blood of the gunman's mangled hand.

"Where is she? Where is the bitch?" Robidi was yelling while coughing non-stop. "Clear the dust away so that I can see! Clear it away now!"

Ignoring the order, the maimed gunman cried out in a voice much louder than Robidi's. "I'm ruined! I'm going to bleed to death! We have to turn back. You've got to take me to the hospital where they can fix my hand. Somebody help me bandage this up. Oh my God, this hurts! Somebody is going to have to pay for this."

"Shut up," Robidi barked as he turned to the driver. "Don't you go anywhere! We don't have time to take him to any hospital. Stay right where you are. They've seen me. We can't let them get away."

"To hell with you," the driver shot back. "We have to drive to the hospital and take care of his hand. This is my cousin. We can't do this to him."

Robidi pointed his gun at the driver. "Now, you listen to me. You're not going anywhere unless you want me to drive a bullet through your fat head. Take this handkerchief and tie a tourniquet around his wrist to stop the bleeding. He's already made a bloody mess of this car. And hurry up."

As the driver worked on the tourniquet, Robidi opened the rear door and sneaked out, taking cover behind the right side of the Mercedes. The shafts of light that were slowly penetrating the dust cloud gave him a line of sight to the windshield of the Jeep. Through it he could just make out Haran's head jutting above the steering wheel. He lifted his pistol to take aim.

Peering through the dust from his side, Regalo managed to catch sight of Robidi's face as he pointed his pistol at Haran, his eyes swelling into glistening, glassy beads, his bony hands wrapped around the pistol butt, the gnarled right index finger fondling the trigger.

As Robidi's lower lip twitched with anticipation and he began to pull the trigger, Regalo jumped out of the Jeep with his gun blazing, deliberately running straight into Robidi's line of fire. In the exchange, one screaming bullet caught Regalo in the neck before Robidi ran out of ammunition.

Bleeding badly, Regalo stumbled back to the Jeep. As soon as he was inside, Haran revved the engine and they moved out in a fresh cloud of dust.

"Step on it, Haran. We have a head start. Let's get out of here!" Alain cried out, while he took his shirt off, tore off both sleeves, and wrapped one around Regalo's neck.

"It's lucky the bullet didn't hit your spine."

"But not so lucky that it hit my carotid artery. We've got to stop the bleeding."

Wangetha took the other sleeve and carefully wrapped it on top of the first sleeve.

In the Mercedes, Robidi, who was unscathed in the shoot-out, was screaming at the driver. "Get going! We have to catch them!"

"I'm not following them," retorted the driver. "I have to take care of my cousin."

Robidi glared at the gunman with the mangled hand. "The tourniquet stopped most of the bleeding. Now stop crying about your hand. You've got another one left." He nudged his gun into the back of the neck of the driver. "Move this thing! I said move it."

But the driver wouldn't budge.

Inside the Jeep, Alain was now ripping the sleeves off Regalo's shirt. "I need yours, too. Mine weren't enough to stop your bleeding."

"I know," Regalo moaned in pain. "It's hard as hell to stop the carotid artery from hemorrhaging when you get shot there. We have to get to a hospital."

"Which one?"

"Nairobi Hospital. I know some of the doctors there."

Alain turned to Haran. "Do you know the way?"

"I can find it."

"Then let's step on it."

It was dark when the Jeep pulled up to the emergency entrance of Nairobi Hospital. Robidi had not been able to catch up with them, but Regalo had fallen unconscious. By the time the emergency technicians arrived with a stretcher, he was dead.

CHAPTER 30
HARAN VERSUS ALAIN

∽

Haran and Alain walked out of Wangetha's hospital room into the hallway.

"From what the doctor said, she's going to need a lot of medical attention and rest for her injuries to heal," Alain said. "He also wants to test her for slim disease."

"She's been through hell, but she's as resilient as they come," Haran responded.

"As resilient as beautiful?"

"For sure."

"It's very encouraging to hear you say that. Let's go down to the cafeteria for some coffee," Alain suggested. "You seem so distracted. It's Regalo, isn't it?"

"Yes, it's Regalo," Haran said as they headed to the ground floor. There is a Kikuyu proverb that comes into my head now, as I think of him. It goes, "*Gutiri mundu wonaga wega wake, no kuonwo wonagwo,*" which means "Nobody can see his own goodness: it can be seen only by others."

"That's nice, Haran," Alain responded. "You had quite an argument with him once."

"Yes, but I never questioned his goodwill, only his methods. There was never any doubt about his skill, either. He was in his own category. What about your feelings toward him? Didn't you resent some of the things he did?"

"I have to admit that I wasn't always comfortable with his need to be in control," Alain said, "even as I have to acknowledge that he was a natural leader. I'm sure you felt the same way at times."

Haran nodded.

After they ordered their coffee, took their cups to a table, and sat down, Haran took a deep breath. "I have to confess that there is something else bothering me, Alain, bothering me very much."

"What is it?"

"This is very difficult for me to tell you, Alain, after all that we've been through."

"Don't tell me then. We succeeded in spite of everything. Don't trouble yourself now."

"I don't want to tell you, but I have to."

"Then tell me if it will make you feel better."

Haran sighed deeply. "I was the one who tipped off Robidi that you were at the Ngong Hills Lodge. He knew you were with Wangetha and had already learned about the double-cross. But he didn't know where you were staying or where the safehouse was. His people were asking around and were ready to pay a lot of money to get this information."

"But I was also paying you to get information, and I was paying you well," Alain said incredulously.

"Yes, but Robidi offered serious money, money that would re-establish me in this town."

"And you obliged him, knowing full well he would have me beaten to a pulp in trying to find out where she was?"

Alain slammed his cup to the table as he stood up and glared at Haran. "So you were the one! You, Haran! I once wondered about you being the culprit. But then I became convinced it couldn't have been you because of all the doubts you managed to raise in my mind about Rebecca. Don't you remember? Don't you remember all your insinuations?"

Alain's voice was rising in anger. "How could you possibly have done such a low thing, especially when I was trying to help your own sister? I'm getting out of here. I never want to see you again."

"Alain, please wait," Haran pleaded as he quickly arose and put his hand on Alain's shoulder to keep him from going. "Please, let me try to explain."

"There's nothing to explain," Alain muttered, brushing off Haran's hand.

"Just give me the chance to try. Please, Alain, you have to listen. You have to try to understand. You owe it to me out of your love for my sister."

"What does your sister have to do with it?"

"She's my blood, Alain. If you see some good in her, there must be some in me as well."

"I don't see it."

"Please, just sit down for a few minutes. Then you can go."

After hesitating at first, Alain slowly sat down.

"You are a man. You know how important it is that we have some power to show if we are to win the woman of our dreams. Don't flatter yourself to think that it was just your European charm that made Wangetha fall for you. We know here in Africa what most of the journalists like you earn and the quality of life you enjoy. She knew it, believe me. It figured into the way she looked at you. It made you that much more appealing in her eyes."

"So what are you driving at?" Alain responded impatiently.

"The power that comes to you so easily and that you take for granted comes very hard in this country. Very hard. The money required is extremely difficult to get. It is a man of means that most women want. It doesn't matter who she is. She could be a whore sitting on her barstool or the spoiled wife of a corrupt politician, demanding more household help. She could be the comely young thing singing in the choir."

Alain frowned. "You've let your bitterness carry you away, Haran. This is your excuse? That you wanted money? Why do

I need to listen to any of this?" He rose from his chair again and started to walk away.

"You need to listen and you need to know, because this is what spoils us," Haran said as he stood in Alain's way to keep him from leaving. "No one asks how anyone gets his money. The only thing that counts is if you have it."

"That's not so uncommon in the world," Alain said as he slowly sat down again.

"I know that. But in this part of the world there are so few ways to get money – and I mean an amount of money that translates into any kind of power."

"And Robidi, as we well know, had that kind of money," Alain added.

"Yes, and he gave me plenty. It was enough to rent a new office, buy better clothes, get a good car, acquire everything that I need to make myself a man of consequence in this country."

"And so you were even willing to risk your sister's rescue, if not her very life. Yet you expressed great concern about the lives of others when Regalo was laying out his plan to attack the safehouse. Have you forgotten already how you objected to the attack Regalo wanted? You said you had enough of bloodshed. You pressed for another way. You did it with heart and conviction, and you persuaded us. That was a different Haran from the one I see before me now."

"No, Alain, it's the same Haran. I believed then and I still believe in the other way. I compromised my convictions and I stand condemned, not only in your eyes, but in my own eyes, for what I've done. I thought I could undercut you with Robidi without endangering Wangetha, but I was only deceiving myself. Selling any person out will always have consequences for others as well. I could see that after the beating you received from Robidi's boys. Your resolve to continue helping her faltered, and I encouraged you not to give up. Remember?"

"Yeah," Alain nodded.

"Even then, even after my disgraceful act, I pleaded with you not to give up on my sister. I hadn't turned my back on her completely. There was a part of me that still knew what was right."

"So how did you find out where I was? Was it Rebecca or Regalo?"

"It was Regalo. He told me after you met him at the Nyama Choma bar. I was worried that you would ask him if he had told me, but you never did."

"I should have asked. Maybe I didn't want to know." Alain turned his face away.

"I'm asking for your forgiveness, Alain."

"That will be very difficult so don't expect that of me right now. You've caused too much pain."

"And you have never caused anyone pain?" Haran asked.

"I didn't say that."

"Maybe the more you will think about the pain you have caused in your life, the more you will find the strength to forgive me. I don't want to lose your friendship, Alain. If I didn't value it, I wouldn't have confessed to you. We Kikuyu know that true friendship has to be based on candor and trust. There would have been no real friendship with you in my own eyes if I didn't come clean, even if, in your eyes, it appeared that there was nothing wrong."

Haran paused. "I would have been robbing you of the friendship that you deserved because my own guilty conscience would have kept me from being the complete friend that I know I can be. Besides, at a deeper level and at some later point, you would have sensed that I was nothing but a poser anyway."

Alain turned to face Haran again. "Now that you've admitted informing Robidi about my staying at the Ngong Hills Lodge, I suppose that you also tipped Robidi about our plans to raid the safehouse."

"No, Alain, that I didn't do."

"How can I believe you? You lied to me once already. How do I know that you're not lying now?"

"I swear to you, Alain, that I didn't do it. Just think. If I admitted to you that I informed Robidi about the first part, why would I now lie about the second part? It doesn't make sense. Remember, I was Robidi's target in the chase as well."

"The first betrayal still doesn't make sense to me, in spite of your trying to link it to becoming a man of consequence. Is that what being a real man means for you, Haran? To have power and money?"

"I learned a great deal in these last few days, Alain. I never felt more of a man than when I was risking my life to help my sister."

Alain acted as if he hadn't heard him.

"You have to believe me, Alain. I never tipped him off about our rescue operation. I never told him where the safe-house was, either. He asked, of course, that first time I called him, but I had nothing to tell him. I hadn't yet received the information that I was tracking down with the money you gave me.

"Once I learned where the safehouse was located, yes, I was tempted to tell Robidi and get even more money. But I couldn't justify it to myself. I had run out of excuses that could explain away doing something that low. Wangetha was becoming too real to me again. I hadn't seen her for so long and now we were close to freeing her. I couldn't excuse myself for what would have happened to her had I played around with Robidi again, as big as the money might have been."

"It's nice to know that you drew a line on how far you would go after selling me out," Alain said bitterly. "So if you didn't tip Robidi off about our raid on the safehouse, who did?"

"It had to be the way Regalo suggested. The fourth kid-napper that took up with Robidi had a contact in the safehouse, somebody he either befriended or paid off. It was this contact who then let them know about our surprise visit. There's no other way to explain it."

"Except, of course, if you were the one who alerted Robidi as to when we would be at the safehouse. You know that you are asking me to believe a lot now, after already admitting that you turned me over to Robidi once."

"I go back to what I said about being part of the chase. If I had gotten more money from Robidi for tipping him about that, why would I stick with you guys and expose myself to fire?"

"How about this? Because he wasn't going to pay you for that tip. He took it and then dumped you."

"Why would he do that? He's got money."

"Simple. He didn't need you anymore. He was brushing you off. Wouldn't that be just like him?"

"I don't know what else to tell you, Alain. Think about how far-fetched your insinuation sounds. Please think also about the fact that there were different people in that house. Maybe it was one of them. Maybe we will never know. I only know that it wasn't me.

"I'll say it again, Alain. I'm truly sorry. I was seduced by the easy way when there was a better way, even if it was a harder way. I didn't want to take it. Yet I did take it. But in the end, we were in all of this together, all three of us laying our lives on the line. Let that be the proof of my sincerity, that in the end I put my life on the line. I value our friendship. I want it to continue. I know that your relationship with my sister won't be complete for you or her if we are at odds. I will always be the shadow on the edges of your sunshine. That's not good."

"No, that's not good," Alain said, looking into his coffee cup and then back at Haran.

"I know it will not be easy for you to forgive me. I only ask that you try."

"I'll try, Haran, only give me time. For right now, let's just try to forget what happened and move on."

"Right you are, Alain. Let's move on."

"Who's going to pick up the tab for the coffee?" Alain asked, rising from his chair.

"You have to be kidding. This one is on me," Haran said putting his hand on Alain's shoulder. Alain did not remove it as they walked together to the cashier.

CHAPTER 31
RACHEL'S DANCE

∽

Regalo's will was brief and left only one executor and heir. Rachel was designated to be both. She had found the will in Regalo's office in a small steel box in the bottom drawer of his writing desk, where he had told her to look if anything happened to him. It consisted of one letter and was signed by him and his attorney, Haran Nakaya. The will stated that she was to receive whatever was left in his bank account, which turned out to be around 250,000 shillings, and his Jeep, furniture, stereo, computer equipment, and book and music collection. In short, he left everything that he owned to her, even the rosary he kept on his night stand. But since the house was rented, she would have to vacate it at the end of the month.

He also left instructions that she should see to it that he was buried in Kenya. She could make whatever arrangements she wished, as he had no interest in what he termed a "fancy kind of funeral."

When Haran had first called to inform her about Regalo's death, she received the news dispassionately. Her forebodings about evil were seldom wrong, and she had been preparing herself for a bad outcome from the moment he agreed to come back to Nairobi to help Wangetha. Even so, she had waited until Haran delivered the bad news before going to the steel box and opening it up. It was only then, after she had opened it and seen Regalo's generosity and the trust he had in her, that she could no longer hold back the tears.

She sat down on the same sofa, in the very same place that Regalo used to sit when he came home from work, put her head down into her hands, and wept until she could weep no more, her flood of tears, trickling down from her face, soaking the top of her dress. Why did this man come into her life and have such an effect on her and now leave so suddenly? She clenched her fists and pounded the coffee table in front of her. "Why, why, why?" she asked herself.

As she sank deeper into her sadness, she noticed the speakers of Regalo's stereo system standing across from her. Maybe she would feel better if she played some of his music. There was one selection that she remembered just now, one that she had heard Regalo play a few times, titled "Folk Songs from West Virginia." They had made her happy before. Maybe they could help lift her spirits now. She knelt down in front of the shelf holding the many cassettes that Regalo kept there until she found it and inserted it into the player.

The song that she especially enjoyed from the collection was *The Rhododendron Song,* about a pretty flower. She had looked "rhododendron" up in Regalo's large dictionary in his study to find out what kind of flower it was and learned it consisted of large pink, white, or purplish clusters with shining green leaves, growing in the Appalachian region of America along its Blue Ridge Mountains. She had decided then and there that they could pass for cousins to the vivid scarlet and yellow flowers with their hooded blooms that she had seen around the base of Kilimanjaro and loved at first sight.

After she slipped the cassette into the player and heard the running and tripping notes of the mandolin introducing the cheery voices, backed up by the bright harmony of the auto-harp, she felt carried away from her sadness to a far-off Appalachian mountain range that nestled those clusters of pink and white and purple flowers.

As she felt the music welling up inside her from toe to head, she found herself tapping her feet and singing in accompaniment to its lyrics:

I want to wake up in the morning
Where the rhododendrons grow.
Where the sun comes a creepin'
Into where I'm a sleepin'
And the song birds say hello.
I want to wander through the wildwood
Where the fragrant breezes blow.
And drift back to the mountains
Where the rhododendrons grow.
I want to climb up in the mountains
Where the rhododendrons grow.
Where the Lord is so near me,
When I breathe He can hear me,
And the whole world sings below.
I want to lay down all my burdens
And forget my worldly woe.
And stay here in West Virginia
Where the rhododendrons grow.

Feeling a little better, she rewound the player and started the music again. This time, as she began playing it she recalled a television program she had seen that the Americans had shown on a local channel about the way people danced in that part of their country. It was called "square dancing," and the men and women stepped along hand in hand, weaving in and out of each other's arms to the rhythm of the same kind of music as *The Rhododendron Song*.

Impulsively, in an effort to blot out her grief even more, she resolved on the spot that she would like to try that kind of dancing, and so began taking the same kind of forward steps that she had seen the dancers on television take around an imaginary circle. The mandolin-picking on the cassette, as crisp and bright as the morning Kenyan sky, nudged her along and the cheerful voices encouraged her to smile to the imaginary partner that was just now rounding the circle in her direction.

She bowed prettily as he came along and weaved her hand into his arm while she extended her other arm to the next partner to come around the bend. Round and round she went, faster and faster until she found herself laughing and smiling, and laughing and skipping, and weaving and stepping smartly, and smiling and laughing some more, and then clicking her heels, making herself so dizzy that the partner she saw coming around the bend was not her imaginary friend any longer, but Regalo. It was her Regalo, glowing with energy and radiating a joy she had never before seen in him, who took hold of her in his strong arms.

Then it was Regalo, still, who was twirling her around so fast, that soon she was on her toes doing pirouettes. And it was Regalo lifting her up when she lost her balance and fell on the floor in a thud, but as happy as she could be. And it was Regalo laughing at her, but then laughing with her until they were both laughing so hard together that they could hardly stop. And then it was Regalo who took her in his arms again, twirling her and twirling her until she felt dizzy again and could no longer see him.

But just as she started to sit down, he appeared behind her shoulder, tapped it, and asked her if he could have this dance. And they were off again, skipping around the circle, faster and faster until Regalo lifted her up on his shoulder and spun her around and around again before setting her down. He then took her by her two hands, bowed deeply, and after kissing her softly on the cheek, drew her close to him and embraced her. Then, as quickly as he had appeared, he was gone.

When she sat down from this imaginary dance, even though she was crying, she didn't feel as sad as before. And when she began to read the will again, she could see more clearly that Regalo expected her to be strong. By putting all his possessions into her hands he had also put all his confidence in her to preserve the only legacy that he had left, his name and reputation. He didn't have to spell this out to her in the letter. This she understood deep in her heart, just as she understood that it was the wound to his good name that had driven him to lose himself in the distractions of faraway Mombasa.

She would not disappoint his spirit, which she hoped would find and meet her grandfather's. She knew that he would see him as he really was, the way that she saw him.

She would sell the Jeep and take the other money that he left her and go up-country, to the shores of Lake Victoria, where she would buy a small boat. With a good boat, she could marry even a poor man, so long as he had a good heart, and together they could start their own fishing business. She could never go back to being a housekeeper again, of that she was sure. And she was just as sure that Regalo would have agreed. Otherwise, he wouldn't have left her this stake to start a new life.

She would find a worthy burial site for him in Kenya, outside of Nairobi under the watchful gaze of the Ngong Hills, in a place where there was always sunshine. There she would lay him and there he would forever be a part of her land and her people.

She got up from the sofa to look out through the curtain of the living room onto the street outside. Only a few cars were passing back and forth, since there was seldom very much traffic anyway this time of day. But now the black, asphalt street looked completely different to her, even though it was a street that she knew well, all too well, because it had no sidewalks and she had to walk on its edges every day to get to the faraway bus station. She both loved this street and hated it.

It was her way to go to work and so she loved it, but it was so narrow and so rough and so dangerous, that she also hated it.

How she felt about the street wasn't important now. She wouldn't have to walk down it anymore. Nor would she have to cram herself into a noisy, crowded *matatu* anymore. This street had served its purpose in her life. She drew the curtain and walked into the kitchen. She had many things to pack and take with her because there was so much that Regalo had left her.

CHAPTER 32
THE MORNING AFTER

༄

When Alain knocked on the door to Wangetha's room at Nairobi Hospital, his mind was a jumble of thoughts. The sight of her after the rescue – disheveled, her face swollen and contorted – was deeply troubling to him. She was a shadow of her former self, and it was hard to reconcile this Wangetha with his vivid memory of the beauty that had first captivated him. Her speech had been halting and tentative, stripped of self-confidence, while her poise had given way to awkward clutching of Alain's hand and pleading looks into his eyes. During the entire trip in the Jeep from the safehouse to the hospital she seemed to be constantly on the verge of tears, while shaking with fear.

But Alain was determined that sympathy would not be all that he would offer her now.

He knocked on the door, "It's me, Alain."

"Oh, it's you. Please come in."

As Alain entered, she continued talking to him.

"Don't be frightened by what you see. I'm not much better than when you and Haran brought me here yesterday. I know that I'm a terrible sight, and I wouldn't blame you if you just walked away from here and never came back. I hate to look in the mirror. I hardly recognize myself."

Alain walked over to her bed. "Don't worry about how you look right now," he said, kissing her on the forehead. "Healing takes time. You must be patient."

"But I'm afraid that I will never be the same – not my face, not my body, not my mind, maybe not even my soul. I suddenly feel old, Alain."

"I've changed too, Wangetha, as you can see," Alain said, pointing to the bruises on his own face and lifting up his shirt so Wangetha could see the other bruises on his torso.

"How did that happen?"

"Robidi and his men."

"Oh, I am so very sorry. Will he ever be punished for all the evil that he's done?" Wangetha sighed. "I already told the police all that I know when they came to question me earlier this morning."

Alain looked out the window. "I did too. But Robidi has diplomatic immunity, so he can't be prosecuted here, though he can be expelled. Your abductors, on the other hand, can still be brought to justice on the basis of your testimony. And then maybe, someday, somehow, Robidi will get what he deserves in his home country."

He turned back to Wangetha, pulling a chair over to her bedside and sitting down. "In the meanwhile, we both have our badges of honor."

"It's nice of you to put it that way. But you must know what they did with me, how they had their way with me."

As Wangetha burrowed her head in her hands and began crying, Alain reached over and put both his hands on her shoulders.

"You can't blame yourself for that. It's not what you wanted."

"Of course not. But there are those who will say that I did and that I enjoyed it. They can't imagine what hell it is to be used and violated like that."

Wangetha shuddered. "You say I can't be blamed, but you are still a man and your instincts must be repulsed by my being with those gangsters, not one of whom deserves to be called a man."

She turned her head away. "I must be an overused piece of flesh to you now, and an ugly piece of flesh at that. What could you possibly want with me now? You don't have to stay. You don't have to play the noble heart when your manly heart is filled with disgust."

"The only disgust I feel is for what happened to you and for the ones responsible for it."

"But what else do you feel, Alain?" Wangetha asked as she turned her head back to look at him again. "Do you still have any feelings for me? Please tell me. I feel so alone, so broken."

"I still care for you very much, Wangetha. I want to see you recover and glow."

"You say you care, but once I felt that there were stronger feelings in you and could sense the desire that you had for me. Is that gone now? Be honest. I need to know."

"Regardless of how you look now, Wangetha, I still love you. I loved you from the moment our two worlds drew together at Lake Naivasha."

"Thank you for saying that, Alain. It makes me feel so much better. I love you, too. I love you very much, I will keep getting better. You will see. I have good blood and good genes, and I will heal faster than you think. Then we will go driving in the countryside together again."

"Yes, I would like that."

"And while I am healing you will come to know what is inside my mind and heart much better also. That is my deep desire. Please let it be yours, also."

Alain gently stroked her tangled hair. Her eyes were dancing now.

"And when I am better, there is something that I very much hope we will do together. I have always wanted to climb Mt. Kenya, but could never find the right partner who shared my enthusiasm. It's over 5,000 meters high, and though not as lofty as Kilimanjaro, it also has snow peaks. Just think how amazing it would be to ascend to the top and see the natural beauty of my country from such a distance. It's another way that I want to show you my country, my home, not just from the street level. I want to climb, and I want to climb with you, as far as we can go."

"And after climbing Mt. Kenya, we could even climb Kilimanjaro," Alain added. "That would be even more of a challenge, but I don't see why we couldn't do it."

"Of course, my darling. With you, I know that everything will be an adventure. Oh, look at the sun. I was afraid that it was going to be one of those rainy days. Do you see the golden sunshine coming into our room? First, you've come, and now we have the sun's warmth. I'm so happy. Please take my hand. I want to feel your hand in mine."

"I won't ever leave you, Wangetha, not ever," Alain whispered as he intertwined his hand with hers.

"Oh, Alain, that feels so wonderful. After all we've been through, just to feel your hand clasp mine."

She looked more closely at his face. "Is there something wrong, darling? Your eyes are becoming teary."

"Don't pay attention to me. It's just that I realize now, as I'm holding your hand, what a friend was trying to explain to me a while ago."

"What friend, Alain?"

"Oh, a journalist by the name of Williams. He wanted me to understand something that was very important to him, something about what happened to a man in Sierra Leone. I thought that I understood, but I realize now that I didn't, not the way he did. No, not the way he did at all."

"Do you understand now?" Wangetha asked.

"Yes," Alain murmured, as he squeezed her hand tightly. "I understand now."

He looked at the clock on the wall over the door. The hour hand and the minute hand had joined together at 12:00 noon, pointing exactly upward. "How could the time have passed so quickly since entering Wangetha's room?" he wondered, remembering that he had arrived two hours before.

"Alain, I feel so thirsty. Could you please bring me a glass of water from the pitcher on that small table in the corner?" Wangetha asked.

"Of course." As Alain came back to Wangetha's bedside with the water, he looked at her anew. In the bathing light of the sun, the bruises no longer seemed as harsh and he could see that the face he once knew so well was there for him to see again, if he would just look for it. He didn't need to imagine things. He didn't need to pretend. He didn't even need to hope. All he needed to do was to see what had been there before him all along this morning in this hospital room. The face smiling at him was the same face that he saw first on the street in downtown Nairobi, then on the road to Molo, at the shores of Lake Naivasha, at the petrol station in Nakuru, and in the safehouse. There was always one enduring face in all these faces, and it was that face that he recognized now as the one that he loved.

He bent over to kiss her lips.

"Do you know what, Wangetha?" he said.

"No, what, my darling? Tell me. Tell me everything..."

www.ingramcontent.com/pod-product-compliance
Lightning Source LLC
Chambersburg PA
CBHW031435240626
47154CB00001B/280